UNICORN

Richard Gradner

Richard Gradner - Unicorn

Copyright © 2016 Richard Gradner

All rights reserved.

ISBN-13: 978-0-620-71479-2

www.richardgradner.com

www.facebook.com/richardgradnerauthor

About The Book

Halim, a Shakti Warrior initiate, lives with his family in Harappa, a fortified city in the Indus River Valley in the year 4518 BCE. His father is injured, so the task falls to Halim to find a cure for his mother, who has fallen prey to a mysterious, debilitating disease. Sanjit, a seasoned Shakti, agrees to accompany Halim to the Kunlun Mountains in search of a sacred medicine from an ancient monastery. Halim's impulsive sister, Taja, insists on joining them too.

When the three travellers confront the Ignogai, a barbaric tribe with a bloodthirsty shaman, they must flee across hazardous and unfamiliar terrain to avoid being captured and persecuted for their Shakti Prana. With a little bit of magic, determination, and some help from unicorns and a few extraordinary people, the trio must fight for their lives to make it back home in time to save Halim's mother from certain demise.

When you finish reading this book, please consider posting a review on Amazon.

About The Author

Richard Gradner is a Director at Mustard, a creative and digital agency. He was the first Red Bull Marketing Director in South Africa and has a passion for brands and branding. He is also the author of Return to Lemuria, Unicorn and Servant of Memory, all stories that fall under the mythical fiction genre. Richard is an ex-Kung Fu and Tai Chi teacher, with a deep connection to all things spiritual. He lives life to the full, maintaining a healthy mind and body through the daily practice of Yoga. To find out more, please visit richardgradner.com..

Richard Gradner - Unicorn

Dedicated to Adam and Jason. Adventure awaits.

Richard Gradner - Unicorn

1 ~ Mantra

Harappa, Indus River Valley, 4518 BCE

Their round, smiling faces appeared hazy, and the sound of their voices muted, as consciousness slowly returned to Halim.

"He has your eyes, Arja."

"And your nose, Shan. Awww. Hello, little Halim. You cute, cute baby boy. You're going to grow up to be a great warrior like your father, aren't you? Yes, yes, yes!" Arja tickled Halim under his chin. He squirmed his little body from side to side, pulling his face into a toothless smile.

"It's been seven days. It's time to do the test," said Shan looking askance at his wife.

"Yes. I guess it is," nodded Arja sombrely.

Shan reached into the folds of his cloak and pulled out a small, round, pale blue stone. It was smooth and shiny as if it had been regularly polished. He gently pried open the tiny fingers of his son's right hand and pressed the stone into his palm. Halim instinctively squeezed his hand around the stone. Shan gently placed his hands, one on top of the other, over his son's forehead, leant in close and whispered, "Halim. My son. By the power vested in me by my father and his father before him, I charge you with the might of the Peraja Stone. May the gods find favour in your chosen path and lead you forward to your destiny."

Shan carefully removed his hands and took a step back. Halim appeared to have gone back to sleep. A moment later, his eyes flickered open, and he began to cry; the shrill sound of his voice piercing the silence like the wail of a startled river bird. Shan pried the stone loose from his tight grip and carefully examined its surface. He smiled.

"The colour is good, and the energy of the stone glows with strength and power."

Arja moved forward for a closer look. The stone had changed colour, from pale blue to sea green. Tiny golden flecks covered its surface like the glittering reflection of the sun's rays on the great, wide ocean.

"Ah. So pretty," Arja beamed with pride. "The gods have blessed us." She turned to her husband, took his hand in hers and gazed up at him affectionately with a smile on her face.

◊ ◊ ◊

"Halim. Give your sister back her toy."

"But mama, I got it first."

"That's not the point, Halim. It's not yours."

Halim clamped his tiny hands over his ears, trying his best to shut out his sister Taja's high-pitched, wailing cry. He picked up the little, wooden unicorn carving and threw it at his sister in annoyance. The statuette clipped the side of her head, resulting in even louder fits of screaming.

"Halim!" Arja reprimanded. "That was unnecessary. Go to your room. This instant!"

"No!" he shouted boldly.

"By the gods, if you do not do as you are told, then you will be severely punished."

Halim folded his arms and stared at his mother in defiance. She glowered back at him. The tension grew but Halim stood his ground.

Shan walked into the room. "What is all this commotion?" he

demanded emphatically.

Arja turned to her husband. "This child of yours is disrespectful," she said, pointing at Halim. "He made Taja cry, and now he refuses to obey my command."

Halim turned and ran away down the hall.

"Halim!" Arja shouted. "Where are you going? Come back!"

Halim ran as fast as his little legs would carry him. He ran away from his mother and the look of disapproval from his father. He ran until the tears dried on his face. He ran until his lungs burned from heavy breathing. He ran until he fell down on the soft earth of the forest beyond the walls of the city, rolled onto his back and stared up at the swaying boughs of the trees caught in the wind around him. A smile creased his little face, and the feelings of anger and resentment were gradually replaced by a peaceful serenity he could not explain. He watched as the trees acquiesced to mother nature's invisible force, his chest still heaving from the effort of the run.

He was drifting, floating, flying. He was an observer, watching the history of his life from above; looking down on his journey, his adventure. He was beyond time. He was beyond space. He was learning. He was the learner. He listened. He was the listener. He became part of the conception that had already been, yet was also taking place now. The memories flowed, and he became a part of them. Again and again.

"Halim. Halim! Do you hear me, boy? Why are you not listening to my instructions? I told you to follow me, yet here you are again, lost in your thoughts." Shan fought to restrain his fury.

"I'm sorry, papa. I cannot help myself," replied Halim timidly.

"That's the problem right there, Halim," rasped Shan indignantly. "You're not focused. You're not concentrating. What have your thoughts got to do with our practice? Hmm? Exactly. Nothing!"

Halim hung his head.

"Look at me when I talk to you, Halim."

Halim slowly lifted his head.

"That's better. Now. I know it's hard sometimes, but you must push yourself. Do not lose focus. What I'm teaching you is the foundation of the practice. If you lose your concentration, then rather lose it to the practice, not some obscure fantasy in your head. You must learn to live in the now. This moment is all that matters."

"Yes, papa."

"When you truly understand the importance of this lesson, only then will you see the value behind my instruction. Until then, you must listen to me, do what I do, and repeat. Constant repetition builds conviction and purpose. It's only once you have repeated yourself time and again, will you realise that this is the path."

"What path, papa?"

"The path to enlightenment, growth and experience," Shan continued. "You see, Halim, everything is constant, moving. That which stands still fades away and disappears like it never was. Our purpose is to find that which moves, and then move with it. Such is life - a constantly flowing river upon which we must sail and navigate. To sail on the river, we need to repeat the foundational practice until it becomes second nature, part of one's very being. Only then do we become worthy to join those that direct the ships of change. As a future Shakti Warrior, this is your destiny, my son."

"I understand papa. I will try harder," said Halim.

"Good. Now follow me. Observe, then do. Bring your hands together in a prayer mudra in front of your heart. Take a deep breath and fold forward. Breath out. Bend your legs, slowly sit down in a comfortable seat and close your eyes. Now, clear your mind and focus on your breathing, nothing else."

Halim closed his eyes and focused on his breathing as his father instructed, imagining the air around him as a silver mist flowing deep into his lungs and then throughout his entire body, charging it with powerful Prana.

"Good, Halim. Excellent focus," said Shan, commending his

son. "Now, just as we repeat the movements, we repeat the mantra."

"Why must we repeat the mantra, papa?" enquired Halim earnestly.

"When we use a mantra, by repeating it, we elicit vibrational energy. These vibrations permeate one's entire being, overcoming and diminishing the current vibrational energy that you may be subject to until all thoughts are replaced, leading to the silencing of the mind."

"So, we become what we chant?"

"In a manner of speaking, yes," replied Shan. "This is the magic of Yoga. We first prepare the body physically, pulling it this way and twisting it that, until we are soft and flexible like clay, ready to accept the vibrational power of the mantra that will shape us into the direction in which we would like to go."

"I don't understand, papa," said Halim, creasing his brow.

"The only way to truly understand is to experience it for yourself, my son. The sacred mantra that I will teach you today is known as laghiman, the power to cancel out gravity."

"You mean levitation?" Halim asked.

"Yes. Levitation. This is the lesson. Its foundation is the mantra. Study it, repeat it until the words become part of you, and then it will take effect. This is why I get upset with you when you lose your concentration because, without it, you become lost. It's all about your intention, Halim. Now focus and chant with me."

"Dish tyaw day vwah tan naw,
Tee awsh vwah sah jaw yah tay."

"Now repeat this next verse over and over again, and bear in mind your intention to levitate, to rise."

"Lah gahah yah yah jaw yah tay,
Ut kah lal lah jaw yah tay,
Ooh daw nah yah jaw yah tay."

(Thank you, Lord, for allowing me to stretch, to breathe easy, to become. To become light, to rise, to fly.)

Halim began to chant the mantra until it became a repetitive, flowing, melody. His father was right. Singing the mantra over and over again, created a vibrational energy, that began to shape itself around his body until he became the intention of the words being chanted. There was nothing else, just the mantra. The words of levitation. Halim could feel his body becoming light and buoyant the more he chanted. The weight of his physical body melted away as he gradually overcame the power of gravity. Both father and son chanting in unison, created a powerful intention, causing them to rise gently away from the earth.

2 ~ The Nine Sages

Halim was just nine summers old when he woke with a start into a night that was dark and cold. He stared at the shadows from the fire outside as they danced across the ceiling like the fleeting remnants of his nightmarish dream. He closed his eyes, and the shadows followed. They seeped into his eyelids, pushing in-between the slits like tiny, wriggling worms, forcing themselves into his sleep-world, expanding into monstrous beasts and horrifying apparitions. His mind raced. He couldn't go back to sleep. He sat up, hopped off his bed and pulled on his thick, woollen coat. He squeezed his eyes shut and shivered once, before stepping out of his room and into the cold night.

The monotonous, droning sound of a voice became more coherent, as Halim edged closer to the group sitting outside by the fire. The heat from the flames drew him closer, its light quickly dispelling the shadows from his mind, as he listened carefully to the words spoken that portentous evening. He gazed, rapt, between two members of the group, at an old, wizened face narrate the most captivating story. It was one of the elders of the city. Halim had seen him before, at the market, but had never heard him speak. His voice was soft, yet surprisingly clear and discernible against the crackling of the savage flames.

"And so it was told to me by my great-grandfather before he passed," said the elder, "that Prasad, his grandfather before him, was there to witness the event with his own eyes."

The group of several men huddled closer together, making sure that they heard the next part of the compelling story.

"The Clan was under attack by a ruthless tribe of warriors, intent on wiping them from the face of the earth. They had retreated into a deep cave, from which there was no escape. They were trapped." The elder looked around at his captivated audience.

Halim pulled his coat in tighter, huddling against the cold. The elder continued.

"Prasad was small enough to conceal himself between two narrow rocks in a corner of the cave. He watched, from his hiding place, as the leaders of his clan opened a small, wooden casket and withdrew the horn. Even in the dim light of the cave, it sparkled with a powerful energy of its own. They ground the entire horn down into a fine, white powder, poured a murky liquid over it, and mixed it until it became thick and golden in colour. Prasad watched in awe, as they each took turns to drink the concoction until it was all finished. He watched intently as the group quietly sat down in a circle, facing each other in Baddha Konasana posture, their knees open and the soles of their feet touching. Even from deep within the crevice, he could feel a warm, pulsing wave of energy wash over him. The group of nine held hands, closed their eyes, and then the very air around them began to vibrate. Prasad struggled to focus on the seated figures. The air was thick, his breathing strained. The circle of nine became a complete blur. Prasad rubbed his eyes in disbelief, looked up, and then they were gone. Missing. Vanished."

Murmurs of astonishment filtered around the group. Even beneath his thick coat in front of the fire, Halim felt a cold shiver run up and down his spine.

The elder looked around at the expectant audience before

continuing his story. "When he heard the group of warriors approaching, Prasad squeezed himself farther into the dark crevice of the cave. The warriors became enraged as they searched in vain for their enemy, shouting and arguing with each other in frustration. Prasad remained hidden from sight, long after the warriors had left the cave, eventually falling asleep and only rising again the following morning."

A length of silence followed, that broke with a question from a young man to the left of Halim. "What happened to the group of nine?"

"They reappeared a few days later, completely safe from harm. They returned with gifts."

"What kind of gifts?" another man asked.

"Gifts of enlightenment," replied the elder. "They came close to the gods and were exposed to a deeper understanding of the Vedas. Then they began to teach others."

"The Nine Sages!" blurted out another man in the group.

"That is correct. These were the Nine Sages of the Vedas."

"But I thought they were thousands of years old?"

"There have been many sages, my son," said the elder bowing his head in reverence. "The Nine are reincarnated every five hundred years or so. They come down to remind us of the ancient prayers and hymns of the Creator, to reaffirm their purity and authenticity."

Halim felt dizzy. He turned and made his way back to his bed to watch the dancing shadows from the fire on his ceiling transform into the Nine Sages seated in a circle in the cave, vibrating intensely, until they disappeared completely from sight.

◊ ◊ ◊

Many moons later, Halim had an epiphany; that would take him back to that cold and fateful night in front of the fire, listening to the elder tell his fascinating story.

He arrived at Bodhan Dasgupta's house early one morning, as he always did, ready to learn. Bodhan was Halim's tutor and a very interesting man. He was well groomed, wore clean, fresh clothes, and exuded a rich, sandalwood fragrance. Despite this, however, he always looked unkempt, as if he had slept in his clothes night after night. His hair was also dishevelled, and rough stubble covered his round face.

"Hello, Halim. You look bright and cheerful this morning," remarked Bodhan with a smile.

"Hello, Mr Dasgupta. Yes, I guess I am." Halim smiled in return.

"Fantastic! Well, then, that calls for a very special lesson today. A lesson of magic and adventure." Bodhan rubbed his hands eagerly together like a little boy ready to receive a prize for good behaviour.

"Oh, wow, I cannot wait. What's it all about Mr Dasgupta?" enquired Halim.

"Hmmm. It's all about the first hunt."

"Ooh. That's going to be exciting." Halim felt his heart skip a beat. "Mine's in two years time, Mr Dasgupta."

"Yes, I know, Halim. Two years passes by very quickly. It's now time for you to learn about your path and the acceptance of your fate. As you know, there are only a handful of Shakti Warriors in the city, so the hunt with your father is a very important event."

Halim smiled with pride.

"It's your duty to stay by your father's side, and take part in this auspicious obligation without question, just as he did for his father, and his father before him." Bodhan amplified his voice to emphasise the significance of this statement.

"Yessir."

"The hunt is symbolic. It stands for Dharma, the path of righteousness and acceptance of the warrior code. The hunt itself will bring you face-to-face with the mythical unicorn, and your successful acquisition of its horn: a powerful talisman imbued with magical properties."

Halim's heart skipped a beat. His throat became dry, and his ears started to ring. Mr Dasgupta's voice turned into a steady drone, as images of the elder relating his story came back to Halim in waves of nausea. He felt the bile rise in his throat. He baulked.

The horn. The sparkling horn with its powerful energy. Of course. It was a unicorn horn.

Halim's sudden realisation caused him to jump up in excitement. "Is the horn ground into a white powder?"

"Yes. So you know. Did your father tell you?"

"Um, well, no, not exactly. And do I have to drink it?"

"Yes. This is part of the Shakti Warrior ceremony."

"But isn't it dangerous?" Halim panicked. Sweat trickled down and into the small of his back.

"No, not really. The Shaman carefully mixes it with datura and other ayurvedic herbs, before blending it into the medicine known as Soma. Then he administers the concoction in a very small dose," said Bodhan. "It gives the user supernatural abilities and heightened awareness for a limited period."

Halim's mouth dropped into a stupor as he gazed at his tutor. "Yes, I'm sure it does," he murmured to himself. "I'm sure it does."

3 ~ The Hunt

"Papa." Halim looked up from his rhythmic chanting, his wide eyes pushing his brow up and into a furrow of tiny creases on his forehead. He had grown into a handsome young man with striking features, dark, wavy, shoulder-length hair and deep brown eyes.

"Yes, my son. What is it?" Shan turned away from tightening his bow to look across at Halim.

"I'm confused. What is astitva?" enquired the boy.

Shan smiled warmly. "Astitva means existence, my son."

"Okay. But then why do the Vedas refer to man's existence as temporary?"

Shan turned back to his bow, placed it gently down on the table, and came to sit down next to his son. He put his hands on Halim's shoulders and looked into his dark, guileless eyes.

"Halim. We are taught that our physical existence in this world is ephemeral; that we are only passing through this time, in these bodies," Shan turned his palms face-up, "to be born again." Halim's eyes narrowed. "The awareness that you are experiencing is a good omen, my son. It is one of the main objectives of the Vedas, encouraging you to be inquisitive, to ask questions."

Halim nodded thoughtfully. "Well then, I have another question, papa." His eyes lit up with excitement as he turned to his father in anticipation. "What is the source of this knowledge? Where does it come from?"

Shan smiled and sat back into his chair with a sigh. "This is eternal knowledge, my son, passed down by my father and his father before him. The Vedas are timeless. Their hymns were taught to the ancient sages by the Creator himself. This is why we place so much emphasis on the pronunciation and articulation of each and every word and verse. The Vedas are sacred. Divine."

There was a long silence, as the deep meaning of Shan's words became momentarily suspended in a dense fog before finding their way into Halim's consciousness. Halim blinked and gently let out his breath, unaware that he was holding it for longer than was usual.

"Come, my son," said Shan as he rose up from his seat. "We must prepare for the hunt."

It was customary for every son of every Shakti Warrior in the city, to embark on a hunt in the sixteenth summer of his youth. A symbolic quest, its origin lost in the annals of time, the hunt represented the coming of age for each young boy and a bonding experience for both father and son. It involved the preparation of weapons, armour and provisions, and a commitment to embrace the code of the warrior. The unique experience of the hunt instantly transformed the boy into a man, and it was now time for Halim to step up to the task. It was late afternoon, and there was still much to do before the sun sank gradually beneath the horizon. Everything had to be ready in time for father and son to depart at dawn's early light.

"Halim, please check your bow one more time. Make sure that your arrows are as sharp as chinkara horns," said Shan sternly. "We cannot afford to slip-up. We only have one chance at this."

"Yes, papa," nodded Halim in agreement.

Shan was as strict as he was fair. Halim felt that his father expected a lot from him at times, but as he matured, he realised that it was for his own good. He had a way of pushing Halim beyond his limits. At first, he thought that he was being punished all the time; made to do hard work that was always way beyond what was expected. He often turned away in humiliation, when his friends caught him working after hours, embarrassed that they may have thought that he was in trouble. He eventually came to despise his father and his scrupulous methods, and then, one day, his animosity turned to respect. His maturity brought him to appreciate the discipline and self-control that his father was trying to teach him. He began to enjoy the tasks, putting effort into everything he did, until they began to pay off. His studies improved, and he started getting rewarded for completing his chores ahead of time. Halim smiled to himself as he checked his arrows, examining them meticulously from shaft to tip.

His bow was made from bamboo, plucked from the banks of the Iravati River. His father had helped him construct it.

"We choose bamboo because it is strong and flexible at the same time," said Shan. "Bend the bamboo, and it does not break. Let an arrow fly, and it is released with force and accuracy from the bowstring. A good hunter becomes an extension of the bow, as he bends it around his arm during the hunt. Patience, focus, fortitude and above all, practice, maketh a good hunter. Now go. Go and practice my son!"

Halim spent day after day practising to shoot his bow in the forest. He focused his time and energy on perfecting his draw and aim, with the same focus he placed on completing his chores. As time went by, he improved, always working to be better, pushing past what he thought he was capable of doing, until he could shoot ten arrows blindfolded and hit the target each and every time.

◊ ◊ ◊

Later that evening, Halim lay wide awake in his bed. He could not sleep. Every time he closed his eyes, he saw himself blindfolded in the forest, shooting his arrow into an animal, while his father looked on, smiling broadly in acknowledgement. Then there was blood. Lot's of it. Everywhere. He felt some bile work its way up into his mouth. His ears grew hot, and a light perspiration broke out across the back of his neck. He pushed himself up into a seated position and threw his legs over the bed. He took a deep breath, stood up to go outside, tilted back his head, closed his eyes, and drank in the cool evening air. His stomach rumbled loudly as he opened his eyes to stare up at the thousands of bright pinholes in the cloak of darkness, which had been thrown nonchalantly over the city. A crescent-shaped tear in the dark, boundless fabric, winked at him mockingly as if the gods themselves were laughing at his naivete. He sat down in the long grass, extended his legs out in front of him and propped his body up on his arms as he stretched them behind him for support. A smile stretched across his face, as he pictured his beautiful mother Arya and his sister Taja, running across the field before him, the hot, unwavering sun beating down on their backs as they moved.

4 ~ Leaving

"Halim, Halim!"

Halim stirred, as rough hands rocked him from side to side. His eyes were glued shut, and his left arm was numb and as heavy as a log. He lifted his head and slowly opened his eyes. Long grass peeled itself off his face, as he blinked into the wan light of the new day. His father towered over him, a dark silhouette against the dim sky behind him. He could feel his father's agitation shimmering off him in layers.

"Halim, what are you doing here?" demanded Shan. His voice was hard. "Come. Get up, wash and eat your fill. We have a long ride ahead of us." He turned abruptly and marched away into the gloom.

Halim dropped his head into his hands. A pang of despair washed over him.

How did I end up starting my day like this? Especially this day. My hunting day.

He jumped up, ran over to the horse basin, squeezed his eyes shut, and dunked his head straight into the icy-cold water. He quickly yanked it out again, pulling a head-full of water with him, like a sea sponge that the fishermen brought with them when they visited the city from time to time, to sell their smelly, salty fish.

Halim ran inside, pulled on his leather tunic, and grabbed his hunting bow and quiver of arrows. He arrived at the stables, tripping over his feet in haste, his mouth full with a thick slice of freshly baked bread from his mother's kitchen. His father was already there, preparing his horse for the hunt. He spoke without looking up.

"Halim. You disappoint me. I pray that your tardiness interferes not with the hunt today. Do not underestimate the significance of this day, my son. Remember, you only have one chance. Come, let us ride!"

Shan pulled himself up and onto his horse. She shook her head, lifted her front legs and whinnied. He stood up in his saddle and leant forward to maintain his balance. Halim looked up in awe at his father. His father, the warrior. A Shakti Warrior. Taja and Arja stepped outside to see them off.

"May the gods protect you and guide you," said Arja proudly.

Halim climbed onto his horse. He turned to wave at Arja and Taja, before following his father through the gate at the front of their property, onto the main road that would lead them past Harappa and on toward the woods on its far side. The dawn's early light cast soft shadows on the ground beside them as they approached the still slumbering city; a city filled with thousands of inhabitants; a bustling, urban metropolis, getting ready to awaken to a new day, a brand new chapter in its glorious history. Halim rolled on his horse, relaxing into a steady rhythm, the thud of his horse's hooves providing a constant beat on the well trodden path. He breathed deeply, taking in the fresh scent of dew from the terrain around him. He felt alive. He smiled and breathed out with a sigh. He thought of the Vedas and the story of Harappa and how it was blessed by Lord Shiva who gave the city its name, long, long ago. The Vedas tell of another Harappa, the first Harappa; a beautiful place beyond the great ocean to the west. A city of magic and beauty like no other. He wondered what it was like to have lived there. He closed his eyes for a moment and imagined the wonders that were, that could have been. He smiled.

◊ ◊ ◊

With the city behind him, Shan rode purposefully into the woods with Halim in tow, following the wide path that began to narrow steadily the deeper they went. Halim nudged his horse forward so that he could ride next to his father.

"Come on Shasta," he whispered into his horse's ear. "Let's catch up to papa."

Halim and his father thundered into the forest canopy. It swallowed them into its midst. Shan slowed his horse down to a trot and then a walk, as the path narrowed even further, forcing Halim to ride directly behind him once more. They continued for a while longer, until Shan pulled his mare off the path and up to a large tree with a small stream running past it. Father and son climbed off their horses and led them over to the water to drink their fill.

"Papa," said Halim gazing up into the tree beside them. "Look there." He pointed up to a tiny, silvery bird that was being pushed out of its nest, by what must have been its mother. It stood teetering on the edge of a branch protruding from the side of the nest, holding on with all of its might. It opened its beak and made a rasping sound. It looked like it was choking. And then it fell. Halim ran instinctively forward to catch the bird, as it plummeted helplessly towards the ground below. Time slowed down to a trickle, and then sped up again in a hurry, just as the creature made a miraculous recovery. The tiniest little wings snapped open and pulled the bird up and away from the ground, saving it from complete catastrophe.

"You must view this event as a lesson, my son," said Shan. "A lesson in survival. But also a lesson in faith and trust in the powers of the gods; those that protect us from losing our way. Those that guide us and watch over us."

Halim watched the tiny bird pull itself, albeit haphazardly, up and into the sky, high above them. "Yes, father," he responded, distracted by the enlightened experience. "I will."

Shan handed Halim a piece of bread and some cheese. He

wolfed it down quickly, forgetting how hungry the morning ride had made him.

"We still have a long way to go before we reach our destination. We ride now." Shan pulled himself up onto his horse. Halim followed without question as the forest welcomed them once again.

Halim gripped his legs around Shasta but kept his upper body relaxed, rolling it forward and back in time to Shasta's steps. He nudged his horse forward to follow his father at a gallop across an open clearing, momentarily closing his eyes as the wind whipped across his face, providing momentary relief from the scorching afternoon sun beating down from above. The horses slowed down to a trot, as they approached an opening in the trees up ahead.

"Papa, how much farther?" enquired Halim.

Shan answered without turning around. "These are the woods where we will find what we came looking for, my son. But we need to venture a bit deeper. Not long now."

The day's last remaining shafts of sunlight filtered through the trees, briefly blinding Halim as he followed his father deeper into the dense forest. He bowed his head down, twisting it gently to stretch his weary neck muscles when Shasta abruptly stopped walking. He looked up to see his father climbing down from his horse.

"We will set up camp here," said Shan. "Come, Halim, help me collect some wood for the fire."

"Yes, papa."

Shan secured the horses to a tree and began clearing the ground nearby for their camping area while Halim ventured into the forest. The air tasted crisp and sweet, kept cool by the shadows cast by the tall trees around him. Halim breathed deeply as he walked, the crunch of his feet on the forest floor, the only sound disturbing the silent space around him. He returned to camp with a bundle of sticks cradled in his arms, dropping them into a shallow trough his father had dug out of the earth for this purpose.

"Good job, Halim." He smiled as Shan handed him some dried meat and a gourd filled with water. "Replenish your energy, my son, for tonight we hunt!"

◊ ◊ ◊

The light from their fire sticks cast an ever-shifting glow around them, bouncing off the foliage as they walked. It was as if they were surrounded by dozens of other Shakti Warriors, their flickering shadows guiding them through the dark and haunting passage of the hunt. Halim hopped as he walked, lifting and shifting his bow and quiver of arrows up and to the right across his back. He settled back into his stride, looking down and ahead at his father's feet as they followed an overgrown path only Shan could see. The shadows cast by the fire sticks began to lighten and then fade away altogether as the trees gave way to a small clearing bathed in the white light of the full moon in the cloudless sky above them. Halim saw the moon as a perfect reflection in a placid pool of water just a few feet away as he stepped up to stand next to his father. His mouth slowly dropped open as he shifted his gaze up to stare in awe at the bright, glowing, magical sphere, casting its light; a reflection of the sun's, down onto the Earth below.

Halim spoke in a whisper, fearful of disturbing the ethereal scene before him. "Papa, it's just beautiful. So very beautiful."

Shan silently doused his fire stick in the waters before him, placed his finger across his lips and beckoned for Halim to do the same. Halim tread as softly as he was able towards his father. He carefully pushed the burning stick into the water and watched, as it let out a hiss of contempt, followed by a puff of bubbles and steam in defeat. Shan filled the gourd with fresh water and then indicated that they sit down nearby for a rest. Halim closed his eyes and listened intently, as the sounds of the forest became clearer with every breath that he took. He smiled as he picked up the most distant sounds emanating from deep within the forest and then listened to the ones nearby, coming mostly from the body of water right next to where they sat.

Crack. An unnatural sound this time; different from the

others. Halim opened his eyes and slowly sat up to peer across the water alongside them. At first, there was nothing, but then he saw movement in the bushes on the other side. He tapped his father's arm gently and gestured in the direction of the movement he just witnessed. Father and son, crouching down between long, slender reeds, carefully made their way towards the water's edge. It was the glittering reflection that first caught Halim's eye. A sparkling shower of moonlight shone off a long, pointed horn connected to a magnificent creature, dipping its head to drink from the water on the other side of the pond. Her white, flawless hide was framed by a thick, silvery mane; that hung down over her head as she leisurely drank her fill.

A unicorn. Right here. Right now.

Halim's head spun. He could feel the presence of the mythical creature as it snorted and nickered, throwing its head back with a neigh. His head was filled with her infinite beauty, like a creature divine, created by the gods to give man hope, aspiration and love for the Creator and all of His beautiful creations. Halim watched the unicorn rise onto its hind-legs, its imposing frame towering high above him and his father, its fore-legs pawing the air like an enchanted beast that had come down from the heavens above, its body framed by the light of the luminous moon behind it.

5 ~ Chase

The unicorn spied Shan and Halim hiding on the other side of the river. It shook its head from side to side, snorting the air in contempt. Halim watched, as the creature lowered its head, pointed its silvery horn directly at him, and charged, spraying water up into the air with every galloping step. Halim knew what he was supposed to do. He could not and would not miss this opportunity. All those arrows fired at all those targets were for this moment. This moment of truth. He already had an arrow nocked in his bamboo bow when his father turned to face him, intending to rebuke him for his apathy. But Shan hesitated, just as Halim pulled back the arrow, took aim, and fired, at precisely the same moment that the creature leapt high up into the air and directly over their heads. The arrow sailed across the night sky, glinting in the light of the moon, burying itself in the neck of the animal. For a fleeting moment, the creature's pain and anguish tore across Halim's chest, leaving behind a tight, aching pang of regret. He gazed up at the unicorn as it landed with a thunderous, double-thud, just beyond his reach and then bounded away into the forest.

Halim turned to look wide-eyed at his father in alarm, and then they ran and ran together, chasing the beast. It tore through the woods, leaving a trail of dust and blood as it galloped. Halim ran until his legs began to burn, but he couldn't give up now. He couldn't stop. Not until he caught his prize. The unicorn. He looked up into the night sky as he ran, wondering if the story about unicorns drawing their power from the light of the moon was true. The blackness of the night stretched into eternity behind the blurry smear of stars, digesting his rhetorical question, offering him nothing but silence in return. Halim fought to keep his negative thoughts at bay as they coursed through his mind. He pushed his legs forward to carry him after his prey. Pushed and pushed.

Shan waved both his hands hurriedly. "Halim, slow down. Listen." The sounds of the creature tearing through the forest had subsided. Their chests heaved, sucking in the air around them to quickly replace the spent energy of the chase.

"I cannot hear anything, papa," whispered Halim.

"It must be tired out. Careful now…"

Father and son moved slowly past several trees and then out into a small clearing covered in long, wild grass. There was no unicorn in sight.

"Where is it, papa? I cannot see anything."

"Look. Over there." Shan pointed to the centre of the clearing. The grass appeared to be flattened. The pair approached with caution. They heard a snort. The unicorn was lying, collapsed, on its side, its breathing erratic. The light of the moon reflected off its glistening hide wet from a mix of blood and sweat. The blood was dark, almost black as if the moonlight had drained the landscape of all colour, transforming it into a bleak and desolate place. Halim's hand shook as he drew back the final arrow.

Thwwwwt!

Silence. Cold silence. The moonlight seemed to dim, yet the sky remained clear. Halim dropped to his knees. The long grass came up as high as his chest, as he looked down forlornly at the lifeless animal before him. He involuntarily relaxed his grip on the bow, and it fell to the earth like a misshapen plaything.

Blood rushed to his ears, as he experienced a wave of mixed emotions that made him giddy and short of breath. He had done it. He had killed the magical creature. He was halfway to becoming a true Shakti Warrior.

"Well done, my son. Well done."

Halim didn't have to turn around to know that his father was grinning with pride right behind him. He closed his eyes and flashed back to the dream he had the night before. He squeezed his eyes tighter, pulling all the muscles in his face together like a sponge. A single tear drop tickled his cheek. It rolled down to the base of his chin and then hung there momentarily, before following the course of his bow to the ground below.

"Come, Halim. We must now appease the gods and find another animal for the sacrifice. We have taken, now we must return the gift. The balance must be honoured." Shan turned and walked back into the forest.

Halim lifted his knees and crawled closer to where the lifeless unicorn lay. He cupped his hands, bent down towards the animal's ear and began to recite the mantra of Avalokiteshvara, also known as the six syllable mantra. He blew over the corpse in between his chanting to purify the negative karma surrounding it and closed his eyes to concentrate on the creature's favourable rebirth in its next life.

"Om Mani Padme Hum"

(Om purifies bliss and pride.
Ma purifies jealousy and need for entertainment.
Ni purifies passion and desire.
Pad purifies ignorance and prejudice.
Me purifies poverty and possessiveness.
Hum purifies aggression and hatred.)

6 ~ Return

The noxious stench of the burning buck was almost as bad as the bitter taste of bile in his mouth. This combined onslaught on his senses made him gag in revulsion. Halim looked up to watch the thick plume of smoke from the sacrificial offering spiral slowly up into the night sky. He looked down at the flames licking the carcass, wondering if the heat from the fire was responsible for transforming the animal's spirit into the smoke that went up to meet its maker. He turned to look across at his father, who was also staring intensely at the flames, as they cast lurching, haunting shadows across his face. Halim's shoulders lifted with a sigh. It was going to be a long night.

The embers from the fire were still glowing brightly when Halim set out to decapitate the unicorn's head. It was a lugubrious, yet customary task for the young initiate. Blood covered his hands and lay splattered across his tunic long before he completed the undertaking.

"Here, Halim. It's ready." Shan stepped out of a shallow grave he had just finished digging, as Halim dragged the rest of the animal across the field and into the hole.

"Papa. I'm going back into the forest to search for a Mukul myrrh tree." Halim turned and walked back towards the canopy of trees. He quickly found what he was looking for, easily identifiable by its beautiful red flowers and strange purple, oval fruit. He broke off several branches from the small, thorny plant, and made his way back to his father who was burying the remains of the unicorn.

"Papa, I found it," said Halim with fervour.

"Good. You know what to do," replied Shan, looking up from his work.

Halim pulled a rolled-up animal hide from his saddlebag and laid it out on the grass. He lifted the unicorn's head, carefully avoiding poking himself with the long, glistening horn, and then placed it on top of the animal skin. Next, he held the branches from the Mukul Myrrh tree over the head of the animal and began to bend and twist them, until a yellowish resin called guggul began to pour forth. He directed the flow of liquid over the base of the head, covering the unsightly wound as best as he could. The guggul was designed to prevent the head from rotting and reeking on the long journey home. He cast aside the branches, wrapped the hide around the head, secured it with some twine and then strapped it to the back of his mare.

The ride back was distinctly sombre. Halim never imagined it this way. Gone was the excitement and expectation of the hunt. It had been replaced instead with a stark realisation that death was inevitable, and, in this case, necessary. Melancholy struck Halim at the thought of his kill; the unicorn, a truly magnificent creature, its life cut short by his hand. Despite the fact that he had been taught why he had to complete this auspicious task, he struggled to come to terms with his current, deeply rooted feelings of angst and chagrin.

Why? Why did the gods choose me to destroy such a beautiful beast?

Halim squeezed his eyes shut, opened his mouth wide, and screamed inside his head. His knuckles turned white as his grip on the reins tightened. All he could see were the piercing eyes of the unicorn, gazing at him intently from the other side of the lake. Try as he might; he could not look away, let alone blink. His eyelids felt like they had been seared off so that the magical unicorn could reach right through him and into his soul.

Why? Why did you do it, Halim? I was a helpless animal, and then you killed me. Why?

Halim shook his head vigorously, clearing his troubling thoughts. He opened his eyes to the flickering of distant lights from the city of Harappa as dusk settled in. For the first time that day, he smiled. He was home.

◊ ◊ ◊

A jubilant, undulating cry echoed across the city square. The inhabitants of Harappa spotted Halim and his father on their approach. Crowds of people quickly lined the streets in anticipation of the arrival of their new Shakti Warrior. Arja, Halim's mother, with the assistance of the Warrior Guild, had prepared a great feast to celebrate the momentous occasion. Row upon row of tables lined the square, covered with mouthwatering foodstuffs and plenty of drink. This rare event, even though hosted by Halim's family, was an open invitation for all to attend and enjoy the festivities.

A visitor to the city turned to stop a local walking hurriedly past him. "What's going on here? Why all the excitement?"

"It's a Shakti feast," he answered. "The young Shakti Warrior is fast approaching," he pointed. "You are welcome to join us in the celebration. Do you have a gift?"

"A gift?"

"Yes. It is customary to bestow gifts and blessings upon the young warrior at the feast. You will receive kismet and good fortune in return," explained the local cheerfully. "Come, join us."

A chaos of young children sprinted past them, their laughter echoing down the street as they ran. They sped up to the top of town to meet Shan and Halim as they passed through the gates of the city. The children crowded around Halim, their little voices showering him with praise like a flock of sparrows and the burden of his ordeal dissipated like a fine mist melting into the sparkling sunlight.

It was surreal, like a soft, hazy dream. Time appeared to stand still as everything around him slowed down. The multitude of voices from the crowds of people that now surrounded him, as he made his way into the square, buzzed like a swarm of bees in his ears. Halim was pulled gingerly from his horse and lifted up to head height by a group of men that were full of laughter and boundless energy. They began to toss him up into the air like one of his sister's raggedy dolls while singing and chanting with gusto. He laughed with them until his insides ached and his head throbbed with giddiness. Thank the gods, he had never felt so alive. So happy and so free.

"Halim!" shouted Shan with urgency from across the square.

Halim turned towards the source of his father's voice, struggling to see him through the crowd.

"The Shaman!"

Halim witnessed the crowd begin to part like a branching river to the sea. He withdrew his hunting knife and forced his way through the mob towards his mare shouting, "make way! Make way!"

The people before him hesitated, saw his blade, and then pushed forward and away like wheat bending in the field to an invisible wind, giving him room to move. He reached his horse, cut down the leather-bound unicorn head, turned around, and sharply drew in his breath. The Shaman stood before him, his big, round eyes surveying Halim with disdain. An elegant headdress with long, colourful feathers and glittering gems, perched on top of a fully painted face, presented a macabre spectacle amongst the sea of revellers.

The Shaman opened his mouth to speak, yet there were no words, just a soft, rasping sound, like a sand lizard defending its territory.

Halim presented the Shaman with the heavy bundle. The Shaman wordlessly received the package from Halim, turned and made his way back through the crowd from whence he came. The hum of the crowd returned as it closed behind the Shaman's departure. They escorted Halim and his father to a long table in the city square laden with a variety of bread, meat, fruit, and plenty of ale.

"Halim, my son!" exclaimed Arja with pride. "How happy I am that you are safely returned from your hunt."

She smiled broadly and held out her arms to embrace Halim, looking past him at Shan in acknowledgement. Shan smiled and nodded his head in return.

"Thank you, mother. It's so good to be home."

Arja leant in closer and whispered. "You know that this is all for you? You'd better show your appreciation by partaking in the feast, but be careful of drinking too much ale. Don't follow your father's example. He's been drinking many years already, and, as a result, has a far stronger constitution."

"Don't worry Mama, I will," replied Halim, hugging his mother firmly.

"My darling." Shan kissed his wife on either cheek. "Let's celebrate!" He threw his hands into the air. There were cheers all round as Shan grabbed a beaker of ale and downed it in a single swig, spilling some of it over his tunic in the process.

"Aaah! More! Come, my son, drink with your father." Shan swung his arm, slapping Halim on his back in encouragement. Before he knew it, he had half a flagon of ale down his throat, much to the dismay of his mother who looked on disapprovingly.

"Halim. I'm so proud of you," congratulated Taja.

Halim stood as his sister approached. He gave her a warm hug. "Thanks, Taj. Really appreciate it."

"So, tell me all about it. I can't wait to hear. It must have been incredible!"

Halim felt the back of his neck grow cold. He looked away from his sister and closed his eyes. He turned back to her and smiled. "Yes, it was. Words cannot begin to explain…"

"Oh, come on Hal. Stop teasing me. Tell me. Tell me all about the hunt of the magical unicorn," pleaded Taja. Her dark brown eyes sparkled like the glistening sun reflecting off the shimmering ocean.

Halim looked away again but this time, he pointed up to the

sky. Taja turned and looked up to where he was pointing. "The unicorn was like the glowing moon, and its horn glittered like the stars scattered across the heavens. It was the most beautiful creature I have ever seen."

"Aaaah…" Taja was gaping up at the night sky, imagining the enchanted beast running through the forest, her father and brother enthusiastically chasing after it.

"And then I watched it jump, its great and powerful body lifting it high, up and into the air. It was truly a sight that I shall never forget," declared Halim in veneration.

The crowd around them fell silent as the Shaman appeared once again, walking towards the main table with a purpose in his stride. He held an old, wooden goblet in his hands, upon which was engraved a mysterious, ancient text. He carefully placed it on the table before Halim.

Halim stared at the goblet. His teacher's voice echoed in the back of his mind, reminding him of the ritual that was to follow.

"Mr Dasgupta, what is the purpose of Soma?" enquired Halim.

"That is a very interesting question. One that will take us a few lessons to learn the answer to," Dasgupta replied with a smile.

Halim's heart skipped a beat, and his stomach twisted itself into a knot as he stared at the goblet. It seemed to glow with a mesmerising, alien energy.

"Soma is ancient in origin. It has been passed down through the ages, refined by the shamanic community through trial and usage," Bodhan explained.

"But what is it used for?"

"It's administered by the Shaman for a variety of ailments. The Shakti Warrior also drinks it after the hunt. Soma gives the user heightened awareness by opening the third eye to the wonders of the universe. It's known as the elixir of the gods."

The Shaman glared expectantly at Halim, gesturing for him to drink from the wooden goblet. Halim looked hesitantly around at his family and the crowd of onlookers. It was now or never. He picked up the goblet and looked inside. The broth was thick and yellow in colour, with a soft, golden hue. Halim lifted the goblet to his lips and closed his eyes. The medicine was warm and malty as it poured into his mouth. Tiny sand-like granules ground against his teeth and a subtle, nauseating odour clogged his nostrils, as he gulped down the heavy mixture, almost gagging in the process.

The Shaman beckoned for Halim to join him as he walked towards a small tent erected on the perimeter of the square. Some cushions lay on the floor of the tent, upon which the Shaman sat. He moved into a full lotus position, twisting and pulling each foot up and into the crook of his groin. Halim sat down opposite him and followed suit. A spicy, aromatic fragrance filled the tent that made his head spin. He closed his eyes just as the Shaman started humming a tune that flowed into a mesmerising mantra. Luminescent imagery flashed across Halim's periphery vision and grew in clarity with every moment that passed. The beauty of the visions seared themselves into his consciousness like the mark from a branding iron, cutting into his psyche like a scalding blade, tearing open his heart and implanting their splendorous seed forever more. Tears of joy poured from his eyes, as Halim journeyed into the celestial ether of enlightenment. The Shakti transformation had begun.

7 ~ Sickness

"Here, Halim, let me look at you," Arja said to her son as he walked into the room. She was lying in bed, sick from a mysterious illness that had befallen her, draining her of her energy and spirit. Her voice was weak and her face a dull shade of grey. She looked frail and sickly, her breathing shallow and strained.

"I can't believe that it's already been two summers since you became a Shakti Warrior. Look at what a handsome young man you have become. You make me so proud."

"Oh, mama." Halim's bowed his head, his cheeks turning a deep red. "Please don't talk. Save your energy," he said in a pleading voice.

Arja smiled. Her eyes filled with tears, that leaked out and onto her cheeks, running freely down her face.

"Now look what you've done," said Halim, annoyed at his mother's embellishment. He quickly moved forward to wipe the tears from her face.

"I'm fine, Halim. Stop worrying so."

"No, Mama. You must rest. Papa says…"

"I don't care what papa says," she interrupted. "Your father is far too over protective."

"But he said he's going to find a cure," Halim said.

"A cure for what?"

"Your sickness, of course. You aren't getting any better," Halim said imploringly.

"Don't be silly, Halim. I'll be fine. It's just temporary. It will pass." Arja coughed and drew in a ragged breath.

"There's no winning with you, is there?" said Halim rhetorically, throwing his hands up in the air. "Why can't you just accept the fact that you're sick and need help?" he said in agitation.

"Halim. Calm down," said Arja. "I'm just trying to stay positive. Positive thoughts create positive energy. Much needed energy required to fight the disease," she continued.

"You need much more than positive energy to fight this disease, Mama," Halim responded. He reached over to pick up a brown bottle next to her bed. "This stuff doesn't seem to be helping." He slammed it down on the table in frustration.

"Oh, but it is, Halim. Without it, I'd be in a far worse condition. Maybe even dead."

"Now don't you talk like that, Mama. You're not going to die." It was Halim's turn to shed a tear. He wiped it quickly away and moved forward to give his mother a hug, knowing full well that it would provide him with more consolation than it would her at this point.

Taja stepped into the room, immediately ran up to Halim and Arja and wrapped her arms around them both. They all began to sob in unison.

"Okay. That's enough," whispered Arja.

First Taja, then Halim reluctantly released their hugs and knelt down on either side of the bed, clasping each of Arja's hands in their own.

"We love you, Mama," announced Taja softly, gazing wistfully through tears at her mother.

Arja turned toward her daughter with a smile. It was then, from an angle, that Halim saw the dark rings beneath his mother's eyes. Dark rings framed by hollow cheekbones. His heart ached, and his eyes welled up again. He closed his eyes and prayed.

◊ ◊ ◊

"What are we to do, papa?" Taja addressed her father in the stables the following morning. "She isn't getting any better. Why can't the Shaman find a cure?"

Shan stood with his back to his daughter, methodically brushing his horse in long, even strokes. He answered without turning around. Taja thought she heard a quiver in his voice."

"I met with the Shaman this morning."

"And? What did he say?"

"He has mixed another potion. He says that this one is sure to break the spell."

"But that's what he said about the last one, papa."

"We must give it a chance, Taja."

"That's the problem, papa. I don't think we have many chances left. Mama is so tired. So weak."

Shan spun around to face Taja, clenching his hands into fists. "Well, what do you want me to do, Taja?! We can only request the Shaman's help and pray that your mother recovers from this ordeal. We have to try. Not trying is worse than failure!"

Taja stood staring wide-eyed at her father, as he reprimanded her in frustration. She pressed her palms over her eyes and burst into tears.

Shan, aware of his insensitivity, stepped quickly over to his daughter and wrapped his arms around her. "I'm so sorry Taj. Please forgive me. It's just that it feels as if I'm trapped in a room with no way out. I have tried everything to help your mother, and you're right, she's not getting better. Let's pray that this medicine works. The Shaman has cured many people before."

Taja wrapped her arms around her father, and squeezed, trying desperately to stop her body from shaking.

◊ ◊ ◊

Days passed, and Arja's condition seemed to remain much the same. The new medicine made her sleep a lot more, so at first, it appeared that she started getting better, but it was hard to see much of an improvement really and her breathing was still rather strained. Halim and Taja sat together by their mother's side late one morning, when Shan appeared, beckoning them to join him outside.

"This is Sanjit," said Shan, gesturing to a resolute character standing silently next to him, legs askance, hands folded casually behind his back. He bowed his head towards Halim and Taja in acknowledgement.

"Hi." Halim raised his hand.

"Sanjit is a seasoned Shakti Warrior. He was one of the first Shaktis that I trained when I joined the warrior's guild."

Sanjit smiled. Shan patted him on the back.

"We've been talking." Shan paused for a moment to look up at Halim and Taja. "And I have learnt much."

Halim studied Sanjit. He looked odd. Like he didn't belong. He had long, dark, unkempt looking hair, and wore a dark-brown robe tied with a burnt-orange sash. The robe was fitted with a hood that lay relaxed across his shoulders and a long broadsword was strapped across his back.

"Sanjit spent time with a bhisaj, a healer, who possesses the knowledge of ancient medicines. He assures me that this healer will have a cure for mama's sickness. I will journey with Sanjit back to these lands to find this bhisaj. I will bring back the cure and Mama will finally be healed."

"How far is the journey?" enquired Taja.

"About seven days there and back," Sanjit replied this time. His voice was gruff. "We travel north-west, towards the Kunlun Mountains."

"seven days!" Taja exclaimed. "Pray the gods that mama will survive that long."

"The Shaman's medicine will help. It's a powerful brew. You must just keep administering it until we return," said Shan reassuringly.

"When do you leave, papa?" asked Halim.

"In the morning. At first light."

"Can I join you on this journey?"

"No. I need you and your sister to take care of your mother while I am gone. She needs you here. She needs your strength."

"But Taja can…"

"Halim," Shan interrupted. He gripped Halim by the shoulders and looked directly into his eyes. "I need you here. Please."

"Okay, papa. As you wish." Halim bowed his head in acceptance.

◊ ◊ ◊

Sleep evaded Halim that night. He tossed and turned in his bed, his mind racing with thoughts of his sick mother, and his father's treacherous journey across foreign lands. His horrifying visions worsened, with Sanjit turning into a ferocious beast and slaying his father in a wild frenzy. This increased anxiety only served to fuel his insomnia. Sleep finally came, but it was so close to sunrise, that, much to his dismay, he slept right through his father's departure.

Taja lifted her head from her mother's bed as Halim approached them later that morning.

"Morning sleepy head. You missed papa."

"I know," Halim replied. "How is she doing?" he quickly shifted focus to his mother who lay asleep on the bed.

"She seems okay. She sleeps a lot more with this new medicine, but the good news is that her wheezing has stopped. Listen."

Halim cocked his head for a moment. "You're right, Taja! That's wonderful news."

"Yes, it is, isn't it?" replied Taja, overjoyed. "I see now how this medicine works. It has a strong sedative effect so that the body can rest and heal itself."

◊ ◊ ◊

Several days passed without any major changes to Arja's condition. Taja continued to administer the medicine, adding a drop to her mother's water every morning and then again in the evening as per the Shaman's instruction. Arja seemed to have stabilised until the night terrors began. Halim was certain he was dreaming when a shrieking wail erupted through the household. It came in fits and starts and continued for quite some time. Halim jumped out of bed and rushed into his mother's room. Taja joined him soon after. Arja was writhing on the bed like a snake, crooning like a woman possessed.

"Mama!" Taja ran up to the bed and grabbed her mother by the shoulders, attempting to constrain her, to hold her down. Halim grabbed her ankles and eventually she settled, falling into a restless sleep.

"How much longer must we wait, Halim?" pleaded Taja. "Where is papa?"

"It's only been five days, Taj. There are at least another two to go. I know it's hard, but we must find the strength to go on and the patience to wait for Papa and Sanjit. We must also be thankful that Mama is still alive."

Taja ran to Halim, threw her arms around him, buried her head in his shoulder and burst into tears.

8 ~ Papa

Halim was tending to the goats in the pasture early the following morning, when a little boy came running up to him, completely out of breath.

"Slow down, boy. That's it. Breathe." Halim handed him his waterskin. He brought it to his lips and gulped down the water without question.

"Thank you," he managed to get out, in-between his erratic breathing.

"Now, what's your name, boy?"

"Yamir," replied the boy, and then without hesitation continued, "It's Shan! He's back!"

"What? What do you mean?"

"I mean he's back, he's here, in the city," replied the boy.

"But he's not due back for several days yet." Maybe he has the cure. Halim dropped everything and ran down to his house.

From a distance, he saw Sanjit astride his mare with his father's horse alongside him. Sanjit appeared to be towing a makeshift wooden sled behind him as he rode. There was no sign of his father. It was only as he approached Sanjit, that he saw a figure in the sled.

"Papa! What happened to you? Are you all right?"

Shan slowly sat up in the wooden stretcher. "Halim. I'm okay. It's my leg. It's broken." He lay down again.

Halim ran up to his father. He had three nasty scrapes across the left side of his face, and his left arm was in a sling. His face was pale.

"And your arm?" questioned Halim.

"It's my shoulder. I think it's just badly bruised," he replied. "We were climbing, and some rocks gave way. I fell…" Shan turned his head, looked into the distance, and screwed up his face as he relived the painful memory.

"Your father was very lucky," Sanjit said. "He fell very far but managed to grab hold of a rocky outcropping that stopped his fall. He has lost much blood." Sanjit climbed down from his horse and began untying the stretcher.

"I'm lucky because of you, Sanjit. If it were not for you, I wouldn't have made it back at all," said Shan weakly. "How is your mother, Halim?"

"She's stable; I guess'" he replied. "Sleeps most of the time. That medicine seems to have helped, but she is still sick. Did you manage to find the medicine, papa?"

Shan closed his eyes. "No. I'm sorry, Halim. We were almost at our destination when I fell. But I have this." He reached down, straining to reach his bag at the bottom of the stretcher.

"Here, let me get that," said Halim. He lifted the bag and placed it in reach of his father.

Shan pulled out a rolled up piece of parchment and a small leather pouch. He handed the parchment to Halim.

"Open it."

Halim untied the strip of cloth binding the parchment and rolled it open.

"A map," he said.

"Yes. This is where we are." Shan pointed to the map. It was yellow with age, but the Sanskrit markings were still quite legible. Halim looked at where his father pointed. He could make out the name, Harappa. "And this is where we were headed." Shan pointed to a tiny, obscure dot on the other side of the map. Written next to it was Aryavartha.

"An ancient monastery," said Sanjit. "Hidden deep within the Kunlun Mountains."

"Aryavartha," repeated Halim thoughtfully. "But does it really exist?"

Sanjit replied. "I too had my doubts until I found this map. I won it many moons ago, in a wager in a town close to this very location." He pointed to the marking on the map.

"But it's just a story, a, a legend," said Halim in exasperation.

"Even legends have truths," Sanjit responded. "This is how they become legends."

Halim gazed at Sanjit as he spoke. Again he looked like a very odd, yet interesting character. He spoke elaborately, yet with purpose. Sanjit cocked his head ever so slightly as if to say. I can read your mind. Halim looked away.

"I have more to tell you, papa," said Halim. "Mama has stabilised somewhat, but she is far from cured. She has had aggressive night terrors that have weakened her further. I fear for her health."

"That is why I am going to return to Aryavartha to acquire the medicine to heal her," Sanjit responded.

"I will join you this time," Halim said. "I will take my father's place and come with you to Ayarvartha."

"Halim, it is too dangerous," said Shan, alarmed. "Let me wait for my leg to heal and then I shall return."

"Papa, don't be ridiculous. We don't have time. The medicine we have is almost finished, and Mama isn't getting any better. I will go."

"Papa!" shouted Taja, running up the road. "By the gods. What happened to you? Are you okay?" She looked at Shan's scratched face and bandaged leg in dismay, wrapping her arms around him with tears in her eyes.

"It's okay, Taj," Shan said reassuringly. "It's just my leg. I'll be all right." He patted her gently on the back and briefly brought her up to speed.

"But how are we going to get the medicine?" enquired Taja.

"Sanjit is going back," replied Shan. "With Halim."

Taja turned to her brother. "I'm going with you."

"Taj…"

"No. I will hear nothing of it. I'm going with, and that's that!" She folded her arms in defiance. "Besides, who is going to take care of you two? Huh?"

Halim looked at Sanjit, raised his eyebrows and shrugged his shoulders.

"Very well," said Halim. "But you're carrying your own gear. And don't come crying to me if you can't keep up."

"Ha! We'll see who can't keep up, mister Shakti Warrior!"

"Okay, that's enough. You two sound like a couple of whining kids, and you haven't even left yet," interjected Shan. "Help me get back home and we can talk this through. I need to wash, change these bandages and get some rest."

Taja glared at Halim before helping her brother and Sanjit carry Shan into the house. They lay the stretcher carefully down in the reception room. Halim began to peel the bloody bandages off his father's leg as Taja filled a pitcher with fresh water to clean his wounds. She began by tending to the cuts on his face and then the open wound on his leg. After applying a thick salve to the wound, she held a wooden splint to the side of his leg and wrapped it securely in a fresh bandage. Halim continued to wash Shan down, wiping away any remaining blood and grime. Sanjit stepped forward to help Halim and Taja carry their father in his stretcher to his bedroom to see Arja. Shan sat up on his elbows and gazed at his wife asleep in their bed.

"My precious Arja. What a joy it is to see you," he whispered. His eyes welled up with tears. "I am so sorry that I couldn't get you your medicine, but Halim and Taja will return with Sanjit to find it for you."

Shan bent his arms, slowly lowering himself back onto the stretcher. Sanjit placed a makeshift wooden crutch alongside him, covered him with a blanket and quietly left the room.

"Halim, my son," said Shan softly. "Come closer."

Halim stepped towards his father, leaning in close to listen to what he had to say.

Shan pulled something out from inside his robe. "Here, take this." He pressed a small leather pouch into Halim's palm. Halim opened the pouch. Inside was a round, dark-wooden amulet that had solidified with age. A spiral pattern had been carved into its surface, and a leather string was threaded through an eye at its apex.

"Put it around your neck. It will protect you."

"What is it?" enquired Halim of his father.

"It's an ancient amulet from a lost civilisation. Sacred geometry. A gateway to the spirit world. In time it will give you a sense of intuition, allowing you to see beyond the material, the perceptible."

Halim studied the mystical artefact.

"Go, my son. Get some rest. You have a long journey ahead of you." And with that, Shan closed his eyes and drifted off into a deep slumber.

9 ~ Responsibility

"Taja!" Halim called to his sister. "Your horse is ready!"

"I'm right here, Halim," replied Taja as she stepped into the stables. "No need to shout."

Tiny droplets of water sprinkled down from the heavens as the three travellers readied their mounts for the journey ahead. The grey clouds that filled the sky above Harappa filtered the light, creating a soft and gloomy atmosphere, and a light breeze stirred the trees on the horizon, signalling a change in seasons. Halim looked up at the sky, closed his eyes and took in a long, deep breath, savouring the cool, moist air in the back of his throat. It was nearing the end of a long, hot summer, and he could feel the energy of the earth drawing in the muggy weather like a thirsty sponge.

Shan was sitting up in his bed when Taja and Halim stepped into the room. The colour had returned to his cheeks, and he was smiling. Shan was holding Arja's hand in his. Her face looked gaunt and pale.

"Oh, mama." Taja ran up to her mother. "You're awake."

"Hello, Taj." Her voice was but a whisper. She attempted a weak smile.

Tears ran down Taja's face. "We're going to find a cure for

you, Mama. I promise."

Arja smiled weakly at her daughter.

"Halim, take care of your sister," said Shan.

"Don't worry, papa. I can take care of myself," remarked Taja. "I'm a big girl."

Shan smiled. "Taja, as obstinate as always. Come here my baby girl."

Taja stepped over to her father and gave him a warm hug and a big kiss.

"Halim," beckoned Shan. Halim stepped forward. "May the gods shine their light upon the three of you and protect you on your journey." Shan gripped Halim's hand in his and pulled him into a fierce hug.

◊ ◊ ◊

Halim involuntarily tapped the amulet around his neck as the three riders set out on their quest. They reined in their horses atop a rise, turning back to gaze wistfully one last time at the city, its spires and parapets glistening in the light of the morning sun. Taja turned to her brother. He grinned and winked reassuringly, as they turned to follow Sanjit down the path and into the forest just up ahead. Halim took up the rear as they entered the canopy of trees, the light receding the deeper they ventured. They rode in silence, the plodding of their horses' hooves on the soft earth, and their occasional snorts and whinnies, the only sounds to be heard amidst the trees and low hanging vines of the damp, misty forest. Halim thought of his mother as he rode, picturing her in a perfect state of health, her infectious smile warming his heart and uplifting his spirit the way that she used to do.

Soon, Mama, soon.

The trio continued through and out of the forest, methodically ascending a narrow path that took them high above the woods. Halim stopped for a moment and turned back to admire the magnificent view. The sun, now at its zenith, had formed an opening in the clouds, illuminating the landscape in vivid splendour. Halim turned his face towards the fiery orb and

49

closed his eyes, feeling its heat and energy pulse through his body in waves of ecstasy.

Taja turned around at the sound of galloping hooves behind her. "Halim, where have you been? I didn't even notice that you had fallen behind," she remarked, surprised.

"I was just having a look at the view from up here."

"We still have a way to go," replied Taja. "Sanjit says we'll camp there for the night," she said, pointing up at an unusual rocky outcropping close to the mountain's summit.

Sanjit waved his arm in a circular motion, signalling for them to follow. The climb to the bulge of rocks seemed to take far longer than Halim had anticipated. The path was narrow and treacherous, and they had to travel attentively as a result. Shasta faltered as the edge of the path gave way. Loose bits of rock and dirt tumbled down the side of the mountain. Halim quickly shifted his weight to one side, pulling at the reins with all of his strength and Shasta recovered. The sun had just slipped over the mountain when they approached their destination. The rocky outcropping was, in fact, a combination of several large rocks that appeared far bigger on closer inspection. The path continued through the rocks and out the other side, with an opening large enough for the horses to comfortably fit through.

Halim entered through the opening in the rock, expecting to continue through a narrow passageway, exiting on the far side, behind Taja and Sanjit. Instead, he was amazed to find that the interior extended quite deep into the mountainside, creating a natural cave that was an obvious place to rest for the night. Sanjit was already setting up camp as Taja and Halim climbed down from their mounts. Halim stepped over to a corner of the cave that had been blackened by numerous fires over time. The charred remains beneath it indicated fairly recent use. He spotted a narrow slit in the roof above the fire pit - a vent designed to carry the smoke safely outside.

"I'm going to find some wood for the fire," announced Halim.

"Great. I'll join you," said Taja, with a smile.

Sanjit sat in a crouch, silently constructing patterns in the sand with the hilt of his hunting knife, completely oblivious to Taja and Halim's departure. He continued to draw in the sand, reinforcing the patterns, pressing them purposefully into the ground, twisting and curving his knife this way and that, but always making sure that he stayed within the lines. By the time Halim and Taja returned with wood for the fire, Sanjit had completed his pattern making and was carefully putting his knife away.

"Wow," exclaimed Taja. "Look at that," she pointed.

Sanjit looked up at Taja with a grin on his face. "Mandala," he whispered. "I have crafted this one to guide and protect us."

"An intentional mandala," said Halim.

"Yes, that's correct," replied Sanjit.

Halim stepped forward to study Sanjit's design etched into the soft sand of the cave floor. It was intricate, yet simple at the same time. The outer circle contained a series of smaller concentric circles within it, common to most mandalas. A large, square block stood out in the centre of the design, and four smaller triangles were drawn over each of the four corners of the square. Sanjit looked up at Halim.

"This is the palace." Sanjit pointed at the square block. "And these are the gates to the palace." He pointed at the four triangles. "The circles over here protect the gates. My intention is here." He pointed at the square block again. "This is where the magic happens. This is where I focus my energy. Will you join me?"

Halim smiled, nodded, sat down next to Sanjit and closed his eyes. Together they focused their intention on the mandala, allowing its pattern of energy to guide them beyond the cave and out into the cosmos. Together they observed and acknowledged. Together they cultivated their feedback and became aware of the safe and secure path to travel on their quest to Aryavartha.

Halim's mind wandered.

"Halim, are you listening?"

"Yes, Mr Dasgupta. It's just that I'm struggling to understand how the pattern connects with the energy of the earth."

"The centre of each and every mandala represents the centre within each and every practitioner," Bodhan explained.

Halim screwed up his brow in concentration.

"This central point inside the circle is where we focus our energy when we begin designing the pattern that makes up each mandala. Imagine the pattern of the mandala as an expression of consciousness; a message encapsulating the intention of the artist."

"So you're saying that the practitioner binds his energy with the mandala, giving it purpose?"

"Exactly, Halim. You've got it," said Bodhan excitedly. "The mandala is alive with energy and purpose. It's a process of self-expression that allows us to produce a powerful message that, by its very design, interacts with the universe and commands a response."

"A response? What do you mean?"

Dasgupta smiled. "By a response, I mean that the unique message of each mandala resonates with the cosmos to produce feedback. You see, we design mandalas as a means to grow as individuals, both spiritually and psychologically. Mandalas are like mirrors but instead of reflecting the external world, they reflect our internal state of mind, of being. They help us determine what is going on inside here." Dasgupta hit his chest with his fist with a thud. "The earth's energy and other surrounding stimuli and events facilitate this awareness. The recognition of this awareness creates enlightenment. Does this answer your question?"

"Yes, I think so," replied Halim thoughtfully.

Bodhan continued. "The next step is the correct interpretation of the design or the pattern. We need to understand the creative process so as to attain maximum benefit from the mandala and its message."

"How do we do this?" asked Halim.

"Mandalas are created with intentional patterns as well as random ones. An intentional mandala is designed to produce the desired result like, um, where you want to predict the outcome of a future event or determine what course of action to take in a drastic situation. A random pattern is where you allow your Prana to flow into the instrument to create a pattern that is guided by your free will and the natural surroundings. This type of mandala clears and focuses the mind, leading to higher states of consciousness. Both types require practice and understanding to interpret the message. This is what we will start learning today."

10 ~ Crossing

The following day, the travellers continued on their way without incident. The skies had cleared, and the sun beat down relentlessly from above. Fine rivulets of perspiration gradually made their way down Halim's forehead and cheeks, as he followed Taja and Sanjit up and over the mountain. He reined in Shasta, stopping momentarily to enjoy a mouthful of refreshing water from his water skin, before catching up to Taja once again. The rocky terrain was beginning to change as the trio made their way down the mountain and into a lush valley filled with a variety of trees and shrubbery.

"Look. Over there," said Taja excitedly, pointing into the distance.

Halim stood up high on his horse. A sparkle caught his eye. A glare. The sun. It's reflection off a body of water. Sanjit picked up the pace. Taja and Halim felt their horses jump forward to follow him, their noses picking up the scent of the water that lay just ahead.

"Race you!" shouted Halim as he bolted past Taja. "Come on Shasta," he whispered into her ear.

"Oh no, you don't!" Taja hollered back. "Yaaa! Yaaa!" she urged her horse into a gallop.

Brother and sister sped past Sanjit, kicking up dirt in their wake as they headed for the body of water at the bottom of the hill. Halim marvelled at its length and breadth, as it came fully into view. It was a river, and it was flowing steadily from the mountain and through the lush valley below. He turned back to find Taja hot on his heels, so he whispered into Sasha's ear again, urging her on. Before he knew it, he reached the river first, coming to an abrupt halt at the water's edge.

"Okay, Halim. This one's yours, but remember, you had a head start," said Taja with a smile so smug, she would have received a stern scolding from her mother, if she was there to see it.

"Ha ha ha! Sore loser," replied Halim mockingly.

Taja pulled out her tongue at him in defiance and then turned to look at the mighty river. "How the gods are we going to cross that?"

"I'm sure we're about to find out," replied Halim as Sanjit approached them at a trot. "After all, this isn't his first time," he said, nodding in Sanjit's direction.

Sanjit pulled up next to them and, as if he was reading her mind, answered Taja's question. "There's a raft hidden beneath those trees, but we must wait for the water level to drop. We cross at sunset."

Sure enough, hidden beneath some carefully placed foliage alongside the river, was a crudely bound raft."

"Are you sure this is going to carry us?" questioned Halim.

"Yes. I built it myself," replied Sanjit. "It just needs some reinforcing. It hasn't carried three people before."

"That's very reassuring," said Taja derisively.

"So what do we need to reinforce it?" asked Halim.

"Not far from here are a grove of trees with long vines. We can strap some more wood to the craft with these vines. This will increase buoyancy and stability." He winked at Taja. She looked away awkwardly.

After securing their horses to a tree by the river, the travellers made their way, on foot, across a stretch of muddy marshland until they arrived at their destination. Halim and Taja gazed, mesmerised, up at the tall canopy of trees. A liana of long, twisted vines grew up and into the trees that swayed from side to side in a gentle breeze. Taja nimbly scaled one of the trees and grabbed hold of a vine, pulling it down from the tangle of branches above her.

"You look like a monkey!" shouted Halim.

"Haha! And you look like a mouse from up here!" she retorted. "Mousee, mousee."

"Stop messing around Taja and cut us some vines already!" said Halim.

"Halim. Go and fetch my horse," instructed Sanjit. "I've seen two logs over there that we'll need."

Using the vines that Taja cut down, Sanjit and Halim strapped one end of each of the logs securely to either side of the horse. The horse dragged the logs behind it as they led it back to the raft.

"There, that should do it," announced Sanjit, as he tied the end of the last piece of vine around the raft. An additional log had been added to each side.

"Yes. It looks much better. Bigger, stronger," agreed Taja. "I feel safer already. Thank you."

"No problem, little lady," Sanjit said with a grin.

Taja felt her cheeks flush. She fought to hold her gaze this time. Sanjit looked away.

"Okay. It looks like it's time to make the crossing. Look over there." Sanjit pointed across the river. "The tip of that rock sticking out of the water means the tide is at its lowest."

"What about the horses?" Taja enquired.

"We will tie them to the raft, and they will swim alongside us," said Sanjit.

"You sure they can swim?" asked Taja.

"As long as we remove all of our provisions and place them on the raft, I don't foresee a problem. Besides, it's only very deep for a short part of the crossing."

After all the provisions had been placed on the raft, Sanjit went up to each horse and whispered words of reassurance in their ears. He took hold of all three horses and led them slowly into the water, deep enough that their legs were immersed, and the water lapped up against their chests. Shasta snorted a few times in irritation, but otherwise, all three animals appeared relatively calm and composed.

"He must first orientate the horses with the river," whispered Halim to his sister. "They need to get used to the water and the current before we cross."

Sanjit beckoned to Halim and Taja with his free hand. Taja climbed onto the raft, and Halim gently pushed it out. He reached Sanjit, and the two of them tied the ropes to the corner of the raft and jumped on. Halim picked up the wooden paddle and began to row. Sanjit tugged gently on the ropes and made some clicking noises. The horses slowly followed them into the river until just their heads were just above water. Deeper still, and they seemed to remain calm and swim freely.

Despite Halim's efforts, the raft began drifting at an angle as the current became stronger the deeper they went. He paddled harder. They passed the protruding rock, and the horses followed. There was a jerk and Halim lost his footing. He fell back, landing with a thump on his back. His eyes filled with tears from the impact and his head spun. He blinked, looking at an upside-down view of the ropes caught on the edge of the rock. The weight of the horses pulling on the ropes with the rock as leverage began dragging the raft backwards. Sanjit tugged futilely at the ropes, trying to free them. In no time at all, the raft reached the rock and continued to be dragged up and over it, tilting precariously the higher it went. Halim rolled over and pulled out his knife, clambering up to cut the ropes. Taja anticipated his move and moved to the edge of the raft as Halim began cutting. Just as the last strands broke loose, Taja leapt off the raft and onto the back of the middle horse. The ropes from each of the three horses were still tied together as Taja grabbed them, coaxing the horses to swim harder towards the shore on the far side. Sanjit and Halim used the paddle to hoist and push the raft off the rock and back into the river.

"Taja!" shouted Halim. "You okay?"

Taja turned and waved just ahead of the raft. She was almost across now as the horses found their footing and began to surface above the water line. Halim and Sanjit touched the shore soon after Taja secured the horses to a nearby tree. Halim jumped from the raft and raced across the beach to his sister.

"Taja," he said, throwing his arms around his sister consolingly. "That was very brave what you did."

She hugged him back solidly. "Yes, I'm fine. That was a close one."

"I'm sorry, it's my fault. I misjudged the strength of the current."

"Don't be silly. You wouldn't have known."

"I should have taken the horses across separately on my own," said Sanjit as he approached the others. "It was I who made the miscalculation."

Halim clapped Sanjit on the shoulder. "Don't worry my friend. No one's to blame. We worked together to make it safely across. That's what's important."

The travellers undressed and hung their clothes out to dry. Sanjit collected some firewood, as the light from the day began to fade, while Halim and Taja managed to catch some fish in the shallows of the river. Soon, the sound of the sizzling fish tickled their ears, and the aroma caused their stomachs to rumble. Halim closed his eyes, savouring the taste of the cooked fish, silently giving thanks to the gods for his good health.

Please protect us on our journey ahead and may we find the medicine for my dying mother and return safely to Harappa, prayed Halim silently to himself.

A shower of sparks exploded into the night sky as Sanjit threw some more wood onto the fire. The flames danced in Halim's eyes as he watched them lick the dry wood like a hungry leopard savouring its kill. He felt his eyes grow heavy as he drifted off to sleep in front of the fire. He dreamed of a lush, green valley teeming with animal life. Tall trees brushed the heavens, and the beautiful scent of flowers filled the air. His head felt light and dizzy as he gazed around in wonder at the dazzling scene before him. He listened to a multitude of chirps and cries from the birds in the treetops calling his name over and over again. Halim, Halim, Halim. He was walking deep in the forest when he caught some movement between the trees just up ahead. A white creature. A unicorn. It stepped out and turned its head to look deliberately at him, its long, silvery horn sparkling in the slivers of sunlight that cut through the forest from above. He froze, unable to move a muscle, as the unicorn's stare sliced through him like a blade. In the time it took him to blink, the creature was gone, disappeared, never to be seen again. Halim felt a pang of regret, a hollow emptiness cutting painfully into his stomach. He looked down and saw red blood, pouring, rushing forth like a river from his body. He was in the river now, a river of blood, the current taking him downstream at a rapid rate. It pulled him down and under, into its depths, twisting and churning with a mighty force. He sank deep and deeper still, into a darkness from which there was no return.

11 ~ Dholavira

Breathe

His lungs burned as he sucked in a deep breath, followed by a coughing fit that painfully racked his body. Tendrils of the nightmare pulled at his subconscious like the vivid memory of a real life experience. Halim sat up, disoriented and confused. He squinted in the dim light of the new day, the sound of the river slowly bringing him back to his senses. He looked around and saw Taja, still sleeping peacefully nearby. Sanjit was gone. He stood up slowly, made his way over to the river, and splashed the icy water on his face. The sound of the flowing river rushed in his ears, as he bent down to sip some water from his cupped hands. He made his way back, to find Sanjit arriving with a bundle of fresh wood for the fire in his arms.

"Good morning. How'd you sleep?"

"Morning. okay, I guess," replied Halim, rubbing his hands over his face and through his hair. "I dreamt of a unicorn."

"That's a good sign."

"Yes, except the dream turned into a nightmare. There was blood. Lots of it."

"I'm no Shaman, but if there was a unicorn, then it can only mean that we are on the right path. Unicorns are the stuff of dreams. I wouldn't look too deeply into it," said Sanjit simply.

"Look too deeply into what?" Taja remarked.

"Morning, Taj. Nothing of importance," replied Halim. "Just a dream I had last night."

"I had a dream too. There was a unicorn," she said with a dreamy smile.

Sanjit caught Halim's eye. He grinned.

"What? What's so funny? What's it mean?"

Halim smiled. "It means that we are truly blessed."

Taja returned the smile, stretched her arms above her head and yawned. "What's there to eat? I'm famished."

After a filling meal of fruit and warm broth, the travellers continued on their way, walking first with their horses in tow, so as to get the blood pumping through their stiff muscles and aching joints. The path continued at a gradual incline away from the river, up and out of the valley. The trees thinned out as they reached the top of a rise, where they paused to take in their surroundings. The river reminded Halim of a silvery serpent, winding through the valley below them, the morning sun shimmering off its scaly surface. They climbed onto their horses, with Sanjit leading the way once more, guiding them boldly across the unfamiliar terrain.

The day wore on, and the three travellers rode on in the silence of their thoughts, stopping only to feed their steeds and drink from their skins.

"Look." Sanjit pointed at the horizon. A thin spiral of smoke rose slowly up into the sky. "Dholavira."

Halim had heard of the city of Dholavira but had never been there. He met many visitors from the city and remembered them as friendly and considerate people. His father introduced him to a trader from Dholavira not that long ago. A jovial old man, with a big, round belly. Halim smiled, recalling his infectious laugh.

Sanjit spurred his horse on, and the others followed, eager to reach the city. The late afternoon sun hid behind a thin veil of cloud, casting a soft glow over the landscape. A cool wind had sprung up, stirring the sand at the horses' feet, rustling Halim's hair, coaxing the travellers into the city. They reached the outskirts of the city, as a lone rider approached them.

"Good day, Dholaviran," said Sanjit in a friendly tone.

"Good day to you, travellers," replied the man with a smile. He was middle-aged, wore a long, brown tunic with pointed shoes, and spoke with a lisp. He rode a mottled brown and white mare and carried a large, swathed bundle on his back.

"My name is Sanjit. This is Halim and Taja. We come from Harappa, and seek lodging for the night. Can you point us in the right direction, kind sir?" enquired Sanjit.

"Harappa! My niece lives there," said the man. He caught sight of a fancy letter 'S' on Sanjit's tunic. He looked across at Halim and saw the same symbol. "Shakti Warriors. Welcome to Dholavira." The man bowed his head towards Taja. "And lady. Why yes, lodging, of course. Follow this path." He pointed towards the city. "You will pass three, no, four houses and then you will see several horses in a field. At the end of the field is another house. This is where you will find Marut. Tell him Suman sent you. He will provide you with lodging. "

"Thank you, Suman," said Taja. "You have been very helpful. Safe travels."

"And to you my lady. May peace and good fortune favour you and your companions." Suman made a clicking sound, and his horse jumped forward. He waved as he passed them.

◊ ◊ ◊

Marut was a tall, lanky fellow with twinkly eyes. He was standing at the gate to his property as the three travellers approached him.

"Let me guess," he piped up. "Suman sent you, and you're looking for lodging."

"How did you…" said Halim, flabbergasted.

"Suman just rode past, so I presumed he bumped into you three heading into the city. I can tell you're foreigners, and you look like you need a good bath, some good food in your bellies, and some well-deserved rest," he continued with a smile. "Come inside." He pulled the gate open to allow them through.

"Thank you, sir," said Taja. "You all seem very hospitable here in Dholavira."

"It's my pleasure. Call me Marut, young lady. And who might you be?"

"I'm Taja, this is Halim, and that's Sanjit. We've come from Harappa."

"I see. And where might you be going?"

"To the distant mountains of Kunlun," Taja replied, squinting at the horizon.

"Kunlun? That's quite a journey. Well, you've come to the right place." Marut turned around, cupped his hands to his mouth and shouted, "Kiran!" A boy of about fourteen summers appeared from out of the stables. "Come here, boy!" Kiran came running towards them. "Take these horses to the stables and give them something to eat. These are our guests for the night," said Marut turning to the travellers with a smile and an extended hand.

◊ ◊ ◊

"This stew is delicious," said Halim with a mouth full of food. The hot meal warmed him up from the inside. He closed his eyes and imagined that he was back home.

"Yes, very tasty," commented Taja. "Thank you for your hospitality once again."

"Good. I'm glad you're enjoying yourselves." Marut took a swig from his beaker.

"Halim," whispered Taja urgently, stabbing her elbow into his ribs. "Stop staring. It's rude."

"Oh, excuse me," said Marut, glancing at Halim. "This is my daughter, Nalini." He gestured to the beautiful young creature at his side that had enraptured Halim in his sights. She smiled demurely, looking down self-consciously. Nalini must have been no more than sixteen summers. She had a shimmering head of long, dark, straight hair and wore a deep blue gown that shimmered alluringly in the soft light of the candles on the dinner table. Halim could not help but marvel at her matching

63

blue eyes that twinkled like stars in his head.

"Please let me know if you need anything for your travels," said Marut.

"That's very kind of you," said Sanjit. "All we really need is a place to sleep and some fresh water and food. We will pay you in silver." Sanjit dropped his purse on the table with a thud.

Marut nodded. "Thank you. You may sleep in the loft in the stables. Kiran has already made up your beds."

The stables were cosy, and the smell of fresh straw filled the air. Halim checked on Shasta and the other horses before climbing a wooden step ladder and into the loft, an open platform filled with hay and suspended on one side of the barn. A chair and work table were stationed at the far end, while three beds had been crudely made up closest to the entrance. Taja and Sanjit were already lying down.

"Halim," said Taja. "I miss Mama. I hope she's okay."

Halim sat down at the foot of Taja's bed. "Papa is looking after her. I'm sure she's fine, Taj. Besides, we're going to find a cure, remember?" He gave her a reassuring hug.

"Good night," Taja said, turning onto her side to go to sleep.

"Night, Taj," Halim replied, standing up and going over to lie down on his bed. He lifted his arms, clasped his hands together and placed them beneath his head. He listened to the sound of the horses shifting restlessly in the barn below, closed his eyes and saw the unicorn again, staring right into his soul. Halim opened his eyes.

"Sanjit, you still awake?" Halim whispered.

"Yes," he replied.

"Are we really going to find this medicine?"

"If my bhisaj is still there, then yes. He's a healer like no other. He develops his medicines with the aid of powerful mantras."

"You mean he sings while he makes his medicine?"

"Yes, but it's more complexed than that. You see, through the intense practice of these yogic mantras, his consciousness becomes purified. He becomes a channel of light while embodied in this state, able to receive and translate yogic healing for others. While within this deep spiritual state, the bhisaj recognises the formula for his medicines. It is a very rare skill that takes a lifetime of dedication and training to develop. I have never experienced anything like it."

"Wow," said Halim. "That's incredible."

Halim closed his eyes again, and this time fell into a deep and dreamless sleep.

"Halim, Halim!" Sanjit urgently shook the sleep out of him.

"Huh? What?"

"Wake up! Come, there is trouble."

Halim sat up and turned to look at Taja. It was still dark, but he could make out her silhouette. She was already awake and climbing out of bed. Halim coughed. Smoke burned his lungs. He jumped up, his senses tingling, as he became fully awake. He heard shouts and screams.

What the gods is going on?

Halim quickly pulled on his boots and followed the others downstairs. They ran into the stables and began ushering the horses out. A corner of the barn was on fire. The flames licked the roof like a hungry monster, eager to consume its prey. The three companions followed the horses out of the barn and into a scene of complete chaos. The main house was also on fire and lit up the field in a halo of light. Six, scimitar-wielding riders on horseback, were chasing Marut and his servants across the field. They wore grotesque looking masks, and long, black cloaks billowed out behind them as they rode. They shouted to each other in an unfamiliar, guttural language as they gave chase. Sanjit pulled out his sword and ran into the melee.

"Sanjit! No!" shouted Halim.

Sanjit targeted the rider chasing Marut. He ran at him from the side, slinking low as he made his approach. The rider turned as Sanjit pounced, raising his sword over his head to strike, but he was too late. Sanjit jabbed his blade hard into the rider's exposed ribcage, and he toppled off his horse with a groan.

Marut turned to Sanjit. "Thank you, Shakti Warrior. Look out!"

Sanjit turned and ducked instinctively, narrowly avoiding the sweeping arc of the scimitar from another rider hot on his heels. He pushed Marut out of the way as the rider, shouting discordantly, thundered past them. Sanjit pulled Marut onto his feet, and the two of them ran in the opposite direction.

"Who are these people and why do they attack you?" asked Sanjit of Marut as they ran.

"They are the Ignogai. A tribe of ruthless savages, intent on destroying everything in their path. They have no conscience. They're barbarians."

"Watch out!" This time, it was Sanjit's turn to warn Marut of the impending danger as two more Ignogai raced towards them. Just when Marut thought they were done for, Sanjit whipped out his blade and slashed it left and then right in quick succession, cutting cleanly through their reins. With nothing to hold on to, both riders lost their balance and fell from their mounts. Sanjit grabbed Marut by the arm, and they both ran hard without turning back.

"Sanjit!" Halim called out, as he ran towards the warrior with Taja in tow. He was brandishing his sword, keeping an eye out for any attackers. "What's going on? Who are these people?"

"Ignogai. A tribe of barbarians," replied Sanjit, as he stopped to crouch down in the long grass. The light from the burning fire danced across his face.

Halim and Taja dropped down onto their haunches as they approached Sanjit and Marut. "But why are they attacking? What do they want?" said Taja.

"They're taking revenge," said Marut dejectedly. "They believe that our people killed their prince. But the truth is very different. He came to our city in search of Bhavani the seer, who foretold of his imminent death. He subsequently killed her in cold blood and in turn was executed by the city's guard."

"Come, we must move," said Sanjit urgently. "They are almost upon us."

Sanjit was right. The thud of hooves was close. A cry from one of the riders indicated that he had discovered their position. They stood up and began to run. Several more cries echoed across the field. Sanjit turned around, and Halim followed, his sword at the ready. They attacked the closest rider together, swinging their swords high. The Ignogai blocked Sanjit's attack with his blade. Sparks flew as their swords connected with a loud clang. But he couldn't defend himself against a double attack, as Halim's blade found its mark, cutting into his neck, slicing it wide open. Blood sprayed out in a wide arc, as the Ignogai's guttural cry came to an abrupt end. His horse continued galloping, taking him away into the darkness of the night.

The shouting became more focused as Sanjit and Halim sheathed their blades, turned, and ran to catch up with Taja and Marut. The thudding of hooves grew louder in Halim's ears, followed by a scuffle right behind him. He felt a bang and a ringing in his head. And then everything went black.

12 ~ Trapped

His head throbbed with a dull, incessant pain that became progressively worse, as he gradually regained consciousness. He blinked slowly, and then painfully lifted his head up from the sodden earth. He looked down at his body that seemed to belong to someone else; it was so numb. He was lying on his side with his legs at peculiar angles as if somebody just threw him onto the ground in a heap. Aches and pains racked his body, as he pushed himself up into a seated position. He rubbed the back of his head instinctively. Bits of sand and mud flaked off his cheek and onto the ground. His lips felt swollen and cracked, as he wiped his face with the back of his other hand. He squinted his eyes to see in the gloom of the dark room, making out other shapes nearby.

"Taja, Sanjit," he croaked.

Silence

"Taj…" His voice sounded like it belonged to someone else. It was dry and broken.

"Halim?"

"Taja! You're okay. Thank the gods," said Halim, relieved. He stood up and ambled over to the source of her voice. The siblings found each other and embraced.

Taja sobbed. "What… what's going on? Where are we?"

Halim squeezed her against him firmly. "It's all right, Taj. He looked around the dark enclosure. It felt clammy and reeked of rotten meat. "We must've been captured by the Ignogai. At least we're still alive."

Halim felt a hand on his shoulder, and a voice spoke from out of the darkness. "We must get out of this place."

"Sanjit!" exclaimed Halim, turning around. "Glad to see you. Where's Marut?"

Taja answered. "When we were running in the field," answered Taja. "He said he was going to find his daughter, Nalini, and ran in the direction of his house. That was the last I saw of him."

"Hmmm. I do hope that he and his family are all right. He was such a generous man," said Halim thoughtfully.

It was dark outside, but Halim could make out the source of the faint evening light that dimly lit the room. He made his way towards the light, where he discovered a securely fastened, slatted bamboo door. It appeared that an additional layer of bamboo had been fitted to the door, making it twice as thick as a conventional one and twice as strong too. There was no visible way out. He heard muffled shouts and strange whooping noises coming from beyond the door. He retreated into the safety of the cell.

"Someone's coming," said Taja softly.

"Sounds like two of them," confirmed Halim.

The pair of Ignogai were arguing with each other. There was a scuffle at the door. Shadows jumped into the cell, flickering against the wall like wraiths. Halim shielded his eyes from the burning torch that was thrust angrily into his face. The Ignogai brought with them the smell of stale sweat and grime. Taja screwed up her face in disgust.

"Come!" barked the one in front. "We go. Now!"

The fire-wielding Ignogai snarled like a wild beast. Thick, black rings framed his eyes, and a hideous, red, snake-like scar marred the side of his face, stretching all the way from his earlobe down to the edge of his chin. It twisted as he spoke, spitting its venom into the dark recesses of the dank cell. His shaven head glistened under the burning torch he held above his head, the flames licking hungrily at the roof above. He turned and marched out. Taja went first, followed by Halim and then Sanjit at the rear. The other Ignogai waited for the captors to pass him before following them out of the cell. Halim glanced at him as he passed. He was just as ugly as the first but shorter and stouter. He brandished a curved scimitar and sneered defiantly at Halim who looked quickly away to stare at Taja's back as they stepped into the night.

The Ignogai led them towards another structure. It was a crudely built, dome-shaped building made out of clay bricks.

"Get in!" shouted the Ignogai in front. He gestured towards the tiny entrance.

The prisoners had to crouch low and squeeze themselves sideways to get inside the peculiar room. A blast of intense heat sucked the air out of Halim's lungs. His throat burned, and his skin crawled. A large furnace roared menacingly in the corner of the room and the walls pulsed with tremendous heat. There were no windows, just a small chimney above the fire. The Ignogai stacked dozens of bricks over the entrance until it was sealed. The heat began to increase in intensity. The pores on Halim's face were wide open, but the sweat dried up before it even had time to do the job of cooling him down.

Sanjit sat down on the floor and gestured for the others to follow. "The air is cooler down here," he said. "The hot air - it rises." He pointed up.

Sanjit was right. No sooner had he sat down, Halim felt some relief. But it wasn't long before air down below began to heat up. His throat was so dry and his tongue so thick, that he struggled to get his words out.

"It's no use," he said slowly. "It's getting hotter."

"What's going on?" enquired Taja. "Why'd they put us in here?" She wiped the back of her hand across her brow.

A blast of hot air swirled around the room. The three captors closed their eyes and buried their heads in their hands.

"This is an Ignogai oven," whispered Sanjit. Halim and Taja leant in to hear him above the roaring flames. "It's fuelled by a bellows that pumps air in from the outside. We're being cooked alive."

Taja opened her mouth to speak. Sanjit placed his finger across her lips. "Shhh. Purse your lips like this," he whispered. Sanjit pushed his lips together, leaving a tiny gap in the centre. "Now suck the air in." He drew in a tight-lipped breath. "And out again."

Halim remembered his father teaching him to breathe this way after running through the forest while being chased by a large, angry tiger. They scrambled up a tree and sat down on a long, wide bough. Halim was completely out of breath.

"Papa. My chest hurts. Can't breathe."

"Look at me, Halim. Squeeze your lips like this and breathe." The air whistled in and out of Shan's mouth. "This forces the air to cool down as it slips in and out of the narrow opening. The cool air helps your body relax and quickly slow down the rhythm of your breathing."

Inside the heated room, Halim closed his eyes and sucked the air in and out of the narrow gap between his pursed lips. He pictured his father sitting with him in the tree, laughing a deep-bellied laugh.

"How are we going to get out?" said Taja in a quavering voice.

"It's a pity we don't have our swords," said Halim, as he deliberately patted his pockets, searching for anything of value.

"Wait!" aid Halim excitedly.

"What? What is it?" asked Taja.

Halim pulled a tiny phial out from beneath his tunic. It was stoppered with the bark from a banyan tree and had a red ribbon tied around it.

"Unicorn horn powder," declared Sanjit.

"Yes. This is the last of the powder from the ground-down horn of my unicorn," said Halim excitedly.

Sanjit pulled out his waterskin. "There is still some left," he said, thrusting the water skin into Halim's hands.

"We must all drink it together," said Sanjit. "It is our only hope."

"But how will this help us?" said Taja. "What will it do?"

"It will guide us to seek and find a solution to our peril," replied Sanjit. "For this is the power of the unicorn's horn, the seat of truth and enlightenment."

Halim unstoppered the phial and poured the contents into the skin. Even in the darkness of the room, the powder seemed to sparkle with a magical energy of its own. He moved the skin around in a circular motion a couple of times, swirling the mixture carefully, and then peered inside in anticipation. He lifted the skin to his lips and took a generous swig before passing it over to his sister. She looked at him apprehensively.

"Your turn. It's not that bad," he said.

Taja threw back the skin. "Ugh. It tastes disgusting," she said pulling a face, before handing it over to Sanjit, who drank the remaining mixture in silence.

"Come, let us hold hands," instructed Sanjit quietly.

They sat in the hot room, holding hands, knees touching, eyes closed. Halim licked his dry lips, curled his tongue up and back in his mouth until its tip touched the roof of his palette. He began to focus on his breathing, in and out, in and out, until this was all that he was aware of, everything else pushed out of his immediate consciousness. His breath merged into one continuous flow of energy and expanded beyond his lungs, enveloping his body like a chrysalis. A bubble began to form, deep inside his belly, expanding outward; a balloon of energy activated through the magic of the unicorn horn powder. He was inside the bubble as it continued to expand, out, beyond the confines of the hot room, and into the night beyond. He sensed a familiar presence. Sanjit. Taja. They were a singularity, moving as one through the cosmos. They felt the life force of everything around them - the trees, the animals, the earth, moving past them in glowing hues of shifting, pulsating, colourful shapes. They observed and moved on, a timeless force of light energy.

Halim felt drawn towards the earth, to a series of patterns moving collectively below. He felt Sanjit leading them, pulling them closer to what emerged as a herd of animals as they roamed the plains. He felt their energy, their life force. They were also connected, a family of elephants, following each other, aware of their surroundings, their purpose, their direction. They acknowledged the singularity that was Sanjit, Halim and Taja, accepting its gentle probing, allowing it to join them and then direct and guide them. Halim felt the great throbbing heartbeats of the elephant herd, heavy, pulsing vibrations that reverberated through him like thunder. A powerful wave of emotion washed over him. It came from the animals, a feeling of love and compassion, an endearing kindness that spoke in a language he could not enunciate. The elephants turned and followed the singularity back towards the village. They began to run, faster and faster. A cacophony of trumpeting blasts echoed through the night as the herd charged, flattening the undergrowth as they ran. Shouts of alarm erupted from the Ignogai village as the elephants approached. They came in full stampede, uprooting trees, smashing through mud huts and trampling Ignogai as they ran. A brave warrior stood his ground, brandishing a spear and shield, ready to defend his tribe. The sweep of a trunk lifted him up and into a tree like a leaf in the wind.

Two large elephants ran towards a round structure, ramming it hard with their long, curved tusks and flat, solid foreheads, their combined force smashing a gaping hole in its outer layer. Sanjit, Halim and Taja collectively released their control over the elephant herd and retreated to their physical bodies still seated inside the ruptured room. They opened their eyes, stood up together, and made their way towards the opening. Most of the elephants had regrouped and were heading out of the village when the trio stepped out into the open, free at last from the suffocating furnace. Maimed Ignogai bodies littered the village, and terrified cries from the injured filled the air. Halim collected three swords from a group of crushed Ignogai before catching up to Sanjit and Taja as they followed the elephants on their thunderous journey out of the Ignogai village and back to more familiar territory.

13 ~ Monk

A silhouette flitted between the trees, steadily making its way up the mountainside, drawn to the rest of its colony tucked away near the summit. It weaved skillfully from side to side, avoiding the tops of the evergreens and then slipped into a crevice, disappearing from sight.

Click, click, scrape.

It was one of thousands, jostling for a comfortable position amongst its peers, after a long, tiring night of feeding on the rich, succulent fruit in the valley far below. Tiny talons gripped the edge of a sharp outcropping, deep inside the dark, damp cave, as it curled up beneath its leathery wings to roost for the rest of the night and into the next day.

A sliver of moonlight illuminated a head of white hair near the entrance to the cave, turning it silver as if it were alive with energy. He sat in a full lotus position, his bare feet twisted into his groin, chest open and spine extended. A solitary figure, as still as the solid rock around him, the rise and fall of his chest imperceptible beneath his long, white cotton robes. His hands rested lightly in his lap, right over left, palms up, thumbs touching. The gentlest of smiles enveloped his face like the blooming of a lotus flower, its magical petals touching the corners of his mouth, his eyes and cheeks, lifting the skin, the sinew and the muscles beneath, into an enlightening effigy that appeared to glow with a light source of its own.

Seven uninterrupted days had passed since he settled himself into a period of meditation and introspection in the great cave, nestled high in the Kunlun Mountains. He prepared himself for this gruelling task many moons ago, through a series of rituals that his father taught him and his father before him. A descendant of a long line of breatharians, the monk, had learnt how to survive solely on Prana, the life force of every living thing on planet Earth. Through years of training, he taught himself how to absorb the energy of the sun, without the need of food or water. He remembered how his father first taught him to stare at the very edge of the sun during the last few moments of sunset when the fiery orb was at its weakest. It took him a while to get used to this practice, before repeating the same task at sunrise. With every day that passed, he stared a little longer, until his appetite began to wane, and he required nothing but sunlight Prana to survive for days on end.

He found a different, softer kind of Prana in the moonlight, sunlight reflected, that gave him a sense of deeper introspection, balancing out the intense daytime energy from the heat and power of the sun. For the first time in days, he sensed an insignificant ripple in the flow of Prana, as it bathed his head in the moonlight. He effortlessly shifted his focus, curiously seeking out its source. He discovered that it was the shift in energy from a distant event; energy that transformed itself into a unique signature that he absorbed and began to decipher. The message was indistinct at first but became clearer as he directed more attention towards it. With the message, came a self-realisation that he was to play an important part in a future event that would affect the lives of many. This was when he knew, with certainty, that it was time to awaken from his deep state of meditation and prepare to receive the visitors.

14 ~ Marching

"Sanjit, what about our horses? Do you think they're in the village?" enquired Taja as she marched briskly behind him. "Maybe we can go back to fetch them?"

Before Sanjit could answer, a shrill cry erupted not far behind them. All three travellers instinctively stopped and turned to face the Ignogai village. Several more shouts blasted through the forest. The trio silently turned back to the path ahead, put their heads down and marched on. Taja's question had been answered.

"Come, we must move quickly. They are not far behind us," said Sanjit.

They watched the elephants as they travelled together through the forest and out into an open field where they stopped to feed on the low hanging trees at its perimeter. The light of the moon cast an eery glow over the huge creatures. Sanjit led Halim and Taja back into the forest and away from the herd. They ran across the flat terrain and scrambled over obstacles at a pace, pushing to increase the distance between them and the Ignogai. They came across a stream and stopped momentarily to quench their thirst and catch their breath.

"Are you sure we're headed in the right direction?" Halim

asked Sanjit. "It feels like we're lost."

Sanjit pointed to the sparkling lights above them. "We can't be too far from Dholavira, and if we follow that star, in that direction," he said confidently, as he drew an imaginary line across the sky, "then we will soon join the path to our destination."

They turned again in reaction to cries from their trackers. This time, they sounded a little more distant. Sanjit led them deeper into the forest, trying to move as fast as possible beneath the canopy of trees in the darkness. The trees began to thin out until they stepped out into a clearing. Sanjit looked up into the night sky to check his bearings before leading them on and up a rocky embankment that slowed down their progress somewhat. More cries indicated that the Ignogai were closing in on them again.

"They won't expect us to climb here, and this route will be difficult for them to track," confirmed Sanjit, pushing them on and further up the mountain.

The climbers scaled the rock face until the sky began to brighten in response to the light from the dawn of the new day ahead. Halim felt his leg muscles begin to ache, weary from the vertical climb. He ignored the burning from dozens of tiny cuts in his hands, as a result of the sharp rocks they were forced to climb over, and pushed on, reciting words of encouragement to his sister just ahead of him.

The climbers reached a long, flat rock, high above the forest canopy below. "We rest here," said Sanjit, pulling out his water skin. Halim looked down. The view was spectacular. The sun was yet to rise from its bed, but a beautiful orange glow spread up and out from the distant horizon to light up the green forest below and the jagged mountains behind them. A myriad of chirps erupted from the treetops, as the birds of the forest signalled the start of the new day.

Soon the travellers were making their descent, down into a valley with another river below. After a quick stop to replenish their water skins and quench their thirst, they continued to travel north, meeting the sun as it rose from the horizon to light up the sky, which became a deep, radiant blue. Halim thought of Nalini with her beautiful blue eyes and matching gown. I hope she's all right. He prayed.

"Haven't heard any more cries from the Ignogai," said Taja to Halim as they walked.

Halim looked at his sister. She sounded tired, and the rings under her eyes betrayed her condition even more so. "We cannot stop yet, Taj. We need to keep on moving so that we can build up a greater distance between them," he replied cheerlessly.

"Here is the path," announced Sanjit.

Halim felt his confidence return, as he looked down at the path beneath his feet. It was a familiar, narrow, slightly worn strip that twisted out in front of them; a line of destiny, leading them into an uncertain future from which there was no going back. Despite this uncertainty, for the first time since escaping from the Ignogai, Halim felt hopeful. He imagined others walking this path before him, treading on the same earth beneath his feet, following their comrades into the rising sun and the dawn of another day. He smiled as he realised that a worn path like this must have an end, a destination of consequence, that those travellers before him successfully reached.

The day wore on, and the trio continued along the path that carved its way through the land, leading them through a small forest that provided a reprieve from the heat of the sun. Halim spotted some movement between the trees. His unicorn immediately came to mind, until he saw that it was a young deer, startled by the presence of strangers in its wood. A gentle wind rustled the boughs, the gentle sound bringing a sense of calm to the travellers as they walked.

Later, in the long shadows of the afternoon sun, Sanjit stopped, scratched his head and looked around as if he were lost. He pointed up to the mountain range that stretched up to the right of them. "That's where your father fell," he said softly.

Halim gazed up at the daunting peaks in the distance. "You mean we have to climb over that?"

"Yes. This is the path we must follow," he replied. "If we are to reach the Kunlun Mountains."

Taja turned to look at the sun behind them. "The day is almost over. We need to rest."

"Yes. Where will we stop for the night?" enquired Halim.

"There is a place to rest. Not much further," replied Sanjit, walking ahead.

Sure enough, the path began to turn towards the mountains, winding up and away from the valley, twisting and turning through the now rocky terrain. Their progress slowed as they clambered over rocks, finding their footing amongst the boulders and loose stones in between.

Just as the sun dipped below the horizon and dusk settled in, Sanjit called out, "over there," pointing to a nondescript collection of rocks up ahead.

They quickened their pace, finally arriving at their destination. A large oblong-shaped rock protruded out of the earth at an angle, as if it was placed there by a giant's hand, made to rest against the side of the mountain, creating a natural crevice for the weary travellers to rest for the night.

"We'll be safe here," said Sanjit.

"It matters not," said Taja. "I cannot go on any longer." She dropped her belongings and collapsed onto a smooth rock beneath the large boulder. "My body is so tired," she muttered, savouring the hiatus.

"Halim, come with me," said Sanjit.

Halim followed Sanjit as he led them a short distance back down the path. "Your amulet," he pointed at Halim. "Take it out," he instructed.

Halim had all but forgotten about the wooden amulet that his father had given him before they left Harappa. He reached inside his tunic to retrieve it. A leather cord suspended it around his neck. The spiral pattern carved into its surface seemed to glow for a moment as he stared at it, mesmerised by its complexed, yet oddly familiar design.

"Okay, now hold it in both of your hands and close your eyes."

The wooden disc felt warm in his hands as if it throbbed with a life of its own. Sanjit faced Halim, placed his hands over his and closed his eyes. Halim felt the amulet grow even warmer as Sanjit began to chant a mantra. Halim recognised the words and joined in, singing in unison with Sanjit as they focused their intention on the wooden disc beneath their hands. The amulet acted as an energy enhancer, magnifying the strength of the incantation, spreading and enveloping its power around them like a cocoon. The mantra was a spell of protection, designed to confuse those wishing to come within its perimeter. They recited it 108 times, enhancing its power and potency with every utterance.

"Aad Guray Nameh
Jugaad Guray Nameh
Saad Guray Nameh
Siri Guru Dev de Nameh."

(I bow to the Primal Wisdom,
I bow to the Wisdom through Ages,
I bow to the True Wisdom,
I bow to the Great, unseen Wisdom.)

15 ~ Berries

Taja was the first to awaken. She slowly sat up, gently rubbed her eyes, and looked around. Both Sanjit and Halim lay unmoving beside her. The pitter-patter of soft raindrops on the rocks just beyond the crevice was the only sound she could hear. The smell of rain was soothing and welcoming, signalling a cooler, more refreshing day ahead. She stretched both arms above her head and yawned, sucking in the moist air and flexing stiff, tired, aching muscles. She took a swig from her skin and munched on some dried fruit, before stepping out to the edge of the entrance of their sanctuary, to stare outside at the rain, as it fell blithely from the heavens above. She looked up and into the clouds, the first light of the new day casting a grey gloom through their ghostly contour. She saw patterns in the clouds, shapes and outlines. A mountain, a face, her mother. Tears came to her eyes and streamed down her cheeks like the soft raindrops falling around her. She pictured her mother, alive and well, with a great big smile on her face as she looked deep into her big, round, bronze eyes.

My Taj. My, how you have grown.

Mama. I love you. I love you so much. Please hold on. Wait for us. We will find your cure. I promise.

She squeezed her eyes tight, pushing more tears out in a steady stream and stepped out into the rain, lifting her face up to feel the raindrops gently fall, mixing with her tears, running down her cheeks. With her eyes still closed, she smiled, dropped her head back further and began to turn, slowly, spiralling, enjoying the giddy feeling that it brought as she laughed out loud, spinning round and round, round and round.

◊ ◊ ◊

The rain subsided, but the clouds remained. They hugged the mountains as the three travellers continued along the path that occasionally disappeared and then mysteriously reappeared, as Sanjit led them onward and upward. They climbed steadily, clambering over rocks, along their sharp edges, always moving, always maintaining their steady pace. The cooler weather made the journey far easier as they walked, saving them from drinking too much of what precious little water they had.

After a brief stop for a bite to eat, Halim pulled out the map his father gave him. It was old and worn, but still intact, the Sanskrit markings clearly legible. He looked at the map and then up at the mountains around them, trying to recognise the curve and shape of the peaks, but the clouds obscured them from view.

Sanjit came to stand beside him. He gazed down at the map. "Another day of travelling," he said flatly. "We're almost there." He examined the path behind them and frowned. "No sign of the Ignogai. Thank the gods."

"Do you think they're still following us?" said Halim.

"Cannot say for sure," Sanjit replied, thoughtfully scratching his head. "That mantra should have misguided them at least."

"I'm sure they gave up," said Taja. "I mean why follow us this way? There's nothing but rocks out here."

"We must remain vigilant," said Sanjit. "Remember, we still need to come back this way, and these people seem to hold onto their grudges. Even if not directly, we have killed many of their people. Either way, they will blame us for what happened back in their village."

"Yes. I guess you're right," replied Taja with a sigh. "Let's keep moving."

It was late in the afternoon when Halim looked up to witness the blue sky break through the clouds. "Look," he said pointing at the clearing. "The mountaintop."

He stopped and pulled out the map again, trying to find something recognisable.

Sanjit looked up. "The Kunlun Mountains."

Halim and Taja followed his gaze and then looked down at the map. The outline of the Kunlun Mountains covered almost a third of the map. Distinct shapes of the peaks jumped out at Halim as he searched for similarities in their design.

"There," said Sanjit, pointing at a sharp, jagged peak on the horizon.

Halim looked down at the map. "This one?" he enquired, pointing at the map.

"Yes. That's it. We're about here." He pushed his finger onto a spot on the map, not far from their final destination. "You see? We're nearly there."

The travellers continued their journey, pushing on until the onset of dusk. The terrain seemed to remain the same, as they edged closer to the peak that Sanjit pointed out. This landmark gave Halim a sense of grit and determination as they marched, a solitary beacon in the distance, guiding them on their way.

Sanjit stopped. "The map," he gestured to Halim.

Halim set down his pack and unfurled the parchment once more.

"Now remove your amulet and touch it to the map."

Halim did as instructed. As soon as the amulet touched the map, he felt a strange tingling sensation in the nape of his neck, like a sixth sense of some kind.

"Look," said Taja. She was pointing at the mountainside, her eyes wide with wonder.

Halim squinted his eyes in the wan light. He blinked. There was a red light coming from a small bush just up ahead. And then another just beyond that one. Halim's mouth dropped.

"What?" He stepped closer. It appeared that the tiny red berries in the bushes were glowing. He followed his gaze even further up the path, and a long line of glowing bushes disappeared up the side of the mountain. "What is this?" he questioned.

"It's the magical path to Aryavartha, the Kunlun Monastery," Sanjit responded softly. "Come."

Sanjit stepped off the path and past the first glowing bush. The others followed. The bushes were illogically positioned where no visible path existed. The travellers found themselves having to climb over rocks and push past overgrown underbrush to reach the next glowing beacon. Halim bent down and pulled a handful of berries off one of the bushes. They glowed eerily in the palm of his hand.

What's making them glow? he wondered. He looked up. It was getting dark, yet Sanjit pushed on, following the zig-zag line of glowing bushes that showed them the way up the mountainside.

"We must continue," said Sanjit, reading Halim's thoughts. "The glow from the bushes can only be seen at night. They will fade when the sun rises again."

The three travellers continued in silence, climbing up and out of the valley below. Just when Halim thought that the line of glowing bushes had ceased, another appeared, a tiny, exhilarating spark of light in the darkness up ahead. Halim's legs began to ache. He pushed his hands down onto his thighs as he walked, hoping to ease their pain. He stopped for a moment, took a thirst-quenching sip from his waterskin, and turned to look back down the path at the string of glowing bushes behind them.

"We camp here for the night," announced Sanjit, indicating a hollow in the mountainside.

"But what about the bushes?" Taja enquired. "You said that the bushes fade in the morning. How are we to find our way?"

"Come have a look here." Sanjit beckoned. Taja and Halim followed him to the next glowing bush. "The path appears again. We will continue this way at first light." He pointed at the ground. The dim glow from the bush lit up what appeared to be a worn section of earth. "This will take us to the monastery."

◊ ◊ ◊

Halim lay on his back, staring up at the stars. "There are so many of them," he whispered. "I wonder what makes them shine."

"So pretty," said Taja. "They remind me of Mama. I pray for her every day."

"Me too."

"Do you think we'll find the medicine?" Taja's voice quavered.

"Yes, Taj," replied Halim. "We've made it this far, haven't we?"

"Yes, but this bhisaj - do you think he will have the cure?"

"Sanjit seems to think so. I have faith in him." He looked over at the unmoving figure nearby, wondering if he was asleep.

"I think he likes you, Taj," whispered Halim. "I've seen the way he looks at you."

"Nonsense, Halim," replied Taja agitatedly. "He's not even my type."

Halim smiled. "Oh, give him a chance, Taj. You're always so critical."

"Don't get me started, Hal. I saw how you gawked at that girl back in Dholavira."

"Oh, you mean Nalini? Yes, she was nice. I think about her often. Those eyes." He looked up dreamily. "At least I admit it, Taj. You, on the other hand…"

"What? What about me?"

"You're just too serious. Lighten up. Have some fun."

"You call this fun? All this trekking puts me in a mood. And those Ignogai. If I ever see one of them again…" She squeezed her hands into fists.

"Yes, I guess you're right. We haven't had time to have much fun," said Halim. "Night Taj."

"Good night."

Halim dreamt he was standing in a great hall, filled with huge, marble pillars. Shafts of sunlight cut lines between the columns, illuminating a shrouded, solitary figure, standing a short distance away.

You cannot hide forever. They will find you.

The voice whispered inside his head. He knew it came from the hooded figure.

Who are you?

You must face your fears. Otherwise, they will consume you, and you will die.

He stared at the figure in front of him, trying to make out the face that belonged to the taunting voice.

What must I do?

Look around you. The answers are there.

Halim turned to look around. The pillars inside the hall had magically transformed into the trunks of massive trees stretching up into the sky above. The ground felt soft beneath his feet, and the sounds of the forest echoed in his ears. He took a breath, tasted the freshness of the trees around him, and smelt the subtle aroma of pollen in the air. He breathed out with a sigh and turned back to the cloaked figure. He was gone. He began to walk through the forest and then heard a frantic cry.

"Halim."

Taja. Panic set in as he began to run towards the sound of her voice. "Taja! Where are you?" he cried.

"Halim. Over here. Help me."

Halim shifted direction, his ears pricking as he ran. He rounded a corner and came to an abrupt halt.

"Taja! No!"

He was stricken with fear as he came across an Ignogai warrior with Taja in a throat lock. They stood on the edge of a precipice, the warrior slowly backing away from him, coming dangerously close to the edge. The warrior wore a mask pulled into a grimace, that writhed and twisted as if it was alive. Halim couldn't look directly at it; it was so macabre.

"Let her go!" he commanded.

"Halim, don't," said Taja. "Don't come any closer."

The warrior backed further away from Halim. A guttural sound escaped his throat. And then he fell backwards with Taja off the edge of the cliff. Halim raced forward to grab hold of Taja's extended hand. She screamed.

"Tajaaaaaaaaa!" Halim dived, touched her fingers and landed on his chest with a thud, sliding out to the edge of the cliff. He watched in horror, as Taja and the Ignogai fell backwards through the air, the agony of helplessness overcoming his very being. They fell into a white low-hanging cloud below and disappeared.

16 ~ Aryavartha

Halim woke with a start, the remnants of the nightmare still plaguing his consciousness. He looked across at Taja sleeping peacefully beside him. He shifted closer to his sister and wrapped his arm around her. She stirred. Halim closed his eyes and settled back into a light sleep until Sanjit shook him awake a short while later.

"Come, we must depart this place. Here." He handed Halim a dried udumbara, a fruit from the fig family.

"Thank you," said Halim gratefully, savouring its refreshing taste.

Taja sat up from her slumber and yawned. "Good morning," she said with a smile. "How far to the monastery?"

"Not far," replied Sanjit as he stared up at the mountain ahead of them.

Halim followed Sanjit's gaze. The path was clearly visible in the early morning light. It wound up the mountain and disappeared beyond some rocks just up ahead.

Sanjit took the lead again, followed by Halim, with Taja at the rear.

"Behold," announced Sanjit, as they rounded the rocks. "Aryavartha."

Halim squinted. Nestled precariously on top of a rocky crag was a structure, it's ochre colour close to the shade of the rocks around it, making it difficult to spot immediately. A ziggurat rose up from inside a mighty wall. The ziggurat was in the form of a pyramidal tower that included several stories with a broad ascent winding around it, presenting the appearance of a series of terraces.

"By the grace of the gods," said Taja in awe. "How are we going to get up there?"

"We climb," replied Sanjit simply.

"But where? How? The wall appears to grow right up out of the rocks. It's an impenetrable fortress."

"Have faith, Taja. Appearances can be deceiving."

Taja closed her eyes and smiled. She loved the sound of Sanjit's deep, reassuring voice.

Sanjit marched on, and the others followed, eager to reach the monastery. The formidable structure appeared much larger, the closer they trekked. Halim gazed up in wonder at its remarkable design. There still appeared no visible way to enter as the travellers approached its base. The path abruptly came to an end, but Sanjit continued walking until he reached a large, flat, rectangular shaped rock sticking out of the ground at a peculiar angle. He turned to Halim and extended his hand.

"The amulet."

Halim reached inside the front of his tunic and pulled out the disc. It was warm from the heat of his body. He carefully lifted it up over his head and passed it to Sanjit who pressed it into a small indentation in the rock that he missed. There was a loud grating sound and the rock began to retreat magically into the earth before them. It continued to disappear, leaving a gaping hole with several steps leading down into the depths of the earth. Sanjit stepped down, and the others followed, ducking their heads beneath the low opening as they walked. The narrow steps led them into a square antechamber, deep underground. As soon as Sanjit stepped onto the lowest step, the flat rock suspended above their heads began to extend slowly back up until the opening sealed behind them. Halim marvelled at the mechanics of this operation. A soft, yellowish glow from a hidden light source lit up the chamber; that was high enough for the three travellers to stand upright quite comfortably. Halim and Taja followed Sanjit through a narrow corridor and into another square chamber. Halim felt a cold breeze find its way across the nape of his neck and down his back. He shivered and looked up. The walls extended up into darkness.

"Where's the ceiling?" said Taja.

Halim spied a wooden lever protruding from the side of the wall. Its surface was smooth with use. Sanjit pushed it down assuredly. There was a click and another, different type of grating sound. Halim felt his knees begin to quiver as the ground beneath his feet began to vibrate.

"The walls are moving!" said Taja, alarmed.

"No. We are moving," confirmed Sanjit. "Don't touch the walls," he warned.

"What's happening?" enquired Halim.

"We are being elevated on a unique system of pulleys and weights."

"Remarkable," whispered Halim, amazed. He looked up again. The darkness above was beginning to lighten as the trio moved slowly up the shaft. "Is this the only way in?"

"I think there may be others, but if there are, I have no knowledge of them," replied Sanjit.

"What if an intruder came to be in possession of such an amulet?" enquired Halim. "He could just enter the way we did."

"This is possible," replied Sanjit. But he would find himself trapped in a sealed antechamber inside the monastery and its inhabitants are alerted each time that the moving platform is activated."

An open doorway of soft light appeared on one side of the wall above them. The platform slowed and then stopped when it became level with the base of the opening. Sanjit led them off the platform and through the doorway, down a corridor that branched left and then right, and then into another room that alight with fire sconces that burned brightly on the walls. A long, empty wooden table stood on one side of the room and a bench on the other. Halim realised that this was the sealed antechamber that Sanjit had mentioned. A clanking sound came from the lock on a wooden door ahead of them that creaked open to reveal a brown-robed character. A hood concealed his features in shadow.

"Sanjit," he said in a soft, foreign accent. "Namaste. I have been expecting you." He pushed his hood back to reveal a bald, smiling face with twinkling blue eyes. "What brings you to the monastery, this time, my friend?"

"Namaste, Aatreya." Sanjit pressed his palms together and bowed his head reverently. "I come with my colleagues Halim and Taja," he turned and gestured to the siblings, "to seek your guidance and wisdom."

"Aah. Wisdom must always precede guidance," said Aatreya with a smile. "An ignorant guide will not lead you to knowledge, my friend."

Sanjit smiled. "Well then, we come seeking your wisdom, that will guide us to what it is we seek."

"What is it you seek, young warrior?"

Halim stepped forward. "We seek medicine. It's for my mother. She is very ill."

"Hmm. Medicine. Yes, I am sure we can help you."

Taja stepped forward and extended her hand. "Pleased to meet you Aatreya," she said with a smile.

"My lady." Aatreya took her hand in his and bowed his head in acknowledgement. "What a beautiful name." He looked away thoughtfully. "Taja. It means crown," said Aatraya with a smile. "A beautiful crown for a beautiful princess."

Taja blushed.

"It gives me great pleasure to welcome you and Halim to Aryavartha," said Aatraya. "Come. Follow me. I'm sure you are tired and hungry. We can chat about your mother once you have some food in your bellies."

"It's good to see you again, Aatreya," said Sanjit. "I have dreamt of this place often. I knew I'd be back."

"It is good to have you back. We don't have many visitors these days," Aatreya said with a smile. "Please, follow me."

Aatreya led the trio from the arrival chamber into a great hall with tall, stone pillars.

Halim gazed around the room. It looked familiar.

My dream. This is exactly like my dream.

He felt like saying something to Aatreya as they walked but hesitated for fear of sounding puerile. He missed the detail of the architecture in his hazy dream. Intricate, spiral patterns jumped out at him from the pillars like slithery serpents, and magnificent, colourful tapestries in hues of red, yellow and green adorned the walls. There was a faint scent of incense in the air that overpowered a more ingrained smell, reminding him of Mr Dasgupta's house. They saw two hooded monks, their hands hidden in the folds of their gowns. They nodded imperceptibly at the visitors as they glided silently past.

"How many monks stay here?" enquired Halim.

"Thirty-six," replied Atreya. "Our numbers are dwindling. We've only had two new disciples in the last ten years."

Aatreya continued walking to the end of the hall and up a narrow, spiral staircase that seemed to go on forever. At last, they reached a landing that opened out into a hallway with several doors either side.

"Your rooms," gestured Atreya. "Make yourselves at home. I shall return later." And with that, he disappeared back down the stairs.

Halim opened the closest door. The room was spacious. A dark, wooden bed was positioned in the centre with a plain-looking, wooden closet to one side. Sunlight from a window on the other side of the doorway lit up the room. Next to the window was a door. Halim dropped his belongings on the bed and opened the door, stepping out onto a terrace with the most astonishing view. He stepped forward to the edge of the terrace, gripped both hands on the waist-high wall at its perimeter and looked down. His head swam until he became accustomed to the height at which he stood. He marvelled at the expertise that must have been required to build such an incredible structure with its many levels, walls and spires. The monastery was a bastion, designed to keep people away, to safely protect its occupants.

But from what? Thought Halim to himself. Why go to the trouble of constructing such a building, a stronghold, unless there was something very important to safeguard? It was near impossible to get into the monastery, let alone find it. What are these monks hiding?

Halim closed his eyes. A fresh breeze carried with it the scent of food being cooked somewhere nearby. His stomach rumbled. He stepped back inside his room and spied a basin filled with fresh water. A handful of mixed herbs floated on top that gave off a familiar smell. He dipped his hands into the water and splashed it all over his face, instinctively drawing in a sharp breath of air at its iciness on his skin. He kicked off his boots, collapsed onto the bed and felt the fatigue from the last several days wash over him in waves. He immediately drifted off into a peaceful sleep.

"Halim. Halim." His sister's voice came to him from afar.

Halim opened his eyes, rubbed the sleep out of them with his fingers and pushed himself up into a seated position on the bed. "Taj."

"Aatreya is back. He says we must join him for dinner," said Taja.

"It's dinner time already?"

"Yes. We've all slept the afternoon away."

Aatreya led them down the spiral staircase and across the main hall. A monk was lighting a row of sconces along the wall with a long fire-rod. Their light cast ghostly shadows that mockingly danced across the stone pillars. Halim imagined them laughing at him as they passed. They turned left and through an entrance to another room filled with a blend of delicious smells that caused Halim's mouth to gush with saliva. Long tables filled with colourful plates of steaming hot food filled the room. Halim counted twenty monks already seated, with several more delivering even more plates of food to the tables.

"Come, my friends," said Aatreya. "Take your seats."

After everyone took their seats, Aatreya stood up to speak once more.

"We welcome our guests to our table this evening. May they be graced with the goodness of our food and the benevolence of our hospitality. Let us pray together."

Aatreya brought his hands together into a prayer mudra at his heart and closed his eyes. The others followed and then began to chant the mantra giving thanks for the food, the sound of their voices ringing loudly through the room.

"Aham Vaishvaanaro Bhutva
Praaninaam Dehamaashritha
Praanaapaana Samaa Yuktaha
Pachaamyannam Chatur Vidam."

(I, the Supreme Spirit,
Abiding in the body of living beings,
As the Fire in their stomachs.
Mingling with the upward and downward breaths.
I digest the four kinds of foods which they eat.)

"Let us eat!" announced Aatreya joyfully.

Halim studied the assortment of food on the table in front of him. Each plate of food was an individual, colourful creation. There was a plate of small, round, green things covered in orange shavings, another with strips of yellow and red and another with what looked like dumplings piled high on top of one another.

"I think it's all vegetarian," whispered Taja in his ear. She picked at the food, scooping a selection into her plate. "Hmmm. This is delicious," she said between a mouthful of the green things. "Tastes like karkati."

95

Halim popped a dumpling into his mouth. "Aaah," he exhaled steam. "It's hah."

Taja laughed. "Careful Halim. You'll burn yourself."

The heat quickly subsided as the dumpling began to melt in his mouth, releasing a profusion of wonderful tastes.

"Wow. That was good," said Halim. "So many different tastes in one mouthful." He helped himself to the rest of the food, filling his plate up with a variety of colourful shapes.

After he had satiated his appetite, Halim turned to Sanjit and whispered, "Sanjit, tell me about the prayer. I picked up some of the words for food but didn't quite grasp its full meaning."

Sanjit pushed his hair out of his face and swallowed a mouthful of food before responding. "The prayer consecrates the food by offering it first to the gods. It becomes cleansed from the three impurities before we eat it."

"What are the three impurities?" asked Halim.

"They have to do with the cleanliness of the food before, during and after preparation," said Sanjit. "Once the food has been offered to the gods through prayer, it becomes purified and then we can eat it without conscience. Our minds become pure as a result."

Halim nodded thoughtfully and continued to eat in silence, enjoying the explosion of flavour in his mouth. The taste of the food began to have a therapeutic effect as Halim slowly chewed his way through the meal. He looked at the monks around him. They ate quietly together, a brotherhood of mysteriously cloaked individuals, living in solitude in a secret monastery tucked away in a remote mountain range. So many unanswered questions ran like wild chinkara through his mind.

◊ ◊ ◊

Sleep evaded Halim. He tossed and turned on his bed, thinking about the monks and their unusual decorum. His ears still rang with their chanting. He thought about Aatreya with his round, beaming face and sparkling, blue eyes, musing over the many mysteries that he held beneath his pious, brown robes.

There was a knock at the door. "Halim." Taja's voice.

"Come in," said Halim.

The flickering light of the candle Taja was holding, cast eerie shadows across her face.

"I can't sleep," she said softly, sitting down at the end of the bed.

Halim sat up. "Neither can I. I cannot stop thinking about Aatreya and the other monks. They are so, how do you put it?"

"Peculiar?" ventured Taja.

"Yes. It's as if they live in their own world. One that we'll never begin to understand. I just keep getting the feeling that we don't belong here, Taj. I mean, how can we relate to this life, this existence? And then there's this place. It's, it's incredible, yet so surreal."

Taja looked around the room. Shadows bounced off the walls. "Yes. Amazing how they built this place. It must have a fascinating history. I keep wondering how that moving platform works that lifted us up into the monastery."

"Sanjit said it works with pulleys and weights," said Halim.

"Yes, I know. But I'd love to see how."

"I also have many unanswered questions. Like when do we get the medicine so we can heal mama?"

"I'm sure we'll get it soon. Aatreya seems like a very nice man. I'm sure he will help us," replied Taja emphatically.

"I just pray to the gods that mama holds on until we return," said Halim. "She is so ill."

Tears streamed down Taja's face. She put down the candle and embraced her brother. "Oh Halim," she said in between sobs. "I pray too for the miracle of healing for mama."

The siblings embraced each other for some time, finding comfort in each other's company.

17 ~ Tablet

Halim opened his eyes. Taja was still sleeping next to him. He turned over, sat up and rubbed the sleep from his eyes. His stomach rumbled. A shaft of sunlight from the window lit up the room. He stood up, stretched, and opened the door to the terrace. The sky was clear and a light breeze ruffled his hair, as he took a deep breath and looked out across the mountainous topography. He smiled. What a view. He watched a solitary eagle glide effortlessly by on invisible thermals, surveying the ground below, searching for prey. The scent of cooked food tickled his nostrils again. He looked down towards the lower section of the monastery, expecting to find the source of the appetising aroma. Taja appeared next to him.

"Morning," she said.

"Good morning, Taj. How'd you sleep?"

"Good. Sorry, I must have just passed out last night."

Halim smiled. "No problem." He wrapped his arm around her shoulder and squeezed, pulling her close. "Come, let's go down for breakfast. I'm ravenous."

Sanjit was already sitting at the table when Halim and Taja arrived. Some monks were also sitting in the room, eating silently.

"Good morning," said Sanjit, in between a mouthful of food.

"Morning," said Halim and Taja in unison.

"The food looks good," said Taja. "Fruit?"

"Mostly," replied Sanjit. "I think."

Halim looked at the spread of food on the table. It looked like fruit, cut up into a variety of small, colourful shapes. He scooped a combination of food onto a plate and sat down next to Sanjit.

"Hmmm. Tastes sweet and succulent," he said. "Definitely fruit. Strange how they cut it into different shapes and then magically stick it together to produce a mix of colourful patterns."

"What's that?" asked Taja. She pointed at a steaming plate of green and white shapes.

"I believe it's boiled vegetables of some kind," said Sanjit.

"Well, whatever it is, it smells delicious," said Taja.

"Good morning my friends!" announced Aatreya warmly as he stepped up to the table. "It's so lovely to have you with us. I trust you slept well?"

"Yes, thank you," said Halim.

"Yes, and the food is wonderful. Thank you for your hospitality," said Taja.

"It's only my pleasure," said Aatreya with a smile. Please, eat and enjoy. When you are done, we will meet in the prayer hall adjacent to this room. The big one that I took you through upon your arrival yesterday."

The trio finished their meal and then made their way to the prayer hall. The room seemed to be filled with all the monks in the monastery. Halim counted at least thirty of them seated silently in five rows of six, one behind the other on the floor. Aatreya was bending down behind a dais in front. He appeared to be looking for something. He straightened and spied the visitors, signalling them to sit down at the back with a wave of his hands.

"Namaste, brothers," said Aatreya as he stood before them. "We welcome guests to Aryavartha," he pointed at the travellers.

The monks bowed their heads into their hands. "Namaste," they said as one. Their voices boomed around the great hall.

"Our friend Sanjit, whom you know, has brought Halim and his sister Taja to the monastery. They seek our aid in helping to cure their mother of a serious illness," continued Aatreya. "Please show them the hospitality they deserve during their stay with us." He pressed his palms together. "I recently returned from my solitude in the caves sooner than expected because I was foretold of their arrival. I believe that they are here for another purpose. I believe that they are the messengers."

Aatreya looked around the hall at the group of monks, gauging their response to his announcement. They murmured quietly amongst other. Aatreya raised his right hand.

"Brothers. I know you have your doubts, but their arrival corresponds with the Navagraha, the nine celestial deities, and their current position in the heavens." He looked up as he spoke.

Halim looked at Sanjit questioningly. Sanjit shrugged his shoulders.

"We must have faith in the gods," said Aatreya to his audience. "Our numbers are dwindling, and soon there will be no one to deliver the message."

"What is he talking about?" whispered Taja. "What does he mean, we are the messengers? And what message is he talking about?"

"I don't know," replied Sanjit. "I'm sure we'll find out soon enough."

Aatreya moved away from the dais and sat down on a raised platform facing the onlookers. He removed his shoes, placed them carefully down beside him and pulled his legs up, one at a time, into a full lotus posture. The monks followed suit, balancing their hands, palms up, on their knees. They touched their thumbs to their index fingers, extending their remaining three fingers.

"The Gyan mudra," said Halim under his breath. "The mudra of knowledge."

The monks took in a deep breath together and then began to chant in one voice. They repeated the mantra over and over again. The hall boomed with the sound, amplified by so many voices chanting at once. Halim closed his eyes and lost himself in the chanting.

"Om Asato Maa Sad-Gamaya
Tamaso Maa Jyotir-Gamaya
Mrtyor-Maa Amrtam Gamaya
Om Shaantih Shaantih Shaantih"

(O Lord, Keep me not in the Unreality of the bondage of the Phenomenal World,
    but lead me towards the Reality of the Eternal Self,
    O Lord, Keep me not in the Darkness of Ignorance,
    but lead me towards the Light of Spiritual Knowledge,
    O Lord Keep me not in the Fear of Death due to the bondage of the Mortal World,
    but lead me towards the Immortality gained by the Knowledge of the Immortal Self beyond Death,
    Oh Lord, let there be Peace, Peace, Peace.)

◊ ◊ ◊

Halim felt his body swaying gently from side to side, long after the chanting had come to an end. He opened his eyes and stretched his hands up above his head. He felt alert and alive. Aatreya stood before him. He smiled.

"Come, my friends, follow me. I have something exciting to show you."

Sanjit pulled Halim to his feet, and they followed Aatreya as he led them towards the back of the hall.

"I know you have many questions," said Aatreya as he walked. "They will be answered shortly."

Aatreya turned left and stopped in front of a large wooden door. A circular seal was carved into the centre of the door in the shape of a lotus flower. Aatreya reached inside his robes and pulled out a bunch of keys that rattled loudly as he searched for the right one. The door creaked as he pushed it open. They stepped into a small, dark room. Aatreya held a small box in his hand. Halim watched him reach out into the darkness, and a tiny flame jumped out of the box. The room became illuminated as a sconce in the wall sprang to life. The flames licked the low roof of the room that now revealed a long spiral staircase descending into the darkness below. Aatreya pulled the sconce from the wall and began to descend the staircase. The others followed.

The air tasted dank and dusty. Halim coughed. The sound of his voice echoed down the staircase and into the darkness below. He wondered how deep the stairs went. After what seemed like ages, they reached the bottom. Halim heard the rattling of keys again, followed by a clank and a grind as they stepped into another room. Aatreya lit another sconce in the wall, and another. Warm light filled the long, narrow room, revealing row upon row of wooden shelves. Without hesitation, Aatreya led them down the length of the room. Halim gazed in awe at the hundreds of scrolls and books that filled the shelves. He had never seen so many in one place before. They looked really old.

Aatreya stopped in front of a large, wooden chest at the end of the room. Halim had seen nothing like it before. It was made of a very dark wood with a thick, protruding lid. Halim imagined a dozen monks struggling to carry it all the way down the spiral staircase and into this room. There were indecipherable; twisted letters carved around the sides of the chest. Aatreya pulled out his keys again, unlocked the chest and lifted the lid. He reached inside and lifted out a cream-coloured, stone tablet about half an arm in length.

"Sanjit, please close the lid," said Aatreya.

Halim could tell that the tablet was heavy by the sound of Aatreya's strained voice. He placed the tablet down on top of the closed chest with a clunk.

"Halim, please pass me that sconce," instructed Aatreya.

The light shone across the tablet, illuminating the intricate patterns carved into its surface. Aatreya bowed over the tablet and blew gently across its surface. A layer of dust spiralled up and into the air.

Halim stared, mesmerised. "It looks old," he said.

"This, my friends," said Aatreya, "is over six thousand years old."

"Where does it come from?" asked Taja.

"Ahhh. The golden question," replied Aatreya with a smile. "It's the last remaining evidence of a civilisation that flourished long before we were even a thought in the minds of the gods. It tells the story of a people that survived a terrible disaster a very long time ago."

"But what language is this?" enquired Sanjit, pointing at the strange inscriptions. "I don't recognise it at all."

"It took four generations of monks to decipher the symbols on this tablet," said Aatreya. "The result is a story that has remained a secret in this monastery to this very day." The three adventurers moved in closer. "The time has come to share this story of humanity's history so that it can be taken into the new world. You have been chosen as its messengers."

"What does it say?" asked Halim.

"It begins over here," Aatreya pointed to the first symbol engraved on top of the tablet. It was a circle within a circle. "The inner circle represents planet Earth and the outer circle, the Creator. This is significant because it means that over ten thousand years ago, the people living at the time were very much aware of a higher power and its role in the creation of our planet. Now, if you look at the next symbol," continued Aatreya, "you will notice that the double circle is repeated, but includes four curved cones, like talons, that extend out in four directions from the circles. The four curved cones represent the four fundamental forces rising out of the divine light, drawing the universe out of chaos and giving it order and purpose. These four fundamental elements are known as the Four Great Architects - water, fire, wind and earth.

"And what about those small triangles sticking out of the cones?" enquired Halim.

"Very observant," replied Aatreya with a smile. "The triangles are like arrows. They indicate that the four elements are energised and moving in a forward direction and that the process of creation is perpetual. Can you imagine that the people living all that time ago, had a foundation of belief and understanding that the Creator and these four elements revolved around planet Earth, infusing it with life and energy?"

"Incredible," said Taja in awe.

"How did you come to possess such an artefact?" enquired Sanjit.

"That my friend is part of the story that follows," replied Aatreya, turning to the tablet. "The next set of symbols tells us that these people lived in a time of peace and harmony. See here? This symbol," he pointed to a hexagonal shape surrounded by another circle," represents the balance of life. A life filled with balance is a life filled with an abundance of happiness."

"What does that mean?" asked Taja, pointing at a rectangle with wavy lines around it.

"This shape represents the homes of the people living on this land, and the wavy lines around it - the sea that rose up to destroy it."

"Destroy it?" said Taja, alarmed. "What do you mean? I thought you said that these people lived lives filled with peace and harmony?"

"Yes, they did," said Aatreya. "But sometimes, there are things beyond our control and understanding that need to take place for the greater good. This event was one of them."

Taja screwed up her forehead. Aatreya smiled.

"You see, if it were not for the cataclysmic event that took place all those years ago, we would not be here having this discussion. In fact, the rest of the story inscribed within the symbols on this ancient artefact, predict the end of one civilisation and the beginning of many more. The seeds of the people from this long lost land were spread over many continents. They were forced to flee from their homeland and settle elsewhere, to begin again."

"So, some of them came here?" asked Halim.

"Yes. They had to escape all the flooding, and so came seeking higher ground and established the very first settlement here as a result." Aatreya looked up into the darkness. "That was a very long time ago. The monastery has evolved over the centuries, with layer upon layer being added, one on top of the other."

Aatreya stepped over to a dusty, wooden shelf and pulled out an old, brown, rolled up parchment.

"This is the ancient text deciphered; the message that you must carry back to the world, to share with your elders and teach to your young." Aatreya handed the scroll to Halim, and the sleeve of his robe slid back to reveal a tattoo on the underside of his right wrist.

"What's that?" said Halim.

Aatreya pulled his sleeve all the way back. The tattoo was a circle, intersected by a line in the shape of a crescent moon. "This is the symbol of the monks of Aryavartha. Every initiate to the monastery is branded with this symbol, a sign that has endured from time immemorial, passed down from generation to generation." Aatreya turned to pull a leather tube from the shelf. The same crescent moon design was branded into the leather of the tube. "Here, place the scroll inside this canister to keep it safe on your travels."

Halim pushed the scroll inside the tube, grabbed the strap affixed to its side and hoisted it over his shoulder. "On behalf of the monks of Aryavartha, I pledge to do my best to deliver this story to the rest of the known world, as you have instructed."

Aatreya smiled and bowed his head in acknowledgement. "Thank you, Halim. May the gods bless you and your comrades. My prayers and those of my brothers go with you." Halim bowed his head in acknowledgement.

18 ~ Medicine

The group of four climbed the spiral staircase and stepped out into the hall. The click of the key in the lock echoed shrilly, reverberating off the walls. Aatreya turned to Halim.

"Halim, tell me about your mother. Describe her condition for me."

"Well, she has been sick for several weeks already," said Halim. "It started when she lost her appetite. She just stopped eating. And then came the coughing."

"What type of coughing? Wet or dry?"

"Wet."

"Okay. And how long was each coughing episode?"

"Long. Hours maybe."

"Any other symptoms?"

Halim closed his eyes. "She has become emaciated from not eating, and she struggles to breathe. Her skin is yellow."

"What medicine does she take?"

"Our Shaman has been giving her a thick, brown, foul-smelling concoction that makes her sleep most of the time. It seems to subdue the sickness, slow it down, but she is not getting any better."

"Hmmm. Sounds like she is suffering from rajayaksmadi - a

rare infection of the chest," said Aatreya. "She must be treated properly. Otherwise, I fear she will die. We will need to collect some fresh herbs for the medicine. Follow me." He led the trio into the elevator room.

"I'll stay behind," said Sanjit. "I need to catch up on some reading in the library. Is brother Vimal still around?"

"Yes, of course," replied Aatreya. "He's still the keeper of the records. He'll be pleased to see you again."

"Here. Please take care of this for me," said Halim, handing Sanjit the canister.

Aatreya pulled the lever, and they descended slowly into the shaft. Halim looked up at Sanjit, who raised his hand before turning to leave. Aatreya led Halim and Taja out of the monastery and around its base. He followed a path that took them higher up into the mountains. They trekked for some time in silence, lost in their thoughts.

"Look. Up ahead," said Taja, pointing at a fine mist that appeared to be spraying out of the mountain.

Halim heard a dull, steady rumbling sound, that became more distinct the further they walked. The path twisted around the side of the mountain to reveal a wonderful sight. Halim stopped. His jaw dropped. The mist was the result of a cascading waterfall, tumbling down the side of the mountain like a herd of wild horses in full gallop. Shards of sunlight pierced the mist, producing colourful rainbows that sparkled and shimmered like magic. Taja placed both hands over her ears to shut out the tremendous roar of the falling water on the rocks below, and Halim closed his eyes and smiled, as the cool mist settled gently on his face.

"There, at the base of the waterfall," said Aatreya, raising the volume of his voice against the thunder of the falling water. "That's where we'll find the herbs."

The path down to the bottom of the waterfall was wet and slippery. Halim twice lost his footing and quickly grabbed hold of Taja when she slid halfway down the path. It was only Aatreya that managed to keep from falling. Halim watched as he hopped nimbly down the path like a mountain goat.

They reached the bottom to find a large pool of water that overflowed down the side of the mountain into a swiftly flowing river. Aatreya was already busy at the water's edge, pulling out several leafy green plants with tiny purple blossoms. He looked up with a smile as they approached him.

"This plant is called Mahamundi - Globe Thistle," said Aatreya. "It is used to treat diseases of the chest. We will mix it with this one," he pointed at another plant with yellow flowers, "known as Gotu Kola, which will help with jaundice."

Taja pulled a purple flower from a Mahamundi plant and raised it to her nostrils. She closed her eyes and took a deep breath through her nose.

"Aaah. Hmmm. Wonderful." She smiled. "Smells bitter and sweet at the same time."

"We just need one more secret ingredient," said Aatreya cheerfully. "And it's in there." He pointed at the base of the waterfall.

"What do you mean in there?" said Halim, confused. "All I see is water."

"There's a cave behind the waterfall," said Aatreya. He stood up. "Follow me."

Aatreya walked around the perimeter of the pool and headed towards the waterfall.

The mist from the falling water turned to spray as they moved closer to its base. The roaring sound consumed them. Halim put his head down and wiped his wet sleeve across his face, struggling to see Taja in front of him. The spray turned to mist again, as they stepped behind the falling water and beneath a rocky outcropping just above head height.

Aatreya turned to face Halim and Taja. *Watch your step.*

Halim read his lips. The falling water drowned out all other sounds. Halim looked down at his feet. A layer of green, slimy moss grew over the wet rocks of the cave floor. He tested a patch with his foot and felt it slide out like he was walking on wet ice. He tried his best to avoid the moss covered areas, until the green mulch gradually faded away, the deeper into the cave they ventured. Aatreya pulled a stick out from beneath his robes. A flame magically sprang to life at its tip, spreading an aura of light around them.

"It's just over here." Aatreya moved deeper into the cave. The others followed.

"How can anything grow in darkness?" said Halim. "It is common knowledge that all living things need sunlight to grow."

"You're right, Halim," replied Aatreya. "But not when it's a fungus. Fungi need very little light to thrive."

Aatreya bent down to retrieve a dark, red mushroom from the ground. "This, my friends is known as Soma, the divine mushroom of immortality." He held it up to the light. "These tiny white spots indicate that it has matured and is now ready to be cultivated."

"Wow," exclaimed Halim. "I've heard tales of this wondrous plant, but this is the first time that I have seen it. Remarkable."

"I will need a day to prepare the ingredients and formulate the medicine," said Aatreya. "Come, let us return to the monastery. We have what we came for."

Aatreya led Halim and Taja out of the cave. They filled their water skins from the waterfall and made their way back around the pool. Halim turned to gaze at the cascading water flowing down the mountain. He closed his eyes and savoured the cool mist on his face once more.

"Halim!" called Taja from further up the path. "Come, let's go, the sun dips and my stomach rumbles. We still have a way to go."

Halim jogged to catch up with his sister. He thought of his mother and smiled.

Hold on mama; we are coming to heal you.

"Brother Vimal," said Sanjit.

Vimal stood hunched over a book at the end of an aisle. He wore a typical brown robe with a hood that lay across his shoulders, revealing a wizened face filled with deep creases like the cracks in a dried up river bed. Sparse, white, wisps of hair clung to the sides of his scalp like wild cotton and a pair of spectacles perched precariously at the end of his nose. He looked up from his reading.

"Eh. What? Who is that?" He squinted over his spectacles. "Sanjit?"

"Yes. It is me, brother. I have returned."

"Aaah. Just in time. Come over here and tell me what you, where did you get that?" Vimal pointed at the cartridge slung over Sanjit's shoulder.

"Aatreya," he replied, lifting the canister off his shoulder. The crescent moon seal caught Vimal's attention. He smiled.

"Do you know the origin of this symbol?" said Vimal, pushing his already creased brow into even deeper furrows. His wispy eyebrows lifted. Sanjit shrugged his shoulders, and Vimal continued. "The Nine Sages of the Vedas use this symbol as their mark."

"But the Nine Sages are a myth."

"Are they? Some of the stories you have heard may be contrived, but in every story there is some truth. They live and have lived many times over. In fact, they are due to return again soon. The Navagraha testify to this." Vimal looked up at the ceiling.

Sanjit followed his gaze. "Ah. Yes. Aatreya mentioned something about the nine celestial deities corresponding with our arrival."

"Yes. This is a time and place where many paths intersect," said Vimal thoughtfully. "Your arrival, the ancient text that you now carry inside that branded canister and the imminent return of the Nine Sages of the Vedas. An auspicious time indeed. Have you heard of the myth of coincidence?"

"Um. No. Don't think so."

"Well, that's it. It's a myth, a fabrication."

"What is?"

"Coincidence. There's no such thing. It's something that was created to explain the unexplainable," continued Vimal.

"Coincidence is for the unenlightened. Do you consider yourself enlightened, Sanjit?"

"Well, there are different levels of enlightenment," replied Sanjit.

"Yes, you are right. This is why coincidence has so much power. It exists at many levels. But there does come a time in your enlightened experience where you come to accept that nothing is a coincidence. Nothing. This is when you come to know that the Divine is in control of everything and coincidence loses its power to this knowledge. When you accept this knowledge and travel its path, only then will you find true happiness."

"And what about faith? How does it play a part in this?" asked Sanjit.

"Faith has everything to do with it," said Vimal. "Without faith, there is no hope, no truth. And without this, there is nothing. The faithless are the servants of chaos. They have no direction and no guidance. They are lost."

Sanjit scratched his head. "And what of good and evil?"

"What of it?"

"Well, how does one accept that coincidence is powerless when bad things happen to good people? I mean, if one has faith in the power of the gods and their control over events, rather than coincidence, then how do you explain the bad things that happen? Why would they let bad things happen at all?"

Vimal smiled. "Now *that* is a different matter entirely. Remember that without evil; good cannot be defined."

"Yes, but it still does not explain…"

"Let me finish and you might begin to understand. The Vedas teach us that the gods created human beings with an eternal soul or Prana. It is our physical bodies that are infused with karma, actions that result in cause or effect. Only until we fully understand the cause and effect as a result of karma, we continue to make decisions based on external stimuli. Our free will is moulded by the things that happen around us. Physical, material things."

111

"Ah, so because we do not fully grasp the future result of the actions we take, we may follow a choice that leads us down the wrong path?"

"Correct. Remember our last discussion? Like attracts like? Choose to act upon something good and the karmaphala or consequence will return to you in the same way. Selfish actions will return suffering."

Sanjit thought of Arja. "But what of people that do good all of their lives and suffer? How do you explain that?"

"Many karmas do not have an immediate effect," said Vimal. "Some karma may accumulate in past lives and then manifest later, while other karma is necessary for a greater good to take place in its stead. But what we must remember is that the things that happen to us are a result of our actions and not that of the gods. The law of karma governs the entire universe and the beings within it. It is beyond our ability to grasp fully the way it works, suffice to say that there is a balance of all things and us as individuals must find our place within this area of cosmic justice. Choose a life of devotion to do good and ye shall be rewarded with goodness in return."

"Thank you, Vimal. I think I am beginning to understand now. With a combination of faith, acceptance and positive action, one can become enlightened." Sanjit laughed. "It sounds like I should become a monk!"

Vimal grinned. "You are a Shakti Warrior, Sanjit. Your path is a different one. You must face greater physical challenges, but that is not to say that you cannot choose faith, acceptance and positive action! And who knows, maybe one day you will become a monk!"

"Well, until that time comes, I will continue to observe the code of the Shakti Warrior."

"Yes, this is a challenging duty and comes with a burden," said Vimal. "But one that can be transferred."

"What do you mean?"

"To become enlightened and one day release the duty of the warrior code, you must pass on your learnings."

"Halim," whispered Sanjit.

"Hmmm? What was that? My hearing is not so good these days." Vimal cupped a hand to his ear.

"Halim. The young Shakti Warrior with whom I am travelling. *He* is the reason I have returned to the monastery."

"Hmmm. Yes. You see, you are already on your path to enlightenment." Vimal patted Sanjit's back reassuringly. "Teach this young warrior all that you know and you will be rewarded with divine providence. Now come, there is something I must show you." Vimal led Sanjit to the other end of the library. He approached a dark, wooden desk upon which was piled a variety of books and scrolls. "Now where is it?" he mumbled under his breath.

"What are you looking for? Can I help?" asked Sanjit.

"No. Don't worry; I will find it. It's here somewhere beneath. Aha! Here it is." Vimal pulled out an old looking piece of parchment.

"A map?"

"Kind of. It's a diagram of the monastery. I had a premonition last night. After Aatreya told us that you were here, I knew that I had to show you this map. I'm not entirely sure why, but I do believe that you will benefit from this knowledge."

Sanjit studied the parchment. "Interesting. I see the entrance here and the pulley system. But what is this? Looks like another entrance."

"Yes, it is."

"But I thought that there was only one way in and out of here."

Vimal smiled. "No. There are others. This one is known to but a few of us. I believe that it was the original entrance before the shaft to the existing entrance was built."

Sanjit studied the diagram some more. "And what of this area? I don't recognise it," he said, pointing to a circular area marked out to the right of the main building.

"That is the initiation chamber. Perhaps you will visit this area one day when you become a monk." Vimal chuckled.

"Haha! Yes, perhaps," said Sanjit. "And perhaps you will become a Shakti Warrior."

Both Vimal and Sanjit erupted in uncontrollable laughter that bounced across the width and breadth of the library walls like the excited cry of the striped hyena.

19 ~ Masks

A row of lifeless, sculpted, wooden shapes lay upside down on the packed earth, waiting for their bearers to awaken the latent forces residing deep within their intricate designs. Carved from the living trees of the Pumbara Forest, these wooden effigies were infused with dark magic, designed to invoke supernatural forces and shadow spirits from mystical realms. Seven Ignogai sat motionless, eyes shut, while the tribe's priestesses painted their bodies in intricate designs. No single design was the same, but they all shared a similar style. There were spirals, geometric shapes and Sanskrit mantras, all part of the ritual designed to protect the physical body and contain the possessed spirits during the ceremony. Three Shamans stood in front of the Ignogai, their hands outstretched, chanting and swaying in unison from side to side. Their ululating cries rang out into the night sky, invoking the mystical mantras in preparation for what was to follow.

The Shamans lowered their arms, bringing them into prayer position in front of their sternums. They bowed their foreheads down to connect with their hands, signalling that their work was done. The priestesses stepped back to allow the Ignogai to rise and make their way to the ceremony area. A large fire raged in the centre of the temple, lighting up the hand-painted tattoos of the Ignogai as they walked in a trance-like saunter around the animated flames. The pungent stench of incense mingled with the smoke from the raging fire clogged the air.

The painted Ignogai bent down, picked up the wooden masks and secured them to their faces. They stood facing the fire, swaying gently from side to side, in tune with the powerful flames, mesmerised by their flickering dance. The Shamans began their chanting once more, triggering the powerful magic of the masks, calling forth the dark spirits to which they were bound. One by one, the Ignogai opened their mouths to release blood-curdling screams, which tore through the night, rippling across the village in waves of terror and dread. The darkness thickened. The fire wavered. The Ignogai raised their arms to welcome the pisaca, the evil spirits, into their bodies. They glowered through the wooden masks into this world with eyes, red with the fires of Naraka. Guttural, incoherent sounds came from each of the Ignogai, merging into one voice, reciting the mantra in time with the Shamans.

A pair of painted Ignigai dragged a limp individual into the temple. Four of his fingers were missing. Irregular stumps of scar tissue remained. A frightened young lamb bleated loudly as it was dragged into the ceremony space to join the listless prisoner in front of the fire. One of the Shamans approached the curious pair, unsheathing a long, sharp blade. Ancient, magical runes were carved into its dark, ebony handle, giving it a macabre, gruesome appearance. The Shaman raised the blade and brought it down across the white, fluffy neck of the innocent lamb. Its bleating came to an abrupt halt as a fountain of red blood sprayed up into the air, splattering across his robe and face. The Shaman lifted the lifeless body and cast it into the fire. The seven possessed Ignogai howled. The Shaman raised the dark blade again, bringing it down across the prisoner's mutilated hand, severing another finger to the fire. The Ignogai howled again, this time, louder than before. The Shaman retreated.

116

The sacrificial offering appeased the dark spirits. They communicated with the Shamans in their sputtering dialect, seeking service in return for their subsistence. The Shamans barked out ancient mantras, charging the spirits with finding the location of the three escaped prisoners, the Shakti Warriors who escaped from their village. They acknowledged the appeal and set out to do their bidding, scouring the land, searching for their victims through spirit eyes that burned through the magical masks, shimmering in the light of the raging fire. The Ignogai swayed in unison to a silent beat, their painted bodies shaking with the powerful entities that possessed them.

20 ~ Unicorns

"They are coming."

Halim, Taja and Sanjit turned to look at Aatreya. They all felt the uneasiness in his voice. Despite the warmth of the room, a quiver raced up and down Halim's spine.

"Who?" said Taja. "Who's coming?"

"You must leave. Tonight." Aatreya went back to eating his food.

The others looked at each other. Sanjit shrugged his shoulders.

"As you wish," said Halim.

"You must exit via the north entrance," continued Aatreya. "It's safer."

"Vimal showed me this entrance," said Sanjit. "I know where it is."

"What's going on?" enquired Taja. "Why the hurry? Who's coming?"

"There are evil forces at work," said Aatreya. "They wish to find you. They are angry." He said this as he looked at the trio questionably.

"The Ignogai," said Halim. "It must be them. Who else would be angry? Who else would be looking for us?"

"Yes," agreed Sanjit. "It is the Ignogai. How far away are they?" he looked at Aatreya.

"Hard to say. Not that far," replied Aatreya. "I feel hatred. So much wrath." He looked to Sanjit for an answer.

"We were attacked and captured," explained Sanjit. "But we managed to escape. "They weren't too happy about that." He looked at the others. "We'd better get ready. I'd rather not encounter these savages again."

After filling their packs with provisions for the journey ahead, Aatreya led the travellers to the northern entrance of the monastery. They arrived at a small trap door set into the stone floor. Aatreya pulled out his keys again and unlocked the large padlock around the latch. He pulled open the door to reveal a round hole cut into the ground. Halim looked inside.

"Wow. It's deep. I can't see the bottom."

"This was designed as an emergency exit only," said Aatreya. "There's no way through here." He lifted a coil of heavy rope from a hook suspended on the wall. One end of the rope remained secured to the hook. He threw the rope into the hole. It dropped down into darkness.

"How do we get down that?" said Taja.

"With these," replied Aatreya. He produced three leather belts, each one carrying a twisted metal coil that was open on one end. "The rope winds through the coil, like so," said Aatreya, twisting one of the coils into the rope. "The bend of the coil causes the rope to twist around it, allowing for a controlled descent. Here put them on." Aatreya gave the trio the three belts.

"You go first Taja," said Halim.

"No, you," she replied. Sanjit can take up the rear."

"Very well," said Halim. He turned to Aatreya. "Thank you, Aatreya for your hospitality and assistance in sourcing the medicine for us. It is much appreciated. We are forever in your debt."

"Nonsense. I am in yours." He pointed to the canister strapped to Halim's back and smiled.

Halim went to sit down on the edge of the hole. He looked down and felt his stomach lurch. Sanjit affixed the rope to his coil. "Okay. Now grab hold of the rope and slowly shift off the edge, eventually putting all your weight on the rope. Good. Now slowly release some of your grip on the rope."

Halim carefully slackened his grip and slid down the rope into the circular tunnel cut into the stone floor.

"That's it. You see, easy does it. If you want to descend faster, simply release more tension on the rope."

Halim gazed up at the circle of light, watching it shrink, the lower he dropped.

"When you get to the bottom," Aatreya's voice echoed down the shaft, "remove your belt and I'll pull up the rope."

Next came Taja, followed by Sanjit. The three travellers watched the rope disappear into the darkness above them for the last time.

"Farewell. May the gods protect you!" shouted Aatreya from above, and then he was gone.

They stood in a narrow passageway with a low ceiling. Halim felt claustrophobic. The passage continued for a time and then opened out into a small cavern. A single shaft of sunlight shone through a narrow opening on the far side, just wide enough for them to slide through. They found themselves standing on a large cluster of rocks, overlooking a narrow gorge. The sun was just rising on the horizon, illuminating an orange sky sparsely dotted with wispy white clouds. Halim carefully navigated the rocks, making his way down and onto an overgrown path. The others followed. They continued for several hours, hiking on and into the narrow cleft, with steep, rocky walls either side. They arrived at a stream and stopped to enjoy some of their provisions.

Taja bent down to drink some of the fresh running water. "Hmmm. That tastes good." She sat up. "I wonder where this stream leads?"

"Aatreya said to follow the stream once we reach it," said Halim. "He said it broadens into a river that leads to a place of exquisite beauty."

"Shangri-La," said Sanjit softly, gazing down the gorge.

"I've only heard stories," said Taja. "Does it really exist? The mythical gardens? The rare fauna and flora?"

Sanjit looked at Taja and smiled. She held his gaze for a moment before looking away bashfully. Her heart raced.

"Yes. It does," he replied. "I read about them in the monastery library, and Vimal, Keeper of the Records, attests to their existence. He said he went there as a child."

"Wow. That's incredible." Taja looked up at Sanjit again and smiled. Her heart beat loudly in her chest and her cheeks flushed hot with excitement.

What is happening to me? Taja thought to herself. *Why do I have these feelings all of a sudden?*

"Here, have some fruit," said Sanjit, his arm outstretched.

"Thank you," replied Taja, accepting his offer. Her fingers brushed his and she felt a quiver in her chest. She quickly dropped her head again, hiding the coy smirk that covered her face.

Halim sensed the awkwardness. He quickly stood up. "Okay. Let's go," he said, hoisting his backpack over his shoulder. "We still have a long way to go."

The stream widened, and the rocky walls of the gorge disappeared. A dense forest emerged, filled with tall, leafy trees. The sound of twittering birds and other forest animals echoed around them as they walked.

"Look at that," exclaimed Taja, pointing at a beautiful yellow flower. "I've never seen anything like it. It's so big. Look, there's more of them." Taja bent down, stuck her nose into the flower, closed her eyes and took a deep breath. "Aaaah. Amazing."

More unusual plant varieties emerged as they walked. The forest gave way to a magnificent valley, and the river broadened even further, becoming a lake. Low, overhanging trees brushed the surface of the water that was home to a flock of spotted-billed ducks. They turned to look at the travellers, bleating out a welcome as they floated by peacefully.

"This is a perfect place for another rest," said Halim. "I'd love to have a swim."

"Great idea," said Taja. She looked at Sanjit. He returned her gaze, and she blushed.

Halim stripped down to his undergarments and dived into the water. He surfaced in the middle of the lake. "Come on! This is incredible!" he shouted to Sanjit and Taja.

Sanjit was aware of Taja's gaze as he undressed. "You coming?" He looked at Taja.

She dropped her head and smiled. "After you."

Taja waited until Sanjit had dived in before quickly undressing to her undergarments. She made sure she was in the water before Sanjit emerged near Halim.

"It's so refreshing," said Taja. She floated on her back, gazing up at the clear blue sky above.

"Yes," agreed Sanjit. "Wonderful."

The three travellers soaked in the afternoon sun on the warm rocks next to the river, while their undergarments dried nearby. Sanjit was rummaging through his backpack when Halim looked up at the sound of movement nearby.

"Look," he pointed.

A herd of eight antelope stood calmly nearby. A few grazed quietly, and others stared curiously at Halim.

"They aren't even frightened," said Taja. "Not one bit." She stood up, and they didn't flinch. "See. That's odd."

"Yes," said Sanjit. "We don't pose a threat; it would seem. Very interesting. It stands to reason that they have never encountered humans before. Otherwise, they would have more than likely run away."

"But surely they've been hunted by predators before? Wouldn't this make them naturally skittish?" said Taja.

"Good point," replied Sanjit. "Very interesting indeed. Perhaps there aren't any predators here?"

"But what about the food chain?" said Halim. "If there aren't tigers to kill the antelope, then there'd be too many antelope."

"Hmmm. Not sure about that," said Sanjit. "Ask yourself,

who kills the tigers so that their numbers are kept in check? This appears to be a very special place." He looked around.

"By the gods," whispered Taja. "Look, just beyond those trees."

"A unicorn," said Sanjit.

Halim felt the hair on his neck stand up. His breathing felt heavy in his chest as he looked to where Taja indicated. The glistening horn first caught his attention. He traced it back to the white body of the animal. It looked odd. Out of shape. Misshapen. And then it dawned on him.

"There are two of them," he whispered gently, dropping down instinctively.

"Do you think they've seen us?" asked Taja. "Perhaps they're tame. Like the antelope." She nodded her head in the direction of the animals.

"Perhaps," said Sanjit.

The unicorns stepped out from behind the trees. They moved together, side by side. Partners. Halim watched as they nuzzled each other, their horns gently touching. They moved closer, unaware of the humans. Halim stood up. He lifted his hand, holding out an apple to the animals.

"Halim," whispered Taja urgently. "What are you doing? You'll scare them away."

The animals turned to look at Halim. He marvelled at their smooth, white hides and long, slender horns that sparkled magically in the sun's light. They gazed serenely at him with large, tranquil eyes. One of them shook its head from side to side and then whinnied loudly. Halim stood his ground, motionlessly holding out the fruit. He noticed a minor difference between the two unicorns. The one standing just in front of the other had a splotch of light grey between its eyes, just below its horn. It turned its head slightly and then stepped forward a few paces, nodding its head up and down, tasting the air. The other unicorn watched its mate move slowly towards Halim, preferring to remain where it was, surveying the encounter with ambivalent eyes. Halim took a few steps forward. The unicorn stopped and whinnied again, blowing air out through its nostrils. Halim's heart raced in his chest. He stepped forward again. The animal watched him. Another step and another. Almost there. The unicorn moved towards Halim, blew some air out of its nostrils in a huff, sniffed at the apple and took it out of his hand in one bite.

"Halim," said Sanjit.

Halim turned. Sanjit threw him another apple. He caught it and turned around. The other unicorn stepped up to meet its mate. Halim held out the apple. The unicorn regarded Halim, surveying him with its dark, boundless eyes. After what seemed like a long moment, it came forward to take the apple from his outstretched hand and then stepped back to stand in the shadow of its mate, chewing methodically, crunching the fruit loudly in between its big, white teeth. Halim slowly moved closer to the animals. He placed his hand over the grey patch on the forehead of the bolder unicorn, rubbing it gently. The other unicorn stepped back a little. He fondly patted the flank of the animal and whispered gently into its ear. He reached out to touch the other unicorn. It lifted its head, cutting the air with its horn in warning but then dropped its head again, welcoming Halim's tender touch.

Taja and Sanjit stood and walked gingerly over to meet Halim. They watched as the two animals enjoyed Halim's interaction with them. The grey-patched one lifted its head, whinnied and then turned to run away. Its mate followed. The trio watched the unicorns gallop playfully along the river's edge, spraying water up into the air as they ran. The pounding of their hooves on the ground caused the family of ducks to explode into the air in a flurry of feathers and loud bleating. Taja laughed with glee, quite aware of Sanjit's penetrating gaze as she finally let her inhibitions go.

21 ~ Taming the Beast

"I have an idea," said Halim. "Let's catch the unicorns and ride them out of here."

"And how do you suppose we're going to catch them?" asked Taja. "I'm all out of fruit."

"These animals are different," said Halim. "They're tame. It shouldn't be too difficult. Wait here."

The unicorns had stopped their playful prancing. They stood at the river's edge, lapping at the water. Halim approached them cautiously. Grey patch looked up at Halim.

"Here boy," said Halim. "You beautiful creature." He made a clicking sound with his tongue on his palette.

The unicorn continued to stare. Halim edged closer, his hand outstretched. The animal whinnied and snorted. Halim gently patted his flank, all the while moving closer until he stood alongside the creature. He slid his hand up its neck, grabbed hold of its mane and deftly hoisted himself up and onto its back. He turned towards Taja and Sanjit, raised his hands in the air and shouted in triumph. The animal whinnied again and then bucked, kicking its hind legs high up into the air. Halim was airborne. He sailed off the creature's back and over its head, landing in the river with a giant splash.

125

"Wa ha ha ha ha ha!" Taja laughed out loud.

Halim surfaced with a frown. "Not funny!" he shouted.

Sanjit laughed with Taja.

"Yes, it is! Very funny!" shouted Taja back.

Even the unicorns looked amused as they shook their heads from side to side. Halim stepped out of the river. He was drenched. He pulled off his top and threw it to the ground.

"Maybe try the other one?" said Taja.

"No, this one's mine."

Halim walked over to the animals again. "Patch. Yes, that's what I'm going to call you, you stubborn creature. And you," he looked at the other unicorn. It gazed back at him with its deep, dark eyes. "Lotus," he said. "Like a beautiful lotus flower."

He walked back to Sanjit and Taja. "I need to find a way to strap myself to its back," said Halim turning to look at Sanjit for guidance. "If only we had that rope from the monastery."

"I have this," said Sanjit, pulling out a cord of twine from his bag.

"Perfect!" said Halim. "Now we just have to make a loop like so and throw it over Patch's head."

"And then you'd better make sure you hold on, Halim," said Taja. "I don't think I could take another sight like that." She laughed.

"Haha. Very funny," replied Halim, glowering at his sister.

"Here, let me secure the other end of the twine to your waist," said Sanjit.

Halim approached the pair of unicorns again. They ignored him as if he wasn't even there. Lotus nuzzled Patch as Halim approached. This time, he rubbed Patch's flank and whispered softly into his ear. "There, there, I'm not going to hurt you. Calm down." Patch shook his head and snorted. "Breathe, that's it. I just want to ride you. I know that you don't like me sitting on your back, but I'm not going to give up, so you may as well listen."

Halim slowly lifted the rope over Patch's head and dropped it around his neck. He continued patting his side and whispering into his ear, hoping to soothe him and win him over. He slid the knot in the twine down, tightening it around the unicorn's neck, grabbed hold of his mane again and hoisted himself up and onto its back. He pulled up the slack on the rope and held on tightly. The unicorn flared its nostrils and jumped, throwing its hind legs high into the air. Halim was lifted up and into the air, but this time, he pulled tightly on the twine to hold on, coming down onto the unicorn's back with a thump; the air knocked out of his lungs. Patch reared up onto his hind legs with a loud whinny. Halim slid down his back but held onto the twine that strained around the unicorn's neck. Patch bucked again. Halim was thrown up and into the air and came down at an angle, landing sideways. A sharp bolt of pain shot up his left leg and into his hip. He pulled on the twine, threw both arms around the unicorn's neck and held on with all his might. The animal reared again and then took off at a gallop. Halim closed his eyes, tightened his grip and dragged himself into a seated position. He grabbed hold of the mane and squeezed his knees in tight. He leant forward.

"Patch!" He spoke assertively into the unicorn's right ear. "I'm not going anywhere, so you'd better calm down." He pulled forcefully on the rope as he spoke. The animal was wild. It ran around in circles, slashing it's horn through the air, trying its best to dislodge Halim. He held on fast. The unicorn came to an abrupt halt in front of Taja and Sanjit. Halim slammed forward into the back of its neck, almost toppling off. The creature lifted up onto its hind legs, and he slid back down, holding securely onto the rope. It landed its front legs on the ground with a thud and snorted loudly."

"Attaboy!" Halim slapped the side of Patch's neck reassuringly. Lotus came trotting up alongside them and nuzzled Patch. He turned away, irritated at having been disciplined. Taja and Sanjit laughed.

"Well done, Halim!" said Sanjit.

"Yes. Well done," concurred Taja.

"I don't think we'll have a problem with the other one," said

Halim looking at Lotus. She stared placidly back at him. Sanjit walked slowly over to the unicorn. She backed away a little and then stopped just behind Patch.

"Haha. It looks like you may," said Taja.

She watched Sanjit nimbly hoist himself up and onto the animal. It whinnied and shook its head in aggravation, but didn't move.

"You were right, Halim," said Taja. "Looks like Lotus takes her lead from Patch."

Halim whispered into Patch's ear again. "Come on boy." He squeezed his knees and pressed his heels into the animal's sides. The unicorn jumped forward at a trot. Lotus followed with Sanjit close behind. Taja watched the men gallop up and down the riverside and grinned with pride.

22 ~ Riding

Taja watched the trees race by in a blur. The warmth from Sanjit's back seeped into her chest like the heat from the glowing embers of a campfire. She closed her eyes and took in a deep breath, savouring his musky-sweet smell. She felt happy and safe with her arms around the Shakti Warrior, rolling her hips in time to the stride of the unicorn galloping beneath her. She imagined they had taken flight and were soaring through the clouds, bounding from one puffy white cloud to the next, wild and free.

"Wait," said Halim. "Did you hear that?"

Taja pulled herself away from her reverie as Sanjit reined Lotus into a halt behind Halim. She drew in a sharp breath and held it, turning her head to listen. She closed her eyes and felt the magical sound travel right through her body, causing the hair on her neck to rise in elation.

"It's so beautiful," said Taja, smiling broadly.

Halim guided Patch towards the harmonious sound. It had a flow and rhythm unlike he had ever heard.

"What animal makes such a sound?" said Halim in a whisper.

The unicorns stepped from the trees and into a small clearing. Perched on a rock in the centre of the clearing was a

129

magnificent bird about the size of an eagle. It had bright red and orange feathers and a long, black beak. It stopped its singing and regarded the travellers with its beady eyes. It cocked its head to one side and then opened its mouth to sing once more. The delightful sound echoed through the forest, bringing tears to Taja's eyes. The bird's melody sounded so familiar to her. She pictured her mother singing to her as a baby, her voice becoming one with the bird's, so soothing and sensual.

"Kalavinka," whispered Sanjit. "Can it be?"

"What?" said Taja.

"The Kalavinka bird. It's a myth, yet this creature," he gestured towards the bird, "in this place..." he looked around in awe, his voice trailing off.

"It must be," confirmed Halim, staring mesmerised at the colourful bird.

"The Kalavinka is a bird said to dwell in paradise," explained Sanjit. "The story tells of a beautiful bird with a magical voice. It is said to start singing even before climbing out of its shell to live in the valleys of the Himalayas and the land of eternal bliss. The bird is known to convey words of truth through its singing. On the last day of its life, the Kalavinka makes its own fire and then dances around it with delight. As the fire grows in strength, the Kalavinka plunges itself into the flames. The circle of life continues as another Kalavinka hatches in the warm ashes of the fire."

"Wow," remarked Taja. "Amazing."

The trio sat quietly listening to the captivating song of the bird.

It is truly magical, thought Taja to herself. Before she knew it, tears of happiness were streaming down her face. She felt as if a spirit had lifted itself from her body, replaced by a feeling of contentment.

"I feel enlightened," said Taja. "So happy, so light, so free."

"Yes, this is the power of the bird's song," said Sanjit, twisting around to look at Taja with a smile."

Taja gazed into Sanjit's eyes and lost herself in their deep, dark depths. She felt overwhelmed with unusually powerful feelings of desire. The song of the Kalavinka pulled her into a trance, drawing her closer to Sanjit. Closer and closer still. Her lips touched his, and they trembled in anticipation. He wrapped his right hand around her waist and gently pulled her over the side of his body. She twisted, turning her face up to meet his. He brushed the hair from her face with his other hand. She closed her eyes and welcomed his embrace, parting her soft, moistened lips as he bent down to give her the most incredible kiss that seemed to last forever, exploding like shooting stars behind her eyelids.

23 ~ Jaya

With the beautiful song of the Kalavinka bird still in their heads, the trio continued in silence through the lush valley.

"Look!" said Halim with excitement. "Smoke."

Taja and Sanjit followed his gaze. A thin, white, snake-like spiral of smoke drifted into the air beyond the tops of the trees ahead. The trees parted, and they came upon a small, stone cabin with a thatched roof. A beautifully tended vegetable garden was growing at the back and a vibrant flower garden bloomed in front. Taja slid off the unicorn and walked over to a colourful bouquet of yellow flowers.

"Oh, how beautiful!" she exclaimed, closing her eyes and taking a deep breath. The sweet aroma tickled her nostrils. "Aaaahhh."

"Welcome travellers," said a voice from behind them, "to my humble abode."

They turned around to find an old woman, wearing a warm, hospitable smile. Her blue eyes twinkled amongst an ocean of wrinkles, and long, white hair hung past her shoulders. She wore a soft, pale green robe with many folds and spoke with a gentle, yet reassuring voice that put the travellers immediately at ease.

"Hello," said Taja. "We're sorry to disturb you," she said

apprehensively, "but we were just…"

"No need to explain," interrupted the old lady. "I've been expecting you."

"You're not the first to tell us that," said Halim. "It seems we're famous around these parts."

"Haha. There was no mistaking your arrival, young man," she said with a chortle. "You made such a commotion further up the river, that I'm sure everyone knows you're here."

Sanjit looked around anxiously, scanning the perimeter.

"Well, we had quite an undertaking," said Halim.

"Oh, you mean the unicorns? They're my friends." She walked over to Patch, withdrawing a golden apple from beneath her long robes. "Did they give you a hard time?" Patch sniffed the apple and then took a sizable bite. He munched loudly.

"Well, you could say that," said Halim, involuntarily rubbing his back.

"Come, let's go inside. I have prepared a pot of fresh vegetable soup that's almost done cooking."

Halim's stomach grumbled at the mention of food. He suddenly felt very hungry. The strong scent of flavours filled the small cabin as they entered. Halim breathed in a mix of herbs and vegetables that reminded him of home. The cabin itself was modestly furnished with a small entrance area that opened up into a room with a wooden table and chairs positioned next to a fireplace. Several pots were suspended over a small counter with a chopping board, and another large, black, wrought iron pot balanced over a crackling fire that warmed the room with its heat. A door in the corner of the room led to a single bedroom, and an old rocking chair was positioned in front of a double set of windows overlooking the flower garden on the other side.

"Please, make yourselves at home," said the woman, gesturing to the table and chairs.

They removed their coats and sat down.

"Thank you for your hospitality," said Halim. "To whom do we owe the pleasure?"

"My name is Jaya," said the old woman with a smile.

"I'm Halim. This is my sister Taja, and this is Sanjit."

"It's a pleasure," said Jaya, bowing her head in acknowledgement. "What brings you to these parts, may I ask? I have not seen anyone for quite some time." She scratched her head thoughtfully.

"We come from the Aryavartha Monastery," said Sanjit. "Do you know of this place?"

"Do I know of Aryavartha? Why but of course. I used to live there."

"Really?" said Taja in surprise. "But I thought only monks were allowed to stay. How did you come to be there and why did you leave?"

Jaya smiled. "So many questions from such a young, beautiful child."

Taja blushed, looking away self-consciously.

"It's a long story," said Jaya.

Taja looked at Halim and Sanjit. "We have time, and ears to listen if you will tell it?"

"Let me serve you some soup first. Once it has warmed your bellies and settled your aching muscles, I will tell you my story."

"Agreed!" said Taja enthusiastically.

Jaya walked over to the fireplace and lifted the large pot from the heat. She placed it on the counter, removed the lid and a cloud of steam billowed up into the air, filling the cabin with a zesty aroma. She dished the soup into four wooden bowls positioned nearby.

How did she know that she would need four bowls? Halim wondered to himself.

"Hmmm," said Taja gingerly sipping the hot broth. "This is delicious."

"Yes, very nice," agreed Halim. "So tasty."

"Why, thank you," said Jaya. "Fresh from my vegetable garden. So you're the quiet one." She looked at Sanjit as he ate.

Sanjit smiled. A rare event. "I prefer to listen," he said quietly.

"Excellent trait to have," said Jaya.

134

"Speaking of which," said Taja. "You promised."

"Indeed I did," replied Jaya. "My story." She smiled again, pushing her face into a furrow of impossible creases. "Now where to begin? It was such a long, long time ago."

"At the beginning, of course!" said Taja, beaming.

Jaya grinned. "Why yes, of course, how silly of me. All stories start at the beginning. Now let me see." She closed her eyes. The embers of the fire crackled in anticipation. "I knew I was different from other children when I started seeing things; things that they could not see. They came to me at first in my dreams, so I dismissed them as childish reflections. But then they came to me when I was awake as well. They were visions; distorted images of people that I knew. Friends and family. Intuitively, I realised that they were visions of real events. What I didn't know was that they were events that were yet to take place."

"So you're a seer?" asked Taja.

"Yes. I guess that's what some people call it, but at the time, I was labelled a freak, an outcast. I was shunned by people that didn't understand me. Fear of the unknown." Jaya sighed. "I was often blamed for strange events or unexplainable phenomena. Eventually, I was forced to go into exile. I was still young, just sixteen summers, yet I was wise beyond my years. Little did I know that this could not substitute experience, something that I was forced to endure until I met Girish."

"Where? How did you meet him?" This time, it was Sanjit who spoke, clearly intrigued with Jaya's story.

"Aaahhh. He speaks," said Jaya smiling. "So you've heard of Girish? He was so charming back then." She gazed up at the ceiling in reminiscence.

"Vimal told me about him," said Sanjit.

"Vimal? How is the master of the archives?"

"He is well. Is it true that Girish was one of the Nine Sages?"

Jaya regarded Sanjit silently for a moment and then smirked. "Yes, it is true. Girish was one of the Nine. When I met him, he was middle-aged and fairly arrogant. He recognised my abilities and taught me how to control them. It was the first time that someone recognised my visions as a gift, rather than a curse. He took me under his wing and invited me into the monastery. At first, the other monks treated me like an outsider. It felt like I was back home again. I felt so alone. In the long history of the monastery, a female had never been inside, let alone taken in by its master."

"The monks must have been upset." said Halim.

"Yes. Angry more like," said Jaya. "They immediately called an audience with Girish to express their resentment towards his actions. I was not invited, but my visions foretold me of the outcome. He told them that I was like him."

"What do you mean?" questioned Halim.

"He said that I was also one of the Nine."

The fire crackled again, and Halim felt a shiver run up and down his spine. There was an uncomfortable silence in the room as the listeners waited anxiously for Jaya to continue her story.

"I had no idea what my vision meant when I saw it, after all, I had never heard of the Nine Sages. All I felt were the monks' reactions, and most of them were condemning. They questioned the validity of Girish's judgement. How could he truly know that I was another like him? Even so, how could he make a decision to bring me inside the monastery, to go against the ancient code as established by the founders of the Order? He argued vehemently that I was not the first female; that the original founders were made up of males and females."

Halim leant forward in his chair, eager to hear the rest of the story. "And then, what happened?"

"Well, a few monks decided to leave the monastery and Girish confined me to my room for fear of further insurgency. I was only allowed to venture as far as the archives. He brought me my meals every day and made sure I never came into contact with any of the monks."

"But what about his statement?" questioned Sanjit. "That you were one of the Nine Sages?"

"As I said, I never knew what the Nine Sages were when I experienced my vision, so I dismissed it at the time until I came across the story in the library. I still remember the day like it was yesterday." Jaya closed her eyes and smiled. "I looked up from a book I was reading on the philosophy of the mind, to find Girish standing before me with a grin on his face. He was holding a large, old, brown book in his hands. He held it up and told me that it was an ancient volume of the Vedas that contained a story of the Nine Sages. He went on to say that the book was written by one of the founders of the monastery and told of the history of the Nine Sages and how they came to be. He sat down and began to read to me. I was enthralled. He explained that the spirits of the sages manifest themselves on Earth every few hundred years. He told me that I was the embodiment of the spirit goddess Durga and that I had an important role to play with him at the monastery."

"What about him?" said Halim. "Girish. What was his role? I mean which of the Nine Sages embodied him?"

"Well, firstly, the name Girish means lord of the mountains. He was the embodiment of Balarama, the eighth avatar of Vishnu, who was a very powerful sage. He was able to manipulate Prana. He explained that he could 'see' the life force all around us. He could sense disruptions in the flow of this energy, and then just by focusing his will upon that energy, he could change its course."

"Wow," said Halim and Taja together.

"Yes, quite remarkable. He was a powerful healer, able to correct the negative blockages in Prana caused by disease or injury just by enforcing his will upon the wounded. He said he sensed my ability when he met me because my Prana glowed around me in a golden colour, unlike anything he had seen before."

"But I thought that Girish was a warrior?" said Sanjit. "I have read the story of Baglarat in the library myself."

"Ah, yes. The attack." Jaya's face turned sombre. "I was there when the monastery was besieged. It was several years after the offended monks had left the monastery. We discovered much later that they had betrayed the location of the monastery to the marauders of Baglarat. In their resentment, they had told these people that the monastery contained great treasures. They came in the night. Hundreds of them."

"How did they get in?" asked Taja.

"There was a secret entrance at the back. It has since been converted into an exit-only passage."

"Yes, I think we used it when we left the monastery," said Halim.

"Aatreya made us leave this way."

"Aatreya," said Jaya. "How is the young monk?"

"Young? He is not that young," said Halim.

"Ah, well when I saw him last, he was young. Have I been here that long?" she said in a quiet voice as she looked around the cabin.

"The attack!" said Taja. "What happened?"

"Ah, yes. Excuse me for digressing. Now where were we?"

"There were hundreds of marauders," said Taja. "And they were attacking the monastery."

"Yes, yes. I woke up in the middle of the night from a terrible nightmare, just moments before the attack. I ran to Girish and told him of my vision. He raised the alarm and woke the other monks. By the time we reached the secret entrance, dozens of intruders were already inside. A few monks were killed while trying to seal the entrance, and then Girish attacked. I witnessed him use his power to maim and kill those wanting to cause us harm. He was unstoppable. It was a ghastly sight. They stood no chance against him. He moved so quickly, weaving in between the intruders, waving his arms about like a bird. Without even touching the Baglarat, he was able to twist their Prana, crippling them where they stood. Their faces contorted in agony as he crafted his magic, crushing them in his wake. Their terrifying screams echoed through the passageways of the monastery, bouncing off the walls like shrieking bats in flight." Jaya closed her eyes, remembering. "I can still hear their painful cries, their torment. Some of them were silenced immediately, while others lay physically challenged, writhing about on the floor like a bunch of disfigured lizards." Jaya gazed out the window. She continued. "It was a sombre day. The rest of the monks called an audience with Girish and demanded that I leave the monastery. They blamed me for the attack, and they were right. If it weren't for me, the other monks would never have left the monastery, and the Baglarat would never have attacked."

"But you warned them of the attack," said Taja. "If it wasn't for you, more monks could have been killed."

Jaya smiled. "Yes, my child, you are right and Girish stood behind me on this, but I had already seen my fate. By the time he came to me, I was already packed and planning to leave. Girish left with me. He helped me build this cottage." She looked around the room, smiling at the memory. Jaya turned to Halim. "The road ahead is layered with obstacles for the three of you. You need to stick together if you are to survive."

"What kind of obstacles?" enquired Sanjit.

"It is hard to see them clearly. My vision is clouded by…" Jaya closed her eyes. The silence was uncomfortable. Her eyes snapped open, and a strange guttural sound escaped her lips. Halim shivered. Taja's eyes widened. Jaya's head dropped. "There are dark forces at work. They are angry. The Talisman." She reached her hand out towards Halim. He turned to look at Sanjit, who nodded imperceptibly. Halim reached into his tunic and pulled out the wooden amulet. He lifted it up over his head and handed it to Jaya. She took it, held it close to her chest and began to recite a mantra, softly at first and then gradually building in amplitude. She continued to chant as she stood and waved the amulet around the room and over their heads several times. Her voice boomed around the small cottage. Halim could feel the power of her chanting wash over them like a magical wave of energy. She sat down abruptly. "There. It is done," she said softly, handing the amulet back to Halim.

"What did you do?" said Taja.

"I placed a spell of protection over you. This will confuse

your pursuers for some time. Now finish your food." She waved her hand over the soup. "It's getting cold."

Jaya stood and stepped outside the hut. Halim watched her through the window as she fed the unicorns a bunch of fresh, orange carrots. He couldn't help but marvel over her amazing story. A true sage of the Nine.

24 ~ Chief

Thick, dark smoke spiralled up into the sky, clouding the sun, casting an abnormal haze over the village. An imposing figure sat, sprawled across a hideous throne, his face twisted into an ugly sneer. His long, matted hair covered most of his face as he chewed on a large bone like the ravenous scavenger that he was. A large, wolf-like creature lay at his feet. It snapped its jaws, catching the scraps of meat he threw at it as he ate. The creature turned its head and snarled, revealing a set of long, vicious, pointed fangs as a solitary figure approached. The man dropped down to his knees and bowed his head in reverence. His face was painted white; his eyes were sunken into their sockets, and he looked emaciated.

"My lord," he rasped. "We have found a trail."

"Good," replied the barbarian. "Where are they?" he growled.

"We have not found them," replied the tracker.

"Then how do you know that it is the right trail?" he said in agitation.

"The spirits are never wrong, my Lord. They have shown us the way."

"But then why can we not find them?!" he shouted.

"I… I do not know, your eminence," he stammered.

The Ignogai chief stood up off his throne. He threw the bone at the man on his knees. It hit him on his head with a clunk. He dropped his head, touching his forehead to the ground and yelped. "You incompetent imbecile!" he bellowed. "Find them immediately! Otherwise, this will be the last time that you kneel before me!"

The creature alongside the throne bared its teeth and growled again. Saliva dribbled out of its mouth. The gaunt looking man quickly stood and scampered away. The chief sat down into his chair, his face red from exertion. He reached across the throne and picked up a long, curved blade. He raised it into the air, admiring his reflection as he twisted the blade from side to side. He sneered, swinging the sword out in an arc, slashing the air right, left, right.

"Hah! Hah!" he roared savagely. "Those warriors are mine! All mine!"

25 ~ Goodbye

Like lithe serpents in the night, the long, winding corridors twisted this way and that, snaking away into the distant horizon. A fine layer of wraith-like mist, clinging resolutely to the soft earth, stirred, swirled and lifted as Halim picked up his pace; the steady stomp of his feet the only sound breaking the silence in this peculiar place. He noticed someone moving beside him. He turned his head to see who it was, but his 'companion' jumped quickly back into his periphery vision, deftly hiding from sight.

Is there someone there? He thought to himself. *Or is it just my shadow following me?*

He shook his head to clear it but still had the feeling that there was somebody beside him, watching, calculating.

Halim.

The voice sounded distant. He stood still and closed his eyes.

Halim.

He recognised it. Nearer now. It was inside his head.

Jaya.

You will need to be strong, Halim. For your sister.

What do you mean? Is she okay?

Don't lose hope, Halim. Stay strong.

The voice drifted away again.

Wait! Jaya! Jaya!

Silence. Halim opened his eyes, and the corridors were gone. They had been replaced by an infinite plain, swathed by an ocean of stars that glittered down upon him from the heavens above. He felt vulnerable and alone, yet humbly connected to the vastness of the universe as it exposed itself to him in all its majestic glory. He dropped to his knees in acquiescence and gazed up in awe at the Creator's masterpiece, His intricate work of art. He witnessed the billions of stars as cogs in the celestial clock, each one turning on its axis, connecting to the others across the endless expanse above. It was then that he became aware. It was then that he understood that despite his insignificance, he was part of Creation. He was significant. And unlike the stars in the universe, he was alive, a human being, capable of forging his own destiny, of creating his own path, his own karma.

Halim felt a heavy weight on his back. He turned to look over his shoulder. The symbol of the crescent moon caught his eye. The canister. The scroll. He felt the burden he was forced to bear. Its weight was difficult to bear. He heard a different voice inside his head. Mocking. Taunting.

Leave the canister Halim. Discard the scroll. You don't need it. It's an unnecessary load. You deserve better.

He squeezed his eyes shut and shouted out loud, "Noooo!" His voice sounded dull, flat. It was as if the environment around him sucked away the energy of his plea, diminishing its power, its strength.

Be strong, Halim. Jaya's voice echoed inside his head.

With effort, he pushed himself up and onto his feet, sucked the air into his lungs and took a step forward and then another.

Come on. You can do this.

The weight of the canister still felt as if it was pulling him back like a resistant force. He lifted his head, strained his muscles, dug his heels into the ground, and the pressure began to ease off a little. Soon he was moving forward easily. His tired muscles ached, but he kept on going, one painful step at a time.

A faint orange glow tickled the horizon as Halim gradually quickened his pace, expectantly looking ahead, yearning for the energy, the source of the light ahead. The glow strengthened, brightened, melting away the blanket of stars like the embers from a smouldering fire. The corners of his mouth turned up into a smile and spread across his face, welcoming the light and warmth that came from the rising sun. He shifted his weight, his centre of gravity, involuntary tilting his pelvis, taking the pressure off his legs, allowing them to fall forward and into a steady rhythm until he was running, his arms pumping effortlessly beside his body, pushing him forward with momentum. The glow brightened until the edge of the fiery orb pushed up and into the sky, forcing him to close his eyes against its brightness as he ran. The energy of the sun enveloped his entire being until he could feel his legs no longer. He was flying, soaring up into the sky like an eagle. With his eyes closed, he could see through the eyes of the bird. The plains below stretched out before him, far into the distance. He was alive. He was free.

◊ ◊ ◊

"The manuscript," said Jaya as she stood at the entrance to the cabin. She pointed at the branded leather canister. "You must keep it safe."

"Yes," said Halim looking up. "Aatreya requested that we share the story with the elders and teach it to our young."

"Girish showed me the text once," said Jaya stepping inside. "The story of our ancestors. And the prophecy."

"What prophecy?" said Taja.

"He didn't tell you about the prophecy of Tarat?" Jaya looked around expectantly at her visitors. "Tarat was a great seer and spiritual leader," she continued. "He was one of the Nine. He lived over one thousand years ago. He said that one day the world would become united through a network of knowledge." She smiled. "Girish believed that I was Tarat reincarnated. Tarat was the one that transcribed the tablets."

"You mean onto the manuscript?" said Halim, patting the

leather canister.

"Yes. The manuscript you carry is one of many transcribed pieces of work carried out by Tarat. It was his genius that was responsible for its translation."

"Aatreya said that it took four generations of monks to decipher the language of the tablet," said Taja.

"My child," Jaya smiled. "That's technically correct. The tablet that you saw and many others like it, were discovered by a monk in a previously hidden chamber beneath the monastery. It was only four generations later that Tarat deciphered them. But he did it on his own. He had no assistance from any other monks or those before him. It is said that he locked himself in the chamber for weeks. Some say that it was the divine light of the gods that showed him the way. Others say that he was visited by the creators of the tablets themselves."

"What of our pursuers?" said Sanjit, changing the subject. "Where are they?"

Jaya narrowed her eyes to slits. "They are coming, but they are confused. Distracted. You will be safe here this evening. But you must leave at first light. Without the unicorns."

"But surely they will catch up to us?" said Taja, concern in her voice.

"The path you must take is too rocky for the creatures to cross. Instead of abandoning them in the mountains, rather leave them here in the valley. Here, take this." Jaya handed a small brown pouch to Halim. "You will need it."

"What is it?" enquired Halim, accepting the gift.

"It's ground unicorn horn. I'm sure you're familiar with its properties, young Shakti Warrior," replied Jaya with a grin.

"It's quite heavy. Feels like there's at least half a horn in here," said Halim, lifting the bag in his hand.

"Yes. More or less," said Jaya. "You must take it all at once. Split it between the three of you."

"But that's crazy," said Sanjit. "That's way too much. It might kill us."

"Trust me. It won't. It will save your lives when you need it

146

most."

"And when will that be?" asked Taja.

"You will know," replied Jaya with a smile. "You will know."

Halim opened the bag and peered inside. Thousands of twinkling stars winked back at him.

"Come, it's getting dark," said Jaya. "Time to get some much-needed rest before your long journey tomorrow." She looked at Taja. "And your mother awaits."

"What?" said Taja. Tears welled up in her eyes. "Will she be okay? How is she?"

"You must leave early tomorrow," said Jaya. She closed her eyes. "She is weak, but she is holding on. Your father is taking care of her."

"Oh mama," sobbed Taja. She stood up from the table and threw her arms around Jaya, burying her head in her robes.

"There, there child," said Jaya patting Taja on the back reassuringly. "It will all be all right. Your mother is a strong woman." This only caused Taja to sob even more. Jaya gently pulled Taja from her shoulder. "I will fix you a nice, hot, herbal tonic that will make you sleep like a baby. In the meantime, you can help me pack some provisions for your journey tomorrow. Okay?"

Taja wiped her eyes, sniffed and nodded her head in agreement.

"That's it," said Jaya. "I want you to focus on the task at hand and the journey ahead. One step at a time, one day at a time and then before you know it, you will be home with your family."

◊ ◊ ◊

"Halim. Halim."

Halim opened his eyes to Taja shaking him gently awake. He smiled. "Taja. My sister."

"We must go, Halim."

Halim reached out his arms, wrapping them around Taja, pulling her into an embrace. She hugged him back. Jaya's voice still echoed inside his mind.

Be strong for Taja, Halim.

147

He closed his eyes, pushed his face into his sister's hair and breathed in her familiar, floral scent. He whispered softly into her ear. "I will keep you safe, Taja, but you must stay close. Promise me."

Taja nodded, her head buried into her brother's shoulder. "I'm fine, Halim. After all, I have not one but two Shakti Warriors to take care of me."

Halim gave Taja one more squeeze before releasing his grip. He smiled up at his sister. "You're all that I have on this journey, Taja. I fear for your safety. I really do."

"If I've survived this far, Halim, I will survive the rest of the journey. Come, let's go home."

Jaya stood at the entrance to her cabin as the three travellers said their final goodbyes. "Halim," she said. "Here, please take this. You may need it." She handed him a package wrapped in a soft white cloth and bound with cord.

"What is it?" he asked, curiously inspecting the package. He held it up to his nose and sniffed. It smelt of mixed herbs.

"It's a powerful medicinal ointment," she said with a smile.

Halim tossed it into the air and then pushed it into his pack. He turned back to Jaya. "Thank you, Jaya. Where's the other unicorn?" he enquired, spying Lotus munching on some leaves in the garden.

"Oh, I'm sure he's around here somewhere," said Jaya with a smile. "Don't worry; they will be fine. I've watched them grow up in the valley."

Halim walked over to the unicorn. She lifted her head to look up at him as he approached. She shook her head, her golden spear cutting through the air precariously. Halim bent down to pick up a handful of fresh carrots from the vegetable garden. He held them out at arms length, and Lotus stepped forward, deftly taking them from his outstretched hand. She munched loudly. Halim smiled and stepped closer to rub her forehead. He stroked the horn. It felt unusually warm to the touch. He marvelled at its length and array of shimmering colours.

"I'm going to miss you," he said, looking into the animal's

big, dark eyes. "Take care of this place." He looked around. "And especially Jaya."

Jaya waved as she watched Sanjit, Taja and Halim disappear beyond the distant rise. She stepped away from her cabin and then dropped slowly down to her knees. She rolled slowly forward and down, stretching her arms out before her, her palms and forehead pressing into the soft earth beneath her. She began to bring a sway into her body, rolling her head from side to side, rocking gently from left to right. She felt the energy beneath the soft sand; a flowing, coursing river of pulsing activity. The position of her cabin was no accident. It was purposefully built on top of an energy meridian, identified by Girish himself. Jaya sensed a ripple in the energy flow. It was insignificant, yet it was there, like the prick from a bee sting that lingered, disturbing the natural flow, if ever so slightly. She knew that it was simply a matter of time before the enemy discovered that they were being misguided; a matter of days before they realised where their prey had gone. She prayed that it was enough time for the three adventurers to escape the clutches of this evil tribe of savages intent on destruction and carnage, but deep down, she knew that it was not so. She had never been wrong before.

◊ ◊ ◊

The day wore on. Halim felt tired. His stomach rumbled.

Sanjit turned to look at him, reading his thoughts. "Let us rest here," he said, shifting his heavy pack off his shoulders and onto the ground. "There is water. Listen."

They froze, straining to hear. The faint, yet familiar trickle of water drifted through the air like bells in the wind.

"Come, this way." Sanjit led them deeper into the forest, away from the path. The trickling sound grew louder until they arrived at a small pool filled with crystal clear water that sparkled in the light of the sun.

"Wow. So beautiful," said Taja. She dropped her pack, bent down and cupped her hands in the pool. She sipped at the water. "It has an unusual taste."

149

"What do you mean? Water has no taste," said Halim.

"Well, this water does. It's kind of sweet."

"Must be from the valley," said Sanjit. "The lush, green valley from whence we came."

"I'll bet it's from Jaya's vegetable garden," said Taja with a chortle. "Did you see the size of those vegetables?"

Halim began to undress. "I'm going for a swim," he said and dived head-first into the pool.

"Hey! Watch it!" exclaimed Taja in alarm. "You splashed me."

"Come on in," said Halim. "It's wonderful. So refreshing."

Taja slipped off her tunic and stepped slowly into the pool in her undergarments.

"Just dive in, Taj," said Halim. "Come on, Sanjit."

Sanjit sat down on a rock by the pool and looked on while munching on some fruit. He removed his shoes and dipped his feet into the water's edge. "Thanks but I'm just going to rest over here," he replied.

Taja took a deep breath and dived in. The chilly water stung her face in a moment of pleasure that rippled right through her body, immediately washing away the stiffness and tension in her muscles from the day's hike. She surfaced near the middle of the pool and smiled. "Aaahhh. Amazing. Come, Sanjit," she said. "Halim is right. It's incredible."

"Very well," Sanjit replied. "Let me just finish this." He raised the papaya he was eating.

Halim turned and stretched out his arms to swim leisurely across the pool. He rolled onto his back to gaze up at the sky above. The water filled his ears with a gurgle until all he could hear was the steady throb of his heart pumping the blood deep inside his head. He closed his eyes for a moment and relaxed his body, his heavy breathing the only other sound echoing in his ears. He thought of his mother and prayed to the gods that she was all right. His thoughts switched to Taja and the concern in Jaya's voice.

Be strong for your sister, Halim.

Halim opened his eyes and looked up at the sky to watch a

single white cloud float desolately by. Its pointed edge reminded him of a unicorn's horn. He smiled with the memory of the exhilarating ride through the forest the day before. He twisted around, diving under the water once more. He surfaced on the other side of the pool and looked back towards Taja. She waved and laughed a sweet-sounding laugh. Sanjit splashed into the pool, coming up next to her. She turned towards him and he cradled her in his arms. Before she knew it, her wet lips found his and the connection of their tongues sent a quiver of excitement through her body. She wanted the feeling to last forever.

She's so happy, thought Halim to himself. *What could possibly go wrong?*

The travellers soaked in the warmth of the sun, allowing it to dry them off after their long, refreshing swim. Sanjit looked up at the sun dipping in the sky as the day drew to a close.

"We must travel a little further," he said. "We need to find a safe place to rest for the night."

"Yes, perhaps in that canopy of trees down there," agreed Halim, pointing in the direction of the waning sun.

Halim led the way, this time with Taja behind him and Sanjit taking up the rear. They hiked towards the setting sun in the west. Halim felt strong, his energy replenished after the long rest and rejuvenating swim in the fresh water pool. They finally arrived at the dense body of trees. A much welcomed, cool breeze washed over Halim's face as he led Taja and Sanjit into the shadow of the tall, imposing trunks, their protective boughs embracing the travellers as they stepped beneath them.

"Look, a stream," said Taja, pointing. "Over there."

"Great, we'll camp right here," said Halim.

They dropped their packs to the ground, and Taja began preparing some food for dinner, while Halim filled their water skins from the stream nearby. Sanjit ventured out alone, deeper into the forest to explore the area some more. He returned at dusk with a selection of fresh mushrooms and deep red berries that he handed to Taja with a smile.

"Thank you," said Taja, smiling back at Sanjit warmly. Even in the early evening's waning light, Halim could not help but notice his sister's cheeks turn a bright red.

After a filling meal, Halim fed the cooking fire with more wood. He blew gently on the embers, coaxing the flames to life. They licked at the edges of the fresh wood like a swarm of ravenous bees in a feeding frenzy. The damp wood began to sizzle from the heat of the fire like the sound of the buzzing bees at work. Halim stared at the flames as they grew.

Taja lay on her blanket, legs outstretched, hands clasped behind her head, staring silently up at the stars between the boughs of the trees in the forest. The smoke from the fire spiralled up into the sky like a ghostly phantom, blotting out the twinkling lights in the heavens above. Taja closed her eyes, pictured her house in Harappa, imagined the smiles on her parent's faces and began to chant a sweet-sounding mantra. Halim lifted his gaze from the fire to listen to the familiar tune. Tears welled up unexpectedly in his eyes, and his heart ached with longing, as what sounded like his mother's voice, escaped from his sister's lips, filling the forest with her presence, her being.

"Lokah samastah sukhino bhavantu," She sang. May all beings in the universe be happy and free.

Halim threw a log onto the fire. The embers responded in a shower of sparks, spraying up and into the night sky as Taja continued her chanting, her magical voice lifting the tiny sparkles of light higher and higher into the heavens above. Silence prevailed long after Taja stopped her singing, its powerful presence bringing a peaceful surrender to everything material.

"I'll stand guard," whispered Halim after a while.

"No," said Sanjit, quickly standing up. "You get some rest. I'll take the first shift."

Halim knew that there was no arguing with Sanjit, so he didn't bother trying.

"Very well. But you'd better wake me for my shift. You also

need rest, Sanjit," he said insistently.

Sanjit pulled out his sword and began to hack pieces of bark from the closest tree. He picked up a long, narrow stick next to the fire and then secured the bark to the stick with some twine he pulled from his pocket. He dipped the end of the stick into the fire until the bark caught alight.

"Sanjit," said Halim. "Do you hear me?"

Sanjit smiled, turned and walked into the forest without so much as a grunt in acknowledgement.

"Sanjit!" shouted Halim after his comrade. His voice echoed into the darkness. "Ah. It's no use," he said, slumping hopelessly against the tree behind him. He went back to staring at the flames as they danced gracefully in the dark of the forest, casting misshapen shadows that danced and jumped about innocuously.

Taja closed her eyes and curled her body around her blanket, drifting peacefully off to sleep. Halim turned to check on his sister, concern layering his brow like ripples across a lake. He watched the rise and fall of her body as she breathed, wondering what lay ahead of their journey home. He shifted his body forward, away from the tree, closed his eyes and dropped his head back, the bright glow of the flames leaving a lasting image in his mind's eye.

26 ~ Fight

The darkness receded from the glow of Sanjit's torch, flickering away like a swarm of startled bats as he trudged deliberately through the forest, squinting into the gloom as he walked. He stopped every so often, closed his eyes and stood very still, listening beyond the soft crackle of the flame in his grasp. The silence of the forest filled the night as if it were listening back. Only when he was satisfied, did he continue on his methodical trek around the perimeter of their camp.

The trees gave way to a small clearing illuminated by the silvery light of the moon that seemed to drain the area from its colour. A lonely tree stood resolutely just off centre of the clearing. Sanjit doused the torch in the sand and then sat down in front of the tree. He removed an apple from his pocket and held it up towards the moon, hiding the shining sphere from sight. He muttered a few words of thanks to the gods for providing him with the fruit and then took a juicy bite. He sucked on the apple, savouring the sweet explosion in his mouth. The crunch of every bite echoed loudly in his ears as he ate.

Sanjit finished his meal, pulled his legs into a full lotus position and closed his eyes. He curled his tongue onto the roof of his palette, opening the circuit of energy as it flowed in through his nostrils with his breath and down into his body. He traced the flow of energy in his mind, focusing on the activation of first the throat chakra, followed by the heart chakra, the solar plexus, the spleen and then the root chakra, situated just below the naval area in his body. The Prana expanded as he reached the end of his in-breath and then began to contract as he breathed out slowly. It found its way down past his genitals, up his spine, around the back of his head into the crown chakra, and then finally into his third eye chakra, where it completed its journey before flowing down through the bridge created by his tongue on his palette, to begin again.

Sanjit continued directing his breath in a constant flow in and out of his body until the Prana took hold and everything else became second-nature. Relinquishment to the Prana was a state of enlightenment that took years to develop. Only once full awareness of Prana was attained, was one able to surrender to its ebb and flow. Like the constantly moving ocean and the rise and fall of the tide, Prana is contained in the air, the breath, as it constantly flows in and out of the body. It was this connection that Sanjit felt, as he moved into a higher state of awareness. He became one with the forest around him, a living, breathing entity, and the many creatures contained within it. He was sensitive to the pulse of Prana flowing through the trees, whispering soft, gentle feelings of peace and serenity into his heart space. He was aware of the smallest of animals scampering through the foliage of the forest floor, to the agilest ones scaling the treetops above. Love. Compassion. Empathy.

The flow was interrupted. A warning. In his mind's eye, he looked up into the treetops, searching for the source of the disruption in the flow of energy, and found it. He saw through foreign eyes. He looked down upon himself sitting beneath the tree and jumped. He moved back into his body, flashed open his eyes and rolled to the side. *Thump.* The thing landed where he sat. It growled savagely. Sanjit reached for his sword, pulled it out of its sheath and stood up all in one motion. The light from the moon cut across the creature as it stepped out of the shadow of the tree to face him. It wore a crudely carved, wooden mask and held a long spear in its hand. Sanjit wrinkled his face in response to the foul stench that wafted from his assailant. He held his sword out at arm's length, carefully gauging the threat before him. He caught site of a dark, twisted tattoo of a snake on his attacker's arm. A shiver of recognition rippled through Sanjit.

Ignogai. How did he find us?

The Ignogai stamped the earth menacingly and grunted loudly.

"Come, you ugly barbarian," said Sanjit with a sneer. "Come and get it!"

The Ignogai jumped forward, jabbing his spear at Sanjit in attack. Sanjit twisted his body to the side, effectively blocking the spear with his sword. The momentum of the jab brought the Ignogai a step closer. Sanjit moved back and twisted the other way, swivelling on his back foot, swinging his sword around in an arc, cutting through the air towards his assailant who dived forward, under the blade and into a roll. The sword whisked harmlessly over his head. The fighters turned around to face each other, and then began to step cautiously around in a circle, weapons at the ready, muscles taught in anticipation. The Ignogai moved again, this time feigning an attack with his spear. Sanjit brought his sword across his body to block the strike again, but the Ignogai had already shifted his weight into his other leg bringing the spear around in an arc, slamming it's blunt edge into Sanjit's leg, just below the knee. He buckled, dropping down to the ground in agony. The Ignogai retracted his spear and jumped up into the air, stabbing his weapon down towards Sanjit with a triumphant roar. Sanjit, still down on one knee, arched back, bringing his sword up in defence. The edge of the spear connected the side of Sanjit's blade with a loud clang, but this time, the thrust was mightier than before. There was a grating sound and a shower of sparks as the spear continued on its powerful trajectory. Sanjit managed to deflect the spear from piercing his chest, but not from burying itself deep in his shoulder. He howled in pain as he felt the jagged spear-head cut through muscle and sinew. His sword fell from his grasp as he clutched onto the shaft protruding from his shoulder. The Ignogai dived forward and onto Sanjit with a growl. He grabbed Sanjit around the neck with both hands and began to squeeze. Sanjit toppled over. Wounded. A surge of pain shot through his body as his shoulder slammed onto the ground with a thud. The Ignogai fell with his side across the spear as he held onto Sanjit, twisting his filthy hands into the soft part of his neck. Sanjit couldn't move. The Ignogai pinned him as the savage lay across the spear that was still rammed into his shoulder. And he was beginning to choke. He had to act quickly. Otherwise he was going to die. He reached his free arm behind his back, withdrew a dagger and brought it around and across the Ignogai's wrists, slicing the skin open. Blood sprayed up and all over Sanjit's face. The Ignogai released his grip and rolled onto his back, hugging his arms to his chest with a howl. He still lay across the shaft of the spear, trapping Sanjit to the ground. Sanjit lifted his feet and kicked at the Ignogai, effectively dislodging the spear from his shoulder with a crunch. The pain was excruciating. A warm, welcoming blanket began to descend across his vision.

No. No. I must get up...

Sanjit fought the pain and the overwhelming feeling of drowsiness that tried to take hold of him. He picked up his sword and stumbled through the trees, willing his legs to push him forward and away from the Ignogai that was writhing in agony on the forest floor behind him.

27 ~ Drink Up

"Taja," said Halim in alarm. "Did you hear that?"

"Huh? What?" Taja rubbed the sleep from her eyes. "What did you say? Where's Sanjit?"

"He's in the forest. Taja. I heard a strange cry. A howl. Like an animal. Except it wasn't an animal."

"I didn't hear it."

"That's cos you were asleep."

"Maybe you were dreaming."

"That's what I thought when I heard it the first time."

"The first time?"

"Yes. But I was awake when I heard it again. It seemed to be coming from over there." Halim pointed into the darkness. "Quick. Get up." Halim pulled out his sword and stepped away from the camp. He peered into the forest, straining to listen. His heart pounded in his ears.

A sound came from the forest. Branches breaking. Heavy breathing. Halim stood his ground, sword at the ready. Taja stood behind him, twin daggers in each hand. A solitary figure stumbled into view.

"Sanjit!" said Halim. "What happened? You okay?"

Sanjit dropped to his knees, dropping his sword to the

ground. He clutched at his shoulder. Blood stained his garments.

"By the gods!" exclaimed Taja. "He's injured."

"Quick, get some water and a cloth," said Halim.

"We have to go. Now," said Sanjit through clenched teeth. "They are here. The Ignogai."

Taja poured water over the cloth and carefully wrapped it around Sanjit's shoulder, securing it as tight as she was able. She fed him some water. He drank it liberally. The trio hastily packed their bags and made their way out of the forest. Halim and Taja supported Sanjit between them as they fled from their camp. The darkness swallowed them up as they pushed ahead.

Halim kept looking over his shoulder, expecting a mob of enraged Ignogai to come bursting from the forest in hot pursuit. "How did they find us?" said Halim. "How many attacked you?"

"Just one," replied Sanjit raggedly. "He was waiting for me. Must have been a scout."

Halim looked up as they rounded a corner. The trees gave way to a clearing that was framed by some rocks. Taja and Halim assisted Sanjit as they climbed over the smooth boulders. The path wound upwards, and the rocky terrain continued for some time. The travellers moved slowly, yet deliberately, gazing back at the forest behind them in anticipation.

"Look. A small cave," said Taja as she dropped over a rock and peered into the darkness beyond. A sliver of moonlight shone through a narrow opening between two rocks. She stooped low and squeezed into the crevice. "I think there's enough space for all of us here," she said from inside. She ducked her head. "The ceiling is a bit low, and we need some light."

Halim helped Sanjit through the small opening and into the cave. The darkness gave way to a soft, yellow light that came from Sanjit's hands as it lit up his face.

"What's that?" said Halim.

"It's a paleo crystal," said Sanjit. I got it from Vimal in the monastery. The monks use them when they study through the night."

He held up the crystal, and its light lit up the cave with a soft glow. Taja pulled the cloth from Sanjit's shoulder. He winced. It was drenched with blood. She cast it aside.

Halim pulled an object from his pack. It was bound with cord and wrapped in a soft, white cloth. He untied the cord and pulled off the cloth to reveal a small, round wooden jar. He opened the lid, and a strong herbal scent filled the air.

"What's that?" said Taja.

"It's a strong medicinal ointment," said Halim. "Jaya gave it to me. She said we might need it for healing."

"Well she was right," said Taja. "She *definitely* knew we'd need it."

"Here, hold this." He handed his sister the cloth. "I need to apply the ointment to the wound." Halim stuck his fingers into the jar. They began to tingle as they slid into the soft mixture. He pulled out a liberal amount of pink-coloured ointment and smeared it over Halim's open wound. He twisted his face in pain. Halim held out his other hand, raised his eyebrows at Taja and tilted his head, indicating that she pass him the cloth. He carefully pressed it over the wound and then secured it in place with the cord. "There, that should do it."

Sanjit took another swig from the gourd. "We have to keep moving," he said.

"No. You must rest," said Taja, concern in her voice.

"I'll be fine. I can already feel the ointment working. It's numbing the pain."

Taja looked at Sanjit. Even in the dim light, his face looked ashen.

"Here, eat these." She handed him a small leather pouch. "Dried berries. They will give you much needed energy."

"Taja is right, Sanjit," agreed Halim, "you are too weak to move. You need to rest."

"But the Ignogai, they will find us."

"I have an idea," said Halim.

Taja looked at her brother questioningly.

Halim reached into his pack and retrieved another small brown pouch. A pang of anxiety washed over him as he opened it to peer inside.

"The horn," whispered Taja. "You think now is the time?"

"She said we'd know when we'd need it most. And I think this is it."

The silence that followed was unnerving.

"But what about Sanjit?" said Taja.

"What about me? I can speak for myself."

"Jaya said that we should split it all between the three of us," said Taja. "But I think you should rest."

"I think she's right, Sanjit," said Halim. "This dosage might kill you. You've lost so much blood."

"Didn't I just tell you that I'm fine. The ointment you applied is working. Besides, I think we should follow Jaya's instructions. She is one of the Nine, remember?"

Halim looked at his sister. She shrugged her shoulders. "Well, only if you sure you're okay," said Halim.

"As sure as I am that the gods are watching over us," replied Sanjit.

"Very well. Pass me some water," said Halim to his sister.

He gave the waterskin a shake to determine how much water was left inside. He threw his head back to take a long swig, shook it again and nodded his head. "Please hold this, Taj." He handed the skin to his sister. "Steady now." He began to empty the contents of the pouch into the skin. The powdered horn shone golden in the light of the crystal as it cascaded into the skin like a mini waterfall. "There, that should do it." Halim stoppered the waterskin and gave it a good shake. "You first, Sanjit." He handed the concoction to Sanjit, who lifted it to his lips, swallowing several times.

He passed it onto Taja. She sniffed the mixture and screwed up her nose. "Ohh. That smells awful."

"Hold your nose Taj," said Halim. "And try to keep it down."

Taja pinched her nose with her thumb and forefinger and took a swig.

161

"One more, Taj," said Halim.

"Yuck! Disgusting. Here. Finish it," she said, passing it onto Halim.

Halim took the gourd and gave the remaining mixture a swirl. He lifted it to his lips. The mixture was thick and granular as he poured it into his mouth. He felt his throat constrict and his stomach turn in objection to the vile concoction as he forced it down. He took Taja's hand in his, looked at her and smiled. "We're going to get through this. Don't you worry little Sis. Don't you worry." He squeezed her hand hard as he spoke.

28 ~ Shaman

The pain tore through Grimak's head like the branding iron that burned into the back of his neck when he accepted the obligation of every new initiate into the tribe. He turned his hands around and watched helplessly as blood pulsed freely from his wrists. He removed the wooden mask from his face and quickly pulled his tunic up, over his head, ripping it into strips, twisting a piece of fabric around each arm. He gripped one end of each strip of fabric between his teeth and pulled on the other ends, tightening the makeshift bandages around his arms. He examined his wrists again. Although the strips of cloth were partially soaked with blood, the pressure against his wounds managed to stem the blood flow. His arms were numb with pain, and he felt light headed as he sat in the moonlit clearing of the forest. He lifted his head and looked around. There was no sign of the cursed Shakti Warrior.

Grimak was built like a typical Ignogai - short and stocky. He had a broad, flat face with an oblong-shaped nose, set amidst a sea of stubble. His bare chest glistened with sweat in the moonlight as he pushed himself up and onto his feet. He bent down to pick up his spear and his head swam. He stumbled forward and steadied himself against the tree, drawing deep, deliberate breaths in and out of his lungs.

I must get back to the tribe and tell the chief that I have found the Shakti Warriors.

He smiled. He looked forward to sharing the news that he had injured one of them. He would be richly rewarded.

"You imbecile!" Grimak dropped to his knees as the but of the chief's spear punched the air out of his chest. He coughed and wheezed, painfully trying to draw fresh air into his lungs.

"Why did you let them go?!" the chief shouted fanatically. Grimak cringed, waiting for the next blow. But it didn't come. Instead, a cry from the Shaman's tent distracted the chief.

"Piju!" the chief yelled. A small, misshapen shape next to the chief jumped in response. "Go and find out what has excited the Shaman."

"Yes, my chief," squealed the midget attendant. He jumped down from the throne and ran to the Shaman's tent. The hairless creature on the other side of the throne bared its teeth and snarled. It's red eyes glared at Grimak. He looked quickly away.

Piju exited the tent with the Shaman in tow.

"My chief!" he said excitedly. "The Shaman has seen the enemy!"

The chief stood up from his throne and climbed down from the dais. He pushed his matted hair from his face. Both Piju and Grimak dropped to their knees as the chief approached. The Shaman stared back with sightless eyes.

"What did you see?" enquired the chief.

The Shaman shifted his head in response to the chief's voice.

"I have seen the warriors. They are not far from here," he rasped. He lifted a scrawny arm and pointed west. A long, black nail quivered at the end of a wiry finger.

"Take us to them," commanded the chief.

The Shaman dropped his arm to his side. "We will not find them," he said dejectedly.

"But you have seen them. You know where they are. What are

you talking about old man?" The chief was agitated.

"They are using magic to slip between realms," he replied. "They are invisible."

"But you are the all powerful Shaman!" shouted the chief in agitation. "You have magic. You *are* magic. Just tell me where they are!"

The Shaman shook his head. "It is no use. I have seen them leave this world. They cannot be found."

"If you have seen them leave then you must be able to follow them?"

"I can try," said the Shaman.

"No. You *will* try. You *will* find them and bring them to me!" bellowed the chief. "Otherwise you'll wish that you were never born, you blind, pathetic old man! Piju. Make sure that he gets the job done."

"Yes, master," squeaked the midget, bowing his head in acknowledgement.

The chief turned and marched towards his tent. The Shaman rested both hands on his staff, took a deep breath and sighed before making his way back inside his abode. Piju followed. Long strings of beads around the Shaman's neck tinkled against each other as he sat down on a large, round cushion in the centre of the tent. His long, white hair contrasted against his dark robes as it fell over his shoulders. He placed his wooden staff down on the ground and groped towards a collection of bottles nearby.

"Which one do you need?" said Piju.

"I need two of them. The one with the circle intersected by a line carved into its side and the one with the square lid. And the bowl."

Piju examined the table. It was filled with bottles of all shapes, sizes and colours. None of them were labelled. Instead, different shapes were calved into their sides. He quickly found the only bottle with the square lid but had to lift each of the other bottles until he found the one carved with the line and circle. He found a wooden bowl nearby. He brought everything before the Shaman who carefully ran his gnarled fingers across each of the bottles. A crooked smile crossed his wrinkled face.

"Thank you," he whispered.

The Shaman unstoppered the bottles and emptied their contents into the bowl. The two liquids swirled together, producing a kaleidescope of dark colours that seemed to pulse with a strange life of their own. He brought the bowl to his nose, sniffed at its contents and poured the concoction into his mouth, gulping it quickly down his throat. He twisted his face into a grimace and dropped the empty bowl noisily to the floor. He thrust both hands up into the air and let out a high-pitched scream. Piju slammed his hands over his ears and squeezed his eyes tightly shut, as the Shaman's voice tore right through his little head. He opened his eyes and watched as the Shaman dropped his arms back down to his sides and swayed slowly from side to side on the cushion, chanting incoherently. Piju blinked. The shadows from the light of the candles jumped around the tent like dark, taunting spirits, wanting to suck him into their ghostly depths. Piju watched as the Shaman continued to sway, silently now, slowly, hypnotic. A shadow fell across the tent. Flames flickered and the Shaman shimmered, faded, reappeared and then completely disappeared from sight.

"Shaman!" Piju shouted. "Where are you?" His squeaky voice was filled with panic. He quickly looked around the tent but the Shaman was gone. "Shaman. What games are you playing? The chief is going to be angry!" The shadows jumped mockingly and the smell of incense clogged the air. Piju's heart pounded loudly in his ears as a bead of sweat trickled down the side of his face. He turned and ran from the tent as he were being chased by a hoard of angry demons.

29 ~ Spirits

The Shaman wasn't born blind. His predecessor gouged his eyes out of his skull one fateful night. His memory of this painful event came back to him now as he drifted between the dark shadows in his tent.

"After I remove your eyes, you will truly see." His master's words echoed back across time.

The medicine numbed the pain beneath his bandages, but he could not understand why his master kept saying that he would see. He saw nothing, just the darkness that came with the blindness and the burning pain where his eyes used to be. It was only days later that this message became clear to him when a young servant girl removed his bandages. She was applying a soothing salve to his wounds when a searing vision came to him so powerfully that it knocked him right over and onto the ground. He witnessed a cataclysmic event. Many people were dying as the earth opened up to swallow them whole. Fiery flames erupted from deep within the bowels of the earth as a mountain exploded before him. He recognised the mountain as the one adjacent to their village. Hot gusts of steam had been pouring from its centre for some time now, sending a warning that the tribe had chosen to ignore.

167

"Master! Master!" he sat up and shouted. "I can see! I can see!"

The young Shaman and his master told the chief that the gods of the underworld were angry and advised him that the tribe should move away from the mountain lest the gods release their fury on his people. He took it to mean that he had to appease the gods, and so sacrificed six young virgins into the fiery crater on top of the mountain with the hope of circumventing the prophecy.

Soon afterwards, the Shaman and his master fled from the tribe along with a band of followers. They had covered much ground before the land rumbled in anger, signalling the onset of the eruption. Even though he was blind, the Shaman remembered turning to face the powerful event that glowed orange inside his head.

◊ ◊ ◊

There were no colours, just shades of light that moved inside his vision as the powerful medicine took hold of his intent and directed it beyond this world and into the place between. It started with the vile taste of the concoction as he poured it down his throat. The taste lingered. It manifested inside his belly and spread throughout his body, first into his chest and then his limbs. He gasped for breath as if he was drowning, and then the magic of the medicine took control and directed his thoughts inward, deep inside himself, searching for the purpose of this journey, this event. His eyes opened, and he could see again - his spiritual sight to which he had become accustomed, developed over years of patient training and hard work. He allowed his spiritual sight to visualise the way forward with the aid of the dark magic that coursed through his body like a thick river, burning with blackened flames. The magic flowed and then his physical form followed until he had completely shifted into the world of the spirits.

The Shaman savoured the moment, in this ethereal place, where he could see with clarity the world around him. It was a dark world; a dangerous world filled with shadows and phantoms, but it was also the world that was home to him and his kind. The Shamans were skilled as guides in the netherworld, leading the blind and the visionless on expeditions of self-awareness, and missions of recovery and salvation. The Shaman of the Ignogai had, on countless occasions, led his chieftain and members of the tribe into the world between worlds to battle against hostile enemies, to find and eradicate the source of scornful attacks in the form of malevolent curses, and solve a host of other complications as a result of inter-tribal disputes. This journey was no different, as the Shaman settled into the familiar landscape like he was born unto it.

The lack of physicality in the spirit realm meant that it was easy to get lost. Without an experienced guide leading the visitor through the multi-dimensional layers of this world, time and purpose would become worthless; the soul would lose direction and find difficulty in returning to the body. The Shaman passed through such a place of souls that had lost their way, their wraith-like forms pressing against his own, trying in vain to latch onto his Prana, like starving leeches without the innate ability to perform their most principal function. The Shaman pressed on, gazing through the field of despair and beyond, searching for the trails left by his prey through an intuitive process that he had developed over many years of practice.

Shades shifted, swirled. The Shaman paused in response to the change he sensed in the environment. He extended his Prana, and it revealed the trace of a familiar vibration that came to him like a dandelion floating across a green field beneath a bright, sovereign sun on a hot summer's day. He reacted instinctively, his Prana leading him towards the evidence left behind by his quarry. Shakti. He could taste their residue. He was drawn to it like an animal on the hunt. He could sense the deep orange glow of the Shakti Warriors' life force as he traversed through the spirit realm. Two flames shimmering in the dark. There was a third. A different signature, vibrating with a distinctive hue. He reached deep within himself, drew back on an enchanted bow and released a multitude of spiritual arrows infused with powerful magic. Their ebony shafts tore across the ether towards their targets, sucking the very light from around them as they flew. The Shaman watched as some of the arrows found their mark. The maimed Shakti turned to face him as he approached. The third entity was untouched, protected by the warriors, a golden source of gentle energy that aroused the Shaman. It was just a matter of time before the Shakti succumbed to the dark magic of the arrows that consumed their Prana.

The Shaman focused his energy to strike again, but the warriors retaliated first. He anticipated the familiar vacuum of pressure before the release of energy; a blast that would have sent him reeling if it were not for a spirit shield of protection that he instinctively manifested in self-defence. He underestimated the strength of the warriors. Even with his magical arrows deeply embedded in their Prana, their combined attack penetrated his protective shield, sending him back and into a vulnerable position. He was exposed. Defenceless. The Shakti were upon him in an instant. The blaze of their Prana burned into his aura. Subjugating. Suffocating. Stifling. Beneath all the pain and anguish, the Shaman smiled. What the Shakti didn't count on were the arrows and the effect that they would have as they came into proximity of the Shaman. The arrows were connected to the Shaman. They were part of him, infused into his Prana. He instantly recognised the familiar presence of his arrows. He drew on the energy that they contained and they, in turn, drew on the life force of the Shakti, literally sucking it out and feeding it back to the Shaman in long, powerful bursts. The crushing force gradually began to subside, as the Shaman willed his spirit shield to return. The Shakti desperately fought back, but the harder they repelled the counter attack, the stronger the magical arrows worked, steadily draining them of their Prana until their defences collapsed to reveal the pure, golden energy of the third entity hiding in their midst.

The Shaman sensed the fear of the female. He tasted it like a snake would with its forked tongue in the air, and it excited him.

He moved towards her as the injured Shakti Warriors began to fade, leaving the spirit world and returning to the sanctuary of their physical bodies, the dark arrows all but draining them of their Prana. To the Shaman's surprise, the female stood her ground. She sensed his hesitation and attacked, releasing an explosive burst of energy that blinded the Shaman momentarily. He knew that she was no match for him, especially in this place, his world, yet her courage and determination intrigued him. He marvelled at how easily she had caused his anguish by attacking the one thing that he treasured most - his sight. The tendrils of Prana finally lifted like a veil as the Shaman quickly scanned the perimeter, gradually picking up her trail. It was faint, but it was there, a golden residue that glowed softly in the otherwise muted environment. He moved forward with purpose and resolve, drawing on the energy around him, stirring the slumbering spirits and disrupting the wandering wraiths, as he followed his mark deep into the netherworld. His Prana trembled in anticipation, fuelled by the newly awakened forces around him, driving him unswervingly towards his goal.

30 ~ Captured

The sound of Halim's voice magically transformed into a kaleidoscope of butterflies, which began to appear at first in Taja's periphery vision and then burst forth in a beautiful display directly in front of her. She reached out to touch the colourful creatures and giggled in delight as they flitted and flapped around her head. She spun around in a circle, following their enchanting flight pattern as they began to melt into streaks of iridescent colour. She blinked. The air was filled with a fine mist that caressed her face as if it were alive. She looked down and watched, as soft, white clouds swirled around her ankles. Halim and Sanjit hovered eerily next to her. They all seemed to be floating beneath the surface of a lake as she peered into its depths from above. She opened her mouth to laugh, but no sound came out. Instead, a pang of anxiety washed over her that was instantly stifled by the sound of Sanjit's reassuring voice inside her head.

Taja. You okay?

Her thoughts formed in response. *Yes. I'm fine. Where are we?*

The unicorn powder has transported us into the spirit world. We have become invisible to our enemies.

But why do we look so strange? Why can't I speak?

This place is governed by a set of rules that prevent us from accessing our full faculties. There is no physicality here.

Taja mulled on this point for a moment. *But if we are invisible to our enemies, then where are our physical bodies if they have not been transported here?*

Taja watched Sanjit's underwater mouth turn up into a wobbly smile. *Good question, Taj. They have not left the world that we know. They are still sitting in the cave. It's just our spirit bodies that have come here, to this place.* His hands shimmered through the mist.

Taja looked around again. The mist shifted. *Okay. But then how are our physical bodies made invisible to our enemies if it's just our spirits that are transported here?*

Any other journey to the spirit world leaves one's physical body visible to others, replied Sanjit, *but the magical properties of the horn keep the window between the physical world and this one open in such a way that the laws of the spirit world apply to our physical bodies too.*

Making them invisible?

Exactly. You got it.

Halim's misshapen face appeared next to Sanjit's. *Taj. Don't be afraid. This is the only way for us to hide from the Ignogai. We will be safe here.*

Come. Follow me, said Sanjit as Taja watched him float deeper beneath the surface of the underwater world. She moved after Sanjit and her brother as they glided through the mist like a shoal of giant squid beneath the ocean depths.

The sound of the screams inside her head tore through her psyche without warning like a hot branding iron. She spun around to complete turmoil. The underwater environment had changed into a hazy, indistinct, grey mass. Long, dark arrow shafts protruded from Sanjit and Halim as they turned to face the source of attack from behind them. Taja felt the dark and potent magic contained in the arrows as they pulsed with a life of their own. She tried to resist their powerful allure as they sucked at the very essence of the world around her. There was a strange pressure around her. Her head felt like it was being compressed between two wooden planks, and then a bright, white light burst forth from both Halim and Sanjit, setting the place aglow like the sun at its zenith on a cloudless day. Their combined counter-attack was directed at a target in the distance.

The Ignogai? How did they find us? Thought Taja to herself. *Invisible in the real world, but in this place, we probably stand out like a swarm of fireflies.*

She followed Sanjit and Halim as they raced towards a silhouette on what could only be called the horizon in this unsettling place. The silhouette became more distinct as they drew closer. It was a man, framed by a deep, red, flickering glow. He lay unmoving on his back, staring up into the haze with white, unblinking eyes. Sanjit and Halim attacked again, their Prana radiating brilliantly, enveloping their foe in a cocoon of light. Taja felt the forces at work like the intense heat from a raging fire. She held her arm up to protect her face and then dropped it again as she sensed a shift in the energy around her. The glowing light shining forth from Sanjit and Halim began to wane. The figure before them began to stir. He slowly sat up and then floated to a standing position, the red, pulsing glow around him growing in intensity, sapping the Prana from Sanjit and Halim like an insatiable, ravenous force. She watched in alarm as both Sanjit and Halim dropped to their knees, succumbing to the draining force of the arrows embedded in their sides. Panic turned to rage as she opened her mouth to scream. A fiery pulse of Prana burst forth from inside her head. There was a bright flash and then she turned and ran as fast as she could.

Time seemed to stand still as the painful, suffering image of Halim and Sanjit flashed before Taja as she ran away from the man with the red glowing aura. She had no idea where she was going. All she knew was that she had to get as far away from him as possible. The eerie world around her shifted in a silvery gloom that had no beginning, no end. Her legs grew heavy, and the back of her neck began to burn. She screamed silently again and then a darkness pulled her eyes shut, and she sank deep, down into a seductive slumber.

31 ~ Prisoner

The golden trail left by the female sparkled in the gloomy expanse like the tears from a hungry child in the light of the sun rising on a brand new day. The Shaman quickened his pace. The trail became more distinct. Brighter. He pressed on, excited by the prospect of capturing her. He could taste her Prana; he savoured it. It tickled the back of his throat, arousing his senses, even here, in the reticence of the spirit world. His white, unseeing eyes saw. They cut through the gloom and identified the fleeing female. A shimmering silhouette against the ever-shifting milieu.

The Shaman smiled deeply to himself. He was powerful and experienced. Spells were no good if they could not be spoken, but, through an intricate pattern of ruins that covered his entire body, he had mastered the art of weaving magic in this intangible place. Their carefully designed sequence was carved onto his skin by his late master over a period of ten seasons. They flared to life like the nostrils of a majestic unicorn in full gallop, releasing his Prana and expanding his consciousness to obscure and ensnare his prey. It wasn't the first time he had weaved this spell, but it was still a complex one, especially from within the spirit world. The spell opened a conduit that helped the Shaman delicately trace the path of the female's Prana to the location of her physical body. He followed the route back through the spirit world and into his tent in the Ignogai village. But something was wrong. A physical transference like this should have taken him some effort to complete, yet it was too easy, too elementary. And then he understood. Of course. He recognised the magic of the unicorn horn, a familiar power that coursed through the female's body, fused together with her Prana, shifting her essence into a state beyond the physical world, facilitating the transfer. The Shaman felt a thrilling tingle through his body. Thank the gods, fortune favoured him this day. He hoped that the Warriors survived his onslaught. Otherwise, the female would just be a useless commodity that would have to be killed. Either way, he looked forward to what was to follow.

32 ~ Pray

A cold wind twisted through the forest, pulling at the trees, lifting their branches, rustling their leaves with a whistling, ill-omened sound. A solitary sun bird perched precariously on a swaying branch, huddled beneath ruffled feathers in an attempt to shut out the wind, as it threatened to dislodge the creature from its place of sanctuary. A powerful gust forced the bird to launch itself off the tree and through the turbulent woods in search of a less exposed location to wait out nature's assault. Foreboding, dark-grey clouds rolled ominously across the sky, casting a gloomy shadow across the land beneath. The bird burst forth from the forest with the wind at its tail. Its tiny wings flapped vigorously, carrying it beyond the trees, across open land and over the city, where it settled on a wall overlooking a house with a column of smoke spiralling from its chimney.

"Looks like rain," said Shan peering out of the window. "Maybe a storm."

He leant on his crutch and twisted around to face Arja. She was awake, lying motionless in the bed, just managing a weak smile in response. Tears flowed down Shan's cheeks. He turned to pick up a log and throw it into the fire. It landed in a shower of sparks, while the heat from the furnace quickly dried the tears on his face. He hobbled over to the bed, sat down, and dropped his crutch. He leant forward, pulled his splintered leg onto the bed beside him and dropped his head into his cushion with a sigh.

"Shan," said Arja faintly.

"Shhh, my angel," he cut her off. "Save your energy. Conserve your strength. Taja and Halim will be home soon with your medicine."

"I just wanted to say," she continued, "that I love you."

Shan's eyes welled up again. "My Arja. I love you more than all the stars in the heavens."

He wrapped his arm around her, buried his face in her shoulder and hugged her tightly. He squeezed the tears out of his eyes and listened to the faint beating of her heart in her frail body.

Please, gods, he prayed silently. *Don't let my Arja die. She is my everything. I don't know what I would do without her. Please save her from this ghastly disease. I beg of you. Please.*

33 ~ Kativa

The atmosphere was stifling. Halim struggled to breathe. His chest was constricted from what felt like straps secured across it. The pain in his head was excruciating, exacerbated by a constant jarring as if he was being dragged by his feet, his head bouncing across a dry river bed. Bang, bang, bang! Then darkness. Then flashes of trees, of leaves brushing against his face, of fresh, forest smells and chattering voices in a musical, lyrical language he couldn't quite understand. He blacked out again, only to wake with a steady, high-pitched ringing in his ears that increased in intensity when he opened his eyes and lifted his head. He closed his eyes again, relaxed his head into a softness and slowly released his breath in a long, heavy sigh. And then a flood of memories rushed into his head like the sudden downpour of rain after a long drought. The pain returned, and he grimaced. But along with the pain came anxiety and confusion.

Taja! Sanjit!

Halim opened his eyes, lifted his head and looked about. He was lying in a strange bed in an even stranger room. He noticed another figure in another bed across from him, but couldn't make out who it was. He dropped his head backed down again, as a numb, throbbing pain tore across his side, just below his chest. Sleep and exhaustion overcame him, and he drifted down into muted darkness.

"Halim. Halim."

Someone was gently nudging him. He slowly pulled himself out of his sleep as if he was swimming up to the surface of a deep, murky lake. He gasped, drawing in a big breath of air and flashed open his eyes to Sanjit's smiling face.

"Good to see you're back with us," Sanjit said softly. He turned to one side and coughed loudly.

"Where's Taja?" said Halim. "She all right?"

Silence.

"Sanjit?" Halim sat up and looked around the room. His head tingled. "Where is she?" His voice faltered.

"She did not come back." Sanjit's monotone voice betrayed his frame of mind.

"What do you mean? Where are we? Come back where?" Halim felt his chest tighten.

"You and I were wounded by powerful magic that brought our spiritual bodies back to the cave. Taja didn't return."

"But where is she? What happened to her?"

"I'm not sure," replied Sanjit. "I can only assume that she was captured by whoever attacked us in the netherworld."

"Well, we have to go back and find her!" Halim proceeded to climb out of the bed. His feet touched the floor, and his head began to swim. Sanjit grabbed him by the arm and helped him sit down on the edge of the bed.

"There will be time for that, young warrior," said Sanjit. "We need to gain our strength back first."

Halim gazed around the room again. The walls were made out of solid wood, and the low ceiling was framed in a soft, white cloth that seemed to float up there all on its own. Semitransparent, white curtains shifted in a cool breeze that wafted through the room, bringing with it the familiar scent of the forest.

"What is this place?" said Halim.

"Look out of the window," replied Sanjit.

Halim placed his hand on Sanjit's shoulder for support before gingerly sliding off the bed and onto his feet again. He paused for a moment, straightened up, and then made his way to the window on the far side of the room. He pulled aside the curtains and gazed out of the window in awe.

"By the gods…"

The giddiness returned to his head in a wave. He gripped the window ledge to steady himself. This time, however, it was vertigo that he experienced, from coming to realise that he was suspended in a tree, high above the forest floor. The first thing he noticed, were the series of wooden walkways connecting the trees around him, like the network of bridges over the waterways in his village. Partly obscured by the canopy of trees, Halim saw that they were connected to other tree-houses, most of which appeared to be much larger than theirs. Some movement to the left caught his eye. It was a female, striding purposefully across one of the walkways connected directly to their room. She wore tight-fitting, brown apparel and looked to be middle aged. Halim stepped back from the window.

"Someone's coming."

"I know. It's Kativa," said Sanjit. "I met her briefly earlier. You were still asleep. She's from the village of the tree people. It was she who found us in the cave. She saved our lives."

The door opened with a creak and Kativa stepped into the room.

"Ah you're awake," she said with a grin. Her accent sounded different, thicker, and her green eyes twinkled as she spoke. "I'm Kativa," she held out her hand.

"Uh, Halim," he stammered, grabbing her hand clumsily. He looked down in embarrassment.

"How are you feeling?" she asked.

Halim took in a deep breath. "Okay, I guess. Still a bit weak."

"Yes, I'm sure. When we found you, you were barely breathing. You were badly injured." She turned to Sanjit. "Here you go," she said passing him a small flask.

Halim looked at Sanjit questioningly.

"It's an herbal tonic," said Sanjit, "mixed by their Shaman. This," he held up the flask, "is what will give us back our strength." He took a swig, screwed up his face and passed it to Halim. "Here, drink."

"How is he?" enquired Sanjit.

"He rests," replied Kativa. "It was an arduous task that sapped most of his energy."

Halim looked at Sanjit questioningly once more.

"Kativa brought us directly to her Shaman after she found us in the cave," explained Sanjit. "He managed to heal us. Look. Even my shoulder is better," said Sanjit pulling his tunic off his shoulder to reveal a secure looking bandage around it.

"Yes," nodded Kativa. "Aside from your physical wound, the Shaman explained that there was some malignant poison that was feeding on your Prana, draining it from your body. A spiritual malady that required a spiritual operation. I don't know what he did exactly, but he went into a trance for some time. When he came out of it, you two were breathing easily and at peace. I've never seen him look so fatigued before."

"Thank you, Kativa," said Sanjit. "We are grateful for your assistance."

"Yes, thank you," said Halim, "for saving our lives."

"No problem," said Kativa with a smile. "I'm glad you're all right. Sanjit here tells me that you have been battling the Ignogai. They are a common enemy. Our Shaman believes that it was them that poisoned you. He said that they have a powerful Shaman that can attack you while you sleep, coming to you in your dreams. He said that he recognised the signature of the poison inside you. He tried to trace it back to its source, but the trail was a dead end."

"We weren't exactly asleep," said Sanjit. "We entered the spirit realm to hide from our pursuers and this Shaman must have found us there and attacked us, poisoning us with his dark magic."

"My sister was with us," said Halim forlornly.

"What happened to her?" said Kativa.

"She must have been captured by the Shaman," replied Sanjit.

"We have to go and get her," said Halim.

"I'm sorry Halim," said Kativa. "We will do what we can to help you find her."

"That's very kind of you," said Halim.

"But first we feast!" said Kativa with excitement. "One of the chief's daughters is going to be wed, and the celebrations begin tonight."

Halim turned to look askance at Sanjit once more.

"We need to build our strength back, Halim," said Sanjit. "It's no use going to fight them in this condition. We also need a plan, and help from these people." He gestured towards Kativa.

"I just pray that she is still alive," said Halim sombrely.

"Me too, young warrior, me too."

34 ~ Wedding

Halim looked down at his garb. The soft fabric was light brown in colour. He lifted his arm to his face, closed his eyes and took in a deep breath. Sweet smells of the forest filled his head. He followed Sanjit and Kativa out of the tree-top room and onto the high, wooden walkway. He looked out, over the railing and saw many more tree people spill out and onto the other interconnected bridges, all making their way down to the wedding ceremony below. The path down took the trio across several trees, down steps expertly carved deep into the tree trunks, worn smooth from years of regular use. They joined many others until Halim lost count of the number of people around him. There was an excited buzz in the air in anticipation of the event ahead. Despite a dull throbbing in his side, Halim felt far less anxious than before. A smile stretched across his face as the spirited atmosphere temporarily replaced the chilling events from the past few days.

They walked for a while longer, until the trees parted to reveal an open plain of soft, flowing grass that reminded Halim of a scene from his childhood where he imagined watching his mother Arja and his sister Taja running beneath the afternoon sun. He closed his eyes and squeezed out unintentional tears. He let them roll freely down his face, gently tickling his skin on the way down to his mouth. He tasted their salty content, licked his lips and smiled. Tears of joy. So this is what they felt like. This is what they tasted like. Oh, how he missed his mother. And his sister. He took a deep breath and wiped his sleeve across his eyes as his tears turned to sorrow. He tilted his head and looked up at the sky as he walked. The setting sun cast soft hues of orange and pink across the streaky clouds that seemed to be frozen in place against the azure blue sky beyond.

Beyond the sea of bobbing heads ahead of him, Halim noticed a peculiar stone structure protruding from out of the earth. "Look. Over there," he pointed.

Sanjit lifted his chin to peer over the heads of the treetop people.

"What is it?"

"It's a sanctum," replied Sanjit. "Their holy place."

"Like Vstu Kirtak?" said Halim.

"Yes. Looks like it."

Vstu Kirtak was an ancient structure built on a mound not far from Harappa. Halim had been there once. He recalled the tall stone pillars, around five-person lengths high, protruding out of the ground in a rough, circular formation. The monoliths, each cut into a crooked letter T, were designed to resemble humanoid forms, some with arms carved into their sides. Others bore low reliefs of dangerous creatures like scorpions, snakes and lions. He learnt that the animals were placed there to protect the sages that partook in the variety of ceremonies conducted beneath the stone pillars; ceremonies undertaken to call on the gods for assistance with matters that affected the community of Harappa. When the sages were immersed in a deep trance together, the animals would come to life and communicate with their mystical sages, guiding them through the spiritual realm and beyond the confines of the physical world. He recalled a time when there was a severe drought in Harappa. Animals were dying, and the river had all but dried up. The sages spent several days at the site, calling on the gods to spare the city and send much-needed rain. Soon, dark, grey clouds rolled in and spilt their contents onto the parched land. The rains filled the river and saved their crops from certain demise. They were blessed.

Halim remembered discussing the design of Vstu Kirtak with Mr Dasgupta one rainy day in class. "So you are saying that we don't know who built it?"

"No. Not really," replied Dasgupta, thoughtfully scratching the stubble on his chin. "It's a very old structure, built long before this city was even a thought in the minds of its founders."

"But the sages. They know how to access its secrets," said Halim. "Surely they know who designed it? I heard tell that the sages can communicate with them, the designers."

Bodhan smiled broadly. "That's here-say, my curious student. I prefer hard evidence myself, and until I meet one of these designers, one can only speculate."

Halim stared out the window at the rain as it splattered steadily on the patio. "Okay, so you are saying that it was built by a civilisation that lived long before us, right?"

"Correct." Bodhan nodded.

"How do we know this?"

"Well, for one, we don't possess the tools required to move the massive stone pillars nor to carve them into the perfect dimensions in which we find them. This is an advanced technology that was somehow lost over time. Such knowledge should have been passed down through the ages, but it was not, which can only lead us to hypothesise that the previous civilisation was somehow wiped out before they could impart this vital information."

"I see. Okay, that makes sense."

Halim and Sanjit approached the stone sanctum. Halim counted six large stone pillars, similar to the ones at Vstu Kirtak. The only difference was that the angle of the T-shaped blocks wasn't as pronounced as the ones back home. He pondered on the significance of this. In the centre of the structure, stood a man clothed completely in white. He looked like a high priest and wore a silver breastplate that reflected the glow of the setting sun. Beside him stood a woman also clothed in white. Her face was hidden from sight behind a silky veil that shimmered in the soft breeze as if it were alive. A group of what looked like more priests, gathered on one side of the temple, facing the high priest and the female. They wore identical brown robes with darker brown headpieces. They began to sing together, chanting softly at first, then building into a louder, more powerful verse. They swayed gently from side to side as they sang, the sound of their voices somehow amplified by the angle of the pillars in the sanctum.

The priests' mesmerising chanting eased the sun into a peaceful slumber as it slipped languidly beneath the horizon in the distance. The crowd surrounding the sanctum stood silently watching the singing priests, enraptured by their song, caught up in the sacredness of the ceremony. A ripple like a wave in the crowd caught Halim's attention. Along with the people around him, he was forced to take several steps backwards, to allow an assemblage of several people to pass through. The group was led by a short, broad-shouldered man wearing a blue robe with gold trim. He carried a sceptre with an opulently designed silver headpiece that extended at least a head taller than the tallest person in the crowd.

That must be the chief of the tree-people, guessed Halim to himself.

Alongside the chief, was a well-groomed young man in a white garment that extended to his ankles. The groom. He walked with confidence and purpose, ready to accept the responsibility of marriage bestowed upon him by his people. Several cohorts in pale-blue garb followed the chief and the groom as they made their way towards the sanctum. The singing priests continued their chanting as the entourage approached the high priest and the bride, stopping just a short distance away. They stood fixed in one spot a while longer as the priests' singing gradually faded into a low, steady hum. The groom stepped forward towards his bride, extending his hands, turning them palms-up in acquiescence. The bride slowly pulled back her veil, dropping her face modestly. She gently placed her hands on his and then slowly lifted her face. Their eyes finally met, and they smiled deeply. She was beautiful. Even from this distance away, Halim could feel the powerful love union between the couple. He blinked away tears that welled up in his eyes and quickly wiped his sleeve across his face. The high priest began to chant, his voice cutting through the emotional silence like a feathered arrow released from a longbow, slicing silently through the air in a long, straight trajectory.

Halim looked up at the first few stars as they twinkled to life in the purple dusk sky. He closed his eyes and prayed. He thanked the gods that he was still alive and then shifted his thoughts to his sister, appealing to the gods, asking them to protect her from the evil forces that engulfed her. He prayed that she was still alive. He prayed for the strength to rescue her from the clutches of the cold-blooded savages that were the Ignogai.

◊ ◊ ◊

"Sanjit. Halim."

Halim looked up at the sound of his voice. It was Kativa. She waved at them from across the crowd, beckoning to them. They pushed through the people who were beginning to disperse.

"Come. Let us make our way to the party," she said with a big smile as they approached.

"Wow," exclaimed Halim. "The chanting from the priests... the energy of the ceremony. It... it was just incredible."

Kativa smiled. "Glad you enjoyed it, young warrior. That was Padma. Her name means lotus flower and she is the youngest of the chief's three daughters and the last to get married. Her groom was chosen by the high priest from several cohorts based on certain attributes known only to the priest."

"You mean they don't get to choose each other as mates?"

"No. That choice is not theirs to make. This is our custom and the way of the tribe."

"But what if they do not like each other? What if they are incompatible."

"The bride is allowed to end the life of her groom if she feels that he does not live up to his role as husband and father. She has one full night and day to decide on his fate."

Halim rolled his eyes in alarm. "That's pretty harsh. How is it that the bride has this choice? What about the groom? Doesn't he have a say?"

"No. Because women bear children and raise them into this world, it is up to them to decide if their partners are compatible and capable of fulfilling the duty of fatherhood. It is up to them to recognise the qualities expected of their husbands."

"So how of often does it happen that there is incompatibility?" said Sanjit.

Kativa smiled. "Not very often. The high priest is seldom wrong, and the men of our tribe are taught the way, so there's little that can go wrong. Unless..." Kativa looked away.

"Unless?" repeated Halim, turning to look at Kativa.

Kativa turned to Halim. Her eyes glistened. "Unless the man happens to come from outside the tribe and knows nothing of the tribe's customs. Unless he is ignorant of our ways and wants to enforce his selfish will upon the woman." Kativa sounded scornful and distraught at the same time.

"Did you...?" Halim whispered.

"Yes. I killed my husband," she said flatly.

"I'm sorry that I..." He hung his head shamefully.

Kativa shook her head. "Haha." The laugh sounded forced. "Don't be sorry, young warrior. It happened a long time ago, and it was meant to be."

Halim looked around. The ceremony was all but over. The priests were still singing, but the bride and groom had left with their retinue. Halim and Sanjit followed Kativa in silence back towards the treetop village, the combined hum from hundreds of voices pushing them on like the steady current in a meandering river. Twinkling lights from the flames of hundreds of tiny lanterns flickered in the trees all around them as they returned to the village. The smoke from burning incense filled Halim's nostrils, and the beautiful, sweet sound of a ravanahatha cast a magical net over the crowd, its twin strings producing a captivating melody. It was joined by several more instruments - a bansuri flute, a pakhawaj drum and a calabash. Kativa led them closer to the source of the music until they reached the base of an enormous tree. Halim lifted his gaze. Several feet up, bathed in the yellow light from dozens of lanterns around them, was the band. A wooden platform had been built on the lowest branch of the massive tree upon which they were positioned. The delightful music felt to Halim like the flow of cosmic energy as it began to build in volume and momentum. He closed his eyes, allowing the music to captivate his senses, to flow through him like the rushing wind in his face while astride Shasta, his beautiful golden-brown mare. He turned to look at his father beside him as they galloped through the Harappan forest, the steady pounding of hooves merging with the beat of the pakhawaj drum as they rode.

The music began to build in both volume and tempo. Halim looked around as more and more people gathered in front of the musicians suspended in the great tree. The tribes-people began to dance, swaying slowly at first, in unison to the steady beat of the pakhawaj drum that reverberated through Halim's body like the constant pounding of the unicorn's hooves on the forest floor. He closed his eyes and felt the energy of the music flow in and around him, a wild, untamed beast with a life of its own.

He opened his eyes to a beautiful, happy face with sparkling green eyes and a magical, infectious smile that instantly ignited in him the desire to laugh out loud. The striking female caught his gaze and held it, swaying her lithe body from side to side like a supernatural creature. She brought her hands up to her face, tilted her head, framing it in a quizzical grin. Strands of long, dark hair brushed across her face as she began to twist her head from side to side in time with the music, her pristine smile permanently etched onto her exquisite face. Halim felt an irresistible urge to join her. He began to move his body in time to the music, gyrating his hips, matching her moves, step for step.

The intriguing girl produced a small, wooden stick and held it out it to Halim who stared at it curiously. He scratched his head. She lifted it to her lips and sucked on one end. It was a pipe. Halim smiled in acknowledgement. A twisted plume of white smoke poured out of her mouth like a serpent coiling itself around an invisible tree, before slowly dissipating into the evening sky. She handed the pipe back to Halim. The smoke was hot as it entered his lungs. He doubled over, coughing hard. His throat and chest burned and his eyes watered. The girl threw her head back and laughed. She closed her eyes and dropped into a rhythmic dance in time with the music, her body connecting instantly with the pulsing beat.

Halim straightened out, dug his fingers into his eyes and rubbed them intensely, before slowly opening them to a very different scene. The lanterns suspended from the trees above were pulsating. Dazzling waves of light came alive all around him, reflecting off the hundreds of smiling faces all moving in unison to the irrepressible sounds coming from the mystical band of musicians in the great tree. He felt alive with energy like never before. He became aware of his breath, flowing in and out of his body like it had a life of its own. His senses were heightened, charged with the Prana of the pipe, while his physical body connected with the music in an extraordinary way. The steady beat of the base reverberated through his chest, moving past his hips and down into his stomping legs of its own accord. The melody spoke to him, and he understood. It was a universal language, and it guided him, focusing his thoughts on the significant aspects of his life, teaching and leading him through the dimensions of his mind. Hurdles and obstacles that he feared to confront, simply melted away, fading into a kaleidoscopic haze of colour. He surrendered completely to the magical energy that flowed through the tribe, succumbing

Richard Gradner - Unicorn

to its beauty and infinite wisdom.

35 ~ Barbarians

The flame of a single candle burning inside the tent flickered momentarily from an unseen force. It steadied and then wavered again before extinguishing completely. A soft, grey trail of smoke twisted up towards the roof of the tent in slow motion. The remaining light in the tent seemed to suck into itself, replaced by a heavy, suffocating darkness that moved of its own accord. The hundreds of stoppered phials began to vibrate gently at first and then more vigorously. They clinked together noisily, some falling over and smashing to the ground, their contents spilling out and seeping into the thirsty earth below. The darkness shifted, flexed and then began to take shape. The Shaman stepped out of the world of the spirits and collapsed onto his cushion in exhaustion. He turned and released the heavy burden of the female onto another cushion beside him. She was unconscious and would remain that way for some time. The Shaman steadied his breathing, sucking in deep breaths of air until he had regained some of his energy. His long, white hair was dishevelled. It hung loosely across his shoulders as he bowed his head to release the tension in his neck. He reached across to his table of medicines, running his hands across the bottles, feeling for one in particular. He paused when he found what he wanted. It was a small blue bottle, half-filled with an obscure liquid. He unstopped the bottle and screwed up his nose in revulsion as the putrid fumes filled the space around him. He threw back the contents, gagging for a moment before swallowing the medicine. It burned his throat as it went down, instantly igniting his chest and warming his belly. The energy from the concoction spread quickly throughout his body, recharging his Prana, gradually replacing what he spent during his escapade.

The Shaman pulled his wiry legs into a full lotus position, took a deep breath and lifted his chest, stretching his spine up and out of his hips. Even though he was sightless, he still felt more connected when he closed his eyelids. He willed his mind to stillness, delving deep within himself, connecting to the ocean of Prana that flowed all around him. He let go of the past, restrained his thoughts of the future and focused his mind instead on the here and now, this moment, the only place of importance. A smile slowly began to stretch across his face as his breathing regulated. The medicine was working. His eyelids flickered involuntarily as his eyeballs rolled vigorously beneath them. He rested his hands on his knees, touching ring finger to thumb in a Prithvi Earth Mudra, designed to replenish the physical energy of the body. The Shaman's skin began to glow with a pinkish complexion as the medicine began to take effect. He flickered his eyelids open. There was a disturbance. It came from the physical. Someone was approaching.

"Piju."

"Shaman! You are back!" squeaked the tiny creature. "Where are you? I cannot see a thing in here. Eeew. What's that smell?"

The Shaman took a deep breath. "Yes. I am back." He smiled in the darkness. He didn't need the light to see. The Shaman placed his hand on the unconscious figure beside him. He felt the gradual rise and fall of her ribcage and the dull throbbing of her heart as it pumped. The Shaman lifted his head in response to the glow from the source of light that Piju held inside the tent.

"A girl!" exclaimed Piju in alarm. "Who is she? Where did she come from? Where are the warriors? The chief is going to be annoyed, Shaman. You were supposed to capture the Shakti Warriors, not some useless girl."

The Shaman swayed from side to side in silence.

"Shaman! I'm talking to you. Answer me." Piju stamped his foot on the ground in frustration.

"Tell the chief that this girl is bait. The Shakti will come for her. She will bring them to us."

"Hah! You tell him yourself, Shaman. You explain why you don't have the Shakti. He is going to be mad." Piju turned and stormed out of the tent on his little legs, leaving the Shaman and Taja alone in the darkness.

The Shaman took a deep breath, grabbed his staff and pulled himself up onto his feet. He rummaged through an open drawer on one side of his tent and returned with some twine that he bound around Taja's wrists. He secured the other end to his waist. He picked up a container filled with yellow powder and sprinkled some over Taja. He gently blew into her face and mumbled a few incantations. She began to stir. She coughed and slowly opened her eyes.

"Uhh. Where… am I?" she pushed herself up into a seated position. "Can't see." She coughed again. "What's that smell?" She screwed up her nose in disgust. "And why are my hands tied? Hello? Who's there?"

"I am here."

Taja jumped. "Who are you? Why is it so dark in here?" Her eyes began to adjust a little until she could just make out a handful of silhouettes in the darkness. "Where's my brother?"

"You are my captive," the Shaman rasped.

Taja remembered. She was running. Her legs burned, then her head exploded in pain. She squeezed her eyes to shut out the memory but all she could see was the man with the pulsing red aura.

"You! You are the one that chased after me. You are the one that injured Halim and Sanjit with the arrows. Where are they?

You better tell me or..."

The Shaman laughed out loud. "Or what? I better tell you or what? You are my prisoner here. Your warriors are gone. Probably dead or dying by now."

"No. They cannot be. They will find you. They will find you and kill you." Taja pushed herself up to stand, but the twine pulled taught, preventing her from getting any further than onto her haunches.

"Haha. That's exactly what I want them to do. They must come. And if not them, then they must bring others. And when they come, they will suffer. They will feel pain. Pain like they have never felt before. And then they will die. And then you will suffer and die too."

Taja sat back down. She silently thanked the gods. At least she was safe for now. She prayed that Halim and Sanjit were still alive.

◊ ◊ ◊

Taja took a deep breath of relief, as they stepped out of the stifling tent. The soft light of the dawn outlined several more tents as the Shaman led them down to a lake nearby. He untied the rope from around his waist, giving Taja some slack so that she could splash some water over her face. She cupped her bound hands in the water and drank deeply. The Shaman handed her a piece of dry bread and some cheese that she wolfed down quickly. The Shaman tugged at the rope, pulling Taja away from the lake and towards a wooden cage on the far side of the village. He lifted a wooden block securing the door, swung it open, untied her bonds and pushed her inside. She tripped on something hard as she went in and fell onto her knees, coming face to face with the bones of a human skeleton. Large, sightless sockets stared back at her from a shiny, white skull. She quickly rolled over and away from the terrifying sight. The Shaman laughed and then shuffled away. Taja listened to the fading thud, thud, thud of his wooden staff on the earth as he walked.

The sun clipped the horizon, sending shafts of light into the cage, revealing more bones, strewn about Taja's cell. It was too low for her to stand upright, forcing her to move about on her knees. She crawled to one corner, pulled herself into a ball and closed her eyes, trying to shut out the fear and trepidation that filled her head. A high-pitched wail sliced through the air. She squeezed her eyes tighter as if to expel the eerie sound. Her body trembled. She took a series of short, sharp, ragged breaths as her throat constricted in angst. She forcibly coughed and watched, enthralled for a moment by the ghost-like vapour that formed momentarily, before dissipating into the crisp morning breeze. She closed her eyes and smiled inwardly as she pictured the faces of Halim and Sanjit, and her breathing eased into a more natural rhythm.

My brother, Halim. She sighed. *And Sanjit. Pray the gods that you are safe. Please, gods, let them find me.* She fluttered open her eyes. *I have to get out of here.*

The beat of her heart increased in tempo as she crawled frantically toward the entrance, grabbed hold of the door's wooden slats and shook them vigorously. A frenzied, frustrated scream erupted from her mouth. It sounded to her that it came from someone else. A lost soul. She let go of the door. It was no use. She was trapped. She dropped to her haunches. She felt hopeless, vulnerable.

"Hey, prisoner!"

Taja looked up and into the face of a tiny little man peering into the cage. His high-pitched voice sounded like a child's.

"What's your name?" he piped.

"Taja."

"Where are the Shakti Warriors?"

Taja looked at the little man. He sounded upset.

"I asked you a question, Taja. Answer me!" he yelled.

Taja jumped back in alarm. "They… they… I don't know."

"Lies! Tell me, girl. Otherwise, I will hurt you." A silver blade flashed in the morning sunlight.

"I'm telling you, I do not know," pleaded Taja. "Your medicine man took me from them. He is the one you should be asking. Now please, let me go. I have nothing to give you."

"Ha ha ha! Yes, you do, yes you do." He jumped up and down in excitement. "They will come for you, your Shakti. They will come and rescue you. They will come to us. Just wait and see. The Shaman is always right. He is powerful, our Shaman. Nothing can defeat him."

"What do you want with them? What have they done to you?" pleaded Taja.

"We want their power. We *must* have their power." His voice changed. It became guttural, animal-like. "We will take it and become mighty Ignogai. The most powerful tribe. Then no one will stand in our way. We will conquer all!"

Taja crawled to the back of the cell. There was no reasoning with this little man. An insatiable rapaciousness consumed him.

"Where are you going girl? There is no escaping this place," he hissed.

"Piju! What are you doing? I told you to leave the prisoner be,' said the Shaman firmly, approaching.

Piju turned, quickly concealing his blade in the folds of his garb. "The chief told me to question her. I told you that he was disappointed in you, Shaman. You did not bring him the Shakti."

"Liar. You have not even spoken to the chief, you miserable, gutless creature. I have just been in consultation with him, and he said nothing of the sort."

"Bah. Shaman. What do you know?"

"Apparently much more than you. When the Shakti come, we will sacrifice the girl. She will be offered to the gods in appeasement for our forthcoming victory."

Taja baulked. *Sacrificed? No.*

"Until then, she is not to be harmed. Especially by the likes of you. Now give me that blade," said the Shaman. "Or face the consequences!"

Taja glanced at the blind Shaman, speculating just how it was that he knew that Piju held a blade in his hand.

36 ~ Yogen

Halim blinked open his eyes, drew in a deep breath and sighed contentedly. He opened his mouth into a wide yawn, quickly snapping his jaw shut in reaction to a wince of pain that cut through his cheekbones, piercing into his head like needles. Smells of the forest drifted into the room, along with the whiff of food being cooked. His stomach rumbled in anticipation. He sat up in his bed and looked across at Sanjit, who was still sound asleep in the bed alongside him. Halim climbed carefully out of his bed and stepped silently over to the window. The morning sun had just clipped the horizon; its golden light, illuminating the leaves on the tops of the trees as they welcomed its powerful, life-giving warmth. He pictured the girl's beautiful green eyes, shimmering in the reflection of the sun's light, captivating his senses, causing his heart to pound vigorously in his chest.

"Good morning."

Halim turned. "Morning brother. How did you sleep?"

Sanjit pushed himself up onto his elbows, squinting past Halim, out of the window and into the blaze of the morning sun. "I think that was the best sleep I've had since leaving Harappa."

Halim smiled. "Yes, me too." He gazed outside again. "What a night."

"Yes, it was phenomenal."

"I've never danced like that before. The music…"

"Powerful."

They sat in silence for a moment, listening to the sounds of the morning, yet still captivated by the enchanting memories of the celebration and the powerful Prana of the music and ecstatic dance of the night before.

"Come, let us rise and find the source of that aroma," said Halim. "I'm famished."

The eating room was abuzz with the tree-top people. They laughed and cajoled with each other while waiting to be served. Halim and Sanjit sat at the end of a long, wooden table. They spooned warm and tasty porridge broth into their mouths and sipped on hot, frothy, malted beverages from a pair of large, wooden flagons.

"Is there space for me here?" said a familiar voice.

"Kativa!" exclaimed Halim looking up. "Good morning."

"Morning, my friends. You enjoy the festivities?"

Halim shifted sideways on the bench. He grinned sheepishly. "Yes, of course. Incredible party."

"And you, Sanjit?" enquired Kativa squeezing onto the bench next to Halim. "Was the ceremony up to your standards?"

Sanjit smiled broadly. A rare occurrence. "Yes, Kativa. It was delightful, thank you. Thank you for your hospitality. It is much appreciated."

"Oh, think nothing of it." Kativa pursed her lips and waved her hand indifferently in front of her face. "Our common enemy makes us family." She lifted her flagon. "May the Ignogai rot in the depths of the underworld. May their carcases be consumed by dark fire and sulphurous fumes, never to rise again!"

"Hear, hear!" Halim lifted his mug and knocked it against Kativa's with a clunk. "Never again!"

They all sipped at the malt from their flagons and then settled back to silently spooning the porridge from their bowls into their mouths.

"So, I didn't really get to asking," said Kativa after several mouthfuls. "Why are the Ignogai after you? And why did they capture your sister? Sorry for being inquisitive, but the more we know about our common enemy, the more we will understand their ways and their motives."

"No need for apologies, Kativa," said Sanjit. "You have saved our lives. We are forever in your debt."

"It's a long story," said Halim with a sigh.

"Well, we have time, and I have ears with which to listen," said Kativa, smiling.

Halim returned the smile. "We're from Harappa," said Halim. "A long way away." He stared into the distance, as the memories of home blossomed like a lotus flower in his mind's eye. Relief washed over him as he shared his story. Tears welled up in his eyes as he pictured the ashen face of his mother.

"Hmm. I have often heard tell of this city," said Kativa thoughtfully. "Some traders that have passed through our village have made mention of it before."

Halim looked across at Sanjit and continued. "My mother is sick. She's dying. We came to find a cure for her. My father tried first but fell and broke his leg in the Kunlun Mountains."

"The Kunlun Mountains. Treacherous place." Kativa nodded her head.

"It began in the city of Dholavira. This was where we encountered the Ignogai." Halim thought back to that night that seemed such a very long time ago. "We were hosts to Marut, a local farmer on the outskirts of the city." Nalini's sparkling blue eyes brought a smile to his face as he remembered them regarding him with curious interest. "There was a fire."

"The Ignogai," said Kativa. "They started it, didn't they?"

Halim nodded. "We were captured."

"How did you escape?" Kativa leant in with interest. "Is this why they are after you?"

"Yes. We called on a heard of nearby elephants. They charged into the village and smashed open our enclosure, allowing us to run free. We haven't stopped running."

"What about your sister?"

"Oh, she escaped with us, but they tracked us, followed us for days. We tried to hide in the world of the spirits, but they found us there and stole her from us."

"Their Shaman," said Kativa nodding. "Don't worry, Halim, we'll find her. See that man over there?" Kativa pointed to a scrawny looking character in a dark-green robe. He had long, dark hair with streaks of grey and was talking animatedly with a young girl by the food table. "That's Yogen. He will help us."

Kativa proceeded to get up from the table and make her way over to the wiry man who was still talking to the girl and gesturing with his hands. The girl turned as Kativa approached. Halim's heart skipped a beat. Those eyes. It was the girl. From the night before. The pipe. The dance. Halim's head swam. His breathing quickened. He couldn't take his eyes off her. Kativa engaged with the man. He pressed his palms together at his chest and bowed his forehead to touch his fingertips in greeting. She followed suit. Kativa turned and pointed to Halim and Sanjit. They waved back in acknowledgement. The girl also turned. Her eyes met Halim's. She smiled broadly and waved in recognition. Halim grinned sheepishly and felt the blood rush to his face. Time seemed to stand still as he found himself cast back to the dance floor. The captivating music came to life inside his head and those mesmerising green eyes, like twin pools of magical water, pulled him into their sultry depths.

"Halim, Sanjit, this is Yogen." Kativa broke Halim's spell. He looked up at a smiling face with the same green eyes as the girl, pushed back his stool and respectfully stood up to greet the venerable looking man.

"Namaste," said Yogen bowing his forehead to gently touch his fingers that were pressed together at his chest.

"Namaste," said Sanjit and Halim, bowing together in response.

Halim looked up at the girl who had also approached them.

"This is Namrah," said Kativa. "Apparently, you two already know each other?" She looked at Halim and raised her eyebrows expectantly.

Namrah quickly bowed her head. "Namaste," she said, with the happiest of smiles.

"Namaste," repeated Halim and Sanjit.

"Yes. We met last night." Halim felt the blood return to his face in a gush.

"Namrah is Yogen's daughter," said Kativa.

"It's good to see that you two have recovered," said the scrawny man in a voice that matched his physique. "You were almost lost to us. The poison was very powerful, very powerful indeed."

"You're the Shaman," said Sanjit matter-of-factly.

Yogen smiled broadly. "Very astute, young man. Yes, I am the Shaman of the tree-top people."

"Well then, I guess a thank you is in order," said Halim. "You saved our lives." Halim bowed his head in gratitude.

"Oh, no matter." He waved his hand through the air, dismissing the compliment. "I was just doing my job."

"We desperately need your help again, Yogen," said Halim. "The Ignogai captured my sister."

"Yes, I know. Kativa just told me. We are going to have to go back to the cave. We will track the Ignogai from there. Come, we have no time to spare. Are you ready?"

"As ready as we'll ever be." Halim squeezed his hands into fists and ground his teeth together in anticipation.

"My daughter Namrah will join us," said Yogen. "She is skilled in the magical arts and will be an asset to our quest."

Namrah looked across at Halim and smiled. Halim's heart skipped a beat.

37 ~ Searching

The five travellers turned back to look at the forest one last time before it disappeared from view. They proceeded to make their way down the other side of the mountain. The terrain became drier as the greenery disappeared to leave a wide rocky expanse ahead.

"Look, a river." Halim pointed to a narrow strip of water at the bottom of the descent. It glistened, reflecting the morning sunlight like a precious jewel.

"Yes, we'll stop there to rest," said Yogen, squinting.

They continued in silence, picking up the pace in anticipation of the refreshment waiting for them in the ravine below. Time slipped by quickly for Halim as he walked behind Namrah, captivated by her moving feet as he followed their steps across the uneven landscape.

"Ahhh. This tastes so good," said Namrah as she sipped the river water from her cupped hands. She turned to Halim as he approached. "Here, let me help you," she said, taking the waterskin from his outstretched hands. She turned back to the river, crouched down and pushed it into the water. The water swirled around the skin and then covered it completely. A gurgle of air followed, bubbling to the surface in satisfaction.

After drinking their fill, the travellers sat down in a circle on a sandy area beside the river. Halim gazed at the flowing water, listening to the gurgling sounds that it made as it flowed. He closed his eyes, releasing the tension in his shoulders, letting go to the flowing waters and the sounds of nature.

"Can you feel it?" whispered Yogen in the silence that followed. "The now. Come back to it. Come back from your wandering thoughts. Close your eyes and feel the energy flowing all around us." Silence followed. "Feel your minds drift like the water in the river. Forever flowing. Constantly moving. Feel them float back into the distant past and forward into the unknown future. Bring them back. Back to the now. Back to your bodies. Your bodies are forever present. Your physical bodies are here. They are always in the now. Bring attention to your bodies and the mind shall return. Feel the Prana flow through your bodies. From your head, down through your chest, into your belly and then deep into the ground. Feel yourself grounded into the earth, anchored here by your body, your physical being. In the now. In the self."

Yogen's mesmerising voice pulled Halim back from the rippling sound of the flowing river and into his body. His heavy body. He straightened his back, shifted in the soft sand and felt a lightness return as he concentrated on his breathing, the soft flow of breath in and out of his lungs.

"Now bring a smile to your lips," continued Yogen. "And feel that smile radiate across your face, from your mouth up your cheeks and into your eyes. Feel the warmth of the sun on your heads melt into that smile. Feel it expand and unfurl like a butterfly awakening from its transformation inside its cocoon, spreading its wings to fly. Feel the Prana build and flow through your body, down into your heart space, your belly and then into your limbs. Feel it flow through your pelvis and into the ground beneath your sit-bones. Feel the pulse with every breath, the heartbeat of the Prana inside your body. Feel it connect with the others in the circle around you as we join as one. Let go. Release your fears. Breathe."

Halim felt a sense of peace and unity like he had never felt before. He was quite aware of the others around him - five magnetic fields of energy all woven together through the Shaman's magical words. The air around him was electrically charged, tickling his ears with an indiscernible buzz that raised the hair on the back of his neck like a cat on guard.

"This connection you feel between you," said Yogen softly, "is a precursor to the next stage of our journey together. An important stage that we will experience when we reach the cave. Feel it. Recognise it. Become it. We are one."

Time seemed to stand still. The tingling feeling in his ears dissipated as Halim felt his connection with the others strengthen like an irresistible force pulling him in every conceivable direction. He succumbed to this force as it quivered through his body.

◊ ◊ ◊

The sun appeared a darker shade of orange as it slowly made its way towards the beckoning horizon. The five travellers reached the top of a rise and stopped, as Yogen dropped his pack to the ground.

"We have arrived," he announced. "There is the entrance to the cave." He pointed towards a few misshapen boulders not far ahead. Halim squinted. They looked like a collection of common rocks protruding from the mountainside. He couldn't make out anything unusual, let alone the cave's entrance, and wondered how the Shaman could be so assured of its exact location. Halim opened his mouth to speak but then shut it again as the Shaman lifted his pack over one shoulder and marched towards the rocks ahead. It was only when they squeezed into the tight entrance that Halim remembered entering the cave that cold and fateful evening. He shivered at the memory of crossing through and into the spirit world with Sanjit and Taja. The cave was dark but soon became bathed in a warm, yellow light.

"Ah. A paleo crystal," remarked Yogen. "I haven't seen one of those for a very long time. Where'd you get it?"

"From an ancient monastery," replied Sanjit.

"Let me guess - in the Kunlun Mountains?"

Sanjit nodded.

"I have heard it rumoured that such a place exists, my friend. Is there truly an immortal living there?"

"I'm not sure about that, but the monastery itself has been there for a very long time, and the line of monks have been around for many hundreds of years."

"I would like to go there one day," said Yogen thoughtfully. "Will you take me?"

"Gladly," replied Sanjit with a smile.

"Excellent! Then it's a deal," replied Yogen, clapping Sanjit on the shoulder in appreciation. "But let's rescue Taja first," he said with a grin. "Okay. Is everyone inside?" he continued, looking around the cave. "Sanjit, please place the crystal on the ground in the centre of the cave and then let's all gather around it."

Halim sat down with Namrah on his right and Sanjit on his left, followed by Kativa and then Yogen.

"Please get comfortable," said Yogen. "Closer. That's it. Now, look at the crystal for a moment, and then, when you are ready, close your eyes." Yogen's voice began to deepen, to slow, into a methodical, hypnotic, ululating rhythm. "Focus on the afterglow, the temporary burn of the crystal's light inside your mind's eye. Use this trigger, this anchor, to root yourself into the present, to prevent your mind from wandering. Now breathe."

Halim found his thoughts drifting to that of his sister. He was anxious, concerned about her safety, imagining her being tortured, cut, maimed. *Nooo!* A bright light burned away the vision, and he came back to the voice of Yogen, the cave, the crystal. His breathing slowed, deepened, as he slowly began to relax, dropping his shoulders and releasing the tension in his back and neck. A curious tingling sensation tickled his eyelids as he sensed the others also deepen their breathing and relax to the sound of Yogen's soothing voice.

"Good, good," whispered Yogen. "Now, make sure that your

mouth is closed, but don't clench your jaw," he added. "Lift your tongue in your mouth and curl it back until its tip is resting gently on the roof of your palette. Now, slowly and purposefully, draw in a long breath of air, deep into your lungs for one, visualise the air as a silvery liquid, two, flow in through your nostrils, three, down your throat, four and into your expanding belly, five. Hold. And, release for a count of five, four, feel the liquid flow through the rest of your body, three, into and out of your limbs, two, and out the crown of your head, one. And repeat ten more times in your own time."

Each time that Halim repeated the exercise, the more he began to feel the presence of Namrah and Sanjit sitting either side of him. It was hard to explain, but it was as if his breathing merged with theirs until they breathed as one. His awareness of this sensation increased and then began to dissipate until a certainty began to manifest deep inside of him. That certainty was the knowledge that he needn't focus on the regulation of his breathing any longer. The connection was made and would maintain, as long as he grounded himself where he sat. As long as he remained connected to the circle of five, he would be connected to a deeper connection of Prana that flowed between them all.

"Good. We are all connected once more," said Yogen "Just like the first time, but stronger. I can feel it. Now, the next step is for us to imbue our collective Prana with intent. Five times the power, five times the force. We need to focus on the flow. Expand the afterglow of the crystal, relax into it, never push otherwise you will push away. Rather, nudge it gently, onward and upward. Yes. Allow it to fill the cave with its light, its warmth... There!" said Yogen earnestly. "See it? A faint trail of energy. Like the tail of a comet in the heavens? It's the energy trail left behind by the surge of Prana that was released here a few days ago. We must follow this trail together. It will lead us to our final destination. Halim and Sanjit, I want you to focus your intention on this residue of Prana as you have been to the Ignogai village before. Release all tension and follow my lead."

Halim experienced a pulling sensation inside his head, dragging him up and out of his body. His body was heavy, yet he was light, light as a feather. He drifted up to the roof of the cave and then passed through the solid mountain rock. He was one with the collective. Guided by Yogen, they shifted into the spirit realm and traversed across the familiar, shadowy world that resembled an underwater cosmos, pulsing with an unnatural, eerie life of its own.

38 ~ Taja

Something shiny in the corner of the cage caught Taja's eye. She crawled across the cramped space to see what it was. She dug her fingers into the soft earth, pulled up a piece of bone and jumped back in fright. It was a decayed human skull attached to a spinal column. Bits of hardened flesh and matted hair still clung to the bone. The empty eye sockets stared back at her ghoulishly. She noticed a leather cord around its neck. She carefully pulled the cord over the skull and lifted it up to reveal a small, diamond shaped, crudely carved metal pendant hanging from it. She rubbed the pendant against her tunic and then twisted the piece of leather around her wrist, pushing it up her forearm so that she concealed it beneath her sleeve.

Taja heard the familiar, methodical, thud, thud, thud of the Shaman's staff on the ground. She shivered. She pulled herself into a tight ball, but her body continued to shake. She squeezed her eyes shut. Piju's irritating voice rang inside her head and sacrificial visions of blood and gore raced through her mind.

"Taja. Taja." The Shaman's voice beckoned. He pulled at the door latch. "Come, let's go."

Taja opened her mouth to speak, to enquire where it was that they were going, but her teeth just chattered inside her pounding head. She crawled grudgingly, like an animal confined against its will, out of the cage on all fours before slowly climbing to her feet. The Shaman gazed at Taja with scars for eyes and tilted his head in contemplation. He somehow sensed Taja's forlorn stance with her arms hanging limply at her sides in resignation, giving him reason enough not to bind her hands once more.

"Walk," said the Shaman, tapping the backs of Taja's legs with his staff. She moved forward in front of the Shaman with a jolt, breaking into a slow, methodical pace. "That's it. Just follow the path."

Taja stepped to the steady rhythm of the Shaman's staff, pounding on the ground behind her as they gradually made their way through the Ignogai village. Members of the tribe came out to cajole her as she passed, but she was blind to their mocking jeers and shrieks of laughter. Her head hung low as she stared spellbound at the ground, watching it pass beneath her shuffling feet. The dense morning mist around them gave way to a looming wall of long wooden spikes with crudely carved tips - a menacing sight. As Taja and the Shaman approached, a solitary figure standing guard at the only visible entrance turned to face them before nodding in recognition. Taja could now see that the wall was one side of an enclosed containment space. She began to wonder what was inside. A pungent smell of burning flesh wafted up her nostrils. She gagged, bringing up what little she had in her stomach. Her throat was on fire and her eyes watered.

"Shaman." The guard bowed his head. "You'd better take care of your prisoner otherwise; there'll be nothing left for the lycanthus. Ha ha ha haaa!" He roared with laughter.

The Shaman withdrew a gourd from beneath his cloak and handed it to Taja. She drank hastily. The water soothed her throat and settled her stomach.

"This is the Pit. It's where we feed the creature." The Shaman gestured beyond the entrance of the enclosure. "The lycanthus." Taja looked up at the Shaman. She had never heard of such an

211

animal. "It belongs to the chief. He is here and wants to meet with you. Come."

This time, the Shaman took the lead, stepping through the entrance. Taja wondered how he knew where he was going. She looked up at the imposing spikes as they passed beneath them and into the Pit. The putrid stench was stronger here. Taja tried to block her nostrils and breathe through her mouth, but the fetor still seeped through and into her lungs like an invasive parasite, intent on causing her intense discomfort. Her head spun.

She was welcomed by shouts and cries from a crowd of unruly onlookers. There were about thirty of them, positioned in a protected space to the right of the entrance. They were all facing the same direction with their arms stabbing the air, jeering and pointing frantically at a flurry of activity in the centre of the Pit. She peered over the wooden beam and gasped. A wolf-like creature was chasing a helpless man in rags. He was covered in blood. Likely his own. He held onto one arm as he ran. It was then that Taja noticed that the arm that he held onto was raw to the bone. His shrieks tore through her head until her heart ached with pity. She wanted to tear her eyes away from the despicable sight, but she was drawn to it like the rip current from a churning river. Bloody gore drooled from the creature's mouth as it pounced high into the air and onto its victim's back. The man was thrust forward and down onto the muddy earth. He landed with a loud thud and a crack of his ribs. He howled in agony, and the crowd erupted with vigour in response. The man clawed at the ground in front of him, trying in vain to pull himself forward and away from the lycanthus. The creature pressed down on his back, baring hideous fangs in a vicious growl that echoed chillingly around the Pit. It sprang forward, clamping its powerful jaws around the soft nape of the helpless man's neck. He spasmed once, arching his back in torment and then went limp.

The hideous creature twisted its prey from side to side, slowly at first, then with a more vigorous shake. Another loud crack echoed around the Pit as the vertebrae in the lifeless man's spine shattered with the force of the jerking movements. Another jeer from the crowd. Taja could see the lycanthus strain as it pulled at the man's neck with its powerful jaws. A huge chunk of meat, flesh and bone tore free in its mouth, spraying an arc of blood and gore across the pit and into the crowd. The Ignogai barbarians welcomed the rain of carnage with outstretched hands and upturned faces. Taja turned away in revulsion, coming face to face with the Shaman, who beckoned her across to the left side of the Pit with a smirk of indulgence stretched across his face.

She climbed several steps, following the Shaman onto a dais with an elevated view of the gruesome scene below. She turned away from the Pit, but that didn't prevent her from hearing the wretched sound of the feeding lycanthus as it feasted on the prisoner.

"Did you see that, Shaman?!" bellowed the chief in a mighty roar. "What a kill!" He turned to look at Taja. "And what have we here? Is this the girl?"

The Shaman nodded. "Yes, my chief."

The chief approached Taja. She looked away. "She's a pretty little thing," he said licking his tongue across his dirty, pock-marked face. He grabbed her chin in his hand and twisted her face towards his. He smelt like a dog, like his lycanthus. Taja swallowed hard. She looked into his face and was appalled. He had a big red gash on one side of his cheek. The skin looked raw like it had been burned there. Blackened teeth protruded from an evil grin and his eyes looked like they were on fire as they poured over her small, lithe frame. His long, greasy hair fell onto some kind of animal skin draped over his shoulders, and a curved sword protruded brutishly from behind his back.

"So you think they'll come?" the chief asked the Shaman.

"Yes. They will. I am certain of it."

"How certain, Shaman? The last time you were certain, you were certainly wrong."

"My chief. This is the sister of the Shakti. They will try and

213

rescue her and then we will capture them."

"What about the girl?"

"Once we have captured the Shakti, we will have no use for her. I suggest we sacrifice her to appease the gods."

"No. I like her. I will have her," said the chief, grabbing Taja by her jaw, pulling her in close. She gagged from his putrid breath as he breathed all over her. Taja screwed up her face in disgust. She twisted her head, prying herself free from his grasp. Her jaw ached.

"Ha! She's feisty. I like it!" he roared. "I will have her now!" Spittle flew from his mouth. Taja cringed.

"No, my chief! We cannot spoil the prisoner. Not before the Shakti come. Your time will come. I promise," said the Shaman with a bow.

The chief took a step back, reached behind his back and withdrew his long, curved sword. He swung it up, down and around, bringing it to rest against the Shaman's neck. Sharp steel pressed against soft skin, releasing a trickle of blood. "You had better be right, this time, Shaman. I grow tired of your empty promises, and soon I will grow tired of you!"

The Shaman gingerly pushed the blade away from his neck and gave a tender cough as if to clear his throat. "I will need to secure the prisoner inside the temple to lure the Shakti into our trap. It's them that you want, remember? We will capture them and their Shakti Prana, my lord. You will become more powerful than you ever know."

The chief's eyes sparkled with lust upon hearing this news. He grinned. "Now *that's* music to my ears." He slowly dropped the blade from the Shaman's neck and then lifted it again to point at Taja. "As for you," he leered. "I will be waiting. Patiently. Hahaha!" he howled, throwing his head back vehemently.

39 ~ Astral

It came back to him now. The familiar sensation was akin to being underwater. His senses were dulled, muted. He felt like a fish, peering at the aquatic world around him with spherical eyes. He could identify the others, but it was more of an intuitive process than a palpable one. Yogen's Prana glowed brightest in the murky environment. Halim focused his attention there, willing his Prana to move towards the captivating light.

You okay? It was Namrah. She was inside his head.

Yes. I've done this before. Halim sensed her Prana. It glowed warmly beside him. He looked at her fuzzy face and smiled a fuzzy smile.

Come, we mustn't lose the others. She turned to glide deeper into the misty environment.

Halim followed. This time, the space around him appeared to be lighter. He wondered if it had something to do with their combined aura's illuminating this drab place. Sanjit had tried to explain how the rules of the spirit world worked, but they were confusing to Halim. The one thing that did make sense, however, was that nothing could beat experience. Sanjit said that the more time one spent in the spirit world, the more familiar it became, and he was right. Halim found it easier to move across the surreal landscape than the last time he was here. He felt lighter and more buoyant and seemed to be able to see farther ahead than before. He gazed around in awe at streaks of colourful ribbon-like clouds that he never noticed when he was with Sanjit. They shimmered in an invisible breeze as he passed.

He looked ahead once more, straining to see the remnants of the trail left behind by the Shaman of the Ignogai. At first, all he could see was the glow from Yogen's Prana; a hazy yellow aura that led them across the blurry terrain. Then he noticed tiny, sparkling grains of light, scattered across the invisible path that they followed. They shimmered in and out of sight like minuscule fairies, frolicking in a world of their own.

Namrah, Look. Halim pointed at the flickering, star-like residue.

Yes. It's so beautiful. She stopped to gaze around with him. Halim sensed her warmth again and felt at peace.

The five visitors to the world of the spirits traversed across a wasteland of shifting energy that had no beginning nor end. There were no landmarks or milestones, no spirit trees or mystical markers that indicated where they were or how far they had to go. Time had no jurisdiction here and distance no governance. They laid their faith in the expertise of their guide. It was this combined faith that gave them unity of thought and strength of purpose in this supernatural place.

Halim looked up. Yogen had paused.

We are here. His voice boomed inside Halim's head. He was communicating to all of them at once.

For us to find this place in the physical world, I need to imprint my Prana here. It will act as a beacon for us to follow upon our return to the cave.

But why can't we just travel here now? Said Halim. *The same way that the Shaman took my sister?*

That would require a serious amount of energy. I could make that journey on my own, but I do not possess the power to take any of you with me, replied Yogen thickly. *Do not move. I will be back.* And with that, Yogen shimmered and then winked out of sight. He returned in an instant, appearing some distance away from the group.

It is done. We can return to the cave now. The journey back will be much quicker. Come, gather in a circle. Okay, now close your eyes and picture the cave. Picture the five of us sitting together as one. Focus. Yes, that's it. Now let's go there.

A powerful magnetic pressure pulled Halim backwards and downward at the same time. The combined thrust of their thoughts all focused on a single destination was a very powerful intention. Wave upon wave of Prana washed over Halim, grounding him in his seat on the cave floor. Gradually, physical sensation began to return to his limbs, and his muted senses began to return to normal. He felt strangely refreshed and completely relaxed. He was conscious of his breathing flowing in and out of his lungs, as he slowly opened his eyes. He turned and found Namrah's beautiful green eyes. He smiled as he gazed into their captivating depths. She took his hand in hers. It was warm to the touch. He closed his eyes and sighed heavily.

"Come on you two lovebirds," said Yogen slapping Halim on the back, it's time to eat."

Halim felt the blood rush to his face. His stomach grumbled loudly. Yogen was right. The pranic journey sapped a lot of energy from his body. He wondered how long they had been gone as he stood up and made his way to the cave entrance. He stepped outside and was surprised to find the morning sun already high in the sky. Soothing sun rays bathed his face in their exhilarating glow. No wonder he was famished - they had been journeying all night long! He closed his eyes and savoured the sun's warmth, stretching his limbs up to the heavens above. Soon after, the sweet aroma of food seeped out of the cave, tickling his nostrils enticingly.

"Halim! Come and eat," called Sanjit from inside the cave.

Yogen had cooked up a spicy vegetarian dish that flared Halim's taste-buds as he wolfed down the sumptuous food. The five ate in silence, gazing up only to refill their plates until the food was all but finished.

"Yogen," said Kativa. "We must plan our quest to rescue the girl."

Yogen nodded emphatically. "Yes, yes, of course."

"Did you see her? When you imprinted your Prana?"

"But how could you?" interjected Halim. "I mean how could you have seen Taja? You were gone for but a moment. I saw you disappear and then reappear in a flash."

Yogen smiled. "The laws of the spirit world are complicated, young warrior. Time works very differently when we navigate through its many layers."

"Hmm, yes, you're right," Halim responded, thinking how baffled he was when he stepped outside the cave to find that many more hours had passed during their expedition into the spirit world than he had imagined. "So, did you see her? My sister?" said Halim eagerly. "Is she all right?"

"It is more difficult than you can imagine to see beyond the world of spirits and into the physical world," said Yogen. He cleared his throat. "I have to rely on my intuition to gather what information I can, and then piece it together like a puzzle to reveal clues and signs rather than outright facts." Yogen closed his eyes. Anticipated silence filled the cave as the group waited for him to gather his thoughts. "I saw... a river," he whispered. "Winding through the village like a serpent. Beyond this was the Ignogai. Many of them. Moving about. A concentration of them in a foul place. Reeking of death. Closer. Must get closer." Yogen was reliving the experience. Halim shifted towards him. "A powerful aura... the Shaman!" he hissed. "Wait... there is another with him. Halim. Is that you?"

"Yes, Yogen. I am here," Halim responded, confused.

Yogen was silent. His eyes remained closed, and he swayed gently from side to side. Halim looked at Namrah and shrugged his shoulders.

"No, it is not you, Halim," whispered Yogen once more. "The girl. Taja?"

"Yes!" said Halim breathlessly. "She is alive! Is she okay?

Yogen?"

Yogen frowned. He was still in a trance. "Must return. Warn them…" Yogen opened his eyes. He sat unmoving for a moment.

"Papa," said Namrah. "Are you all right?"

Yogen rubbed his hands together in a circular motion and then placed his palms over his eyes, pressing them gently into the eye sockets. "Yes, my child." He smiled warmly at his daughter. "I am fine." He squeezed her hand reassuringly.

"You said that you should warn us," said Kativa. "What else did you see?"

"I fear that they are laying a trap for us. The Ignogai. I had a sense of it when I came into contact with the Shaman."

"Did he feel your presence?" enquired Sanjit.

"I don't think so, but I could be wrong. He seemed preoccupied with Taja."

"So you're sure it was her?" said Halim.

"Well, one can never be too sure about anything my son," said Yogen with a grin. "But her signature was very different to the rest of the Ignogai. She was not one of them."

"It *must* be her," said Halim assuredly. "I mean who else not of the Ignogai would the Shaman himself be preoccupied with? What are we waiting for? Let's go and get her."

"Patience, Halim," said Yogen. "We must first put a plan together. They will be expecting us."

"Well, not exactly," said Sanjit. "They will only be expecting Halim and myself."

Yogen nodded. "Therein lies our plan."

"But there are so many of them," said Namrah. "How are we going to get in and save Taja without being detected?"

"One word," said Yogen. "Distraction. We need to create a diversion. This is the only way."

"Yes," agreed Kativa. "You're right. We will distract the Ignogai while Halim finds Taja."

"Easier said than done," said Yogen. "Halim will need your help, Kativa. Then there's the Shaman. That's another matter entirely. Namrah, Sanjit and I will deal with him."

"What's your plan, Yogen?" said Sanjit.

"There's a bridge at the end of the river. You, Namrah and I will create the diversion there. We'll find a way to attract the Ignogai away from the village. This will give Halim and Kativa time to sneak in, find Taja and rescue her."

"What about the Shaman, papa?" said Namrah.

"Sanjit will lure him to the bridge with the rest of the Ignogai. He will recognise Sanjit's Shakti signature. He won't be able to resist the urge to confront Sanjit again, especially in his own territory." Yogen chuckled.

"Papa, from what you've told me about this Shaman, this is no laughing matter." She was clearly agitated with her father.

"Don't worry my child," reassured Yogen. "He won't expect all three of us."

"You overestimate our abilities, papa. What if he overpowers us?"

"We have the element of surprise, my child. He is going to expect the Shakti, not a couple of Shaman. We will be prepared. Do not worry so." Yogen patted his daughter's back.

Sanjit withdrew his long hunting knife. It flashed in the glow of the paleo crystal. He began to scrape a circular pattern into the sand of the cave.

"A mandala," remarked Halim.

"Ah," sighed Namrah. "Papa, look. He knows the way."

"Yes, my child," Yogen nodded. "He is Shakti."

They all watched silently as Sanjit completed his design.

"Halim. The amulet," said Sanjit, his hand extended towards Halim expectantly.

Halim withdrew the wooden medallion from under his tunic and handed it to Sanjit.

"Will you join me?" he said to the others.

Halim noticed that the pattern of this mandala was slightly different to the one that Sanjit etched into the earth at the start of their journey. It appeared to be more intricate with an additional inner circle where Sanjit had placed Halim's amulet.

The rest of the group sat down silently beside Sanjit.

"This is an intentional mandala," explained Sanjit. "It will help us navigate the quickest and safest path to the Ignogai village, avoiding obstacles along the way. Study its pattern for a moment. Good. Now everyone place your right hand on the wooden amulet in the centre of the mandala and close your eyes. Good. Now visualise that pattern in your mind and chant the following mantra with me."

"Om Gum Ganapatayei Namah.
Om Gum Ganapatayei Namah.
Om Gum Ganapatayei Namah."

(I bow to the elephant-faced deity [Ganesh] who is capable of removing all obstacles.

I pray for blessings and protection.)

40 ~ Altar

A haphazard shriek startled Taja as she drifted in and out of sleep. She was exhausted. Her stomach rumbled, and her head hurt. A scraping sound came from the other end of the cage. She looked up at the dirty face of an Ignogai pushing a plate of food under the bars. He grinned a toothless smile. The vile smell of burnt carrion caught her nostrils. She felt a wave of nausea wash over her, but she knew she had to eat to survive. She crawled over to the food, took a deep breath and began to eat. The meat was as tough as leather. She chewed until her jaws ached with a dull pain. The Ignogai stared at her in silence as she ate. She turned her back to him and moved to the centre of the cage. She heard him grunt in indignation and then shuffle away, leaving her to eat her meal in peace.

She closed her eyes and flashes of the savage wolf-beast attacking the helpless prisoner filled her head. She tried to shut out the harrowing vision but the harder she tried, the more distinct the detail became. She swallowed and tasted blood and gore. Her stomach turned. *No. It cannot be. No. Noooooo.* She scampered to the rear of the cage and retched until her throat burned and her intestines twisted in agony. She wiped a dirty sleeve across her face and sobbed. She licked her lips and welcomed the salty taste of the tears that rinsed away some of the vile tasting discharge that filled her mouth.

Thud, thud, thud. "Taja." She turned as the Shaman fumbled with the lock. "It's time to go again. Come, my child." She coughed. "Here, drink this." The Shaman pushed a gourd through the cage bars. Taja grabbed the gourd, and the Shaman went back to the lock. She took a gulp, too fast, choked and spat it out with a cough. She wiped her sleeve across her face again and took another swig. The water flowed down her throat. It tasted like honey after that putrid experience. The Shaman finally opened the door and ushered Taja out of the cage. Her ears pricked to the steady beat of a drum echoing the distance as she followed the Shaman towards its source.

"Where are we going?" she croaked. Her throat burned.

"To the temple," replied the Shaman without turning around.

Taja remembered the Shaman's conversation with the chief. "What's in the temple?"

"The gods of the Ignogai," the Shaman replied. "They will be appeased."

Taja could only imagine what he meant. "How are they appeased?" she ventured to ask.

"Through sacrifice, of course! Yours will be a special one. The blood of a female. A pure female. A virgin."

Taja stared at the Shaman's back as they walked. She could sense his evil sneer. She shivered, closed her eyes and prayed to the gods for forgiveness.

She turned her head instinctively. The toothless Ignogai was following them at a distance. "What does he want?" The Shaman stopped and turned around. Taja pointed. "There, behind that bush."

The Shaman wrinkled his nose and sniffed the air. "Oh, that's Drindash." He chuckled. "I think he likes you."

Taja turned and trudged on, following the Shaman towards the sound of the beating drum. Another wooden structure appeared in the gloom. It was crudely fashioned and circular in design with an open roof. Thick plumes of smoke poured up and out of its centre like a giant pipe.

Another Ignogai stood guard at its entrance. He straightened up as the Shaman approached. "Shaman," he nodded in greeting. He ignored Taja.

"I am taking her in for preparation," said the Shaman, jabbing his thumb at Taja. The guard stood aside as they stepped through the entrance. The first thing that Taja noticed were several Ignogai scurrying around the temple, shifting in and out of the smoke as it swirled around the inner sanctum. They were painted white from head to toe and wore grotesque looking masks with hideous grins and disturbing patterns that seemed to twist and turn with a life of their own.

"Who are they?" said Taja.

"These are the servants of the Picasa, the emissaries of the gods themselves!" said the Shaman haughtily.

The smoke burned Taja's eyes and consumed her nostrils as the Shaman led them through the haze and closer to the source of the drumming. Something brushed passed Taja, and she jumped, spinning around to witness one of the painted Ignogai disappear into the thick smoke behind her. Heat bathed the right side of her face as they passed a raging fire - the source of all the smoke. The Shaman led them to a small clearing with a long, smooth, stone altar-like a table that was tilted at a slight angle so that anything placed on its surface would just slide off. Thick, leather straps hung loosely off the sides of the stone that was stained dark with blood. Taja baulked. The Shaman gestured, and Taja responded, climbing mechanically onto the altar stone. She lay down onto its cold, hard surface. The Shaman bound the four leather straps, one around each arm and ankle. Taja gazed silently at the smoke spiralling up into the sky. She closed her eyes and pictured her mother's smiling, angelic face looking down at her through the haze reassuringly.

Mama. Her heart ached. *Mama. I love you.* Tears rolled down the sides of her face. She felt them trickle down into her ears, tickling them with their wetness. The steady drumming continued, and the Shaman began to chant in a deep, foreign, guttural voice. Taja opened her eyes and noticed a shape moving to her left. She twisted her head to look. It was Drindash. He had followed them all the way to the temple. He was holding an open container as he cautiously approached. Taja turned her head away from him in fear, straining her body against the leather straps. He held out a brush to her face. It was covered in dark, red paint. Taja felt it cold and wet against her skin. She welcomed the sweet, pungent smell of the paint as Drindash smeared it across her cheeks and forehead. He continued painting, covering her exposed skin, from her arms, down to her legs and over her feet. The paint hardened as it dried, tightening against her skin; a superficial layer of protection against the dark forces rising around her.

Boom, boom, boom. The drumming changed. It was more urgent now, faster. Taja's heart raced, pounding inside her head as if it was fighting to keep up with the drum. The Shaman loomed over her, pushing a phial of pungent smelling concoction to her lips.

"Here, drink this," he said.

Taja screwed up her face and twisted her head away, "No!"

A sharp pain shot into her head as the Shaman squeezed the corners of her jaw hard with his free hand, forcing the medicine into her mouth. Taja tried to hold back from swallowing but the liquid bubbled up through her nose. She coughed and choked on the vile concoction as it went down. Tears welled up in her eyes and ran down over the red paint on her face. She blinked through wet tears as the white-painted Ignogai began to gather around her, jumping up and down erratically, chanting in their guttural tongue. They eased their violent hopping into a more synchronised stomp, pounding the earth with heavy feet, sending dirt and dust up and into the fire-smoke. Taja watched the painted mask-faces around her distort and twist freakishly as the powerful medicine began to take effect. Her eyes rolled back into her head, and her body spasmed violently beneath her leather bindings. The Ignogai continued their chanting, swaying their bodies from side to side as they closed the circle around the altar stone. The Shaman pulled something out from beneath his robes and cast it into the fire with a long sweep of his arm. The flames leapt up, high into the sky, crackling indignantly in response.

Taja closed her eyes, trying to shut out the scene before her, but the perverted visions persisted, swarming through her head like a colony of angry bees.

41 ~ Lesson

"Kativa," said Halim in a quiet voice.

"Yes, Halim. How can I be of service?" she replied.

"May I ask you a question?"

"Well, that depends." She smiled.

"On what?"

"Well, you have already asked me two questions without permission and…"

"When?"

"That's three," Kativa chuckled.

"Kativa! Stop teasing me so."

"Oh, I couldn't resist. You looked so serious when you said to me, *may I ask you a question?*" Kativa mimicked Halim's deep voice.

Halim looked around the cave. The others were packing their things ahead of the journey. "Can we step outside for a moment?"

"Is this about our quest?" enquired Kativa. "To save your sister?"

Halim ignored Kativa's questions until he left the cave. The sun had climbed to its zenith. It was hot on his head. "No, it's about Namrah," Halim finally replied. He sat down on a flat rock near the cave. "I take it you have known her a long time?"

"Since she was born," said Kativa, gazing up into the distance with a smile. "I was young then and carefree, and she was... such a beautiful baby." She turned back to Halim. "Why do you ask?" Halim was also looking out across the mountains in the distance with a faraway look in his eyes. "Ahh. I see," said Kativa grinning. "You and Namrah..."

Halim's cheeks turned crimson. He looked away, embarrassed. "I cannot stop thinking about her," he said softly.

"And you want to know if she feels the same way?"

"Well, I... Yes," he nodded.

"Hmm. I could just ask her."

"No! Don't. Please don't."

"Well, I can tell you that she doesn't have an interest in anyone else as far as I know," said Kativa. "She has been very preoccupied with her studies of late, with very little time for anything else. Her father is a relentless teacher."

Halim smiled sheepishly. "She is so very beautiful. Every time I see her, I can think of nothing else. And her eyes. They see right through me. Into my heart!"

"Sounds like you are in love, my boy," said Kativa with her familiar chuckle.

"I don't know what to do, Kativa. I'm a wreck," he said, running his hands through his hair despairingly.

"Haha. Don't sound so forlorn, Halim. You should be happy. Excited. Not upset and depressed."

"But I don't know what to do. I feel so helpless," he pleaded.

"I guess I can give you some advice. I was in love, once." Kativa looked to the sky again with a sigh.

"What happened?" said Halim. "Is this the story about your husband? The one you were forced to kill?"

"No. This is a story about my very first love. I must have been younger than you are now. Probably your sister Taja's age when I met Padak. He was the son of a master-builder. He was incredible."

Halim looked up at Kativa, puzzled.

"Ah. A master-builder is a highly skilled craftsman in our tribe. He is responsible for building the houses that make up our village in the treetops," she explained. "And Padak, being the son of a master-builder, was in training to become a master builder himself. He didn't have time for girls. He was too busy being taught the trade by his father. Every day I used to watch him. First in the forest, climbing trees to cut down their branches and then back in the village where he applied his craft, shaping the wood and then joining it to create replacement parts and new designs of exquisite beauty and style." Kativa sat down next to Halim.

"I fell in love with Padak long before he even noticed I was around. I marvelled at his muscles and finesse, as he worked in the forest, climbing trees and chopping wood. I was in awe of his craftsmanship, watching him produce the most magnificent designs time and time again. Then one day it happened. He noticed me. I was sitting there, as I always did, watching him work when he looked up at me. I must have looked amusing to him, just sitting there watching him, because he laughed. At me! I was so ashamed. I looked away, but he came right up to me. He approached me and told me that I was beautiful. My heart melted, and my head swam. I'm not sure what happened but the next moment, he was holding me, helping me up. I must have fainted."

Halim was rapt, caught up in the intriguing story. Kativa took a deep breath and continued. "We quickly got to know each other. I continued to visit him, and we spent more and more time together. It was tough in the beginning because his father was very strict. He made Padak work very hard. We used to run into the forest, to a tree-house he built for me there. We had so much fun. Climbing trees and exploring the forest beyond the village. We were young and carefree." Kativa was silent for a while.

Halim couldn't contain himself. "How did Padak feel about you?"

"Oh, he was very much in love with me too, although he tried not to show it," Kativa smiled.

"But why not?" said Halim.

"A man should not display too much affection for fear of driving his woman away. A woman likes a man who is in control of his feelings."

"But how do you control your feelings? That's impossible."

"Maybe. But you shouldn't show it. You may be feeling overwhelmed inside, but on the outside, you should appear calm and collected."

"That's hard," said Halim looking down at his hands despondently.

"No one said love was easy," Kativa smiled again. "Don't try to understand it, just go with the flow. The flow of Prana. Don't use love to make rash decisions, just allow it to take you on its beautiful journey and in time it will settle, and you will come to understand its lessons. Just as time is a healer, so too is it a teacher in this game, this game of love."

"I'm not sure I understand. So what must I do? Nothing? I seem to be getting more confused."

"Halim, you are but a seed in the life of a tree. The seed has only just been planted, and you still have a long time to grow. As you grow, you will learn how to stand tall and strong. You will learn how to move in the wind, and you will learn from your experiences as you lose your leaves and replace them with new ones. You must embrace these things, these experiences of life, of love. Don't be afraid for this is part of the journey we must all take."

"Okay, I will try."

"Just use your intuition and above all, show respect and appreciation for the one you love. If you show her that you care, she will respond with affection. At the same time, women are attracted to things that maketh a man - strength of character, confidence, a sense of humour and sincerity. Don't be afraid of being who you really are, Halim. Don't try, just be."

Halim sighed. "Thank you, Kativa for your insight and guidance. I definitely feel like I understand things a bit better."

"Aaahhh." Yogen stepped out of the cave and stretched his arms up into the sky. "You two look like you're in a serious discussion. I'm sorry to disturb, but we need to get moving."

Kativa grinned. "We were just having a chat about life, but we're done now. Good timing."

"Ah yes, life. The mysterious condition that distinguishes us from all non-living things. Let us enjoy it while it lasts. No?" Yogen laughed. "I trust that it was a good chat? A valuable lesson?" He pushed his eyebrows up, creating a crease of deep furrows on his forehead.

"Yes, it was," said Kativa. "It sure was." She looked toward Halim, who smiled gratefully in return.

◊ ◊ ◊

The afternoon seemed to go quickly for the travellers. They journeyed in silence, thinking deeply about the events ahead. Dusk soon set in and they stopped to rest near a small stream. Halim met Sanjit crouching at the water's edge.

"Halim, my brother. How are you doing?" enquired Sanjit as he filled his waterskin.

"I'm doing okay, I guess."

"You know that Kativa is one of the treetop people's best fighters?"

"Really?"

"Yes. Yogen told me that she has fought the Ignogai many times. She is particularly skilled with bow and arrow. Yogen told me the story of how she killed many Ignogai single-handed."

"Wow!" Halim's eyes widened in awe.

"She is also skilled at climbing trees. He said that she is a tree-climbing champion amongst the tree people. She attacked the Ignogai from the trees as they were planning to raid the treetop village. She never even set foot on the ground before over twenty Ignogai were slain by her arrows."

"Incredible."

"By the time the rest of the Ignogai reached the village, there were but a handful left that were easily overwhelmed by the perimeter guard. She is a hero amongst her people. You are in good hands, Halim. Besides, there shouldn't be too much to contend with once Yogen, Namrah and myself lure the bulk of the savages away."

"I'm more worried about that Shaman of theirs. I get the chills every time I think of what he did to us. We almost died."

"Yes, that is a concern, but it is no concern of yours. You need to focus on finding and retrieving your sister. We will deal with the Shaman." Sanjit tilted his head back and took a swig from his waterskin. His hair hung long down his back.

"Sanjit, please do me a favour?"

"Sure, what is it?"

"Please keep an eye on Namrah. I wouldn't want her to meet the same fate as we did." He felt the blood rush to his face as his concern became visible.

Sanjit smiled. "Don't worry, Halim. She has both me and her father, a very powerful Shaman in his own right, to look out for her safety. I have seen you two together. I know that you have feelings for her."

"Is is that obvious?" said Halim, taken aback.

"Love wears a mask of beauty that is often difficult to hide," Sanjit replied. "Namrah is a strong woman. She has a good teacher. I think she can stand her ground. In fact, I have a strong feeling that she'll be looking out for me instead!" Sanjit laughed. "Speaking of which..." He looked up.

Halim swivelled around to find Namrah approaching. He stood up to find himself swimming in the depths of her sea-green eyes. He was at a loss for words as her beauty enveloped him like a veil.

"Sanjit. Halim." She smiled, and Halim's heart exploded into a million little fragments.

"Namrah." Sanjit bowed his head.

"Um, can I fill your waterskin for you?" said Halim, his heart thumping loudly in his ears.

"Why thank you," she smiled again, handing Halim her gourd. Their fingers touched. Halim quickly bent down to the stream.

"Are you ready for this?" said Sanjit turning to Namrah.

"Ready as I'll ever be. My father says he has a plan."

"I sure hope so because that Shaman is powerful."

"Halim," said Namrah as he stood to hand her the gourd filled with water. "My father requires your assistance."

"Of course. How can I help?" Halim said.

"Your amulet. He would like to borrow it. He has another one. He says it comes from the same forest."

"Really?"

"Yes. They could even be from the same tree."

"Wow. Now that would be something," said Halim pulling the wooden amulet out from beneath his tunic. He studied it closely, this time, tracing the spiral carving with his finger. Round and round, round and round. He pulled it over his head and handed it to Namrah. "Can I see the other one? The other amulet?"

"Of course. Come." Namrah turned away.

Halim followed, mesmerised by the way that she moved her lithe body. He was fascinated with every part of her as she walked. He traced her figure from the backs of her calves up to her hips, her back, shoulders and finally her head. He closed his eyes for a moment.

Come on, Halim. He urged himself. Strength of character, confidence and above all, respect. Kativa's voice rang inside his head.

Sanjit followed them as they made their way over to Yogen, who was chatting to Kativa.

"Ah, the amulet," Yogen beamed as Namrah handed him the wooden medallion. "Thank you kindly, Halim. I'm sure Namrah told you about mine, he said, withdrawing a similar looking wooden amulet from his pouch. Where did you get yours?"

"My father," replied Halim stepping forward to examine Yogen's amulet. "He said it was an ancient artefact from a lost civilisation. Mmm. This one is almost identical, but the spiral is in relief, where mine is carved. Interesting. How do you know that it comes from the same forest? They look similar in age but…"

"I sensed the Prana signature when I touched it last," said

233

Yogen with excitement in his voice. "It spoke to me the same way that this one does when I draw on its energy. Your father was right. These magical medallions are hundreds if not thousands of years old. See how the wood has hardened."

"Yes, and darkened over time," said Halim.

"They belonged to a civilisation that preceded ours. I am certain of this," said Yogen.

"What makes you so sure?"

Yogen held up the amulets, one in each hand. "These amulets have been imbued with the ability to draw Prana from their surroundings, and in the right hands, their energy can recharge the user. This much I have discovered. This is lost knowledge, ancient knowledge that I have no idea how to imitate. Whoever made these, had access to some kind of magical formula or recipe that was part of their design." He pressed them together; Halim's one with its carved spiral and Yogen's with the same spiral but in relief, connecting like two parts of a puzzle.

"Would you look at that," Halim said in awe. "It's a miracle. How they just fit, like they were made for each other."

"Like the lingam-yoni," said Yogen. "Male and female. Independently, your's is the yoni, the vagina and the symbol of the goddess Shakti, while mine is the lingam, the phallus, symbol of the god Shiva. The union of lingam and yoni, of Shiva and Shakti, represents an indivisible convergence, the passive space and active time from which all life originates."

Halim's head tingled. He felt more aware of things around him, like Yogen's words had unlocked a door to the universe of truth and enlightenment. He looked at the group and smiled. For the first time in a long time, he felt confident that they would succeed. He looked to the heavens, closed his eyes and prayed that Taja was okay.

42 ~ Stars

Dusk set in over the five travellers as they marched, the methodical plodding sound of their footsteps echoing into the gloom. Sanjit took the lead with Yogen, casting the light of his paleo stone ahead of the group as they continued along a makeshift path. Halim lifted his head in response to the distant howls from a group of nocturnal hunters. The darkness pressed in, and he returned his gaze to his feet on the ground ahead.

"We have reached the river," announced Yogen, coming to a halt. "We will camp here and then continue at first light. The river will lead us to the Ignogai."

"This place seems familiar, said Halim, looking around."

"That's because we have been travelling in a big circle," Sanjit explained. "The Ignogai village is north from here, upriver. When we escaped from the village days ago, we travelled north-west until we reached Aryavartha. Then we travelled south-west through the valley where we found the unicorns and met Jaya. From there we went south to the cave where we were attacked by the Shaman of the Ignogai. The tree-top village is just west of the cave, and now we have been travelling east, back towards the river."

"Okay, then that means that Harappa is north-east?"

"Correct," said Sanjit. "You've got it. It's on the other side of the river."

Kativa opened her backpack, producing some bread and meat which she generously passed around. They ate in silence, each deep in thought over the events that were to follow. Halim finished eating and made his way to the river to wash his face in preparation for bed. He returned to his sleeping mat and lay down. The soothing sounds of the flowing water did little to ease his anxiety. He gazed up at the night sky. The stars winked at him mockingly. He twisted his head around, stretching his neck to take all the stars in, feeling exposed beneath their watch. He closed his eyes only to hear Dasgupta's voice ringing in his ears.

"Halim, what is your question today?"

"Where do the stars come from, teacher?" said Halim.

"They were placed in the heavens by the gods themselves, my boy." Bodhan was wearing a creased, brown tunic. His hair was dishevelled like he had just rolled out of bed.

"For what purpose?" said Halim.

"Without the stars, there would be no svarga," explained Dasgupta with a smile. "And without svarga, there can be no place for the righteous souls to exist before their next incarnation. Life would cease to exist without the stars, Halim. Every human being has a Janma Nakshatra, a birth star. I will teach you how to find yours, and you will see how it shapes you and your life. Understand its place in the heavens and it will guide you until the end of your days. If you ever feel lost or confused, look to the night sky, and you will find your way."

Halim slowly opened his eyes and gazed at his Nakshatra. It twinkled amongst the millions of others in the great sea of stars, suspended in the heavens above him, watching, waiting, unmoving.

"Halim," whispered Namrah. "You awake?"

"Yes. Can't sleep."

"Me neither."

"I can't stop thinking about tomorrow," he said. "I just pray that my sister is alive."

"I'm sure she is," said Namrah. "Halim."

"Yes?"

"Tell me about your mother. Kativa says she is not well?"

"It's the reason we left our home - the city of Harappa - to find a cure for her. She is suffering from rajayaksmadi, a rare chest infection that could kill her if we don't get back soon. We journeyed to Aryavartha, a monastery in the Kunlun Mountains. Sanjit took us to meet his bhisaj, a powerful healer. He gave us some medicine. I just pray that it will heal her."

Halim felt her hand find his. She squeezed it reassuringly.

"Your hand is so warm," he remarked. He thanked the gods that the darkness concealed the blood rushing to his face.

"I want to meet her - your mother," said Namrah softly. "After we rescue your sister."

"Yes. Of course. I would love for you to meet her," responded Halim.

"The stars are so beautiful," said Namrah. "Magical."

Halim gazed at the twinkling sky above. "Yes. And there are so many. When you look in one spot, more appear in the place you were looking at before, just at the edge of your vision, and then when you look back, they disappear. I wonder why that is so?"

"I think it's because there are just too many to look at all at once. When you focus your attention on one star, its light fills your vision, blotting out the light coming from the others close to it. It's only when you look away when you turn your focus away from that one star, do the others appear around it again."

"Hmm. I guess that makes sense," said Halim. "It's that same feeling that you get when you think you're being followed and then turn to find there's no one there."

"Haha. That's a funny way of putting it," Namrah chuckled.

Halim smiled, savouring the melodic sound of Namrah's voice. It reminded him of the tiny birds in the trees of Harappa singing their *songs of sunrise*, as his mother used to call them. Tears welled up in Halim's eyes at the painful memory. *Sincerity.*

Kativa's voice whispered inside his head.

"Namrah."

"Yes, Halim?"

"You have a beautiful voice. I love the way it sounds."

"Why, thank you."

Halim could hear the smile in Namrah's voice and imagined the blood rushing to *her* face this time. He squeezed her hand and rolled onto his side to face her. He pushed himself up onto his elbow and gently brushed the hair away from her face. He lost himself in her eyes, aware only of his quickened breath as he edged his body closer. Her lips parted as he touched them with his, brushing past them with the slightest of gestures. They were moist with desire. She took in a short, sharp breath as he pressed his lips down softly on hers into a kiss. She lifted her head and wrapped her arms around his body, pulling him down into a strong embrace. Halim closed his eyes and let go of all inhibition, relinquishing himself to unbridled passion. He was flying amongst the stars, an angel of light. Free. Euphoric.

43 ~ Fishing

"Halim, Halim." The voice was distant, yet urgent.

He was floating, suspended. Blissful. At peace.

"Halim." Closer, louder. Other sounds came with it now. The trickling of water. Another voice.

He opened his eyes, rubbed them. There was a little light. The first light. The sweet smell of Namrah tickled his senses. She stirred, turning over to face him. He smiled. "Good morning."

"Morning," she whispered.

"Come on sleepy heads," said Yogen. "It's time." He stomped over to the fire and stoked its embers. "We still have a way to go. We must reach our destination before day's end."

Sanjit was on his knees, meticulously rolling up his sleeping mat, while Kativa sat in full lotus, facing east, eyes closed, motionless. Her wrists rested lightly on her knees, palms up, with the tip of her thumb and index finger touching in a Gyan mudra.

After a tasty meal of hot broth, the group cleared the camp and began their journey along the river's edge. Halim looked up, catching the light from the sun as it peeked up over the horizon in the east. The cry from a yellow-billed river tern broke the silence. It's grey plumage contrasted against its red legs and black cap as it sat on the other side of the river bank scrutinising the visitors to its territory with beady eyes. Yogen led the party upstream of the meandering river that gradually widened as the day progressed. Occasionally they were forced to navigate away from the river and around several boulders but adhered mostly to the river's sandy bank as they walked. The river was framed by a canopy of trees that, together with a light breeze, provided much-needed respite from the beating sun overhead. Halim closed his eyes and took in a deep breath of cool air. He tasted the river's energy, a sweet, revitalising aroma that lifted his spirits.

"We rest here," announced Yogen, turning to the group.

Halim looked around. They were standing on a beach framed by unusual looking trees whose exposed roots covered most of the rocks in the area.

"What kind of trees are these?" he asked.

"Rubber fig trees," said Kativa. "They have a secondary root system which grows above ground."

Halim spied some maroon coloured fruit hanging from the closest one. "Are these ripe?" he pointed. "Can we eat them?"

"As long as they're not green," said Kativa.

Halim managed to reach one of the figs. He pulled it off the tree.

"Mmm. Definitely ripe," he remarked, biting into the fig. He deftly climbed the tree to grab a few more for the rest of the group.

"How are we doing?" asked Sanjit of Yogen. How much longer?"

Yogen turned to face north and closed his eyes. "We're making good progress, he replied after a moment's contemplation. "Not far now." He opened his eyes again and smiled.

"When do we split up?" Sanjit enquired.

"After we cross the river, just beyond the Ignogai village," replied Yogen. "You, me and Namrah will proceed further upriver, leaving Halim and Kativa to wait for our signal before proceeding into the village."

Namrah removed her shoes and stepped into the river. "Aaah. That feels so good," she remarked, closing her eyes and lifting her face to the sun. "Papa."

"Yes, my child."

"Please pass me my waterskin so that I can fill it."

Halim jumped at the opportunity to engage with Namrah once again. "Here, I'll pass it to her. I also need to refill mine," he declared, taking the skin from Yogen before removing his shoes and walking over to Namrah in the shallows.

"Thank you, Halim," said Namrah with a smile. Her long, auburn hair glistened in the sunlight as she brushed it over her shoulder before bending down to refill the skins.

"Where's Sanjit?" said Halim looking around for his Shakti brother.

"Over here," Sanjit answered, stepping into view. He carried two long branches with freshly carved, sharp tips on each end.

"What are those for?" said Halim quizzically.

"Fishing," replied Sanjit. "I saw a couple of big ones earlier."

"Excellent!" said Yogen clapping his hands excitedly. "I'm tired of all the bread and dried meat we've been eating."

"I'm going to need your help, Halim," said Sanjit.

"Sure," he replied.

"Start by collecting as many small rocks as you can. We're going to make ourselves a natural catchment area." Sanjit took a few paces into the river. "Create a small wall here, two or three rocks high, in a wide semi-circle."

Halim followed his instructions, carefully building an underwater row of rocks.

"Now, we wait," said Sanjit, crossing his arms and looking on in approval.

"How is this going to work?" said Halim scratching his head.

"Let me explain," replied Sanjit. "You'll notice that the semi-circle of rocks faces against the current, right?"

Halim nodded in affirmation.

"Okay. So, what happens to water when you place something in its way?"

"It flows around it?"

"Correct. The water bends. It finds another way, through or over the obstacle. The current is now greatly diminished inside the catchment area that we have created. The fish are attracted to this tranquil area, protected from the river currents. Their natural instincts tell them that the tranquil parts of the river are where they will find food and maybe even other fish."

"Wow. Amazing!" said Halim. "And then we just jump in and stab them?"

"Haha! Don't be so hasty my young Shakti. The water is calm, the fish are calm, so we must be calm."

Namrah began to hum a beautiful melody. Halim lay down on the sand, closed his eyes and pictured the two of them floating away on a raft across the meandering river. The gurgling sounds of the water, Namrah's captivating voice, the gentle sigh of the trees in the wind and the broken shards of sunlight on his face, sent Halim into a light slumber for a few blissful moments.

"Halim." He woke with a start. "Come, it's time," said Sanjit urgently. "The fish await."

Halim's stomach rumbled loudly. He picked up the spear, tested its tip, adjusted his grip and lifted it over his shoulder in an attacking posture. He followed Sanjit gingerly into the water, looking beyond and into the enclosure they created for any signs of movement. The water was clear. A silvery flash rippled through the water, and another. Fish. They were there. Several of them. Halim's heart raced, and his breathing quickened in anticipation. Sanjit slowed until they were barely moving and then stopped just beyond the stones. They looked into the calm pool, watching at least a dozen fish swimming, the small ones darting about with vibrant energy, and the larger ones gliding through the water more casually, enjoying the peaceful environment. Halim glanced at Sanjit and then back to a big, silvery-green fish making its way towards the middle of the catchment area. He saw Sanjit move to strike out of the corner of his eye and moved with him, diving forward and into the water with his spear, stabbing it down. Hard.

Halim pulled his spear out of the water, and a large, flapping specimen came with it. "Yes! I caught one!" he shouted with glee.

Sanjit dived right past him at the same time, stabbing the water several times. A fish jumped right out of the water. Halim watched it splash down and disappear beneath the churned-up surface. He scanned the pool. All the fish were gone. Sanjit pulled himself up out of the water with the butt of his spear. There were no less than three fish pinned onto its end.

"By the gods Sanjit, how did you...?" Halim was at a loss for words. His mouth gaped.

"Practice, my brother. Practice."

"Sadhu! Sadhu! Well done!" Yogen clapped again, jumping up and down excitedly.

After a sumptuous, hearty meal, the travellers continued on their journey upriver, stopping only to refill their water or to relieve their bladders. Time seemed to pass by very slowly. Halim wiped his brow with his sleeve - the air had become very humid towards the end of the day.

"Stop." Yogen held up his hand. The travellers froze. "We're almost there." He closed his eyes.

The rippling water was all Halim could hear. The river had grown much wider now. He looked to the opposite bank and imagined swimming no less than five hundred strokes to get there.

"Just a bit farther." Yogen marched forward again.

Halim began to see a higher concentration of Rubber Fig Trees in this area. And they were bigger. Much bigger. Their external roots stretched over rocks and boulders like a plague. They were everywhere.

"Look. A bridge," said Kativa, pointing further upriver.

Halim looked up ahead. The bridge looked odd. Warped. Twisted. In some places, it was fully exposed, while elsewhere, it was fully enclosed; protecting its pedestrians like it was designed for that purpose. Perhaps it had been damaged in a bloody battle that lasted days. Weeks. Halim couldn't be sure. And then he thought that his eyes were playing tricks on him. The bridge. It seemed to be to the riverbank in a most peculiar way. It swayed in the wind as if it were alive, testing its limits like it was part of the forest.

"It's a living root tree," announced Yogen matter-of-factly. "It will take us to the other side of the river where I have placed my marker."

"The Ignogai village," said Kativa bluntly.

"Yes," nodded Yogen. "We have all but arrived. After we cross the river, we'll split up as planned. Sanjit and Namrah with me, and you and Halim into the village. You'll need to hide at first so that we can draw the Ignogai away. Enter any sooner, and you are doomed to failure."

"How will we know when they have been drawn away?" Kativa questioned.

"Oh, you will know," he grinned. "You will know."

Halim looked up at the bridge. It was more magnificent than he imagined it to be. "Wow. Remarkable," he said in awe. "Whoever built these must have spent years twisting the roots and feeding them into each other, helping them grow into pillars of natural strength and beauty." He couldn't imagine the Ignogai even contemplating such an arduous task.

"Udyana," said Yogen. "The gardeners. They used to live near here but were wiped out by the Ignogai. They tended these bridges. Generation after generation. Taking care of them, helping them grow. Fifteen seasons. That's how long it takes to grow one bridge and then, over time, it grows even stronger. This one," he pointed to the bridge, "looks to be close to five hundred years old. By far the oldest and biggest that I have ever seen. My guess is that it could hold over fifty people at once." The group stared, mesmerised by this strange, yet intriguing feat of design. "Come, let's go," urged Yogen as he stepped onto the bridge.

Halim could now see that the bridge was a combination of

roots from several trees, some with trunks the width of five men side by side. The root system covered the entire riverbank before spreading out across the water. Some roots had grown down from the bridge and back into the ground along the river's edge, providing further support for those crossing it. Halim was surprised at how solid the bridge felt beneath his feet as the party crossed. He looked down, watching the river water flowing steadily below.

A single cry of alarm cut through the air, a guttural, short, sharp, *whoop, whoop*. A chill shot up and down Halim's spine. He crouched down on the bridge, instinctively drawing his sword, scanning the trees around him, searching for the source of the potential threat. Sanjit had also drawn his sword. He crouched down next to Halim.

"Do you see anything?" whispered Halim.

"No. Nothing," he replied.

Halim looked down at the water again. They were about halfway across. He looked at Namrah. She was with her father, pressed against the other side of the bridge, trying to remain hidden. Kativa was the only one that stood, rooted to the centre of the bridge, arrow drawn, longbow stretched taught, pointing an arrow in the direction of the canopy of trees on the other side of the bridge.

"We are exposed," said Halim.

"Yes," said Sanjit. "We will have to face whatever is coming."

"We could go back." Halim looked behind him.

"I think we should make that decision once we know what it is we are facing," said Sanjit. "Look. Movement," he whispered.

A solitary figure stepped onto the bridge. Three more joined him. They stood side-by-side, brandishing weapons in a defensive stance. They shouted something incomprehensible. Yogen stood up and waved. "We don't want any trouble!" he shouted. "Let us pass!"

"Come!" the one in front bellowed in a deep voice, beckoning.

Yogen turned to the others, indicating that they should lower their weapons. Sanjit and Kativa moved ahead of Halim, Namrah and Yogen. The four foreigners stood silently waiting for the party to cross. Their features became more distinct as the distance between them narrowed. Their faces were painted white, and in direct contrast, their eye sockets black - an eerie sight. Their open chests were also painted, but in a deep red ochre colour, and they all wore the same dark, tight-fitting pants. They were most definitely Ignogai. Halim turned to look at Yogen, praying that he had something miraculous up his sleeve to save them from this predicament.

Another loud cry came from behind them. The party turned to witness four more painted Ignogai drop down onto the other side of the bridge from the trees above. The travellers were outnumbered, trapped between a total of eight threatening looking savages.

Sanjit put his head down and broke into a run, charging directly at the first group of Ignogai on the far side of the bridge. "Akrama! Attack!" he yelled at the top of his voice. Halim and Kativa followed right behind him, drawing their weapons in mid-stride. Namrah and Yogen stood their ground, facing the second set of four behind them. The Ignogai advanced from the rear, shouting a mingled roar-scream together, that bounced across the rippling river water like an angry wraith in defiance.

Yogen squatted on the bridge and rubbed his hands together vigorously. Faster and faster he rubbed, until they became a blur. Then, without warning, he plunged them down inconceivably into the bridge at his feet. They disappeared into the thick, solid roots, right up to his elbows. Like magic. And then the bridge lurched heavily, throwing the attackers off balance. Small shoots burst out of the bridge floor. Little roots. Little roots that continued to grow. Rapidly. Until the entire width of the bridge had come alive. The roots twisted into each other like surreptitious serpents, spreading their winding bodies up into the air. Up. Faster. Until they formed a solid, impenetrable wall, cutting off the Ignogai behind them from the rest of the group.

"Akrama!" shouted Halim. The Prana flowed through his body like white fire. Rushing. He was alive with spirit and energy.

Kativa ran beside him; her arrow nocked and ready to fire. Halim followed Kativa's gaze. She had her sights on the Ignogai second from the left, which meant that it was probably safe for him to target the savage on the far right, considering that *her* target would be first to fall.

Thwit.

He was right. The arrow found its mark. Second from the left. It hit the Ignogai with an ominous thud in the middle of his chest. Kativa reached back for another arrow from her quiver. She was still running. The longbow creaked with strain.

Thwit.

This time, the arrow slid delicately into the stomach of the Ignogai to the right of her first kill. The Ignogai dropped to his knees, but quickly stood right back up again, blood oozing from his wound. He stared at the shaft protruding from his belly and then tore it from his body with a howl, his contorted face holding the effort for a while longer than was necessary.

Halim jumped with Sanjit, up into the air, their swords swinging in unison like two silver Shakti angels. Kativa tossed her bow to one side and dived into the fray, brandishing two small short-swords like the extended claws of a tiger in a powerful attack. Three on three. The movements were so sudden, instinctive that it was hard to tell what was going on. Sanjit's sword was blocked by his opponent, but the powerful overhead swing brought the Ignogai to his knees. Sanjit swung his sword around in an arc. The Ignogai twisted his body to parry the attack, but he was too slow. The sharp metal blade sliced into his arm above the left elbow, cutting through muscle and bone, rendering it useless. Sanjit pulled away bits of flesh and blood as he tore his blade free, swinging it around in a circle again, aiming for the neck of his opponent. The Ignogai jumped up onto his feet, this time successfully bringing his blade up in defence. *Clang!* Their swords rang loudly across the bridge. Sparks flew. A river of blood poured down his useless arm as the Ignogai turned to face Sanjit. He lunged, stabbing his sword forward. Sanjit stepped nimbly out of the way, easily blocking the thrust with the side of his blade. He followed up with a powerful punch to the Ignogai's face, connecting his jaw with a crack. The Ignogai stumbled, disorientated. Sanjit buried his blade deep into the side of the ugly savage's body. The Ignogai wheezed his last breath and crumpled to the ground.

The overhead swing of Halim's blade glanced off the defensive block of his opponent's sword, severing the last two toes of his left foot as it hit the ground with a thud. The Ignogai dropped to the ground, howling in pain. Halim took another swing, but the Ignogai miraculously rolled out of the way, sword still in hand. Halim stepped after him, swinging wildly. The Ignogai managed to block another swinging attack, despite the fact that he was still on the ground. He climbed to his feet, placing all of his weight on one foot. Blood poured from the wound in his belly, but he seemed undeterred. Halim blocked a thrusting attack. The Ignogai was a good fighter, but Halim had the advantage. He lunged forward, stepping on the Ignogai's injured foot, jabbing his sword forward in a fatal thrust to his opponent's chest. The Ignogai dropped to his knees, choking on his blood. He was finished.

Kativa faced the last of the Ignogai this side of the bridge. Her blades tore across his chest, cutting into his flesh like the razor sharp claws from a mountain bear. Blood oozed from his wounds, running down his red painted torso. He looked around at his defeated comrades, dropped his weapon, turned and ran back towards the Ignogai village.

A scream from Namrah interrupted the melee.

"Leave him, Kativa," said Sanjit. "We must help the others." He pointed at Yogen and Namrah. The wall of roots was being hacked apart by the four other Ignogai. Yogen withdrew his arms from deep inside the bridge, produced a short blade from his robes and joined Namrah, stabbing at the Ignogai through the widening holes in his defensive barrier.

Halim raced to keep up with Sanjit as they ran back along the bridge, while Kativa stopped to retrieve her bow before following. Namrah swung her blade, slicing into the arm of one of the Ignogai as he was climbing through an opening in the wall of roots. He howled in pain but continued to force his way across. Sanjit came running. He extended his leg and booted the Ignogai back to the other side of the root wall. The other three savages continued to hack away at the twisted roots. One at a time, they dived through a new opening, rolled onto the bridge and came to stand, facing their adversaries. The burly one raised his sword with a yell and charged at Halim.

Thwit.

Silence. Kativa's arrow pierced the Ignogai's forehead, killing him instantly. He keeled over, landing with a thump on the bridge. Halim turned to Kativa with a grin and winked.

Halim and Sanjit stepped in front of Yogen and Namrah as the remaining three Ignogai attacked. Another flurry of movement, swords slashed through the air, connecting, metal on metal. *Cling, clang. Cling, clang.* The sounds rang out loudly across the bridge.

Thwit.

This time, Kativa's arrow buried itself in the shoulder of one of the remaining Ignogai. He sliced his sword across the shaft, snapping it clean off. He bared his teeth in a snarl, turned and ran at her. She dropped her bow and withdrew her short-swords just in time, dropping to one knee and raising her blades at an angle to block the powerful overhead strike. She pushed away the sword with hers and took a swing at her opponent's legs. He jumped back and counter-attacked, jabbing his sword into Kativa's face. She instinctively lifted her head and arched her back, only just managing to avoid the deadly thrust. Her steel reflection stared back at her coldly. She rolled onto one side and jumped to her feet as the barbarian followed through with his lunge. The fighters circled each other, slowly pacing, watching, anticipating. Kativa concentrated on her opponent's panting breath. In, out. In, out. He drew a longer, disproportionate breath in and then, anticipating his movements, she deftly side-stepped his attack, blocking his sword with her two shorter ones. She allowed her blades to slide along his as she moved forward, pushing her arms with all the force she could muster, her blades an extension of her wrists. She watched them slice through the hilt of the Ignogai's sword and then into the soft flesh of his neck, decapitating his head in an instant.

The Ignogai that Namrah had injured faced Halim. His left arm was drenched in blood from the gaping wound. "Aaaaah!" he shouted, running at Halim with his sword. Halim parried the powerful blow that left his wrist numb with pain. The Ignogai stepped back, preparing for another attack. Halim lifted his blade up and over his head in a counter-strike. *Clang!* The two blades connected, bringing the swordsmen face to face with each other. The Ignogai roared pugnaciously, spraying spittle into Halim's face. Halim cringed at the foulness of his breath. He kicked the savage in the groin with his boot, and he bowed down instinctively. He held the back of the Ignogai's head down and rammed his knee up and into his chin with a *crack!* He ended it by bringing the pointed edge of his sword down into the Ignogai's back. He wheezed one final breath and slumped down onto the ground. Defeated.

Halim turned to watch Sanjit swinging his sword impossibly fast, advancing on the last remaining Ignogai, forcing him back to the edge of the bridge. He put up one final effort of defence before succumbing to Sanjit's blade as it sliced open his chest like a ripened fruit. The maimed Ignogai lost his footing and fell off the bridge. Halim watched him sink beneath the bloodied water, the stain eventually dissolving in the current.

"Halim, Kativa," said Yogen, an urgency in his voice. "You two must hide while Namrah, Sanjit and I head further upriver as planned. The Ignogai that ran off will bring more of his tribe to find us. And they are not going to be happy. I will lure the Shaman away too. Otherwise, you will not have a chance to find and rescue your sister."

Halim walked over to Sanjit. They embraced each other. "My

brother," said Halim. "May the gods protect you."

"And you, Shakti," said Sanjit.

Halim turned to Namrah. "You take care now, you hear?"

Namrah stood on her toes and wrapped her arms around Halim in an affectionate hug. "I'll be fine. Don't you worry." She smiled warmly.

Halim turned to the Shaman, bringing his hands to his chest in supplication. "Namaste."

"Namaste, young warrior. Kativa." He bowed his head. "Remember, wait for my signal."

"Namaste," Kativa responded. "Safe journey. Come, Halim, let's see if we can find a hiding place beneath the bridge."

Halim watched Yogen, followed by Namrah and then Sanjit, disappear into the tangle of fig trees along the river's edge. He turned to follow Kativa as she led him down the side of the bridge.

"Look. Over there," she indicated as they stepped under the long roots.

Halim bent down and saw a natural cavity between two trees; that was otherwise completely hidden from view. Halim squeezed into the hollow alongside Kativa. "What's that?" said Halim, pointing to a thick root above them. It was covered in a white, gooey substance.

"That's tree sap. These trees are full of it."

Halim followed the trail of tree sap down the root. It formed a thick, white mound at the bottom. He poked at it with a stick. It was soft and wet. He pushed the stick deep inside the sap-mound. When he pulled it out, the tip was covered in a dry, white powder.

"Hey, I have an idea," he said. "Let's make a paste with this powder and paint our faces. That way, we'll be less conspicuous when we enter the Ignogai village." Halim prodded the mound of sap, pulling away the thick, sticky membrane with his stick to reveal a small cache of fine, white powder beneath.

Kativa poured some water from her skin over the powder, while Halim mixed it with the stick to form a thick paste which they painted over each other's faces. Halim closed his eyes and felt the paste tighten against his skin as it dried. Namrah's beautiful smile and sparkling green eyes filled his head. He sighed deeply, and his heart ached with longing.

44 ~ Escape

Her head ached and her eyes burned from the smoke as she blinked them tearfully open. She must have passed out for some time because the fire had waned and the jumping, chanting Ignogai had disappeared together with the Shaman. Her shoulders were numb with pain and her wrists burned from the constricting leather bindings. Taja lifted her head and looked down at her painted body.

Whose body have I inhabited? What manner of magic is this?

She closed her eyes and dropped her head back down onto the hard stone of the tilted table with a thud. And then it all came back to her. In a rush. Halim. Sanjit. The Shaman. The Ignogai. More tears poured down her face. She screwed up her eyes and pulled at the leather bindings with all of her might, but to no avail. She was tied fast. There was no going anywhere for her.

No, no, no. I must... break... free...

Taja twisted her arms in the bindings. They chaffed against the table edge, cutting painfully into her wrists. She closed her eyes. She was inside her cage, Something small and shiny caught her eye. She flicked open her eyes again. The metal pendant. She remembered tying it around her wrist. She concentrated on shrugging her shoulder up and down, so that her forearm rubbed against the table, pushing the leather-bound pendant down her arm until it reached her wrist. She concentrated on rubbing her wrist against the table, feeling the leather cord work its way around until the pendant dropped into the palm of her hand. She curled her wrist, stretched her thumb and index finger until she could reach the diamond-shaped, metallic pendant. She lifted it up and started rubbing its edge against the leather binding until it began to cut gradually through the leather. The muscles in her forearm burned with the effort. Taja paused, waiting for the pain to subside before continuing. Her shoulder began to cramp, but she soldiered on, twisting her wrist up and down, rubbing metal against leather. Time seemed to stand still as Taja twisted and rubbed, twisted and rubbed. She pulled her arm. Just a little more. Eventually, the binding was cut wide enough for her to pull her arm free. She let her arm hang down the side of the table, breathing heavily from the effort, waiting for the cramping to abate before lifting it up and across her body so that she could untie the binding on the other side. She slowly sat up, bent her knees, sliding her torso down to meet her bound ankles, so that she could release them from their constraints.

Taja looked around the temple, straining to see movement through the swirling smoke. She hopped off the table and picked up a rock - the nearest thing she could find that could be used as protection. It felt warm in her hand. She heard voices and quickly hopped back onto the table, closed her eyes and lay as still as possible. She recognised the grunting sounds as he approached. Drindash. She prayed that he was alone. She half-opened her eyes, shifting her eyeballs in their sockets, squinting through her lashes, watching, waiting.

Closer. That's it. Ready. Now!

Taja swung her arm around and down with as much force as she could garner, connecting the rock with Drindash's skull. *Bang!* Her arm reverberated with the force of the blow. He fell to the ground with a groan. Taja jumped off the table and

254

hurled the rock at Drindash with a yell. It hit him in the chest, and he cried out in pain, curling up into a foetal position like a baby. Taja looked around for another weapon. She pulled a burning log from the fire as Drindash climbed slowly to his feet. Blood poured down his face from the gaping wound in his head. It ran into his eye, blinding him momentarily. He wiped his sleeve across his face and charged, howling at the top of his lungs. Taja side-stepped the enraged Ignogai and swung the smouldering log across his back. An explosion of sparks lit up the temple momentarily. Drindash fell onto his hands and knees, winded from the powerful strike. He pushed himself up with a grunt, turned and charged at Taja again. This time, he extended his arm to block Taja's anticipated strike. The log bounced off Drindash's arm, and Taja lost her grip. Drindash collapsed on top of her, his weight toppling them over and onto the ground. He grabbed Taja's neck with both hands and squeezed. She felt the pressure of the restricted blood in her head. She coughed, straining to breathe. The temple swam.

Remnants of the smouldering log were still attached to the tunic on Drindash's back, and they began to burn, smoking at first and then turning to flames that spread quickly across his garb. Drindash released his grip from around Taja's neck and jumped back, frantically beating his arms over his shoulders. It was too late. Drindash howled in pain as the flames flared, covering most of his body. Taja stepped away as the fire consumed the Ignogai. She watched as he flailed around in circles, flapping his arms like a flightless bird.

Taja ran across the temple. There was nowhere to hide. *How am I going to get past the guard?* She wondered to herself. She spied one of the hideous looking Ignogai masks lying on the packed earth of the Temple. She picked it up and placed it over her face. It reeked of something foul. She stepped out of the temple. The guard looked at her and nodded in acknowledgement. She quickly moved away from the temple and into the Ignogai village.

45 ~ Cave

Sanjit turned back to look at the root-bridge in the distance. He made a quick, silent prayer to the gods to protect Halim and Kativa on their mission to rescue Taja before turning back to following Namrah and Yogen upriver. The rubber fig trees gave way to smaller, low-hanging foliage along the riverside and the water became rougher, churning amongst large rocks and boulders as it flowed. The trio continued hiking, following the river as it twisted and turned like a huge serpent. Sanjit looked down at the narrow but well-worn path alongside the river. It turned, leading the group up the river bank, out of the trees and onto a plateau. Yogen stopped.

"We go there," he pointed at a formation of rocks in the distance.

The sound of the flowing river dulled to a distant babble, as they continued in silence, the foliage concealing them from the outside world like a cocoon. Soon the trees gave way to another clearing. They had been gradually climbing through the forest and emerged on a precipice overlooking a breathtaking sight. Below was the River, glittering in the golden light of the setting sun like a bed of diamonds. To the north was a magnificent waterfall, cascading majestically down and into the river below, sending a fine, white spray framed by an exquisite rainbow of colourful light into the air. Sanjit gazed at the scene before him, allowing its natural beauty to wash over him like a cleansing wave of Prana.

Yogen led them down towards the river again. The cool, refreshing spray was welcomed by the three travellers as they filled their gourds at the water's edge.

Sanjit had to shout to be heard above the roar of the cascading water behind him. "How much farther?"

Yogen smiled. "We are here."

Sanjit looked around. "But we will be too exposed. They will find us."

"There is a cave hidden behind the waterfall. We will hide there," said Yogen.

"You never told me that you've been here before, papa," said Namrah.

"It was a long time ago, my child," said Yogen closing his eyes, savouring the memory. "And the funny thing was, I was also hiding."

"From what?" Namrah asked.

"My teacher. I took his ward stone and used it without asking. I ran away when he found out."

"But how did you find the hidden cave?" said Namrah.

"Well, it was by chance. I approached the waterfall from the other side of the river, drawn to its splendour and beauty. As I drew nearer, I noticed that the rocks behind the falling water curved in, creating a natural depression. A cavernous hollow big enough for one to walk through without getting wet. Naturally, I stepped into this hollow, and that's when I discovered the cave. Come, let's go."

Yogen led them along the river's edge. The terrain was rocky and uneven - Sanjit was compelled to watch his footing as they clambered over the loose stones. Finally, they reached the foot of the waterfall. Sanjit tilted his head to gaze up at the rocky cliffs that disappeared behind the falling water. He closed his eyes and cherished the feeling of spray on his face, as the tumultuous roar of the cascading water crashed down into the river below. The wall of falling water hid them from view as they stepped behind it, making their way deeper into the natural rock depression until they reached a large, triangular-shaped hole cut into the rock.

"The cave," announced Yogen. "It's still here," he said, excitement in his voice.

Sanjit ran his hands across the opening. "It looks like the rock was cut open. These lines are so straight and smooth. Doesn't look natural."

"It is said that the river god, Apam Napat, created this opening," explained Yogen.

"But Apam Napat is the supreme god of creation," said Sanjit, "credited with the creation of all existential beings. Why would he concern himself with cutting a hole in a rock?"

"That is correct, Sanjit," said Yogen. "Apam Napat is the god of creation, but he is also the lightning form of Agni, the son of the waters." Yogen led them into the cave. "It is said," he continued, "that Apam Napat helped the people of this land overcome a serious drought. This river was dry when the people prayed to him for assistance. He came to this wall of rock and blasted his way in." Yogen pointed to the symmetrical entrance behind them.

"Why?" questioned Namrah. "Why did he blast open the rock?"

"He spent a week here, in this cave. He called on his brothers, the other gods of nature, to bring rain to this arid region. The rain came and continued for ten days. The river overflowed and the waterfall cascaded down this rock face once again. It is said that this region has never seen a drought since."

Yogen led Sanjit and Namrah deeper into the cave. His paleo stone came to life, casting tall, animated shadows amongst the jagged rocks as they walked. He stopped, thrusting his staff into the sand, indicating the end of their journey. Namrah prepared some food as Yogen settled into a lotus position. He brought his hands to his chest in a prayer position and indicated that

Namrah and Sanjit follow suit.

"You never told us the outcome of your story," said Namrah.

"Which one, my child?"

"The one where you found the cave. What did the ward stone do and what happened to it?"

"Ahh. That is another tale for another time," said Yogen with an impish grin. "Right now, we have work to do. First, we must cast a web of concealment over Halim and Kativa. Then we must lure the Ignogai away from their village."

"I've been wondering how we are going to do that," said Sanjit.

"You mean lure the Ignogai away?" said Yogen.

"Yes. They don't possess any form of magic, those savages." Sanjit spat on the ground in distaste. "Don't they need to be enchanted to some degree to recognise the magical lure?"

"Very good, Shakti. You understand the way. But there is something you have missed. The Shaman. We will seize his attention. He will recognise the call. He will come, and the Ignogai will follow. But first our friends." Yogen closed his eyes. "The Ushnisha Sitatapatra is the White Umbrella Goddess, also known as the Victorious White Parasol. She is one of the Nine Sages whose parasol protects us from all forms of misfortune. She has a thousand eyes and a thousand arms, watching over all living beings, symbolising the power of active compassion and protection. Chanting her mantra invokes an extremely powerful spell."

Halim and Kativa closed their eyes.

"First, you must visualise the entire universe in the colour white," continued Yogen softly. "See the universe dissolving into a white Om symbol. From this Om symbol, Sitatapatra arises on a beautiful white lotus flower. See her many arms and eyes. In her left hand, she holds a parasol, and her right hand is positioned in the wish-bestowing mudra. Now we shall recite the four-syllable mantra together." Yogen cleared his throat and took a deep breath. "*Ja*. Visualise Sitatapatra moving into this cave with us, sitting on her white lotus. *Hum*. Now she moves

259

into the space above our heads. *Bam.* She floats with her lotus flower into your heart. *Hoh!* Sitatapatra starts to grow inside your heart, expanding, until you become the goddess Sitatapatra. Visualise the white parasol of protection covering us in this cave. Her parasol extends beyond the cave, to Halim and Kativa. Finally, visualise your crown chakra opening to reveal a white Om to seal the mantra and blind those searching for us. We will chant Om together 108 times. Become one with the vibrations. Feel the magic at work, visualise the protection of the goddess at all times and the spell will be activated. Now, let us take a deep breath and begin."

Their combined voices reverberated around the cave, bouncing off the walls like a cacophony of Malabar whistling thrush birds in full song. Sanjit lost all feeling in his body as the powerful vibrations dislodged his Prana, sending it up and out to Halim and Kativa in an umbrella of powerful protection.

After what seemed like a very long time, Yogen whispered. "He senses us."

"The Shaman?" questioned Sanjit.

"Yes. He is aware of a shift in the void. Our magic has created a ripple of Prana that cannot go undetected."

"Does he know where we are?" said Kativa.

"No. Our spell of protection will hide us for a while yet. He knows that we are close and can probably tell that we are upriver, but he does not know our exact location."

"This is what we wanted, right?" said Kativa. "To lure the Shaman away from the village?"

"Yes. I have a feeling, though that he may send the Ignogai warriors and remain behind in the village to safeguard Taja. I may need to provoke him a little more. We'll have to wait and see."

46 ~ Village

"What's that sound?" Halim whispered.

Kativa cocked her head. "It's just the river, nothing more."

"No. Wait. Hear that? Drumming."

"You're right," said Kativa sitting up.

The cramped hiding space beneath the bridge was uncomfortable. Halim wanted to move, to get out and run into the village to rescue his sister. He knew it was suicide but the wait was agonising.

"What exactly are we waiting for?" said Halim.

"A sign from Yogen to say that it's safe to go into the village."

"What kind of sign? What will it look like? How will we know?"

"Yogen told us to wait," said Kativa. "He is never wrong, and he has never failed our people."

"I'm sure that we can go once the Ignogai pass? He said that he was going to lure them away from the village. I'm sure that he has already done so, otherwise, why would they be here already?"

The drumming grew louder.

"It's the Shaman that I'm worried about, or have you forgotten what he did to you?"

Halim quivered at Kativa's mention of the Ignogai witchdoctor. "Yes, he did say he would lure the Shaman away too but how will we know if he's with the Ignogai that approach us?"

"Shhh. They're here," said Kativa, silencing Halim.

"...gut them and hang them," came a gruff voice from above.

"No. I say we feed them to the chief's lycanthus," said another voice.

"Ha ha ha! Yessss. The lycanthus," came a third voice. "We can watch. It will be so much fun!"

"No! You imbeciles!" Another voice. This one held some measure of authority. "The Shakti are mine. You can have the girl. Soon she will be of no use to us."

Halim turned to Kativa, wide-eyed. She placed a finger to his lips and gently shook her head from side to side.

"Search the bridge," instructed the last voice. This is where your brother said he was attacked. Remember, there are five of them. They can't be far. But be careful - don't underestimate them - they have already defeated the river watch."

"Yes, Shaman."

Halim felt a tremble in his spine from several footsteps overhead as he sat pressed against the trunk of the tree below. He held his breath. The sound of the blood pumping inside his head pounded in his ears and beads of sweat trickled down his temples. He closed his eyes and prayed.

Thud!

One of the Ignogai jumped off the side of the bridge, landing just a few steps away from Halim and Kativa. Halim pushed himself deep into the crevice between the two trees. The Ignogai walked directly under the bridge and looked around. His white painted face and black eye-sockets gave him a ghoul-like appearance. Halim slowly curled his fingers around his blade, ready to strike. The Ignogai stared directly at them.

Why can he not see us? Halim tightened his grip on the hilt of his sword, but the Ignogai straightened up and ambled over to the river's edge. He placed his hands on his hips, spat into the water, turned around and made his way back up the river bank. Halim could hear the others marching up and down the bridge.

"Shaman!" called one of the savages. "This is powerful magic. The roots from the bridge have been pulled up to form some sort of barrier."

"This is not Shakti magic," Halim heard the Shaman say. "This is the magic of the tree people."

"The Udyana? But I thought we wiped them out."

"No, you idiot. The tree people of the tree-top village. This is the work of their Shaman. Yogen is his name, I believe. I have encountered him before."

"So, it's not the Shakti?" said the other voice. "What are we going to tell the Chief?"

"Nothing. From Bagdam's description of the five intruders, the Shakti may be with Yogen. This makes things interesting."

"Shaman!" This time, the voice came from upriver. "We have found some tracks. They're fresh, and they're headed upriver."

Halim let go of his breath. "I guess that's the sign?" he whispered to Kativa.

She nodded as they listened to the Ignogai run across the bridge and into the forest. "Yes, but let's wait a while longer. I can still hear them."

Halim closed his eyes. The sounds of the flowing river soothed his anxiety.

"Okay. I think it's clear now," said Kativa.

Halim pushed himself to his feet and turned to pull Kativa up to hers.

"Thank you, Halim."

"My pleasure."

Kativa led Halim up the riverbank and towards the Ignogai village. The sounds of the river abated as the well-worn path took the pair over a rise and down the other side. They hiked slowly and in silence, straining their ears for any sounds of approaching Ignogai. Halim's forearm throbbed from the taught grip of his hand on the hilt of his sword. Halim looked around, noticing the forest begin to thin out and then Kativa raised her fist into the air, signalling a halt. She turned to Halim and pointed wordlessly ahead. A plume of dark, grey smoke drifted into the sky not far from their position. Halim took a swig from his waterskin and then resumed his step, following Kativa towards their destination.

Taja, can you hear me, my sister? Halim said to himself. *Pray the gods that you are still alive in there. I'm coming for you, you hear? I'm coming.*

The trees gave way to open ground and then they saw it - the Ignogai village. It was surrounded by a dark, wooden wall; thick beams, crudely built, but strong enough to create a compact barrier that kept undesirables out.

"I cannot believe that I'm back here again," said Halim. "Do you think this face paint is good enough to conceal our identities? I think we need to think of something more convincing to get inside undetected."

"I have an idea," said Kativa. "I'll pretend to be injured. I'll climb onto your back and lie across your shoulders as we approach the gates. You call out to the guards. Tell them that we were ambushed at the bridge. This will get them distressed. Their concern will overcome any hint of suspicion. Maybe even tell them that the Shaman and the other Ignogai are engaged in a big battle and require assistance?"

"Great idea, Kativa. I pray this works."

They continued along the widening path towards the Ignogai village and stopped when they could make out the silhouette of the guards at the gates. Kativa climbed onto Halim's back and twisted her body around until she was lying across his shoulders as planned. She let her arms and legs hang limp as Halim began to slowly make his way towards the village gates. Halim smiled. Their timing was perfect - dusk was settling in, which helped to hide their true identities.

"Who goes there?!" shouted one of the guards.

Halim looked up. A large, stocky Ignogai stood at the gate, his spear planted into the earth. His menacing look was enough to drive anyone away.

Halim took a deep breath, preparing to speak in the deepest, most guttural voice he could muster. "We were ambushed. At the bridge. Need help."

The guard shifted, turning to look up and behind him at another guard positioned on top of the wall. "Where are the others?" questioned the guard. "Where is the Shaman?"

"They are in a fierce battle and need your help. The enemy is strong."

"But I thought that there were just five of them? Five is no match for our Shaman and the Ignogai warriors," said the guard arrogantly.

The other guard made his way down from the wall. Halim twisted his shoulders, carefully rolling the motionless Kativa carefully off his back and onto the packed earth.

"Is she dead?" said the first guard stepping up to Halim. "I don't see any blood."

"That's because she was injured by magic," replied Halim. The guard stepped back a few paces, clearly unsettled by Halim's mention of the taboo word.

"What must we do?" said the second guard.

"Take me to the Shaman's tent," instructed Halim.

The guards looked at each other. "We cannot do that," said the first guard. "The Shaman is not here, and no one goes inside the Shaman's tent when he is not here."

"Except Piju," said the other one.

"Maybe we should call the chief?" said the first guard.

"No, not the chief, said Halim. Just send more men to the bridge and take me to some place where I can tend to her." He pointed at Kativa.

The guards stepped back, clearly not interested in touching one who had been injured by magic.

"Okay. Come this way," gestured one of the guards.

Halim lifted Kativa in his arms and followed the guards back towards the gates. The big one shouted some kind of instruction as he approached. There was an audible rattling of chains and the gates swung slowly open.

"Gabal. Assemble the rest of the guard and head out towards the bridge. The others need help."

"Yessir!" shouted a young Ignogai in response. He turned and ran inside.

"Malak. Take this warrior and his fallen comrade to the Shaman's tent. And call Piju."

Halim smiled at the mention of the guard's ironic description of him. He breathed a sigh of relief. Things seemed to be going according to plan. *With so many white faced Ignogai, it must be hard to tell them apart,* he thought to himself. He bent down to pick up Kativa again and then followed Malak inside the village, struggling to keep up with the weight of her in his arms. A repulsive, choking odour burned his nostrils with every breath he took. He passed several tents, noticing a handful of inquisitive Ignogai staring at him from inside.

"Wait here," instructed Malak gruffly. "This is Shaman's tent." He pointed at a large, brown tent covered in painted spirals and strange-looking motifs before trotting off to find Piju.

They're a persistent bunch, these Ignogai, Halim thought to himself. *And now here we are, back inside this despicable place again. Taja, where are you? Please, gods you're okay.*

"Halim." Kativa sprang out of his arms. "Thanks for the lift." She grinned and the white paint on the corners of her mouth cracked.

"Very funny, Kativa. My back hurts."

"Careful, Halim. You don't want to insult a woman, especially the likes of me. By the gods, what's that hideous smell?" She wrinkled up her nose in disgust.

"I don't know, but it's making me feel sick," said Halim. "Come, let's see what's in the tent. Taja could be tied up inside. We have to find her."

47 ~ Prana

Yogen closed his eyes again. Sanjit watched him in the light of the paleo crystal. He swayed gently from side to side like a tree in an invisible wind, settling into a deep trance on his own. He slowly opened his eyes.

"Is he coming?" enquired Sanjit. "Have you sent a message to Halim and Kativa?"

"Yes," Yogen nodded. The Shaman comes. Halim and Kativa are safe."

"The question is, are we safe, papa?"

Yogen turned to Namrah and smiled. "Our mantra protects us, and we are in the cave of Apam Napat, who protects us too."

"But the Shaman. He is strong."

"Yes, this is true, but he is with Ignogai, who do not see as well in the dark as he does. He won't risk expending his powers in trying to find us at night. No, he will rest and wait until dawn."

"How will we fight the Shaman *and* all the Ignogai?" said Sanjit, concern in his voice. "There are just three of us but many of them."

"We must use the element of surprise and strike at the head

of the serpent before the body has time to react. We need to battle the Shaman in the spirit world before they find our physical location."

"And pray that we can overcome him there," said Namrah.

"Yes," said Yogen. "Namrah is right. This is the only way we will be able to strike fear into the hearts of the Ignogai. If we injure or weaken their Shaman in the spirit world, before they find us, they will lose all confidence in their ability to defeat us and then we will have a chance at overcoming them."

"So why not attack him now?" suggested Sanjit.

"If we attack him now, he will retaliate. We will also give up our position by doing so."

"But we are protected by the mantra. Is this not enough to safeguard us?"

"Hmm. It's a little more complicated than that. You see, we need more time to prepare our defences." Yogen pulled the pair of wooden amulets out from inside his robe and placed them on the ground next to the crystal. Their spirals appeared to shift and swirl in its glowing light. "We must pair the amulets and invoke their magic. This is the only way that we will succeed in overcoming the Shaman. The amulets will funnel our Prana into a collective force when we attack, while at the same time, help recharge our spent energy."

"How is this possible, papa?" said Namrah.

"As I've explained before, these are powerful talismans from the ancient world. I do not fully understand their workings, but I do know how to activate them. I have invoked the magic of one of these wooden artefacts before and experienced its power, so I can only imagine what two will do."

"How long will it take us to activate them?" enquired Sanjit.

"Well, there appear to be different levels of access."

"What do you mean?"

"I mean you have already experienced the power of Halim's amulet, right? You recognise that it can be used as a conduit for Prana, enhancing your intention?"

Sanjit nodded.

"Okay, good. So, this is one level. The primary level of access. In other words, you have successfully tapped into the first level of protection afforded by the amulet. Now we need to advance to the next level. The strength of our combined Prana will activate the true power of these two magical artefacts. We need to connect them together as before and focus our intention on them to release their true power. To answer your question - I am not sure how long it will take us to invoke the full power of the amulets but the more time we have, the better prepared we will be when we confront the Shaman."

Yogen opened his bag and produced a small, yellow-coloured phial. He removed the stopper, stuck out his tongue and poured several drops onto it. He passed the phial onto Namrah.

"What's that?" Sanjit enquired.

"It's an ayurvedic blend of my own; its recipe passed down to me by my master and his master before him. It will enhance your Prana and focus your intention."

Namrah passed the medicine to Sanjit. He sniffed it first before shaking out several drops onto his tongue. "Aah. Disgusting. Not sure which is worse, the smell or the taste." He screwed up his nose.

Yogen smiled. "The more potent the mixture, the more powerful its effect. Come, let us begin." He placed his palms together in prayer at his heart. Sanjit and Namrah followed suit. "Look at the amulets. Study their design, follow their spirals, appreciate their beauty and craftsmanship. Now close your eyes but still visualise the amulets. See them joined in perfect harmony. See how they connect to the universe. Soham. I am He. Soooooo hummmmmmm. Soooooo hummmmmmm." Yogen repeated the ancient Vedic mantra, symbolising the connection of the self to the universe of ultimate reality.

"Soooooo hummmmmmm." Sanjit and Namrah joined in. "Soooooo hummmmmmm," they repeated, deepening their breathing with every chant.

Sanjit was no stranger to the spiritual path, yet this experience felt like his first. He remembered the time like it was yesterday while being guided by his teacher, Amitabha, the great monk of the Tabha monastery. Sanjit was just fourteen years old. He had been studying the Vedic scripts for some time and was eager to apply his knowledge to practical experience.

"You must become one with the universe, young disciple." The old monk's voice rang like a bell in his ears. "Imagine your lungs as the bellows used to drive the Prana through your body."

"But I only feel my breath, master," said young Sanjit. "How can I drive the Prana if I cannot feel it?"

"The breath and the Prana are one and the same, my son. Just as the tree sways gently in an invisible wind, so too must you yield to the breath as it flows in and out of your lungs. If you just focus on your lungs and your breathing, then that is all you will feel, but if you give in to the breath and allow it to flow beyond your lungs and through the rest of your body, then you will experience the flow of Prana, guided by the breath. You will feel the wind on your branches."

Yogen closed his eyes and followed the monk's instructions, succumbing to the flow of air in and out of his lungs, allowing his mind to focus on breathing beyond the confines of his physical body until his breath became light and ethereal. And then it came - a tingling sensation in his throat that expanded into his lungs as he breathed, continuing down into his belly and throughout his body. It was a feeling of enlightenment and bliss, peace and fulfilment.

Back inside the cave, Sanjit allowed the breath to flow through his body; to expand beyond his lungs until the Prana enveloped him. It pulsed through and around him, beating to the steady rhythm of his heart. He focused on the wooden amulets, tracing their spiral carvings, beginning in the centre and expanding outward. Round and round, round and round he spun, faster and faster, until he was part of their never-ending flow of energy. He traced a single drop of Yogen's yellow elixir, admiring its golden beauty as it coursed through his body, awakening every cell of his being. The amulets began to glow in the same yellow colour, transforming into pure, white lotus flowers, bathing his very essence in their fiery brilliance.

The flower petals unfurled in a never-ending bloom, drawing him into their spiralling depths. Deeper and deeper. A purring sound emerged; a singularity that enveloped his body in a shimmering, a vibrational cocoon of Prana, layer upon golden layer. The purring transformed into a sonorous ringing; a rippling wave of energy that solidified the cocoon into an amorphous shield of protection around his physical body.

Sanjit experienced levels of enlightenment beyond his wildest assumptions. He sensed his connection to the amulets as they facilitated and sealed the flow of Prana moving through his body. He was a spectator, watching, spellbound by the magical journey of energy moving through his chakras like a steady flowing river of fiery lava. The frequency of the ringing shifted, and Sanjit became aware of Yogen and Namrah beside him - two more golden spheres of energy also connected to the ancient amulets. The three were united, a tripartite fusion of mind, body and spirit, ready to face the Shaman of the Ignogai in mortal combat.

48 ~ Vritra

"Shaman!" An Ignogai scout came running back towards the Shaman and the group of Ignogai making their way through the dense forest.

"What is it?"

"The tracks. They've disappeared."

"You sure? How?"

"Well, it's getting dark and…"

"Imbecile!" The Shaman back-handed the Ignogai scout through the face with a loud thwack! He fell to his knees, holding the side of his face. "The tracks are there; you just cannot see them." The Shaman marched to the front of the group. "Come, show me," he called to the scout. "Show me where the tracks disappear."

The scout ran ahead, and the Shaman followed, quickly picking up his pace.

"Look. Here," pointed the scout. "And here," he indicated the outline of a boot in the sand and then ahead of it, nothing. "See? They just disappear."

The Shaman dropped to one knee and waved his hand across the smooth sand several times. The sand shifted in an invisible breeze, and the outline of a boot appeared, followed by another and another in front of that.

"Magic," whispered the scout in awe.

"Yes, our enemies have used magic to cover their tracks," confirmed the Shaman. He scanned the area with sightless eyes, twisting his head from left to right, sniffing the air like some feral creature. "We will camp here tonight and then continue at first light."

"But what if they get away? What if they continue in the dark?" said the scout.

The Shaman smiled. "They may continue, but they must also eat and rest. These are the only constants. We all need food and sleep to survive in the physical world. If they rest now or tomorrow, it matters not because we will still catch up to them. I need to meditate, to find the residue of their Prana." The scout looked at him in confusion. The Shaman continued. "It's the by-product of magic use, and it lingers for some time. I will find it and trace it to its source, revealing the direction in which they travel or better yet, their actual location."

The Shaman settled into a comfortable seat in front of the fire while the rest of the two dozen Ignogai prepared the camp for the night. The Shaman swayed from side to side several times before coming to perfect stillness. His breathing deepened and became more pronounced as he delved into a deep trance-like state. He tasted his surroundings like a serpent darting its tongue in and out of its mouth in quick succession. The residue of the energy left behind tasted sweet like honey, and the Shaman savoured it, enjoying its texture and composition. He expanded his reach beyond the camp and out, into the forest, tracing the trail of Prana as it flowed upriver like grains of glimmering pollen dispersed by bees in the spring time.

Something was wrong. The taste in his mouth turned insipid. The trail had died. *Impossible.* The Shaman's confidence wavered. He doubled back down the trail.

Could it be a trick? A false path? The Shaman took a deep, focused breath and weighed out all the possible options. *Could the Shakti have falsely drawn me away from the Ignogai village so that they could rescue the girl?*

No. The trail he followed was real. The magical residue was still fresh. They were close.

But why did the trail die? How? Unless...

He went back in his spirit form to where the trail disappeared and then ventured up, high above the trees. He gazed back down to the earth, taking in all the life force energy below; the signature of the trees with their sluggish, deep-amber Prana and the rapid, bright-blue energy of the flowing river a little farther away. And then he saw it, an opaque, nondescript shroud that stretched out and over the northern area of his awareness. From the ground, it was too translucent to see up close, but from his position high above the ground, it shimmered faintly, catching the corner of his eye. It was a cleverly concealed aura of protection, a magical shield of energy manifested by the Shakti and, he guessed, with help from Yogen, the Shaman of the tree-people.

The Shaman smiled to himself. They were close. They were waiting. And so would he, he decided. He would preserve his energy and attack with the rest of the Ignogai just before dawn.

The Ignogai settled down for the night, but the Shaman remained awake. He wore a mask, the wooden effigy of a dark spirit from the netherworld that gave him the gift of spiritual sight. He began with a series of incantations, which began as imperceptible, guttural utterances of a foreign language from an ancient race. The chanting grew louder and more pronounced until the Shaman's body shook with the effort of intoning the powerful necromancy. He entered the Nerakan wasteland in search of Vritra, a demonic entity also known as the King of Dragons. Vritra was vanquished by Indra, the deva of rain and thunderstorms and incarcerated in Neraka for all eternity. Through an age-old rite of passage, the Shaman planned to temporarily bring Vritra to aid him in the elimination of Yogen and the capture of the Shakti Warriors. Bound by his shackles in the fiery pit of Neraka, he would be forced to return to his eternal prison but not before a brief but welcomed respite from his confinement.

The Shaman's voice carried over and into the netherworld, reciting the many names of Vritra, calling forth his spirit, urging him to awaken and serve. A high-pitched shrieking sound echoed across the burning skies of Neraka in response to the Shaman's invocation. The shrieking grew louder, as Vritra drew nearer, enthralled by the promise of freedom through the magical spells intoned by the Shaman. He took the true form of his spirit - a magnificent dragon with three heads, appearing before the Shaman in all of his fiery splendour.

"Who dares call me from the depths of Neraka?" His many voices bore through the Shaman like the hot embers from a fiery furnace.

"It is I, Shaman of the Ignogai, son of Krathra, servant of Hiranyaksha. I call on you to rise and obey my command as I release you from your shackles."

"Ha ha haaa! You cannot release me. I am bound to this place by forces beyond your mortal comprehension." Vritra's voices boomed across the scorched landscape.

"I possess knowledge of a powerful, ancient magic that will grant you the temporary freedom to leave this prison, this dark hole of despair, and join me in the physical world in a battle against the forces of light and the followers of Indra. Surely you would consider this as an opportunity to exact your vengeance on your enemy?"

The dragon heads roared ferociously together. "What do you know of Indra, mortal?"

"I know that he imprisoned you here," said the Shaman, "for all eternity. I know that you long to leave this world, if even for a brief moment, to taste the cool night air, to hear the sounds of the living creatures and feel the soft earth beneath your feet." And with that, he turned his back on Vritra, intending to leave the fiery underworld.

"Wait."

The Shaman froze in his tracks without turning around.

"I will join you, mortal. I shall return to the world of the living and battle your enemies," bellowed Vritra. "But if you betray me in any way, I shall hunt you down and destroy you, and your spirit will join me in the netherworld, tormented for all eternity."

The Shaman shuddered at the thought of a life of endless suffering in this forsaken place. He turned to face the three-headed creature and continued his chanting, fulfilling his vow by completing the ancient magical incantation that would release the King of Dragons into the world once more.

◊ ◊ ◊

The Shaman returned to the physical world. The sound of his deep-belly breathing consumed him, rasping in the back of his throat as he sucked the cool night air into his lungs. The darkness was at its most dense. It bore down all around him like a heavy weight, pressing out all the light it encountered. Even the stars seemed dulled by its encumbrance. He rose to his feet, careful not to wake the Ignogai, collected his staff and walked in the direction of the river. He quickened his pace, eager to reach the flowing waters, knowing that there was precious little time before the light of the new day made its appearance. He needed to use the element of surprise if he was to stand a chance at defeating the Shakti and the tree-top mage.

The Shaman could taste the sweet river water in the air as he approached the shore. He planted his staff in the ground, raised his other arm into the sky, adjusted his mask and continued to chant in the ancient tongue. The water in the middle of the river began to hiss and churn, twisting around aberrantly with a life of its own.

"Vritra, King of Dragons," the Shaman declared. "Rise. Come forth. Join us. May the river waters be your uterus. May they deliver you into this world. Rise! Come forth Vritra!" He lifted his staff into the sky. There was a flash of lightning followed by the deep rumble of thunder in the heavens. The river water continued to bubble, heating up as the Shaman continued his chanting. The waters finally ceased their churning as a dark, scaly form broke the surface. It continued to rise, a long, hideous snake-like creature, twisting out of its womb, free at last from its subterranean prison. Water ran off its silvery-green scales, and its three heads opened their mouths and shrieked together triumphantly.

"Vritra!" commanded the Shaman. "Find the enemy. Flush them out, cripple them but do not kill them. I must take them alive as my prisoners. Be warned, they possess powerful magic."

Vritra roared. "I will take pleasure in crushing them but will not kill them as you have commanded." Three blasts of fire shot out of three mouths, lighting up the night sky momentarily.

The Shaman lifted his staff again. "Then go! Find the enemy!"

Vritra's scales rippled as he twisted his body high above the river before diving down into its depths with a great splash, spraying water up into the air. He surfaced again and soared up towards the stars and then disappeared into a slither of pitch black that appeared in the sky, swallowed into its fracture, as it closed abruptly behind him, leaving not a trace of his ubiety behind.

◊ ◊ ◊

Sanjit sensed a distortion in the flow of Prana. He knew that Yogen and Namrah sensed it too. It was a warning, a premonition. The Shaman was coming. He had found them. The tripartite braced themselves. A ripple reverberated through the spiritual realm in anticipation of the encounter and then Vritra appeared, tearing through the fabric of the world with an ear-splitting shriek. Sanjit watched in horror as three mouths opened, blasting three pillars of fire in their direction. They reacted, drawing on their combined will to repel the attack. The fire blasts fizzled into a wall of manifested Prana. Sanjit felt the amulets come to life to replenish their spent energy in an instant.

"Who are you, demonic creature?" said Yogen.

"I am Vritra, King of Dragons," he bellowed. "I was summoned to destroy you, followers of Indra."

277

"I know you, Vritra. Indra vanquished you, but you are mistaken, he is not our ally, nor do we serve him."

Vritra roared. "It matters not, mortal. You are warriors of the light, that much I can see. You will feel my wrath and succumb to my power."

Yogen, Sanjit and Namrah attacked together, enveloping the fiery serpent in a bright, white shroud of suffocating Prana, preventing Vritra from opening his mouths to retaliate. They surrounded the demon, feeding the shroud with energy and strength to contain Vritra as he twisted, struggling to break free from his confinement.

"Cannot hold him much longer," said Namrah, strain in her voice.

"We need to get to the Shaman," said Yogen. He controls the demon. If we find a way to attack him, he will be forced to relinquish his hold on the creature."

"But that means we will have to split up," said Sanjit. "How else will we fight on two fronts at once?"

"I will go, papa," said Namrah.

"No, my child, the Shaman is too powerful for you. I must go and find him and end this. But for you to contain this beast, I am going to have to break my connection with the amulets."

"No, papa! You need their power to defeat the Shaman."

"I am relying on the fact that his Prana will be weakened through the control of Vritra. This is my only advantage."

Sanjit felt a surge of energy as Yogen severed his connection to the amulets and disappeared. Vritra sensed the shift in the flow of Prana, taking the opportunity to rip through the energy shroud, breaking free from his transient prison. He turned towards Sanjit and Namrah blasting several fireballs in their direction. They dodged and ducked the attack, narrowly avoiding the powerful blasts. They withdrew their swords; twin spiritual blades of energy, and attacked the fire-beast as he swam past them, piercing his hide, disrupting his assault.

Another rancorous shriek tore through the fabric of the spiritual plane as Vritra turned to retaliate. Sanjit and Namrah drew on the amulets, absorbing their Prana, charging their blades in defence. This time, the King of Dragons came at them head-on, giving Sanjit and Namrah little time to react. Sanjit pushed ahead of Namrah to absorb the majority of the attack. He spun his spirit blade in an arc, creating a shield of energy with his Prana, bracing himself as the fire-demon connected. Sanjit strained against the force of the attack. His shield wavered, thinned and then shattered in a shower of sparks. Vritra roared triumphantly, twisting his long, snake-like body, lifting Sanjit up and then throwing him down in a heap.

"Sanjit!"

Namrah drew on the power of the amulets, transmitting their energy through her body and out of her palms, directing the Prana at Vritra in a powerful blast that shook the very fabric of the spirit realm. The Dragon King was forced to retreat as Namrah glided quickly over to Sanjit. She placed her hands over his motionless body and closed her eyes, feeling for his life force. It was gone. Vritra twisted around for another attack. Namrah opened her mouth and started to sing. Her beautiful, harmonious voice filled the spirit realm, transforming the dense darkness in every crevice into incandescent particles of light. Vritra faltered, reacting to the powerful effect of Namrah's voice as it rang across the expanse, filling the void with a magical melody.

◊ ◊ ◊

The thunderous sound of falling water grew louder in his ears as Yogen returned to his physical body in the cave behind the waterfall. He opened his eyes to find Sanjit and Namrah sitting like a pair of statues in the glow of the paleo crystal. He picked up his staff and made his way out of the cave. Shafts of morning sunlight cut through the falling water, creating a rainbow of vibrant colour in the spray. Yogen continued around the edge of the waterfall, making his way up the embankment so that he had a better line of sight down-river. He followed the path into a canopy of trees that hid the river from view and then cut through the forest until he reached the flowing waters once more where he saw the Shaman. He was standing at the water's edge, hands extended, chanting loudly. Yogen knew that the Shaman had to continue his chanting to maintain control over Vritra. He carefully retreated into the forest and circled round so that he would come up behind him. He closed in on the Shaman, raising his staff to strike him and then the unthinkable happened. The Shaman turned around. Yogen, surprised by the hideous mask jumped back in alarm.

"Yogen. It's been a long time," said the Shaman maliciously.

"Not long enough," replied Yogen.

"You have made a fatal error."

"How so?"

"You have befriended the Shakti. They will be captured by my fire dragon, and then I will finish you."

"The fatal error is yours, Shaman. You have stopped your chanting. Vritra is no longer under your control."

"Don't be concerned, tree-mage, my spells will continue to feed the demon while I end your miserable life!"

The Shaman brought his staff down in a crushing blow. Yogen twisted his staff, deflecting the strike with a thwack. He stepped forward and spun deftly around, swinging his staff low, aiming to sweep the Shaman off his feet. At the last moment, the Shaman jumped into the air, narrowly missing the attacking strike. He reached into a pouch at his waist and threw a handful of yellow powder at Yogen as he moved past him. Yogen howled in agony, bringing both hands to his face. Dozens of red, seeping welts covered his skin. They burned, hissing, as the magical powder took effect. Yogen turned towards the Shaman. His vision was blurred, his face swollen in pain. He began to incant a mantra as he lunged for the Shaman. A bolt of white fire erupted from his staff, enveloping the Shaman completely and bringing him to his knees. The magical flames burned through his defences, sapping the Prana from his body as he fought to keep the fire at bay. Yogen took the opportunity to swing his staff around, striking the Shaman across the side of the head, so hard that he went crashing into the river, disappearing from sight. Yogen stepped into the shallows and gazed hard at the flowing waters, looking around for his adversary to surface.

The water erupted as the Shaman burst forth with a roar, hurling his staff hard at Yogen. The wooden rod twisted in the air and then began to split into a thousand tiny splinters, flying towards him like a rain of arrows shot from a multitude of bows. All Yogen could do was raise his arm to protect his face as the tiny needles pierced his skin. He fell into the shallow water with a splash, pain tearing through his flesh like the stings from the swarm of a thousand bees.

◊ ◊ ◊

An ear-splitting shriek tore through the skies as Vritra appeared through a tear in the heavens above. The Shaman turned around to face him.

"Vritra! Where are the Shakti? Have they been vanquished?"

"I must return to my prison, Shaman," bellowed the fire dragon.

"No! You must complete your duty as I have commanded you." The Shaman began his chanting again.

"It is too late, Shaman. You no longer control me. My shackles beckon, but first I am taking you with me!" Vritra twisted and rolled in the sky and then charged directly at the Shaman, his three heads spitting columns of fire.

"Nooooo!" The Shaman raised his arms as the flames washed over him. The sickening stench of burning flesh filled the air. Vritra opened his three mouths and engulfed the Shaman, taking him down and into the seething waters of the river with a splash. The waters bubbled loudly, sending clouds of steam into the air, before finally settling, leaving no trace of the demon or the Shaman.

"Papa! Papa!" Namrah came running down the path towards the river with Sanjit hot on her heels. Her father floated, unmoving in the shallows. She dropped to her knees and cradled Yogen in her arms. "Papa. Oh no," she sobbed.

"My child," said Yogen weakly. Red, swollen welts completely covered his face. "You're alive. What happened?"

"The demon attacked us, broke through our defences. He picked up Sanjit and threw him down to the ground. I thought he was dead. Then Vritra came at us again. I drew on the power of the amulets and cast a shield of protection. I knew that I couldn't hold him for long. I prayed to the gods for help and then began to sing a magical mantra. You must have distracted the Shaman from his hold on Vritra because he just disappeared. I turned to Sanjit and redirected the flow of Prana from the amulets through his body. He breathed again. It was a miracle."

Yogen wheezed. "Namrah."

"Yes, papa?"

"My time here is up."

"No, papa. You'll be fine. You just need some rest." Namrah turned to look forlornly at Sanjit. Tears streamed down her face. "The amulets. They can save you," she said to her father.

"No, my child. It is too late for me. I have been poisoned. The Shaman…"

"The Shaman is gone, papa. We saw Vritra take him."

Yogen wheezed one last breath and then was silent.

"Papa! Noooo!" Namrah held her father close. Her body shook with grief.

49 ~ Rescue

The smell inside the tent was almost as bad as it was outside. Halim still felt nauseous.

"Look," said Halim. "Some bindings."

"And some shoes," said Kativa lifting a pair of sandals up for Halim to see.

"Those are Taja's!" exclaimed Halim. "She was here." He looked frantically around the tent. "Nothing. There's no one here."

"I wonder where she could be," said Kativa.

"Maybe in one of the holding cells that they kept us in when we were captured the last time we were here. Shht. Someone's coming. Lie down, Kativa," instructed Halim, in a whisper. "Pretend you're unconscious again."

A little person stepped into the tent. Malak and another Ignogai accompanied him.

"Is this the one?" said the little person to Malak.

"Yes, Piju," replied Malak. "He says he needs the Shaman's help. His comrade has been injured by magic."

"Who are you?" said Piju in a squeaky voice. "I don't recognise you." Piju turned to look at Kativa. "A female? Who sent her into battle? This is against regulation!"

"My name is Bhag," said Halim. "I fought the Shakti on the bridge."

"But I know the river watch," said Piju, "and you're not one of them. Who is your commander?"

The Ignogai guards shifted around uneasily.

Halim looked at Kativa. She nodded imperceptibly. Halim moved. He drew his sword and attacked, swinging his blade at the guards. Malak was faster than Halim expected. He parried the blow with a sword he pulled out of nowhere. Kativa was on her feet in an instant, her short swords drawn and ready.

"Kill them!" squealed Piju, diving under Halim's blade.

The other guard swung his blade down at Kativa. She rolled to one side and his sword smashed against the hundreds of glass bottles and phials on the table. Kativa came in low, slicing her blades, cutting into the guard's leg below the knee. He dropped to his other knee, bringing his blade across his body with a grunt. Kativa twisted her body, bringing her blades up in defence. The tent resounded with the sound of metal against metal.

Halim and Malak continued to spar, trading blow after blow, until Halim's wrists ached with the effort. Piju ducked beneath the skirmish, heading for the exit. One of Kativa's swords flew through the air on a direct trajectory towards the fleeing little person. Her blade found its mark, sinking into Piju's back with a thwack! His high-pitched scream tore through the tent. He fell to the ground. Kativa blocked another blow with her other sword and then spun around quickly, pivoting in a clockwise motion, burying her blade into the guard's right shoulder, forcing him to drop his blade to the ground with a clatter. She withdrew her blade together with a spurt of blood and tissue and stabbed it into the soft skin of his neck before he had time to react. He stared at her in disbelief, choking on his blood as he went down.

Malak glanced at his comrade, briefly exposing himself as Halim attacked. Halim brought his blade up in a cutting motion, slicing open Malak's chest with its tip. Malak staggered backwards, and Halim advanced, swinging his blade down with a yell. Malak brought his sword up in defence, but Halim smashed it away. He swung again. This time, Malak barely managed to block the powerful blow. Halim stabbed his blade forward. It glanced off Malak's sword and sunk deep into his chest. Blood gushed out of his mouth. He convulsed once and then fell lifelessly to the ground.

"Come, quick, before others arrive," said Kativa diving out of the tent. Halim followed. They walked briskly away from the Shaman's tent, trying not to attract too much attention to themselves in the process.

"Hey. You!"

Halim bowed his head as he walked.

"Aren't you the Shaman's prisoner?"

This time, Halim looked up. A burly looking Ignogai was talking to a girl with long, dishevelled hair. She wore a dirty, bedraggled tunic and kept her head down.

Can it be? "Taja?"

"Halim!" Taja looked up and ran over to Halim, throwing her arms around him ecstatically.

"Hey, what's going on here?" said the Ignogai. "Who are you?" He looked Kativa up and down.

"Don't get any ideas you ugly brute," said Kativa. "She's coming with us."

"You are not of the tribe," he said, drawing his blade menacingly.

Halim pushed Taja behind him protectively and turned to face the Ignogai with Kativa. Taja screamed. Halim spun around. Another uglier looking Ignogai with long, matted hair had his arm around Taja's neck.

"My chief," said the other Ignogai. "These two know the prisoner. He pointed at Taja. "They were trying to take her."

"Drop your weaponsss," rasped the chief. "Otherwise, she dies." He tightened his grip around Taja's throat. She started to choke.

"Okay, okay," said Halim, placing his sword on the ground.

Kativa dropped her short blades and raised her arms into the air in surrender. The burly Ignogai ripped her bow off her back and kicked her to the ground.

"Take them all to the cage," said the chief, shoving Taja towards Halim. "And send someone to call the Shaman. For once he was right. His Shakti have come to us. Ha ha, ha ha!" he bellowed with laughter.

"Where's Piju?" demanded the chief from atop his raised dais. The lycanthus seemed to mirror his agitated mood as it paced restlessly from side to side. It snarled, baring its yellow-stained fangs. Saliva drooled languidly out of its mouth.

"I don't know, my chief," replied the grovelling Ignogai. "We cannot find him."

"Then send someone, anyone, to get the Shaman. I need him here. Now!" he roared, jumping to his feet. The lycanthus growled loudly at the Ignogai. It looked like it was going to pounce on him. The Ignogai cowered in fear.

"Yes, my chief. I will go myself to see that it is done," he said bowing low. He turned and trotted off.

The chief collapsed onto his throne with a grunt. The lycanthus settled down beside him, still baring its menacing fangs, panting copiously. The chief tossed a strip of bloody meat into the air. The creature sprang up, deftly catching it with a snap of its jaws. Using one of its paws to hold the meat in place, it tore savagely at the food, emitting soft, guttural sounds of satisfaction as it ate.

Like a light breeze on the surface of the river, a cowled figure silently appeared before the chief. He looked up in surprise.

"Who are you? Reveal yourself before the chief of the Ignogai!" he demanded. The hood fell back to reveal a face of infinite beauty. "By the gods," he whispered, mouth agape. He quickly cast his gaze around the village. "Where did you come from? How…?" His voice trailed off. His mind raced. His breathing quickened. The girl stared at him. He felt the power of her gaze. It bore right through him. His chest constricted.

286

And then she spoke, and her voice sounded like honey. The chief felt light-headed. His left hand shook of its own accord. "I have come for your pleasure," she said with a smile.

The chief felt the blood rush to his face and then to other more sensitive extremities. He opened his mouth, but words failed him. She seemed to glide as she moved closer. Her fragrance was sweet, seductive. A gnawing sensation of uneasiness probed his senses, but he quickly dismissed it, rather giving into his yearning desires.

The lycanthus, distracted by its meaty treat, ignored the girl as she approached the throne. She was close now. The Chief closed his eyes and breathed in her aroma, her essence. His head swam. He smiled, inebriated by her presence. She whispered in his ear, and he obeyed, rising from his seat, making his way down the dais and through the village. The girl followed. He knew that what he was doing was what the girl asked him to do against his will, but he didn't care. He was the chief. He could do anything he wanted to. But he didn't want this. Why was he doing it? That gnawing feeling again. Questioning. Probing. He pushed it aside. Why was it irritating him so? Why couldn't it just leave him alone? He stopped and looked around. For a moment he wasn't sure where he was and then she whispered in his ear again, and it started all over again. He closed his eyes and smiled. He felt so calm, peaceful. He breathed deeply and then continued walking through the village until he reached the cage.

"Namrah!" Halim cried from inside the cage.

Namrah raised a finger to her lips.

The chief looked about again, confusion marring his face. He shook his head vigorously. "You! What am I doing here? You bewitched me!" he roared, withdrawing his curved broadsword. He lunged at Namrah, who gracefully sidestepped the attack.

"Namrah! No!" Halim shook the bars of the cage in frustration.

The Ignogai chief was quick on his feet despite his rotund appearance. He turned, swinging his blade in an arc. It sliced through the air, cutting through Namrah's clothing as she moved away. She looked down in dismay at a growing red patch on her tunic.

"Sanjit!" yelled Taja.

"What took you so long?" said Namrah.

The chief spun around twisting his blade up to deflect Sanjit's powerful blow. Their swords rang loudly with the impact. The Ignogai chief returned the attack, and Sanjit blocked it. Left, right, left, right, backwards and forwards they moved, stirring the dust up off the ground as they parried. The chief feigned an attack, twisting his sword the other way. Sanjit just managed to avoid the furtive jab by rolling his body sideways. He came up close to the chief, lifted the elbow of his sword arm and drove it hard into his belly. The chief doubled over in pain. Sanjit followed up with a powerful kick, sending him up into the air and onto his back with a thump. He brought his blade down with a howl of triumph, but the chief quickly rolled out of harm's way, turning to come up to a standing, defensive position. A look of horror crossed the chief's face as he looked down to find a silver blade gradually making its way through the front of his chest. He slowly turned around as Namrah let go of the blade. Blood seeped out of his mouth as he dropped to his knees. He grabbed the sword with both hands and squeezed, trying to push it back and out. The sharp blade cut into the soft flesh of his palms. Blood ran over his hands and dripped onto the earth below like the red juice from wild berries. He looked up at Namrah and grinned at her through bloodied teeth. Sanjit swung his blade as hard as he could through the air, severing the chief's head clean from his body. It hit the ground with a thud. A red fountain of blood sprayed into the air from the neck of the lifeless torso, as it toppled lifelessly to the ground.

Namrah dropped to her knees, cradling her stomach. Sanjit released his blade and ran over to assist her.

"I'll be all right," she said softly, screwing up her face in pain.

"Here, let me see," said Sanjit, peeling back her hands from her belly. Her face was pale. She was losing blood. "It's quite deep. We need to stitch it closed."

Namrah nodded silently. "The others…" she whispered, pointing at the cage. "Kativa. She will know what to do."

Sanjit stepped over to the cage, lifted the wooden block and pulled open the door.

Kativa was the first to exit. She acknowledged Sanjit and then ran over to Namrah, removing a small pouch from inside her tunic. She rolled it open to reveal a collection of medicinal herbs and multi-coloured phials.

"Sanjit, my brother," said Halim as he gave Sanjit a quick hug before joining Kativa at Namrah's side.

Taja stepped out of the cage and collapsed into Sanjit's arms, exhausted. He held her tenderly. He felt whole.

"Here. Pass me that stick," Kativa instructed Halim.

Kativa withdrew a small knife, sliced off a piece of the stick and then began to whittle it down to a thin, sharply curved splinter. She opened one of the phials and poured its contents onto a cloth that she pulled from one of her pockets. She used the cloth to wipe away as much blood from the open wound as she could. Namrah groaned in pain. Kativa picked up a small ball of twine from inside the pouch and twisted one end around the splinter. She pushed the splinter into the skin around the wound, meticulously sewing it closed. The flow of blood from the wound abated as she dabbed at the skin with her cloth.

"I need a long strip of cloth," said Kativa. "We need to strap the wound; to keep it from tearing open."

Thin beads of sweat covered Namrah's ashen face. She closed her eyes. Sanjit removed a blanket from his backpack and began ripping it into narrow strips.

"Where's Yogen?" said Kativa looking around. Her gaze fixed on Sanjit and she read his eyes.

"Oh no," her voice cracked. "What happened?"

"He was a true warrior," said Sanjit. "He fought well but the Shaman, he…" Sanjit dropped his gaze. "I'm sorry," he said in a whisper.

Kativa turned to Namrah. "Poor girl. She's been through a lot."

"We let him go with the river," said Sanjit. "He's with Agni, the water god."

Taja came to crouch next to Halim. He put his arm around her. She looked a mess.

"Oh, Halim." She buried her head in his shoulder and sobbed.

Halim felt tears sting his eyes. He couldn't hold them at bay. He rocked gently, forwards and backwards. "Taj. I'm so glad you're alive."

Kativa wrapped two blanket strips securely around Namrah's waist and carefully poured some water into her mouth. Namrah opened her eyes and lifted her head, coughing once, and again as the water struggled to find its way down.

"Here, chew on this," suggested Kativa, pushing a small, dry, hard, ball through her lips. "It will give you back some of your strength."

Taja lifted her head from Halim's shoulder and rubbed her eyes with the back of her hands. "You must be Namrah. Kativa told me about you." She looked at her brother and smiled. "She's beautiful, Halim."

Namrah smiled weakly. "Taja," she whispered. "I see Halim in you. A dirty version of Halim."

Taja laughed. "And a sense of humour too. I like her," she said to Halim. He looked away, embarrassed.

"We need to leave this place," said Kativa looking around. "And quickly."

Halim and Sanjit helped lift Namrah to her feet.

"Do you have any more of that white paint?" said Taja, pointing at Halim's face.

"Sorry Taj, we found some near the river and applied it there. I'm surprised mine's still on! How does it look?" He turned his face from side to side.

"Hmmm. A bit patchy but it'll pass."

"Good. Kativa and I will lead the way, but then you're going to have to help Sanjit with Namrah. She can barely walk on her own."

"No problem. I'll manage," said Taja taking over from Halim.

"I have a plan," said Kativa. "It's the only way we're going to make it out alive." She glanced at Namrah as she spoke. "I saw some horses stabled near the entrance. We need to get to them. Soon someone is going to find the bodies that we left in the Shaman's tent and they aren't going to be happy. We don't have much time."

The group of five slowly made their way across the Ignogai village. It seemed strangely quiet, almost empty. More truer words could not have been spoken when cries of alarm sounded from inside the village. They had found the bodies. Kativa and Halim picked up the pace, widening the gap between them and the rest of the group as they pushed to reach the stables. The discovery of the bodies seemed to work in their favour as Ignogai guards ran past them, focused on investigating the source of the alarm, instead of the curious group of trespassers.

Halim and Kativa arrived at the stables. A pair of Ignogai stood blocking the entrance.

"Quick!" shouted Halim pointing behind him. "The chief! He is under attack! The Shakti are here!"

One of the guards picked up his spear and ran into the village without hesitation but the other more burly one paused and turned to Halim.

"I know you," he said slowly, pushing his brow into a furrow of lines. "And you," he pointed at Kativa. "You were sick, wounded by magic. How is it that you are healed? Where's Piju?" The guard looked past Halim and Kativa as Taja and Sanjit arrived with Namrah between them. "What is this?" He took a step back to reassess the situation and then lifted his spear into the air defensively. "Intruders!" he shouted, jumping forward and jabbing his spear aggressively.

Kativa had her twin blades out in a flash, twisting to block the powerful attack. She sidestepped the guard, giving Halim the opportunity to follow through with a slice of his blade. The guard brought up his spear, successfully blocking Halim's strike.

He spun quickly around with a yell and charged, stepping to the left, thrusting his spear at Halim, who used both hands on his sword to deflect the jab. His shoulders shook with the force of the blow. The guard was strong. Kativa took the opportunity to strike at the guard's exposed side, but he anticipated the attack, diving into a roll and away from Kativa's blade as it cut through the air with a swoosh. Halim and Kativa advanced cautiously together, like a pair of leopards cornering their prey. The guard was still on the ground. He pulled his arm back and hurled his spear at Kativa with a grunt. She sidestepped the deadly weapon. It flew dangerously close to her head before landing harmlessly on the ground several paces away. The guard pulled out a short knife and jumped to his feet.

"Come, you filth. Come meet your doom!" he said, snarling aggressively.

Halim and Kativa continued to advance. Halim's blade flashed through the air. The guard blocked the strike leaving his ribs exposed once more. Kativa thrust her short-sword forward, burying it deep into his side. He roared loudly from the pain, but that didn't stop him from reaching out his hand and gripping Kativa forcefully around her neck. He squeezed and Kativa choked, pulling frantically at his powerful grip around her throat. Halim's blade cut through the air, severing the guard's hand at his wrist. He dropped to his knees, cradling his blood-soaked stump with his other hand. Halim stabbed his blade into his chest. The guard let out one final wheeze of air before tumbling over.

"Looks like four horses," said Halim as he ran into the stables. "I will go ahead with Namrah on one horse and the rest of you follow on the other three," he instructed.

Sanjit nodded in agreement and smiled.

The young boy becomes a man, he thought to himself.

Sanjit and Halim helped Namrah up onto a magnificent, black mare. Halim secured the leather tube with the sacred parchment to the side of the horse and then hoisted himself up in front of Namrah so that she could wrap her arms around him as they rode.

"You okay?" he asked her.

Namrah nodded and smiled. "I'm always okay when I'm with you."

Halim felt his face go hot. He turned to grab the reins and quickly guided the horse out of the stables for fear of being seen. Taja, Sanjit and Kativa untethered the other three animals and followed close behind.

50 ~ Hide

"Hold on tight," said Halim picking up the pace. He was concerned for Namrah's safety as they rode out of the Ignogai village. The constant pounding of the horse's hooves on the ground as it galloped must be excruciating for her, he thought. He knew that they had to travel east, away from the river but the only path in and out of the village was west towards the river and the rest of the Ignogai that were probably getting quite restless waiting for the Shaman's return.

Halim turned to steal a quick look behind him as he rode. Taja, Sanjit and Kativa followed at a pace. He breathed out a sigh, relieved that there were no Ignogai chasing them. The trees lining the path created a secure canopy, concealing them from sight. Shards of sunlight flickered through the boughs and several forest animals scampered away as the four horses whipped up a whirlwind of their own, sending fallen leaves flying and a cloud of dust in their wake.

Halim slowed his horse down to a trot and then leant forward to slap its heaving flank in appreciation. "There, there. Good boy."

Sanjit came up alongside Halim. "The rest of the Ignogai are up ahead."

"I know."

"What is your plan?"

"There are too many of them for us to fight," said Halim. "And they're all on foot. I say we just ride through them. Surprise them."

Sanjit reached into his pack and produced the two wooden amulets. They looked as nondescript as before.

"How are those going to help us?" said Halim.

"We'll recite a mantra of concealment. The combined power of the amulets will enhance the mantra and protect us all. We will be invisible to the Ignogai."

"So we hide and wait for them to pass?"

"That's the plan," said Sanjit.

"But how will we get them to pass? Or how will we pass them?"

"Kativa," said Sanjit. "She'll head upriver, past the bridge to where the Ignogai are stationed. As soon as they see her, the Ignogai will give chase. Kativa will double back towards the bridge and then cross it, drawing them away. This will give us clearance to head upriver to the waterfall and then east to Harappa."

Halim glanced back at Kativa, who nodded with a smile.

"She wants to go home too," said Sanjit. "The Ignogai will never catch her on foot, and they'll lose interest fast without their Shaman to guide them," said Sanjit.

"What about Namrah?" said Halim

Namrah squeezed Halim tightly. "I'll stay with you," she said. "Besides, I don't have the strength to run. I'm already quite weakened by the short sprint from the Ignogai village."

"There's another problem," said Halim. "The root wall that Yogen created on the bridge. How will Kativa get past it with the Ignogai hot on her tail? You all saw how those Ignogai struggled to break through."

"It was created by magic," said Namrah. "Although constructed from the roots of the trees, it needs to be sustained by the source of energy that created it. Otherwise, it will wither and die. By now, there's probably not much of it left."

Sanjit dropped back to converse with Taja and Kativa, reaffirming their plans. Several rubber fig trees appeared, signalling their proximity to the river. Halim reined in his horse and turned to face the others as they approached.

"We must hide here," Halim announced, climbing off his horse.

"I will prepare the amulets," said Sanjit as Taja and Kativa climbed off their mounts.

The group led the horses off the path and into the forest, securing them all to a nearby tree. Halim and Kativa carefully helped Namrah down, and Sanjit kicked away leaves and loose stones to create a circular clearing for them to sit. He placed the amulets in the centre, their sides interlocking to form a solid piece. Halim blinked tears away as he gazed at the amulets and thought of Yogen. He missed his cheerful disposition and twinkling green eyes. He looked at Namrah, squeezed her hand and smiled reassuringly.

"Kativa," said Namrah, hugging her affectionately. "You take care now, you hear? Please be careful. I will pray for you. Namaste."

"Namaste, Namrah, my child," said Kativa. "You take care of her, Halim," she said sternly.

"Yes, mother," Halim replied with a sarcastic grin. "Safe journey." He hugged her affectionately. "Thank you for your assistance. Without you, we would never have made it this far."

"Kativa." Taja bowed reverently. "Thank you for your help and support. It was lovely to meet you. You will be sorely missed. Namaste." She touched her forehead with her fingertips.

"Taja. I'm so happy that we found you in one piece," said Kativa. "Sanjit and your brother are true Shakti Warriors. You are lucky to have them by your side."

She turned to Sanjit. "You are a good man, Sanjit. May the gods protect you and guide you home. Namaste."

"Namaste," said Sanjit, bowing his head to his hands.

Kativa climbed onto her horse and rode back towards the

path. She pulled her horse around, lifted her arm in a final farewell and then disappeared.

The four remaining travellers sat down around the amulets and closed their eyes. The breeze on Halim's face was soft and gentle. He lifted his chin and filled his lungs with a deep breath. For the first time in a long while, he felt at peace. Taja was back; they were headed home, and the danger that lay ahead was nothing compared to what he had been through on this adventure. Sanjit led the chanting, reciting a short but powerful mantra over and over again. The words were unfamiliar to Halim but before long he joined in along with the others until their voices became one, long, steady chant, reverberating through the forest like the drone from a swarm of flying locusts.

"Om devee kaalee, ham tum hamen hamaare dushmanon
ko anadekhee karane ke lie praarthana karana.
Apane prakaash mein chhipa hai aur hamen
unake paraakram om shaanti se bachaane ke."

(Om goddess Kali, we beseech you to make us unseen to our enemies.
Hide us in your light and protect us from their might.
May peace be with you.)

51 ~ Arrows

Kativa pulled on the reins of her horse, bringing it to a slow walk as she approached the river. Two Ignogai guards stood at the entrance to the root-bridge.

"Halt!" one of them shouted. "What is your business here, soldier?"

Kativa was taken aback at the way he addressed her and then she remembered that she was still wearing white face paint.

"I'm looking for the Shaman," she said with as much authority as she could muster. "Tell me where he is immediately."

"He's further upriver," said the guard pointing. "Wait. I don't recognise you. You're not Ignogai," he said, as Kativa passed by. "Who are you? What do you want with the Shaman?"

The guards withdrew their curved blades and began to advance. Kativa quickly reached behind her back, pulled an arrow from her quiver, nocked it in her bow and let it loose, all in one, fluid movement. She was already reaching for a second arrow as the first one found its target, burying itself deep in the neck of the guard. He brought his hands to his throat as the blood pumped out viciously. The other guard ran at Kativa with a growl just as she released the second arrow. He swung his blade, chopping the arrow away before it could reach him. He swung again, this time at Kativa, who withdrew her double short-swords to deflect the powerful blow. Their blades rang. She kicked hard with her boot, connecting the guard under his jaw, sending him sprawling. He climbed back up and charged again. This time, Kativa turned to face the guard head-on, dug her heels into her horse's ribs and pulled back on the reins. The horse reared up onto its hind legs and then came down on top of the guard with all its weight, crushing him to the ground in an instant. There was a crack from the sound of the Ignogai's spine breaking beneath the horse's hooves and then silence. Kativa led her horse to the river's edge so that he could drink his fill before heading off, upriver in search of the other Ignogai.

Smoke in the distance, drifting east in the breeze caught Kativa's attention. She reined in her horse and climbed off. She removed her quiver and emptied the arrows onto the ground, counting eight in total. She replaced a single arrow in her quiver and slung it back across her back. Then she cut each of the remaining arrows in half, discarded the blunt halves and pushed the other pieces into the ground at an angle with their points just sticking out. She measured a single stride up the path away from the arrows and then, using her twin-blades, she hacked at the hard earth on the path, digging a long, narrow trench across its breadth. She collected an armful of leaves from the forest floor, covering both the trench and the deadly arrows from sight. She stood back to admire her work, climbed back onto her horse and continued along the path towards the fate that awaited her beneath the rising smoke in the distance.

Kativa reached the top of a rise and looked down on the Ignogai camp. She counted almost thirty Ignogai, most of whom were pacing up and down restlessly. She unstoppered her gourd, poured some water onto her sleeve and wiped it across her face to remove the white paint. She brought her fingers to her mouth and blew as hard as she could, emitting a loud whistle that rang across the valley below. The Ignogai turned to look up at Kativa. She lifted her bow, withdrew her last arrow, and snapped it onto the bowstring. She took aim, pulled and released. The arrow flew high, landing with a thud right next to the fire amidst the startled Ignogai. They cried out in alarm, brandished their weapons and gave chase. Kativa smiled, sitting atop her horse, waiting for the Ignogai to draw closer before turning to ride back down the path from whence she came. She glanced back to see the horde crest the rise not far behind her. She pulled on the reins, guiding her horse off the path to circumvent the trap that she laid for them. Kativa grinned as the painful cries from some of the unfortunate victims echoed from behind her as she rode on towards the root bridge. She stepped around the two dead guards and made her way to the centre of the bridge where she stopped to wait patiently for the arrival of the Ignogai. The magical roots had withered just as Namrah had predicted. Kativa prodded them with her boot, and they turned to dust. The Ignogai burst from the forest, shouting and screaming in anger when they saw Kativa. She turned, nudging her horse across the bridge, luring the ignorant Ignogai after her and away from her comrades hiding nearby.

Sanjit opened his eyes. "Come, friends, they have passed. Kativa has done her duty. We must go now, quickly, before the Ignogai return."

Sanjit collected the amulets and then together with Halim, helped Namrah back up onto her horse. They all made their way out of the forest, back onto the path and down to the river.

"Look," said Taja pointing at the guard with an arrow protruding out of his neck. "Kativa's been busy."

Sanjit looked across the bridge. "I hope she'll be okay," he said, concern mirroring his voice.

The four travellers continued upriver, following the path north before heading east, back towards Harappa.

52 ~ Banyan

"It's been eight days," said Halim to Taja as he rode up next to her.

Taja's dirty face was wet with tears. "I hope we're not too late to save her."

"Your mother?" said Namrah.

Halim nodded.

"I thought the monastery was a myth."

"No, it's real," said Taja. "It's where we met the monk Aatreya who gave us the sacred medicine for our mother."

"May the gods have mercy upon you and your family," said Namrah. "And may the medicine heal her from her illness."

"Thank you, Namrah," said Taja.

The group, led by Halim travelled east without rest until the sun disappeared behind them. They set up camp in the forest, alongside a small stream that trickled down from the mountains ahead of them. Halim tended to Namrah while Sanjit and Taja foraged for wood and food.

"Tell me about your mother," said Namrah to Halim as he peeled back the layers of cloth around her wound. She winced from the pain.

"You okay?"

"Yes. I'll be fine."

"I have some ointment in my pack," said Halim. An old seer gave it to me." Halim pulled out the small brown jar. He twisted the lid off the jar and was hit by its pungent herbal aroma.

"Where did you say you got that?" said Namrah.

"From an old seer in the forest. Jaya is her name."

"I know that smell," said Namrah. "It's been infused with seeds from the banyan tree. Here, let me apply some over the wound."

"Don't worry, I'll do it," said Halim, dipping two fingers into the soft paste. A tingling sensation rippled up his fingers and into his hand. At first, it felt like he was being bitten by a thousand ants but then the pain subsided, until he felt nothing but a dull, warm throbbing sensation.

"What are banyan seeds?" he remarked. "What do they do?"

"The banyan tree is a magical tree, replied Namrah. "One of the Nine Sages once told one of his disciples to pull a fruit from the tree and remove one of the seeds. Then he was told to open the seed and relate to his teacher what he saw inside. He explained that he saw absolutely nothing and the Sage told him that it was from nothing that the banyan tree sprang forth. This is a lesson about how so much life and abundance can come from so little. It is also believed that the banyan tree's roots never stop growing so that if it is ever hacked down, it will use its powerful roots deep below the surface to rise again."

Halim stared at the ointment on his fingers. "Wow."

"The life-giving properties of the seeds promote a very fast healing process."

Halim carefully smeared a generous amount of ointment over Namrah's wound. She closed her eyes and sucked in a short, sharp breath, wincing from the pain. Halim removed the last two strips of cloth from her pack and wrapped them securely around her waist. He opened his waterskin and lifted it to her lips so that she could drink.

"Thank you, Halim," she smiled. "Now, about your mother…"

"Ah, yes. My mother," said Halim, closing his eyes. He held back the tears as her face came to memory. "She is the most beautiful, caring and affectionate woman I know." He sighed. "I pray that she lives to receive the medicine we have journeyed to find."

Halim lay down next to Namrah, slid his arm beneath her neck and pulled a blanket over them both. Within moments, they were both sound asleep, exhausted from the full day's ride.

Halim blinked open his eyes. He was still lying in the same position with Namrah curled up next right to him. He twisted his head to gaze at the beautiful features of her face in the soft light of the dawn and smiled. He was so very warm and cosy, he wished that he didn't have to rise again. He turned to look up at the canopy of trees above, listening to the creaking sounds of the boughs shifting in a gentle breeze. He closed his eyes and drifted peacefully off to sleep again.

"Halim. Halim."

Halim screwed up his eyes against slivers of sunlight that stole through the trees. Namrah was sitting up next to him.

"Good morning," she smiled.

"Hi. How are you feeling?"

"Much better, thanks. The ointment helped."

"Great! Don't know about you, but I'm famished. You know we never ate last night."

"Yes, I know. We were both so tired. Here." Namrah held out her hand. "Berries."

"Thanks," said Halim taking the juicy orange berries. "Hmmm. These are good," he said as he chewed. "Where are Sanjit and Taja?"

"They went to find more wood for the fire," said Namrah pointing at the smouldering embers.

"Ah! Good morning mister sleepyhead," said Taja as she approached with Sanjit in tow. She tossed some wood onto the fire.

"Morning. Ow!" exclaimed Halim as he sat up. "My aching

body."

"Time for some yoga," remarked Sanjit. "Let's practice while the girls prepare the food," he said, tossing a pair of freshly caught rabbits onto the ground.

Halim climbed to his feet and reached his hands up into the air for a stretch. "Sounds good. Let's do it."

Halim cleared away leaves and twigs next to the stream for his and Sanjit's mats. They began the practice by sitting in a full lotus position, hands relaxed in their laps, breathing deeply in and out of their noses. They moved together as one, flowing through chaturanga several times, increasing the circulation of fluid through their muscles and joints and awakening the flow of Prana in their bodies. Halim closed his eyes as he moved, attuning himself to the flowing movements of the practice, relinquishing his body to the Prana that flowed in and around him. He sank into Virabhadrasana, extending his arms like arrows out on either side of his body, feeling his chest open up wide, and his back extend, stretching the muscles apart like wings so that he could fly. The muscles in his legs burned as he pushed the soles of his feet into the earth. Every breath was like a current of energy, flowing in, charging his body and then out again. He pulled the corners of his mouth into a smile, feeling so grateful to be alive.

53 ~ Home

"How much farther?" enquired Namrah as the four travellers left the protection of the forest.

"The city of Harappa lies just on the other side of these mountains," said Sanjit.

They continued in silence, following the sandy path as it took them up and over the mountain pass. Halim looked up towards the midday sun as they began their descent. Namrah turned her head, closed her eyes and gently rested her cheek on Halim's back. He breathed deeply, and Namrah's scent filled his head, making him giddy with pleasure. The travellers entered the forest at the foot of the pass. Halim looked around as familiarity set in, along with feelings of trepidation and excitement.

"This is where I grew up," he whispered to Namrah. "See that tree?" He pointed to a tree in the forest, larger than all the others and covered in a speckled vine. "I used to climb that tree. Right to the top." He lifted his hand, and both he and Namrah followed its aim.

Namrah squeezed his torso. "I can't wait to see your home, Halim."

Halim closed his eyes, allowing his horse to follow the path unguided. He listened intently to the sounds of the forest and tasted the sweet smells that wafted through the cool canopy of trees surrounding them. The forest finally gave way to the grass plains on the outskirts of the city. The four travellers crested the next rise and stopped to gaze down upon the magnificent city of Harappa framed in a dazzling orange glow from the setting sun. Tears ran down Halim's face. It was the most beautiful sight he had ever seen. His heart ached with an abundance of feelings. He was home.

Halim, followed by Taja and then Sanjit, thundered down the path to his house. Shan hobbled out to greet them with open arms.

"Halim! Taja! Sanjit! You're home!" he shouted with glee. "And who is this beautiful creature?"

Namrah blushed.

"This is Namrah, papa," said Halim. "Namrah, this is my father, Shan."

"Pleased to make your acquaintance, my lady." Shan bowed honourably.

"Papa," said Taja jumping down from her horse. "How is Mama?"

Shan looked down forlornly. "She's barely breathing," he said softly. "It's as if she has been waiting for you to return so that she can say goodbye before departing this world."

Taja burst into tears. "Oh, papa. Don't speak like that." She wrapped her arms around her father, sobbing heavily. "Halim has the medicine, papa. *We* have the medicine. We will save her," she implored. "We must save her, papa."

"I will call for the Shaman," said Sanjit. "We need his assistance."

Sanjit pulled his horse around and spurred it forward in the direction of the city.

Halim climbed off his horse and helped Namrah down.

"Namrah has been injured, papa. She needs rest."

"Yes, yes of course. Come. This way."

Shan led them inside, directing Namrah to Taja's bedroom at

the back of the house. Halim and Taja stepped into their mother's room. A sweet smell filled the air, and the windows were covered with thick cloth, blotting out the sunlight from entering. Arja lay motionless on the bed. Her face looked gaunt and pallid. Taja fell into Halim's arms and sobbed uncontrollably.

"Halim," she blurted in-between her crying. "She looks terrible."

Halim hugged his sister reassuringly. The siblings swayed gently from side to side. Halim closed his eyes and prayed to the gods for strength.

Sanjit returned with the Shaman. He held out his hand wordlessly to Halim, who withdrew a small bottle from inside his tunic, placing it carefully into the Shaman's outstretched hand. The sacred medicine. The shaman unstoppered the bottle and sniffed its contents. A fresh, herbal fragrance filled the room. He moved silently over to Arja and gingerly poured the bottle's contents into her mouth. Shan, who had quietly entered the room, put his arm around Halim's shoulders in a comforting embrace. The Shaman stepped back, gesturing to the others to circle the bed. He began to chant the ancient Vedic Maha Mrityunjaya mantra for healing. Halim closed his eyes and remembered Dasgupta's teachings. His voice echoed inside his head.

"The Maha Mrityunjaya mantra is one of yoga's most important mantra's, restoring health and happiness and bringing calmness in the face of death. Its power is omnipotent, and it's daily repetition will keep the spirit of death at bay."

"But how is this possible?" questioned Halim. "How can the utterance of a mantra keep death at bay?"

Bodhan smiled. "It is said that Shiva explained this to his wife Parvati one day when she asked about his eyes and how they came to contain the immortal elixir. He responded by explaining that she had to be joined in yoga to understand this. You see, Shiva held the ability to destroy and create with the power held in his eyes. It is said that his eyes embodied his radiant vitality, the source of immortality and the ultimate force of all healing and nourishment. The recitation of the Maha Mrityunjaya mantra taps into this divine energy; the blinding light that is stronger than a million suns."

Halim knew that for the mantra to take effect, it had to be recited thousands of times. He looked around at the determined faces of the Shaman, Shan, Sanjit and his sister Taja chanting in unison. He closed his eyes and joined in. It was going to be a long night.

"Om. Tryambakam yajamahe
Sugandhim pushti-vardhanam
Urvarukamiva bandhanan
Mrityor mukshiya mamritat."

(Om, we worship the three-eyed one,
Who is fragrant and who nourishes all beings.
May He sever our Bondage of Samsara, the worldly life,
Like a cucumber severed from the bondage of its creeper
And thus Liberate us from the Fear of Death,
By making us realise that we are never separated from our Immortal Nature.)

54 ~ Mantra

They took turns to relieve themselves as the night wore on, returning quickly to their places beside Arja so they could continue the methodical chanting. Halim's body ached, and his head grew heavy as he fought to resist the urge to lie down and sleep. Now and then he would glance at his mother as she lay corpse-like on the bed in front of him, her emaciated features making her look almost unrecognisable. The longer he repeated the mantra, the more it awakened in him feelings of enlightenment and inspiration. At first, Halim thought that he imagined things, but then the more he thought about it, the more he realised that the magic of the Maha Mrityunjaya mantra was beginning to take effect, to almost take a life of its own. It was as if the mantra itself was gaining substance and developing awareness. With every repetition, it grew stronger. With every iteration, it became a thing of purpose, seeking out the reason it was called forth into the physical world. Guided by four powerful intentions, all focused on a common goal, it yearned to live, to breathe, to heal, to restore, and to banish the forces of darkness and death whose intention it was to extinguish the fire of life from the fragile soul that lay in the bed before them.

Halim relinquished himself to the magic of the mantra. He became the conduit, the channel of transmission for the intention. He was the Shakti Warrior of light, riding in a golden chariot across the turbulent seas of the Swarga. He looked up to find three more chariots coming from different directions, all headed for the same destination. He entered the void, coming face to face with a heavy burden, a senseless entity that devoured all desire, all purpose. Death. He climbed off his chariot and sat down next to the nonentity. He closed his eyes, afraid to gaze upon its cadaverous nature, but then forced them open to see. It had the face of his mother. She stared back at him with dark, sightless holes for eyes. He looked into those eyes, and they drew him in, sucking his Prana from his body and into a whirlpool of affliction and torment. And it was then, faced with total obliteration, that the Maha Mrityunjaya mantra returned to Halim's lips. Stronger than ever before, banishing all fear, all doubt and despair, coursing through his body like a living thing, charging him with intention, tearing through the darkness with a light so bright he was forced to shield his eyes from its brilliance.

It was done. The ordeal was over. He opened his eyes. His face was wet with tears. He felt surprisingly light and energised like he had just woken up from a good night's sleep. He turned to look at his mother. Her cheeks were pink with colour and her chest rose and fell gently with the breath of life. Halim knew then that she was going to be okay. He looked up at the others and smiled. They had successfully invoked a powerful mantra and saved his mother from maut - certain death.

55 ~ Epilogue

Halim gazed at the flames, listening to them engulf the wood with a sizzling crackle, staring until his eyes watered with the effort. He squeezed his eyes shut and witnessed the bright, white silhouette of the fire emblazoned across his vision like a fiery phoenix on its moribund flight into the sun.

"Halim, my son. Tell me of your journey. Did you find it difficult?"

Halim opened his eyes and smiled. He looked to Shan and Taja sitting across from him for moral support. Shan winked. Taja sighed deeply.

"Papa," answered Halim. "It was a journey of a lifetime. We were faced with the impossible, but the gods were watching over us and showed us the way. I'm just glad that we all made it back alive." He thought of Yogen and dropped his head. "Well, not all of us," he murmured.

"What do you mean, my son?"

Halim looked up at his father. "Yogen. Namrah's father. He died trying to save us from the Shaman of the Ignogai."

"The Ignogai!" exclaimed Shan. "That cursed tribe." He spat into the fire with disdain.

"They kidnapped us," said Halim. "We managed to escape,

but they pursued us all across the valley until their Shaman captured Taja again. If it weren't for Yogen and Namrah, we would never have saved her."

"Oh, my poor child," said Shan turning to give his daughter a consoling hug. "I'm so sorry."

"It's okay papa," said Taja, sobbing gently into Shan's shoulder. "I'm just happy that mama is going to be all right. I've feared for her life all this time. May the gods continue to protect us."

Shan released Taja and sat up to gaze across at the leather canister lying next to Halim. "What's that Halim?" he said pointing. "And that symbol? The crescent moon."

Halim lifted the canister. "This is the symbol of Aryavartha, the secret monastery in the Kunlun Mountains. Aatreya, Sanjit's bhisaj gave it to me." Halim opened the canister and withdrew the scroll inside. "He charged us with spreading the story contained in this scroll, sharing it with the elders of the city and teaching it to all of the children." Halim rolled open the scroll. Shan, Sanjit and Taja gathered in for closer inspection. The light from the fire cast a flickering shadow across the old parchment.

"It's written in Sanskrit," remarked Taja.

"Yes. Remember, Aatreya said that it was a translation of the story from the tablets," said Sanjit.

Shan scanned the words in the scroll. "That's odd," he said. "It looks like some kind of riddle." He began reading out loud. "Deep within the bosom of mahi and far beneath the jala of the mahasagara it rests. The embryo of the sthiti. The eternal fire. Nine shall find it. Nine shall release it. Nine shall control it."

"What else does it say?" enquired Taja.

"It seems the rest is unrelated to the riddle," said Shan. "It tells of a people that lived across the seas and then fled rising waters to find higher ground. It mentions Aryavartha."

"The secret monastery," whispered Sanjit.

"But what does the riddle mean?" said Halim. "Maybe Bodhan Dasgupta will be able to decipher it."

"Perhaps," said Shan. "But that is for another day. It's late, I'm tired and need to rest," he said standing up and dusting off his robes.

Halim replaced the scroll and hoisted the canister over his shoulder. "Good night Papa," he said hugging his father.

"Good night, Halim. May the gods watch over you. Good night Taja. Sanjit."

"Night you two," Halim said to Sanjit and Taja. "I'm going to check on Namrah."

"Good night papa. Good night my brother," said Taja.

"Good night Shan. Good night Halim," said Sanjit. "May your Shakti spirit find rest this night and may you dream of peace and happiness always."

"Thank you, my brother. Namaste," said Halim bowing his forehead to meet his hands in reverence. He turned to follow his father into the house.

Taja snuggled up next to Sanjit as they stared silently at the dancing flames. She turned her face up to his and smiled. He dropped his head, gently meeting his lips with hers for a long and passionate kiss.

THE END.

Thank You

I really hope you enjoyed reading my book. Thank you for reading it! Reviews are very important for authors. If you enjoyed the book, please consider posting a review on Amazon.com.

Please visit my website, richardgradner.com for more information about my other novels, *Return to Lemuria, Servant of Memory and Acoustic Alchemy*. By registering for my monthly newsletter, you will receive a link to download a complimentary digital copy of my first novel, *Return to Lemuria*.

Thanks in advance for your support!

Richard

Servant of Memory

SERVANT OF MEMORY

Richard Gradner

1 ~ New World

Mount Ararat, 2104 BCE

The perpetual barrage upon the world had brought with it a deep sense of grief and despair, blurring the days into nights until there was nothing but a dismal, suffocating atmosphere that seemed to clog the very pores of the survivors with its anguish. Now that the torrential deluge had all but dissipated, shafts of radiant colour shimmered vividly in the morning sunlight, cutting through the thick, granite clouds with hope and purpose. Winds of change buffeted the deck, swirling around an indomitable figure, whipping his long robes about him in earnest. The skin across the knuckles of his left hand stretched white and taut around a solid wooden staff, planted firmly beside him, as he gazed up toward the heavens through slitted eyelids. His long, iron-grey, matted beard reached almost to his waist, twisting from side to side in the turbulent wind. He sucked the icy air into his lungs, savouring the moisture brought down from above, and he smiled.

Deep in the bowels of the vessel, a woman screamed in pain.

317

Beads of sweat mingled with tears of agony ran down her face as she lay on her back with her knees bent and her garments pushed up past her waistline. Another maiden knelt behind the afflicted woman, gently cradling her head in her lap while dabbing her face with a soft, damp cloth and whispering words of faith and encouragement. The woman drew in a deep, ragged breath and screamed again.

"That's it," said a third woman reassuringly. "Push."

After another intake of breath, the woman lying on her back grunted and groaned with visible effort.

The third woman's eyes widened. "Just a little more. Nearly there. Push, push!"

The intermittent screams of labour were replaced by the high-pitched wail of a newborn child that echoed shrilly through the cavernous hold as the midwife held the infant up into the air exultantly. "Behold," she said with reverence, "a miracle." Her voice was strong and unwavering. "The Lord is merciful. He is forgiving. He has not forsaken us. He gives us life!" Tears ran down her face. "Mankind will be fruitful and multiply!" She sobbed as she spoke. "Blessed is the Lord our God!"

And so it came to pass, that a first-born son was begotten to Japheth son of Noah and Adataneses, daughter of Adah. He was named Gomer, meaning to complete, symbolising the end of the Great Flood on Earth. Together with the sign of the rainbow, shining vividly across the heavens, God established a covenant with Noah, promising to never again cause the waters to become a flood and destroy all life on the planet.

◊ ◊ ◊

Gomer grew into a handsome, fair-haired boy with deep, brown, compelling eyes. He was mischievous, inquisitive, and filled with boundless energy, always testing his parents, tempting their patience. He was just four summers old when his father found him standing precariously on the edge of a wooden stool, preparing to jump onto one of their sheep.

"Gomer," said Japheth in an exacting tone. "No."

Gomer looked up at his father with an impish grin. The stool wobbled and his grin turned to consternation. He turned back to face the sheep and the stool steadied.

Japheth raised his voice. "Gomer! I said No!"

Gomer was oblivious to his father's admonition. He bent his little legs, thrust his arms back behind him and jumped, landing squarely on the back of the sheep. The sheep jumped forward in a panic, bleating loudly. Gomer gripped the thick, woollen hide of the animal in his tiny fists to save himself from being flung off its back as it ran. A look of dread flashed across his face that fast turned into a wide-eyed grin as soon as he gained control. A high-pitched laugh of glee escaped his lips, infecting Japheth with its magic, instantly turning his chagrin to cheer. Japheth placed his hands on his hips and smiled whilst shaking his head in wonder.

The Lord was true to His word and blessed Japheth and Adataneses with six more male children, born to spread their seed all over the Earth and establish powerful nations unto themselves.

◊ ◊ ◊

"Magog, Madai, Javan!" Gomer called to three of his siblings. "Come, let's explore the fortress."

"Gomer, I told you to eat your breakfast first before running off to play," said Adataneses admonishingly.

"But I'm not hungry," he replied, dashing out of the house with his brothers hot on his heels.

Adataneses shook her head in dissatisfaction. "Gomer. What am I going to do with you?" she said rhetorically.

Gomer sprinted through his grandfather's vineyard, dodging the serpentine vines as he ran. He grabbed a handful of succulent, green grapes and stuffed them into his mouth without pause, laughing out loud as he ran. His infectious giggling caused his brothers to follow suit and the vines came alive with their sweet cries of joy. Gomer huffed and puffed as he pushed his legs to carry him up the mountainside. He burst forth from the vineyard and across a field of long grass that tickled his legs as he ran. The morning sunlight bathed his face with warm, invigorating energy. He closed his eyes and felt the sun's radiance wash right through his body, charging his very being and elevating his soul.

The journey took the boys most of the morning as they climbed up the mountain to their final destination. The sun reached its zenith and then disappeared, blotted out by a massive structure rising stoically out of the Earth. Gomer slowed down to a walk, gazing up at the colossal fortress that towered high above him. He stopped to catch his breath, in awe of every visit, this one being no different. His mouth dropped open as he marvelled at the sheer size of the wooden construction that stretched right across the mountain. His brothers caught up to him, panting and gasping for air. Madai collapsed on the grass, rolling onto his back with a sigh.

"Gomer, why do you run so fast?" enquired Javan, the youngest of the siblings.

"Because I am the eldest," replied Gomer smugly, his fists pressed squarely against his hips and his chin lifted up in pride.

"I think it's because he's scared of Mother," said Madai with a chuckle. "He's scared of being caught and punished for disobeying her wishes."

"Ha-ha-ha very funny," said Gomer. "Come, let's race to the entrance!"

The four young boys ran further up the mountain. The great Ark towered above them as they ran, its dark, stained exterior an ominous reminder of the old world; a world of pain and torture, of violence and suffering. It was a story told to them many times over by their grandfather:

"God had forsaken mankind because he had sinned." Noah's unwavering voice echoed ominously around the room. Gomer felt a chill run up and down his spine. He pulled the blanket up to his chin and snuggled up close to his mother.

"He spoke to me," continued Noah. "He came to me in a dream. But this was no ordinary dream." Noah closed his eyes, reliving the memory. He paused and took a deep breath. "God was angry with all the violence and evil that mankind had unleashed upon the world. He said that he was going to cleanse the earth with a great flood. In my dream, God showed me how the incessant rains would come down from the heavens, together with water erupting from the bowels of the Earth and completely cover the planet. Every living thing drowned. Every tree was destroyed. Every mountain was covered. There was nothing but water everywhere." Noah's voice softened to a whisper. "A great despair washed over me and I felt myself drowning beneath the waves. A dreadful darkness blanketed the world and I felt myself being consumed by it."

Noah paused again. His eyes flashed open. "And then I saw it!" he cried out. Gomer jumped with fright. "The ocean was wild. It was angry. But amidst the churning waters, there was a light. The Ark!" Noah pushed his hands together in prayer and extended them up to the sky. "That was when the Almighty told me what I had to do to save my family from the flood. That was when He told me to build the Ark, to construct a vessel out of gopher wood, covered in pitch inside and out. I toiled 120 years with my sons to construct it. 120 years it took us and here we are. A divine miracle. Saved by the hand of the Lord."

Gomer and his brothers reached the entrance to the Ark. The great wooden monstrosity loomed up into the sky, dwarfing the boys as they prepared to enter. The midday sun shone across the opening, illuminating the interior and banishing the shadows as Gomer and his brothers climbed up the wooden ramp and stepped inside. They entered at the lower level, with two more levels set above it. Several doves startled the boys, bursting forth from the darkness within, flying out, into the sunlight.

Gomer could hear his grandfather's voice again as if it were coming from deep within the deep, dark, cavernous belly of the Ark.

"For forty days and nights, the rain pounded the roof of the Ark, a constant reminder of the fury unleashed by the Lord. For many months thereafter, we were tossed about the churning oceans of the world like a plaything, while all manner of life was erased from the Earth. Together with the animals, we were trapped inside the Ark like prisoners with an uncertain fate…"

Gomer and his brothers made their way to the front of the vessel where they climbed a series of ladders until they arrived at the uppermost level. The boys reached the only opening, set at an angle in the roof. It was wide open but just out of Gomer's reach.

"Magog. Come. Climb onto my shoulders," instructed Gomer.

Gomer crouched down onto one knee while Magog climbed onto his shoulders. Gomer lifted his left hand and Magog took a hold of it, while Gomer slowly pushed himself up to a standing position. Magog lifted his right hand up towards the window, grabbed hold of its edge and pulled himself up and through it. Next went Madai and then Javan with Magog helping them up. To lift Gomer up and through the window was a little more arduous a task. Magog and Madai grabbed a hold of Javan's ankles and then lowered him down through the window towards Gomer's outstretched arms. Javan extended his arms, grabbing hold of Gomer's in a firm forearm-grip. With visible effort, Magog and Madai gradually pulled Javan and Gomer up and through the opening. Finally, all four boys collapsed in a heap on the other side, panting visibly with the effort it took them to reach the top of the Ark.

"Gomer, you're getting so heavy!" Madai exclaimed.

"And you are getting weak, little brother," he retorted with a chuckle.

The four boys slid down a short distance on the roof of the Ark and onto a small deck below. From this vantage point, they turned to look back across the Ark, all the way to the rear of the vessel. It was an impressive sight to behold.

"Look!" Javan pointed towards a spiral of smoke in the distance. "That's our home."

The brothers turned to stand at the helm of the Ark and gazed out across the valleys and hills below. The flight of white doves sailed past them, their wings whistling gently in the breeze, and their soft, drawn-out lamenting calls echoing forlornly across the mountainside.

www.ingramcontent.com/pod-product-compliance
Lightning Source LLC
Chambersburg PA
CBHW050553260626
47157CB00002B/549